Unforeseen Destinies

Book Three in The Walking With The Moon Series

Rhiannon Hailey

Copyright © 2024 by Rhiannon Hailey
ISBN: 979-8-9901689-2-3

Written by: Rhiannon Hailey
Published by: Rhiannon Hailey~Author~
Edited by: Victoria Quistgaard
Cover art by: The Black Fern Art

This book contains explicit sexual content, violence, and mentions of trauma. This book is intended for readers 18 and older.

Prologue

We often confuse destiny and fate. Destiny is something you can choose to follow. Fate isn't. Fate is something you can't run or hide from. It will find you no matter what you do to conceal yourself from it. The question is: how long can you run before it takes its course?

Unforeseen Destinies

Chapter One

VINNIE

"I should have stayed my ass out of Corfu! Fucking Corfu. Fucking seer. Fucking puppies. Fucking witches," I complained to Kal after little witch left. We made basically no progress; she mainly sat there like she was waiting for me to eat her. Even after I told her she smelled like cabbage, and I wasn't interested.

"Perfectly fine being around a shit ton of wolves, but *I* scare her." I knew it shouldn't bother me. Most vampires love being feared. I, on the other hand, was not like most vampires.

"Give her time, Vin. She'll come around," Kal reassured me.

"How much time does she need? I don't want to fucking die!" I complained as I took a long drink from my cup. The final death wasn't exactly something I wanted to experience.

"Would you calm down? Always so dramatic. You have to remember this is a lot for her," Kal started before I cut her off.

"First, no I won't. Second, you love my dramatics, so shush it. Third, we don't have time for her to come around. She should have come around last week," I told her as I got up and started to lap the room, tidying up as I went.

"Can you slow down? You're getting all blurry and it gives me a headache," Kal complained, and I slowed down.

"Vin, I'm going to suggest something, but you have to promise you won't get pissed." I already knew what she was going to suggest. My answer would be no, but I humored her.

"I promise," I replied.

"You could do an allurement on her."

"Kal, you know I won't do that," I told her, not hiding my disappointment in the fact that she even asked.

"I swear, you are the only vampire in existence that has a conscience. You could just do it long enough for her to relax and get to know you a little bit," she continued as she tried to convince me.

"Kal. The. Answer. Is. No. I will never do that to someone who doesn't know it's being done." I was starting to wish I had never told Kal about it in the first place.

"Ask Jameson then. He has some kind of weird crush on you. I'm sure once you tell him what it is and why you need to, I bet he would let you," she countered.

"I'm going to do it the old-fashioned way. I refuse to ask Beta puppy if I can essentially hypnotize his girlfriend, so she feels all warm and fuzzy around me. I'm also pretty sure Alpha puppy wouldn't like it either," I told her, my irritation on full display.

"Like I said at the beginning, it was only a suggestion," she told me as she raised her hands defensively. "Now, come brush my hair," she continued with a smile.

"Are you sure he ate, Jam?" I heard little witch ask her mate as they approached my door.

"Yes babe, and how many times does he have to tell you that he doesn't want to eat you? Give him a chance. Try to look at him as just a regular guy and not a vampire," Beta puppy told her as they stood outside my door, not knocking.

"You sound like Dani. Fine, I'll really try," she responded as I heard a knock on the door at last.

I looked down at my current outfit: silk pajamas, gossamer robe, and matching kitten heel slippers. Nothing about that screams normal guy, but I was determined to get her to not be scared of me. I didn't want to die, but I was also willing to walk into the sun without her help to save Max if I had to. That little boy had a hold on me that I couldn't explain. I let them knock one more time before swinging the door open dramatically.

"Beta puppy! Little witch! I'm so happy you came back to see me. Please come in! Kal made snacks!" I welcomed them as I stepped aside, so they could enter.

"Can you eat real food?" little witch asked me suddenly.

"This is it. Don't screw it up," I whispered to myself. This was the first time she ever asked me something first. "I can, but it doesn't have any nutritional value for me, and it tastes like dirt," I told her as we sat down. She and Beta puppy sat on the loveseat that was farthest from my chair. I watched as she shifted uncomfortably in her seat. I didn't like that she was that uncomfortable around me.

"You're killing me! What do I have to do to get you to relax? I just want to get to know you. I didn't realize that was too much to ask. It's starting to hurt my feelings. I'm glad to see that vampire biases also got passed to the 'I grew up in the human world' crowd. I thought vampires were in." As soon as the words were out of my mouth, I could hear what Kal would have said to me. *"Stop being so dramatic."* But I couldn't help it. I was dramatic.

"I didn't mean to hurt your feelings. I'm just wicked nervous. I don't want to say or do anything that offends you. I'm not exactly known for thinking before doing, and it's got me into a lot of trouble recently," she confessed.

"Oh, little witch, you don't have to worry about that with me. It takes more than you got to offend me. I've walked this earth for over five thousand years. Ask me anything you want. I have seen and heard it all. I'll even make you a deal. If you can offend me, I'll give you five thousand dollars." As I spoke, she just stared at me.

"You're five thousand years old?" she finally asked after a few minutes of staring.

"Give or take a couple hundred years. I stopped counting a long time ago," I told her as I stirred the air with my finger. Everyone always gets so caught up on my age.

"Have you always been so flamboyant?" she asked me as Beta puppy lightly elbowed her in the ribs.

"No need for violence, Beta puppy. It's not the first time I've been asked that. Short answer, yes. I have always been this fabulous," I told them both with a laugh.

"How old were you when you got turned into a vampire?" she immediately asked. It was quickly turning into twenty questions.

"Twenty-six. An old man in those days. Can you believe it? Me, considered old, with this face," I told them as I posed my hands around my face and pursed my lips.

"Why aren't you pale?" she asked next.

"Why aren't you?" I countered and she giggled. "Honestly the whole paleness thing is just a story. Crafted to help us blend in, just like werewolves only shifting on the full moon."

"Is your skin hard?" As she asked me questions, I could see her relaxing.

"Not that I've been told. Chilly yes, but hard, no. Would you like to feel for yourself?" I asked her as I lifted my hand out toward her. I watched as she thought about my offer and slowly nodded her head.

"Do you want me to come to you or you to me?" I asked in response to her nod.

"I'll come to you," she told me as she started to stand.

The look of sheer determination on her face was almost comical. I had to stifle a laugh. I didn't move, keeping my hand out as if I was waiting for her to shake it. Once she was close enough that she could touch my hand, she paused and looked into my eyes. It surprised me, causing me to shut them. Not many people, no matter the species, make intentional, full eye contact with me. It's dangerous for vampires to make direct eye contact for more than a few moments.

I'm not sure what she saw in the brief instant that her eyes locked with mine, but she slowly raised her hand. Lightly, she ran her fingertips over my skin. After a couple of passes, she added a little more pressure.

"Ouch!" I called out, not being able to help myself.

"I'm so sorry! I didn't mean to hurt you," she exclaimed as she dropped my hand. The look on her face caused me to break out into laughter.

"No. No, little witch. I'm sorry. I was just messing with you. It takes way more than that to hurt me," I told her as I tried to get myself under control.

"That wasn't very nice," she told me as she smacked my hand. I watched as Beta puppy froze, waiting to see what my reaction would be. I just laughed and shook my finger at her.

"You shouldn't hit someone faster than you."

"What does that mean?" she asked me.

"It means, you shouldn't hit someone who can move faster than you can see," I explained with a sly smile.

She asked me question after question for the next three hours. Having over five thousand years of stories and experiences gave me a lot to pull from. I hadn't had someone ask me this much other than Kal. I could tell as we talked that I was winning her over. Finally, she asked the question I was hoping she wouldn't. The one question I never wanted to be asked.

"How were you made, and do you talk to the vampire that made you?"

"That is a story for another day. I'd rather tell it when everyone is here, so I don't have to repeat it later. It's not my favorite to tell. To answer your second question, no, I don't speak to my maker. When I tell you how I was made, I will also explain what happened to my maker," I told her honestly.

"Vin, I'm home!" Kal called as she opened the door, having spent the day with Fern and Luna puppy. It was nice to see her have actual friends. "Cy, Jameson. I didn't think you would still be here. I can leave and come back later," she started before Cy stopped her.

"It's okay, Kal. We should be going. Jam still has to take me home," she said. A blind man could see the sadness in her eyes. "Vinnie, let's exchange numbers so we can text," she told me as she shifted her gaze to me. The Luna puppy had gotten Kal and me local numbers. Alpha puppy was complaining about the international rates when we were all technically under the same roof.

"Love it!" I exclaimed as I typed her number into my contacts.

"It looks like everything went well. Did you use allurement?" Kal asked me not but two seconds after the door was closed.

"No, Kal. I didn't," I snapped at her. She was getting on my nerves with it.

"Then how did you do it?" she probed.

"The same way I did with you, baby. My glowing personality and witty comebacks. I'm going to bed," I told her as I got up and flung my robe out dramatically.

"Of course you did. Goodnight, Vin. Love you," she told me with a laugh and a smile.

"Night, Kal. Love you too," I told her as I walked to my room and shut the door.

I knew to the outside world our relationship looked strange. We were an unlikely pairing, but I genuinely loved

Kal. A feat said to be impossible once I was turned. I was glad to find out that wasn't true. Another lie spun just for me by Konstantin.

Chapter Two

DANI

For the next ten minutes, Stefhan told me the CliffsNotes version of what happened with Marcus. I didn't have time to process what he told me before Phoenix's cries came through the baby monitor. And it was a lot to process.

"I'll get her. You get Max," I told him as I started to move. I knew it wouldn't be long before he was up too.

"Mama, Papa," Max called out before Stefhan was even off the bed.

"I'll have Fern, and my mom take the kids later, so we can finish talking," Stefhan said as we made our way to the door. I could feel his nervousness.

He threw so much at me so quickly that I was more focused on catching it all, not understanding it. It was times like that when my "gift" actually felt like one. As I got Phoenix changed and started feeding her, I replayed what Stefhan told me. Since he wasn't able to go into detail due to the time restriction we were under, I was left with more questions than answers after my instant replay. As I finished up with Phoenix, Max ran into the living room with Stefhan not far behind.

"You never catch me, Papa! I the fastest wolf ever!" Max screamed as he ran toward me.

"Oh, I'm going to catch you. Where do you think you got your wolf speed from?" Stefhan called after him.

I loved watching them together. Stefhan was an amazing father, and he was doing everything he could to make up for the time he lost with us. Right as Max was going to jump on the couch and into my lap, Stefhan grabbed him.

"Careful, bub. You have to watch out for Phoenix," he told Max while swinging him up on his shoulders. "Are you ready for some breakfast?" Stefhan asked me.

"Yes! Breakfast!" Max screamed and clapped his hands, answering for me.

"Then it's settled. I'll link Iris and have her bring us up something," Stefhan said with a laugh.

"Don't link Iris. I want to cook," I quickly interjected. It had been a long time since I cooked. I loved Iris and her cooking, but I wanted to make breakfast for my family.

"Even better," Stefhan said with a smile.

Seeing Stefhan try to put on Phoenix's baby wrap might have been the funniest thing I had ever witnessed. It looked so small on him, and it didn't fit.

"Who in the hell said this was a one-size-fits-all?" he complained as he tried to loosen the straps more.

"It says, one size fits most," I corrected him, not being able to stop myself.

"Shit!" he whispered in frustration as he pulled the strap once more, tearing it in two.

"I'll just carry her, love. You can roll her bassinet into the kitchen," I told him as I started walking. "Come on Max. We can make pancakes."

Max and I made pancakes, eggs, bacon, and sausage. It was a meal that made me think of Gram. I felt like I was passing on her secrets when I made it with him, even though there wasn't anything special about the recipe or the way it was prepared. Once everything was done and we were fed, Stefhan linked Fern and Sarai to sit with the kids. It was time to finish our talk.

We walked in silence to the garden and sat in the grass where he took me on our first date. Stefhan was barefoot and his heart was pounding. He only had time to tell me the very basics. All I really knew up to that point was Marcus was dead. Marcus told him he was a Deus Interfectorem and Marcus told him what happened to Gram.

"I know I wasn't able to tell you everything earlier, but I'm going to tell you everything now. I'm not going to leave anything out. I just really hope you still look at me the same as you do now," he whispered as he took my hand and told me everything that happened in the dungeon.

There was no part of his story that didn't shake me to my core. I sat in shocked silence as he told me about the demon voice, cutting off Marcus's manhood, being the Deus Interfectorem, the shift that he went through, Marcus's accusations against the God of the Witches–Salix, Marcus welcoming death by Stefhan's hand, Helen, and finally Gram.

My brain was broken, I couldn't even find a starting point to try and begin to comprehend what he said. For the briefest of seconds, I went back to when I thought I was in a coma dream or had a tumor. Stefhan sat without saying a word, while I tried to wrap my head around what was happening. I could feel Stefhan's hand, but I couldn't speak. I replayed everything three times before I could say a word.

"That was a lot, and I need a minute," I finally managed to choke out. I needed to pace.

I gently removed my hand from his, got up, and started pacing. As I paced, tears filled my eyes and pain swirled through me. Out of everything Stefhan said, the one thing I refused to believe was what he said about Gram.

"She wouldn't do that. She wouldn't just leave me like that! You don't know her and Marcus is full of shit!" I screamed as the sobs came in full force. Right as I was going to drop to my knees, Stefhan's arms were around me. He didn't speak, he just held me while I sobbed.

The sobs rocked through me like a boat during a storm. I knew there were other things that I needed to focus on, things that needed immediate attention. Like my husband being some God Killer demon. But I couldn't.

"Marcus said that Gram told him to kill her." Stefhan's words repeated in my head like a broken record. That's why I call my gift a curse. No matter how much I wanted to turn it off, it just kept repeating. I don't know how long I sobbed, but I finally ran out of tears.

"I'm sorry," I whispered into his massive chest once I was able to speak again.

"Why are you apologizing?" he asked me as he kissed my head.

"This wasn't the time for me to have a complete meltdown," I started before he cut me off.

"Stop. You can have a meltdown anytime you need to." I tried to interrupt him, but he covered my mouth with his hand. "You said it yourself. It was a lot. You're allowed to have feelings. Especially when it comes to Gram. I don't know if everything Marcus said was true, but that's why we have to look into it. All of it."

I knew he was right, and I was determined to prove Marcus was nothing but a liar. At least when it came to Gram.

I finally had some control over my thoughts and was able to start processing the other things Stefhan told me. It was then that I remembered something I had read when I was doing research with Jameson. Something that at the time wasn't relevant to what I was looking for but had just become super relevant. Deus Interfectorem.

"Come on. We need to get to the library," I told him suddenly as I grabbed his hand and started pulling him through the garden.

"My love, are you going to tell me why we're going to the library?" he asked as he let me pull him down the path.

"One day when I was doing research with Jameson, I read something about the Deus Interfectorem. The thing is, I just glanced over it because it wasn't relevant to what I was looking for at the time. So I can't remember what it said." I quickly explained as I pulled him through the packhouse. Once we were in the library, I pulled him straight toward the restricted section.

"It looks like a tornado came through here," Stefhan whispered as he shut the door behind us.

"Jameson and I have a system. Don't worry, once everything is figured out, you won't even know we were in here," I told him with a quick smile.

I was cursing myself for not paying more attention to what book it was in. I knew it wasn't that long ago when I saw it, so I grabbed the stack that I was looking at the last time I was there. Quickly I started thumbing through the books. Four books later, I finally found it in Stefhan's family book.

"Here it is!" I exclaimed. "'Deus Interfectorem, Latin meaning God Killer. The only creature that is able to kill a God or Goddess. A true Deus Interfectorem is only born about every one thousand years. Once a millennia, a male wolf will be blessed not only by Selene but also by Death. This son is hand-selected by Death herself and will possess two wolves. The first will be like all the wolves that came before him, but the second is nothing like the first. The second is a servant only to anger and rage. The son must be able to not only harness the anger and rage but also give it full control. Only a true grounding force can make the selected son capable of walking with the beast. Failure to find this grounding force and complete the full mark will result in rage consuming them and will end the life of the wolf, reuniting the beast with Death.'" By the time I was done reading, I had more questions than answers.

"What does that even mean?" I asked more out of frustration than looking for an actual answer. Cryptic shit never came with an immediate answer.

"I know what it means," Stefhan whispered as my eyes met his. "Well, not all of it, but part." I could feel the fear rolling off him as he took my hand and started guiding me back outside to the woods.

"Why are we going into the woods?" I asked him as I rubbed circles on his hand with my thumb.

"There's something I have to show you."

Even if I couldn't feel his fear, I would have been able to hear it in his voice. He guided me deep beyond the tree line before he stopped and looked at me for the first time since we entered.

"Please tell me what's going on. I can feel how scared you are," I pleaded as soon as he turned. All I wanted to do was comfort him, but as I went to wrap my arms around him, he pulled away.

"I promised you that I would never keep another secret from you, and I'm going to keep it. But if there was ever a time, I wished I never made that promise, it's now. I wasn't lying when I told you I don't deserve you and that I'm a monster. If anything, I just have undeniable proof now." He paused and took a deep breath. "In order to show you what I need to, I need you to tell me something that's going to piss me off."

"Hold on a second," I said, cutting him off. "First off, stop it. You do deserve me, and you aren't a monster. Second, are you really asking me to pick a fight with you?"

"Yes, I am. I do have to warn you if what Marcus said held any truth, it's scary as fuck. I promise I won't hurt you. I could never hurt you. You're my grounding force, and we've already completed the full mark," he told me as he touched his neck.

His fear was hitting me like a tidal wave. He was terrified. Terrified that I wouldn't want him after he showed me. I was determined to be the support he needed me to be in that moment.

"Okay. How pissed do you need to be?" I asked as I reached out and touched the back of his hand. Sending waves of electricity dancing between us.

"More pissed than you've ever seen me," he responded as he closed his eyes.

"I don't know if this is a good idea," I confessed. I wasn't sure I wanted to see it.

"You don't understand. I won't be able to control it if I don't show you. It's part of the process." His voice was pleading, and his eyes bore into mine with an intensity I had never seen before. It was life and death. I shook my head and took a breath. I could only think of one thing that would get him that angry.

"I'm letting Cy move back into the pack house." I tried to say it with enough confidence that he wouldn't be able to tell I was lying.

"You wouldn't," Stefhan's voice was deep and gravely

"You have to keep going, child," Enya's voice echoed in my mind.

"I already did. She's moving her stuff as we speak," I instantly replied. I watched as he began to shake. "Love?" I asked him as I reached out to touch him.

"Stay back." A deep, demonic voice left Stefhan's mouth. He took a step back, his skin started to vibrate and the shaking intensified. While still standing, his bones began to pop and snap into new positions. It wasn't fluid like a normal shift, it was extremely jerky and looked painful. The sounds his bones made as they found their new positions were a cross between grinding and crunching. If I wouldn't have been so terrified, I would have gagged. Tufts of dingy gray fur began to sprout from his sun-kissed skin. It didn't come in like Kane's fur, it was patchy and looked like it would scratch you if you touched it. The bones in his face stretched and popped. His beard was replaced with the same patchy, gray fur that covered his body.

Kane was massive, majestic, and beautiful; what stood in front of me was none of those things. It looked more like a movie werewolf with a bad case of mange. I had to cover my mouth with my hand to stop the scream that almost escaped. Terror rocked through me, and the hairs on the back of my neck stood up. Every single one of my body's fight-or-flight responses was telling me to run. I could hear Enya trying to tell me something, but I was too terrified to be able to make out what she was saying.

Up to that point it hadn't acknowledged my presence. Wanting to put as much distance between us as possible, I slowly started to back up. I had taken only a few steps when I stepped on a twig. The second the twig snapped under my foot; it whipped its head in my direction. Large black voids with green swirls stared at me where Stefhan's eyes used to be. Quickly I looked down, so it couldn't lock eyes with me.

"Please don't be afraid. I won't hurt you. I could never hurt you," the demonic voice pleaded to me.

Slowly, I raised my head to look at it. The moment I lifted my head enough to see its face, the voids locked with mine.

"Please," it pleaded again.

"I just need a minute. This is a lot," I confessed.

It nodded and took a step back to give me space. Suddenly Stefhan's words came rushing back into my head: *"We've already completed the full mark."* The realization of what that sentence actually meant was enough to break my brain once again.

"That's what I've been trying to tell you, child. You are mated to him." Enya sounded like she was underwater. I didn't know how to process what was happening.

"No, no, no. That's not how this works, mate implies equals. You are Kane's mate. I'm Stefhan's mate. Both sets are equal. I don't turn into whatever the hell that is! This is not equal!" I shrieked at her. I was on the verge of having a panic attack.

Suddenly I was hit with a wave of sadness that stopped my budding panic attack in its tracks. For the first time since Stefhan shifted, I was able to feel his emotions. It was beyond sadness–it was anguish. My terror caused him so much pain. It took my breath away and my heart ached. Unconsciously, I took a step toward him and my hand started to rise. I couldn't bear feeling him in so much pain. I took one of Gram's deep breaths.

"Can Stefhan hear me?" I asked it.

"Yes, my love," the demonic voice answered.

While they were words I had heard Stefhan tell me hundreds of times, hearing them said by that creature was too much for my brain and everything went black.

I was back in the all too familiar field and immediately looked toward the bench. Gram was already waiting. These encounters never lasted long, and I always ended up with more questions than answers. But I cherished every second. I ran full speed toward the bench and launched myself into her arms. I couldn't stop the tears that rolled down my cheeks as she wrapped her arms around me.

"My sweet Dani girl. Why are you crying?" she asked me as she leaned her head back to look at me. Gram was always my safe place. I could tell her anything. The second I opened my mouth, the word vomit started and didn't stop.

"I don't know how much more I can handle, Gram. Why can't anything just be fucking easy for a little bit? It's been non-stop! We have a vampire living in the basement. Cy is struggling to get her powers under control. Stefhan won't let her anywhere near the packhouse. He's making her live with her

parents. He tortured and killed Marcus. Speaking of Marcus. He said that you told him to kill you and that the God of the Witches was behind everything." The tears were freely falling down my cheeks. Gram didn't interrupt me, she just listened and rubbed circles on my hand with her thumb.

"Stefhan is some God Killer. He shifts into a monster! I don't mean that in the figurative sense, he really shifts into a hideous creature. He sounds like a demon and his eyes are black voids with green swirls. It's terrifying! Why does my husband have to kill a god? Why is it always us? I'm so fucking sick of hearing 'it's your destiny' and Selene will never give me more than I can handle. Well, let me tell you, I'm there. I'm at my limit! I just want to raise my kids in a safe environment! What Stefhan turned into tonight didn't look or sound safe."

I was talking myself back into a panic attack. Images of the creature flashed in my head. Gram suddenly gave me a little shake.

"Danielle, listen to me. No road in life is easy, there will always be challenges. You just have to choose what path you take when those challenges arise. You have to decide whether you stay and fight or walk away. Will the choice always be simple? No, but anything worth fighting for seldom is. This creature is part of

Stefhan. It always has been and always will be. If you truly love him, then you have to love all the parts of him. Even the ones that aren't so pretty. I wish I could answer all your questions my lovely, but this is your destiny, and you have to decide. Just remember. Sometimes it helps to go back to the beginning."

"Please wake up. I need you to wake up."

I heard Stefhan's muffled voice pleading to me as I regained consciousness. I could feel his arms around me, holding me to his chest. Quiet sobs shook his massive frame, and his face was buried in my hair. My heart ached in response to his pain, causing me to stir. The second I moved, Stefhan repositioned me so that he could look at me. Gram's words swirled in my head as his tear-stained face entered my line of sight. Fear and pain were rolling off him and hitting me like a bullet train. I didn't need to think, my mind was already made up.

"I'm so sorry!" he started before I stopped him.

"It's okay," I whispered as I placed my hand on his face. A face I couldn't live without.

"You were so scared of me you fainted. That's the opposite of okay and don't try to say you weren't. I could feel it. I've put you through so much. You don't even have time to recover from one thing before I hit you with another. It's a never-ending cycle. At some point you're going to get tired of it and go running for the hills," he whispered as he pressed his face against my hand.

"I was scared, and a little warning would have been nice," I started as I placed my other hand on the other side of his face. "Gram told me that things worth fighting for are seldom easy. Has our relationship been a cakewalk? No. But I will always fight for you. I will stand by your side no matter what is thrown our way. True love is loving all the parts of someone, not just the pretty ones," I told him and pressed my lips gently to his. I didn't tell him about my visit with Gram. That could wait until later. I needed to be his strength in that moment, and that's exactly what I was going to be.

"Are you sure?" he asked me, his lips still touching mine.

"I'm sure that I love you more than someone has ever loved someone else. I'm sure that I will love you always and forever, no matter what. And positive that I can't live without you," I told him as I leaned back and locked my eyes with his.

"You can't be afraid of it. I can't fully control it if you are," he whispered as he looked down. He didn't want to expose me to that again. I took a deep breath.

"Let's try this again. Now that I know what to expect, it won't be so bad. I promise," I told him as I started to move off his lap to give him space to shift. As I moved, I could see the cords of our bond. They were brilliant gold and were so bright it was like looking at the sun, only it didn't hurt my eyes.

"Do you see them?" he asked me as I moved.

"Yes. I think it's showing us that this needs to happen," I answered as I kept moving. I didn't want to give him any reason to change his mind. I was also reassuring myself. I watched as Stefhan removed his sweats and closed his eyes. Slowly his body started shaking. I wasn't ready to watch him shift again, so I closed my eyes. My eyes being closed didn't save me from the sounds his body made. I took deep breaths, so I didn't gag.

"You can do this, child. Remember, he is still Stefhan," Enya encouraged me.

"Please open your eyes," the demonic voice called to me before I could answer Enya. Quickly I let my mind replay the images of the creature, so I wouldn't scream when I opened them.

"Stefhan?" I could still see the cords of our matebond linking us together.

"Yes and no," the demonic voice said as it started walking slowly toward me. It held its claws up in a defensive position to show it didn't want to hurt or scare me. Taking each step slowly and deliberately, it inched closer and closer to me. Rather than focus on the creature that was making its way to me, I focused on the cords that bound me to Stefhan.

"I don't understand," I told it honestly, still focusing on the cords.

"I am Abaddon. You will soon, I will explain everything. Will you sit with me?"

Unforeseen Destinies

Chapter Three

I stopped focusing on the cords and looked at Abaddon. For the first time, I willingly locked my eyes with his, and for a split second, I saw Stefhan's eyes in the blackness. It was like he was reassuring me that it was okay. I knew this needed to happen, and I couldn't let fear get the best of me. Slowly, I sat down and patted the ground. Abaddon sat close but made sure we didn't touch and took a breath.

"It's amazing the calming effect you have on me. I never thought I would get to experience it," he whispered as he took a couple more deep breaths. I didn't speak, just waited for him to continue.

"In order for you to fully understand, I have to start at the beginning. What I'm going to tell you has never been written down or verbally told before. It is information given directly to me by Lilith. Only to be shared once fiet unum was finally completed." He paused briefly. "Abaddon means the destroyer. I'm the physical manifestation of pure unfiltered rage. Created for one purpose, to kill a god. No one besides Lilith knows who or the reason for her selection. Once she had selected a son, she pulled me from the void and planted me like a seed, allowing me to tap into the rage all people are capable of and amplifying it steadily as they aged. It was then up to the son to harness and control the rage before it consumed him. None of them tried to control me early. Instead, they allowed me to grow uncontrollably and unchecked." Abaddon paused and took another breath.

"I have killed every son I have been gifted to; the rage too strong for them to control. Causing the shift to happen too early, killing them instantly. The first two steps of the bonding process have to be completed before the first shift. Without them being completed, the son wouldn't be able to shift back. Leaving me completely free to kill anyone or anything I wanted. Not wanting to risk that, Lilith made a clause that if the shift happens before the first two steps are completed it kills the son. The son and his wolf would go into their afterlife with Selene. I would return to the void and wait for Lilith to start the process again. Fiet unum, or becoming one, is a four-step process. Stefhan is the only selected son to complete any of the steps."

As he spoke, I found myself subconsciously leaning closer to him.

"He completed the first when he started trying to control the rage early. Doing that, he was able to keep me in check until he completed the second step. Finding you and completing the matebond. You are his true grounding force; you are what gives him the ability to see past the rage and shift back. Third was his willingness to allow the first shift to kill Marcus. Fourth was last night when you completed the full mark. The first three steps are him becoming one with me, and the last is the new him becoming one with you." At some point, while he was talking my hand reached out and rested on his. His fur wasn't scratchy, it was the exact opposite. Instead of feeling like a Brillo pad, it felt like silk.

"The relationship that I have with Stefhan is nothing like the one he shares with Kane. I'm not connected to Kane in any way and I'm not a wolf. I'm purely the physical manifestation of concentrated blind rage. Unlike with Kane, Stefhan has equal control while in this form. He is the Deus Interfectorem. I am just the vessel that will be used when Stefhan deems it's time."

I needed a minute to go back over everything Abaddon had told me. To say it was a lot was an understatement. I could feel the nervousness and fear coming from Stefhan as he waited for me to speak. I started rubbing small circles on his hand. Even after replaying his story four times, I still had no words.

What do you say to something like that?

"Please say something, my love," Abaddon pleaded for Stefhan.

"You need to speak, child," Enya's voice echoed in my mind.

"Your fur is super soft," I whispered as I ran my hand over his. I could feel faint, electric sparks dancing between us. I knew that wasn't what Enya was looking for, but it was all I had at the moment.

"It only feels that way to you. Anyone else would be scratched and a poison released. While I was created to kill a god, I am fatal to all," he replied as he wrapped his long, talon-like fingers around my hand. Max and Phoenix suddenly filled my mind, followed quickly by panic.

"You won't hurt the kids, will you?" I asked as I started to pull my hand away.

"No! I could never hurt them. While you are the true grounding force, and I would have killed Stefhan without you, once the children were born, they became part of that grounding force," he quickly answered as he grabbed my hand.

Before I could respond, I felt a wetness on my shirt. I looked down to discover that it was apparently time for Phoenix to eat.

I didn't watch as Stefhan shifted back. Seeing him shift into Abaddon was something I never wanted to see again. I wasn't scared of him anymore, but it was still disgusting to watch.

"You can open your eyes now," Stefhan's beautiful voice called out to me.

I opened them to see Stefhan reaching for a pair of sweats. Seeing Stefhan naked was something I would never get tired of. He turned and caught me staring.

"Do I have something on me?" he asked as he started to brush his hands against his face.

"I'm just enjoying the view," I told him with a smile.

We walked hand in hand back to the packhouse, and I told him about my visit with Gram. Normally I would have waited until we were home, but I needed something to get my mind off the electricity that was shooting between us. It flowed even where our skin didn't touch. I knew Stefhan could feel it too, but we didn't address it.

"What do you think she meant by 'go back to the beginning'?" he asked me.

"I'm not sure." I hadn't had time to process it, let alone decipher it yet. I needed to pace and talk it out. "Once we get the kids and I address this," I told him, pointing to my breasts, "we can figure it out."

"I wish just once she would just tell me something straight. It would have been helpful if she would have at least said what beginning," I complained as I paced in the living room. For over an hour, we racked our brains trying to decode Gram's message. "I really hate when you do this Gram! Tell me where to start!" I yelled at the ceiling in frustration. Suddenly a commercial on the TV that had been playing quietly in the background caught my attention.

"Are you looking to get out of the woods? Get your fill of sand, fun, and sun! Dip your toes in the water and stay awhile. Come find the answers you seek in the sunshine state. It all starts in Florida." A woman's voice played over a picture of the ocean with the word Florida written in huge letters.

"The letters," I whispered as the memory of looking in Gram's treasure chest replayed in my mind.

"What letters?" Stefhan asked me when I didn't elaborate.

"Letters I found in Gram's treasure chest. We have to go to Florida. I have to go home," I told him as I started walking toward the bedroom.

"Now? What about the kids?" he asked as he followed behind.

"They'll be coming with us, and we're leaving as soon as we're packed and can get to the airport. Please get the plane ready to go," I instructed him as I turned into the bedroom.

I didn't need to pack much for me. I still had a closet full of clothes at Grams. I headed straight to the closet and grabbed three big suitcases, one for kids' clothes, one for Stefhan's, and one for me to bring clothes back to Crimson Diamond. Everything in me was screaming that we needed to get to Florida as soon as possible.

Within an hour we had everyone packed and were on the road. I could feel Stefhan's nerves as we drove away from the packhouse. He was nervous about leaving Cy and Vinnie. I was surprised he didn't try to talk me out of leaving so soon. Between having a vampire in the basement and Cy still not having control of her powers, it really wasn't the best time for us to leave. But there was no way he was letting me go alone. I couldn't lie, I was just as nervous, but not for the same reasons he was. Ryland's prejudices against any supernatural species other than werewolves was more than apparent.

"Why baby Pheenick sleep so much?" Max asked as soon as we were driving.

"That's what babies do," Stefhan answered.

"But I want to play with her. Pheenick boring!" Max complained.

"She won't be small for long, bud."

I loved listening to their conversations. He would talk to Max for hours, about anything and everything. Jameson even joked that Max was taking his place. Max continued to ask questions the entire drive. He was still rattling them off one after the other when we boarded the plane.

"Alpha, Luna. Welcome, it's so nice to see you!" Monday welcomed us as we boarded.

"Thank you, Monday," Stefhan greeted her.

"Hi! My name Max!" Max yelled, waking up Phoenix.

"Hi, Monday. It's nice to see you again," I told her as I adjusted Phoenix in my arms.

Stefhan got Max settled in his seat and then sat next to me. The electricity ricocheted between us, causing my pussy to clench. I tried to ignore it and fed Phoenix the second we were in the air. She couldn't eat the whole flight, so eventually I had to put her in her car seat. Stefhan kept shifting in his seat and adjusting himself. It was doing nothing helpful for the situation I had going on in my own pants. I took some deep breaths and tried to focus on anything other than Stefhan. Max had fallen asleep, so I put in my headphones. Hoping some music would distract me, I closed my eyes and tried to go to sleep.

"I know you aren't sleeping. Let's go to the back," Stefhan's voice suddenly filled my mind. I didn't respond or open my eyes. *"You're really going to do that to me?"* he asked when it was obvious that I wasn't going to answer.

"Yes, I am. We can't leave the kids out here with Monday," I finally responded. As much as I wanted to take him up on his offer, I didn't know Monday. I sure as hell wasn't leaving my sleeping kids with someone I didn't know to go and have sex.

"Okay, but once we get to Grams, you better be ready."

Thankfully, the kids woke up not long after and Max stayed up the rest of the flight. I watched, just like everyone who came before, as Monday fell in love with Max.

Stefhan had a rental waiting for us when we landed and started loading the car as I got the kids buckled in. The feeling that I needed to get home was intensifying.

"King of the one trip has finally been thwarted," Stefhan whined as he skillfully loaded more bags into the trunk. Like he was trying to win the ultimate game of Tetris.

"Kids will do that. Well, that and the fact that you won't let me carry anything other than Phoenix," I told him with a smile.

I made Stefhan let me drive since I knew the route without GPS. It was the first time I was more familiar with our surroundings than he was. I drove my favorite route from the airport. It wasn't the fastest, but it went right past the ocean. It was dark, so I couldn't see the beach, but I rolled down my window to smell the salt water and let the breeze hit my face.

In what seemed like only a couple of minutes, I was pulling into the driveway. Before the car was even in park, Barb was peeking out her curtains. Cy had asked her to keep an eye on the house when she left. As Stefhan was helping me out of the car, Barb appeared in the driveway.

"Dani? Is that you?" she asked as she squinted in the darkness.

"Yeah, it's me. Hi, Barb!" I greeted her as Stefhan went to get Phoenix out of the car.

"Don't get the kids out yet!" I linked him before he had a chance to open the door. Barb was nosy to the hundredth degree. She would definitely have a ton of questions if she saw the kids. Stefhan didn't question it, instead, he went to the back and started getting out the luggage.

"Oh, Dani! It's so good to see you! How are you doing? How is the fellowship going?" Barb cried as she walked closer to me.

"It's good to see you, too. I'm doing really well. The fellowship is going great," I quickly lied to all her questions. I just wanted her to go away.

"Oh, I remember you! You're looking much better," she said suddenly when she saw Stefhan bringing suitcases from the back of the car toward the house.

"Thank you," Stefhan replied, not sure what to say.

"Did he get you the things you needed?" Barb asked me.

"Yes, he did," I quickly answered.

"Are you two going to be in town long?" she asked pointedly. Right when she was done, Phoenix started to cry. Barb started to crane her neck to see in the back seat.

"Mama! Papa! Pheenick crying!" Max screamed. This caused her eyes to bulge from their sockets.

"I just realized I didn't introduce you. This is my husband Stefhan, and I think you heard our kids, Max and Phoenix. We had a long flight, and we just want to get the kids to bed. We can have lunch sometime and catch up." I had no intention of having lunch with her, but I was willing to say anything at that point to get her to leave.

"Oh, that would be wonderful! It looks like we have a lot to catch up on. I'll leave you all to get settled," Barb told me with a nosy smile.

Not giving her the opportunity to say anything else, I started to walk toward the house. It seemed surreal as I pushed the key into the lock and turned it. It felt symbolic, like I was unlocking secrets.

Chapter Four

CY

"God dammit, Cypress! Your magic isn't tied to your emotions! It runs in your very blood. Stop trying to use anger as a way to manifest it. Just will it to be!" my dad screamed at me.

"Stop screaming at me! It's not fucking helping!" I screamed back as I threw another energy ball at the tree.

"Oak, she's right. We are more to blame than anyone for her lack of knowledge. Ultimately it was our decisions that led her to not knowing how to tap into it properly. Physical manifestation without incantation is difficult even for seasoned witches! The fact that she's able to produce anything without any training is unheard of and we won't get into the power of her blasts. Stop being such an asshole!" my mom said as she crossed the yard toward me. "You have to find your method; every witch is different. You control it, not the other way around. Will the magic to do your bidding. You have to look within and focus. Watch how I do it," she told me as she came and stood beside me.

She closed her eyes and slowly started moving her hands in a circular motion. I continued to watch as her hands began to glow faintly. With steadily increasing speed, she moved her hands faster and faster until they were glowing as bright as burning embers. Suddenly her eyes shot open, and she pushed her hands toward a tree about twenty yards away from us. What looked like a fireball shot from her palms and struck the tree, causing a few pieces of bark to go flying.

"That's enough for today. Let's go home and get something to eat," my dad huffed as soon as her blast hit the tree.

So much was riding on me learning to control and use my magic. I still had to tell Jam that I wasn't randomly throwing energy balls when I got pissed. I didn't like keeping it from him, but I didn't want him pressuring Stefhan to let me move back into the packhouse. But after the conversation I had with Stefhan, I had to come clean to Jam. The list of people that scare me is very small and the list that makes me fear for my life is even smaller. Stefhan was currently number one on both lists. How quickly the hunter becomes the hunted.

More and more I was wishing I would have just stayed in Florida. At least in Florida my fuck ups only directly affected me. If there was one thing I was good at, it was fucking up. More than once, Dani bailed me out due to my stellar decision-making skills. Coming to Oregon was turning into the most epic fuck up of my life.

Jam was the only person who didn't look at me completely different. Not that I cared. I really didn't give a fuck what anyone thought of me other than Dani. While we were definitely in a better place, we still weren't back to where we were, and I was afraid we never would be.

"Come on babe, she didn't let anyone hold Phoenix before you. I think you're looking into it too much. She has a lot on her plate," Jam tried to convince me as we sat on the back deck.

"You're right. But have I seen them in person since? No. She didn't even tell me they were going to Florida. If you hadn't told me, I wouldn't have even known," I said with a sigh.

He didn't know Dani like I did. In all our years of friendship, I had never seen her that angry at anyone. Not that it wasn't warranted, I did almost kill her son. The craziest fucking part was that wasn't even the reason she was so pissed at me. She was pissed because I didn't tell her about my powers. Even though I could have told her, I didn't. I didn't take any precautions to make sure the people I loved were safe.

"Again, looking too much into it. She has a newborn and a toddler. They left in a crazy hurry. She probably just didn't think about it, and before you know it you'll have your powers under control. Then you can move back into the packhouse with me, and you'll be able to see Dani and the kids more." The confidence was ringing in his voice. I hated that I was going to smash it. Just like I had with every other good thing in my life.

"About that. There's something I need to tell you," I started as I took a breath. "I can control my powers." His stone-gray eyes that were locked with mine went wide in disbelief. Oregon had turned me into a liar, and I needed to come clean. "Well, sorta. I don't randomly throw energy balls when I'm pissed, every manifestation is deliberate. Weak as fuck but deliberate. I can barely blow a leaf off a tree. It's like I traded extremes. 'Learn to call the magic and find my method.' Whatever the fuck that means. I liked it a lot better when I thought my parents were just crazy.

"Before you ask, I didn't tell you because I knew you would start asking Stefhan to let me move back in. I wasn't going to add any more stress to Dani's plate. I put her through enough. The only reason I was allowed to come to the hospital was because Stefhan showed up here after Dani asked him if I could. I ended up telling him everything. I even apologized for the way I treated him. The only reason I was allowed within sight distance of the hospital was because I wasn't a danger to anyone. He told me that I needed to tell you myself and that he wasn't going to.

"I'm not sorry that I didn't tell you. I understand if you're pissed at me, but Stefhan isn't going to let me move back into the packhouse any time soon. I refuse to be a burden anymore." The tears rolled down my cheeks as I watched the pain of my words flash across his beautiful face.

A face I didn't deserve.

"I understand why you didn't tell me, but please don't keep something like that from me again," he begged as he wrapped his arms around me. His love for me was truly endless, and I still didn't deserve it.

Before I could say anything, my phone went off. I didn't have to look to see who it was. Only three people texted or called me. Jam, Dani, and Vinnie. Jam and Dani had their own ringtones, and I guess by default so did Vinnie. Jam let me move just enough that I could pull it from my pants pocket.

"Little witch! What are you doing? Come see me! Kal went with Fern, and I'm bored!"

"I'm so glad you're here! I was so bored I could've died. Where's Beta Puppy?" Vinnie welcomed me as he dramatically threw open the door.

"I told him I'm a big girl and I didn't need him to chaperone me," I said with a sly smile as I walked in. I finally was at the point where the hairs on the back of my neck didn't stand up around him. I had to develop a real bond with Vinnie, and I couldn't do that with Jam drooling over him. He had some weird man crush on him.

"It will be nice for it to be just us. We can have girl talk and really get to know each other! I'll grab us some drinks," Vinnie exclaimed as he clapped his hands together and headed toward the kitchen.

Only mere moments later he was sitting beside me on the couch with his usual bedazzled cup in one hand and a glass of wine in the other. I jumped as he materialized out of nowhere. It was the only thing he did that still freaked me out a little bit.

"Will I ever get used to that?" I asked as my heartbeat slowed back to normal.

"Oh, I hope not! It's so funny to see you jump like that," he told me with a laugh as he handed me the glass and pulled his legs into his chest.

"Well at least one of us thinks it's funny when I have a heart attack," I said with a laugh.

"Oh, my sweet little witch, I can hear your heart better than you can feel it. I would know before you had any clue that something was wrong," he retorted as he pointed to one of his ears.

"How well can you hear?" I asked him before I could stop myself.

"Better than you," he said with a laugh. "But seriously, I can hear better than every species and most vampires. Just to give you an example, I can hear through that door," he continued as he pointed at the soundproof door that led into the hallway. I thought about all the conversations I had with Jam that I thought were private outside that door. I suddenly felt very exposed and embarrassed.

"How is training going?" Vinnie asked me, breaking my train of thought.

"The same. I still can't blow a leaf off a fucking tree. I don't understand! How do I go from one extreme to the other?" I confessed, repeating the same words I used with Jam.

"Don't fret, it will come in time. You were pulling your magic from a place of anger. Accidental magic is easier to manifest than intentional magic. Learning to pull your magic from your blood and not your emotions is a difficult thing to do. Most witches start training at a very young age to learn how to draw, hold, and manipulate the magic." Vinnie told me with such confidence I couldn't help but want to believe him.

"How do you know that?" I asked before I could stop it.

"Reading. I swear, you're just as bad as the puppies. Maybe it's not all your fault. My maker insisted that I study all species and learn all I can. He didn't want me to be weak. I had an image to uphold after all," Vinnie retorted and took a long drink from his cup. He didn't talk about his maker often and I never brought it up. I was surprised when he continued after his sip.

"When you come from the line that I do, there are certain behaviors that are expected. It was one of the reasons our relationship ended the way it did." His red-tinged eyes looked almost fogged over. I could tell he was thinking about a certain memory. It was almost identical to how Dani would look when she was recalling a memory. Curiosity was overtaking me; I had been spending time with Vinnie for over a month and he still hadn't said more than two sentences about his maker. He said he only wanted to tell the story once, but I had no clue when Dani and Stefhan would be back.

"What happened?" the words suddenly flew out of my mouth. Before I could apologize, Vinnie smiled.

"I think it may be time, my little witch, for me to tell you my story."

Unforeseen Destinies

Chapter Five

VINNIE

As much as I didn't want to tell her about my history, it was time. The Alpha and Luna puppies had gone on a trip to Florida with no return date, and I didn't have time to wait for them. I had to form a true relationship with little witch ASAP. I took a long sip from my cup and then took a deep breath.

"I don't remember what year I was born; we didn't really keep track of time like they do now. I came from a well-off family and didn't see the poverty that most endured. Back then there wasn't gay or straight, everyone slept with everyone. And before you ask, yes, I've slept with women. I would frequently attend sex parties that were thrown by the rich families in the area. Sex wasn't looked at like it is now. It was celebrated, not shunned. People didn't live as long as they do now. I told you before that I was considered old when my human life ended. Living to thirty was almost unheard of. Between disease and famine, most died young. Girls were married off as soon as they were able to produce children, and you were expected to carry on the family line." I took another deep breath before I continued. I knew once I said the next sentence it was going to prompt a lot of questions, and I had to be ready. When I told Kal, it turned into an hour-long integration.

"I was married at sixteen, but we never had children. I was shooting blanks, as they like to say." I watched as hundreds of questions danced across her face. I held a finger up to keep them at bay. "I did what I was expected to do. My family was highly respected, and I had to maintain the image. My wife and parents died from illness four years before I was turned. I had also gotten sick but somehow survived. I was alone and had more money than I could possibly spend. I began to throw elaborate sex parties, charging a fee to attend to keep money coming in. My sexual appetite was hard to fill. While I preferred the company of men, I could never say no to a beautiful woman. People say today that I was a whore. But it was at one of these parties that I met him.

"Konstantin was the most beautiful man I had ever seen. Painfully beautiful. I was drawn to him like a moth to the flame. He attended four different parties before he even spoke to me. He just watched me make love to countless people. Always disappearing before sunrise. When he arrived for the fifth, I was already engaged with someone. He walked up, pulled her off me, and handed me a drink. As his eyes locked with mine, all I wanted was to make him happy. I was willing to be anything he wanted or needed me to be.

"As he handed me the drink, he leaned in and whispered in my ear. 'My name is Konstantin, and you are now mine. Take me to your chambers.' I didn't hesitate to fulfill his request. I guided him right to my bed. I don't remember a lot of what happened due to being under allurement." I paused and took yet another breath. The next part was gross, and I was trying to figure out a way to word it delicately.

"He left before sunrise and returned the following night. When he returned, he didn't waste time taking what he wanted from me. Things that I was more than willing to give him. He asked me if I wanted to live forever and if I believed in vampires. Before I could respond, he bit me in the neck." The memory of the pain shot to the forefront of my mind. "He nearly drained me before making me take his blood. Not only is it painful, it takes a week to complete the process. Most don't make it through the change. Every night he would nearly drain me and then make me take his blood. I begged him to just kill me. I didn't want to be a monster."

Cy's eyes were as wide as saucers, and I could see the questions forming in her mind. She didn't interrupt, just listened, compiling her mental list of questions.

"He denied my request, telling me that he had put in way too much effort to just kill me. I prayed to every God and Goddess I could think of. I begged them to save me, save me from this horrible fate I was going to endure. As you can see my request was again denied. Finally, after seven agonizing days, my human life was over. And my new, never-ending life began.

"As I mentioned earlier, he was adamant that I read and study. That was on top of teaching me how to be a vampire. 'No weakness, Vincent. You can never show weakness!' he would scream at me. For years he kept me at his massive estate. I wasn't allowed to leave. He had to make sure I wouldn't embarrass him because he had a reputation to uphold. He made sure to tell me over and over how he picked me above everyone else, how he could have taken anyone he wanted, and that I should be thankful for the life he had given me.

"But I wasn't thankful, I was pissed. That bastard took my soul and expected me to be happy about it." I watched as confusion crossed her face. I then remembered that she wasn't there when I told the puppies the creation story. "As I read, I learned that one of the reasons the change is so painful is because it kills your soul. Vampires aren't allowed to cross into the afterlife, but that's a story for another day," I explained quickly. A vampire can only reveal so much trauma in a single story.

"He made me memorize vampire history and where we came from. I was also expected to know the same about all supernatural creatures. For over a hundred years, I read every book in his obnoxiously large library. Of course, not all my time was spent reading. When I wasn't reading, we would train. He taught me how to do all the things that make people fear vampires. The things that make the hairs on the back of your neck stand up." I paused just long enough to take a sip of my drink.

"He made sure that no one would ever catch me unless I wanted them to. I know what you're thinking. Why didn't I just leave? It's not that simple. A vampire is bound to its maker. I had to obey him, I didn't have a choice, he forbade me to leave. I wasn't able to cross the threshold of his property. The only way to break the bond is for your maker to either release you or they die. For hundreds of years, I did what I was told when I was told. Hating myself more and more with each passing year. I killed thousands of people. He didn't believe in letting food walk away.

"About five hundred years after I was turned, he found another that he wanted. We had to go back to his estate while she went through the same training I did. We bonded over our mutual hatred for Konstantin, eventually becoming lovers. When he found out, he released her and ordered me never to see her again. I asked him why he would release her and not me. He then confessed that he was the cause of my family's illness and deaths. He poisoned us, making sure that I only consumed enough to make me sick and not kill me.

"He told me that he looked for years for an heir to carry on his legacy, and he wasn't just going to let me walk away. That was when I decided that I was going to kill him. I won't go into the details, but within two weeks he met the final death, and I never looked back. I spent years trying to repent for the monster I was for so long. It took even longer for me to unlearn the lies he filled my head with.

"I didn't want to be a murderer; I was better than that. Konstantin was the last time I committed murder. Now, have I ended lives since? Yes. But it was always in self-defense. While this life wasn't one I chose, meeting the final death isn't something I want to experience. So, I will protect my own life. You may find this hard to believe, but people tend to think because of the way I present myself that I'm not a threat. That I couldn't hurt a fly. When in truth, I'm *always* the most lethal thing in the room.

"You also may have noticed I talk to myself. The amount of time I've spent alone would be unfathomable to you.

For a while, I tried to develop friendships with my donors. But watching them all grow old and die, leaving me alone, got to be too much. Loneliness is usually the main reason a vampire becomes a maker. I would never make anyone suffer this fate, so I accepted the fact that I would just be alone. I traveled, never staying in one place too long, finding donors along the way. Eventually, I had donors in a couple of places that I would rotate. I lived this way for thousands of years. Until I met Kal."

When I finished, I watched as she processed all the information I gave her. The funniest part? It was the extreme CliffsNotes version; little witch didn't have enough lifespan for me to give her every detail of my existence. I made sure to answer all the questions Kal had, but I was sure little witch would come up with at least a couple. Cy was getting more comfortable around me, and I could see her true personality coming through.

"How did you meet Kal?" she asked me suddenly after a long silence.

"I wasn't expecting that to be your first question. I was walking home one night when I heard someone screaming. I went to investigate and found Kal being attacked by rogue dogs. Normally I would have just walked away. I didn't get involved with dogs or their affairs. But there was something in the way she was screaming that made me want to save her. Within minutes, they were all dead and Kal was near death. I picked her up and carried her to my house where I cared for her until she was better. She didn't even realize I was a vampire until she had been with me for days. Things got dicey for a minute when she finally realized what I was. I was never more thankful for her gift as I was then. I didn't want to kill her, but if she would have attacked me, I would have. She was able to see I only spoke the truth. We were kindred spirits, both of us wanting to be something else. We bonded over that." I was hoping that she wouldn't ask me any more questions about Kal.

"I'm glad you found her. You don't deserve to be alone," she mused more to herself than me. I answered her anyway.

"While I appreciate that very much. Before long, I will be alone again."

Cy looked at me with the most confused expression. I often forgot that only vampires understood what the word eternity truly means. Sure, Kal had many years of life to live. Werewolves typically live over one hundred years, but before I would be ready Kal would be gone. I tried not to think about it.

"You shouldn't think that way. Cherish the now," she told me as she shifted closer to me.

"I do. Believe me, I do. Is that all the questions you had?" I quickly responded, hoping to change the track of the conversation. Kal lived a rough life and not one that most would ask for. It wasn't my place to tell her secrets.

"No, but I'm not sure what's appropriate to ask," Cy confessed.

"Ask me anything. I'm an open book," I told her with a smile.

"When was the last time you slept with a woman?"

I could see her trying to picture me with a woman. I couldn't help but giggle before answering her.

"Are you offering, little witch?" I asked her between my giggles. I knew when I actually answered the question it was going to prompt fifty more. "Total honesty, Vin," I whispered to myself before turning so that my body was fully facing her. "About two weeks ago." I watched her face as her mind tried to comprehend what I had said.

"But you don't leave. How would that have even been possible?" she finally asked after a long pause.

"I didn't have to leave," I told her, trying to give her enough that she would put the pieces together herself.

"The only women you see are me, Fern, Dani, and Kal."

I looked at her very pointedly, my eyes wide and eyebrows high. I was honestly surprised that it was taking her so long to put two and two together. I watched as finally it clicked and her eyes widened.

"Hold the fuck on! You have sex with Kal?"

Chapter Six

DANI

A feeling of comfort and familiarity grabbed hold of me as I walked into the house that I shared with Gram. It was then I caught a very faded scent: Stefhan's scent. Instantly I was pulled back to what Barb said.

"How does Barb know you?" I asked him as he entered the living room carrying both Max and Phoenix.

"Can we talk about it later?" he asked me as he nodded toward Max.

That boy was smarter than most adults and didn't miss anything. There were a lot of things that now had to be discussed in private to avoid his questions. I didn't verbally answer his question, instead I just nodded my head.

"We can put the kids in Cy's old room. Her mattress is on the floor, so we don't have to worry about Max falling out of the bed. The bassinet will fit in there too, so we can have the pack-n-play in the living room," I explained as I took Phoenix and pointed at what I needed him to carry.

"Alright bub, I have to put you down so I can carry things for Mama," he told Max as he placed him on the floor.

"I help Mama, too! I big, strong wolf!" Max exclaimed as he walked to our pile of luggage and necessities. Stefhan handed Max a pack of diapers and then loaded up the bassinet.

"King of the one trip is back!" Stefhan whispered as I walked down the hallway toward Cy's room. The second I opened the door, it hit me.

"I didn't tell Cy we were leaving!" I almost yelled and guilt consumed me.

"It's okay, my love. I'm sure Jameson told her," Stefhan said as he wrapped his arms around me.

"No, it's not okay. Once we get the kids settled, I'm calling her," I told him as I shifted Phoenix to one side so that I could start unpacking the bassinet.

Cy and I still weren't back to where we were, but it was coming along. Between all the restrictions Stefhan put in, her need to bond with Vinnie, learning to control her powers, and me having a newborn and toddler, it was really hard for us to spend time together.

"Will you get Max ready for bed while I finish getting the room set up and Phoenix settled?" I asked Stefhan, already knowing what the answer would be.

"Come on bub, you heard Mama," he said to Max as he scooped him up and headed toward the bathroom.

I wasn't surprised that he didn't ask for directions. I knew he had already been inside before. That was something else I planned to ask him about. I didn't waste any time emptying the bassinet, so I could lay Phoenix down and get the room set up.

Once I had all the necessary items in logical places, I turned my focus to Phoenix and getting her to sleep. I changed her diaper and got her into a sleeper before settling in the rocking chair that was nestled in the corner of the room.

"Now remember bub, you have to be quiet and go to sleep, so you don't wake up your sister. If you wake her up, she'll start to cry," I heard Stefhan explaining to Max as they walked down the hallway to the bedroom.

"I no like when Pheenick cry, Papa. It so loud," Max complained as they turned the corner.

Stefhan quickly pointed to Phoenix and lifted his finger to his lips. Max looked, shook his head, and covered his mouth with his hands. The look of sheer determination on his little face was comical. His little black eyebrows furrowed with concentration; his eyes squinted. I had to hold back a laugh. Stefhan quickly got him settled in bed, and then he took Phoenix from me and placed her in the bassinet. I got up and walked to Max.

"Goodnight, little one. I love you," I told him as I placed a kiss on his cheek.

"Night night, Mama. I love you too," he said as he wrapped his arms around my neck and pulled me closer to him. I took a deep breath of his scent and let it fill me.

I waited for Stefhan in the hallway as he told Max goodnight for the fifth time. It was like this every night, the bond they shared was amazing. Finally, Stefhan emerged and closed the door behind him. I didn't say anything, just started walking toward the living room.

"I would say let me show you around, but since you've been here before, I don't think that's necessary," I told him with a coy smile.

"I thought for sure my scent would have been gone by now," he confessed as he sat on the couch and put his arms out for me to sit with him. I sat on his lap and laid my head on his chest.

"I came here when I was looking for Luan. I was flying out of Florida to go to Brazil. When I realized how close I was to your house, I had to come here. I needed to feel close to you, to smell your scent. It wasn't until I got here that I realized I had no way of getting into your house. Well, I did, but it would've been illegal. It was while I was sitting in the driveway looking suspicious as fuck and plotting how I was going to break into your house when Barb knocked on my window. I told her I was a friend of yours from the fellowship and that you asked me to stop by and grab some of your things. I told her that I forgot the key you had given me at my hotel, and it was an hour away. I asked her if she had a key, and she said yes and gave it to me. I was honestly shocked that in the state I was in she gave it up so easily.

"I was like a junky in desperate need of a fix. I made my way inside and was instantly disappointed. Since it had been so long since you had been here, your scent was so weak. Like a maniac, I made my way through the house until I found your room. I was hoping your scent would be stronger in there, and it was. I laid on your bed and let your scent consume me until I fell asleep. When I woke up, I looked around and tried to imagine you here." The emotions pouring off him were crushing.

He shifted us just enough to pull out his wallet. Slowly, he opened it, pulled out a small picture, and without a word handed it to me. I had to flip it over to see what it was. I was beyond shocked when I saw it was a picture of me at my white coat ceremony.

"I took it," he whispered before I could say anything. "I realized I didn't know what you looked like as you were growing up. So, I started looking at all the pictures on the walls. I missed you so much. I wanted to go home. I was going to go home, but Kane said we had to finish what we started. When I got to this one, you looked so happy, and there were more than one, so I took it. I needed to be able to see your face other than in my dreams."

I could feel his tears soaking into my hair. I wrapped my arms around him and pressed my lips to his chest. I knew I had to change the tone of the conversation fast.

"Well, if you like that one, just wait till you see these," I told him as I got up and made my way to the bookshelf.

I pulled out six huge photo albums labeled "Dani" and carried them back to the couch. My entire life was chronicled in those photo albums. Gram was addicted to taking pictures and documenting milestones. I settled in next to him and flipped open the first one. Slowly, we flipped through album after album, while he asked me question after question about each picture. He wanted to know the entire backstory, and thanks to my gift, I was able to provide it. By the time we got through the last album, he knew my life story from five years old to right before Gram's death. We had taken a trip to the Keys a month before she died. She had just put the pictures in three days before she was rushed to my hospital.

It was a little before midnight, and I still had to call Cy. I was tired and just wanted to lay down, so instead of calling I sent her a text apologizing for leaving in such a rush and not telling her. I told her to call me in the morning when she got up and we would talk. Once I sent the text, I got up and put the photo albums back on the shelf.

"Are you ready to go to bed?" Stefhan's voice suddenly whispered in my ear.

"Yes," I breathed back as I took his hand and led him to my room.

The sparks danced between us as I guided him down the hallway. It wasn't large enough for us to walk side by side. The closer we got, the more intense the sparks became. My pussy began to clench, and I could feel my panties getting wet.

"If you don't hurry and get us to your room, I'm going to take you right here in the hallway," Stefhan growled as he placed my hand on his rock-hard cock.

The reaction my body had to him was overwhelming. I increased my speed as I pulled him the rest of the way down the hall and into my room. Before he had time to process what was happening, I launched myself at him, knocking him on my bed. I straddled him and crushed my lips to his.

The electricity exploded between us as I ran my tongue along his lips. Our tongues danced in perfect harmony. I pulled at his shirt with one hand and mine with the other. I needed as much of his skin touching mine as possible. Without breaking our kiss, he sat up and with one yank ripped his shirt off, flinging the pieces to the side. I broke the kiss just long enough to pull my shirt off. I really liked the shirt I was wearing and didn't want it to meet the same fate as Stefhan's. With one deft hand, he unclasped my bra, stripped it off, and pulled my body against his.

"The things you do to me," he moaned against my mouth as he pressed his cock against me.

With feather-like touches, he kissed his way from my mouth to my jaw, slowly and methodically working his way down my neck until reaching my mark, scraping his teeth against it, sending a wave of pleasure rippling through me. I pushed him back so he was laying down again, before he could continue on his path.

Languidly I kissed my way down his neck, biting his mark as I worked my way down. The deep growl that emanated from his chest sent another wave of pleasure through me. I continued kissing my way down his chest to his stomach, running my tongue over the grooves of his perfectly sculpted abs, before making my way to his V-line. His breath hitched as I slid my fingers into his sweats and started pulling them down.

His cock sprung out like a jack-in-the-box and into my waiting mouth. A low hiss escaped his lips as I wrapped my mouth and both hands around him. Slowly, I slid my mouth up and down on his cock, each time taking a little more than the last. Due to the angle I was at, I wasn't able to take as much of him as I wanted.

"Stand up," I instructed him as I stopped and got off the bed.

Without hesitation, he stood in front of me. Thanks to our massive height difference, his cock was basically lined up with my mouth. I flicked my tongue against the head as I wrapped my hands around his shaft once more, while I swirled my tongue around the tip before quickly sucking him into my mouth. With measured movements, I slid my mouth farther down his shaft, keeping my hands and mouth in sync as I took more and more of his cock down my throat. When I couldn't take anymore, I started to increase my speed. With each stroke, I went faster and faster. The sounds that came from Stefhan were more than enough to keep me going. Feeling the tears streaming down my cheeks, I continued to take as much of his cock as I could. He had one hand wrapped in my hair and the other on my shoulder.

"Don't stop," he moaned as he squeezed my shoulder.

Knowing he was close only turned me on even more. I fought against my gag reflex and tried to take even more of him down my throat. I kept my rhythm and after a few seconds, Stefhan squeezed my shoulder even harder, and hot cum shot down my throat. When I released him, he lifted me up and placed me on the bed.

"So beautiful," he whispered as he leaned over me and placed his lips on mine. He didn't waste any time peeling my now-soaked leggings and underwear off. "So wet for me," he growled hungrily in my ear, sending goosebumps all over my now naked body.

He ran his tongue from my jaw to my breast, lightly tracing around my nipple before continuing his way to my clit, stopping just before his tongue made contact with my swollen bud, making my body tremor with anticipation. I wound my hand in his hair and tried to push his head down.

"So impatient," he teased as he flicked his tongue out, barely grazing my clit. While the contact was brief, it was enough to send a wave of electricity coursing through me. A low growl escaped my mouth as I tried again to push his head down. Stefhan let out a small laugh before wrapping his arms around my legs and locking them in place. He kissed each of my inner thighs before starting his oral assault on my now throbbing pussy. Like a skilled surgeon, he explored every crevice and fold.

Wave after wave of electricity flowed through me as he slid his fingers deep inside me. I had to grab a pillow to stifle the screams of pleasure I was no longer able to keep in. My body shook and thrashed against his hold as he continued to punish my pussy in the best way. Right as I was going to cum, he stopped.

"Not yet," he told me as I felt him adjusting his position.

I still had the pillow over my face, so I wasn't able to see his movements. It was kind of exciting not being able to see him. Only feeling his eyes on my naked body, I pushed myself into him until I felt the tip of his cock press against my pussy, causing just the head to go inside me. The electricity that rocked through me was like nothing I had ever experienced, causing me to go into a near frenzy.

Without warning, I threw the pillow off my face, wrapped my arms around his neck, and pulled his mouth to mine. Running my hands down his back and started pushing his ass down. I needed him more than I needed air, and I wasn't going to wait anymore. Stefhan pulled back and locked his eyes with mine as he repositioned himself and rammed his cock deeper inside me. We hissed in unison as he filled me completely. Stefhan grabbed onto the posts of my bed and rammed his cock in and out of me like a jackhammer. The mix of electricity and pure pleasure caused screams to exit my mouth one after the other. Stefhan placed his hand gently over my mouth in an attempt to stifle them, but he never decreased his speed or his intensity.

Knowing I was close, he rammed me with a speed and intensity that I didn't know was possible. The faster and harder he went, the harder and faster I wanted him to go. I clawed at any part of him I could as I reached my orgasm. As I rode the high the overwhelming need to claim him suddenly came over me. Without thought, I grabbed his neck, pulled it to my mouth, sunk my teeth into his mark, and came all over him. A low growl left Stefhan's mouth as he rammed his cock in and out two more times and released his load deep inside me.

He collapsed on the bed next to me with one arm draped over my body. We were both covered in sweat and our breathing was labored. I waited until my breath and heart rate went back to a normal rate before trying to move.

"Where are you going?" Stefhan whispered as he wrapped his arm tighter around me.

"I'm not going anywhere," I started as I continued to try and sit up. "We are going to take a shower. I can't feed our daughter covered in our sex juices. Then I'm going to change the sheets. We made quite the mess," I finished as I lightly smacked his ass.

"Fine," he whined. I knew he just wanted to go to sleep, but there wasn't a dry spot on us or the sheets, and I couldn't sleep like that.

Showering took a little longer than I had expected. I didn't realize until we were both in the shower how small it was in comparison to Stefhan's.

"Is the main bathroom shower bigger?" he asked me as he crouched down to wash his hair.

"No. It's the same size as this one," I said with a giggle.

After some acrobatics, we were clean and out of the shower. I then got to work on changing the sheets. Once they were changed, I wasn't anywhere near sleepy. Suddenly the letters were at the forefront of my mind. I was like a woman possessed. Without a word, I just walked out of my room and headed toward Gram's room. I could hear Stefhan following behind as I opened her door and marched inside.

Her scent hit me like a train and took me by surprise. I wasn't expecting it to still be so strong. It had been over two years since she passed, it should've been gone. I stopped so suddenly that Stefhan ran into me, almost knocking me to the ground, needing to grab me before I completely lost my balance.

"I'm so sorry! Are you okay?" he asked once he made sure I wasn't going to fall over.

"Yeah. I just wasn't expecting to be able to smell her scent," I whispered as I looked around her room.

"You can smell it?" he asked cautiously.

"You can't?" I asked in return.

"No. I could barely smell it when I was here last," he confessed.

"I think Gram is telling me that we're on the right track," I told him as I walked to her closet. Not hesitating before opening the door and grabbing her treasure chest. "Come on, we'll look at them in my room," I said as I closed the closet door and started walking back to the hallway. I heard Gram's door shut as I walked back into my room. I was already sitting in the middle of my bed with my legs crossed when Stefhan entered.

"In a hurry, my love?" he asked me as he shut the door and sat on the edge of the bed.

"I need to know what's in these letters," I told him as I opened the treasure chest. The letters were still sitting on top and bundled together with twine, just as I had left them. As I started to separate them, I realized that not only were they bundled together, but they were already separated into groups. Some had more letters than others. All the envelopes had Gram's elegant handwriting on the front. I spread the bundles across the bed like a fan, so I could see them all at once. As I got to the last bundle, I was shocked to see the name on the top envelope.

Danielle

My heart skipped a beat as I grabbed the bundle of letters and started taking off the twine that held them together. There were small numbers written in the corner of each envelope. Slowly, I flipped to the letter with the number one in the corner and opened the flap. Even slower, I slid the letter out of the envelope and unfolded it.

The feeling in the room shifted as I started to read.

My Sweet Dani Girl,

There is so much I have to tell you. So much you don't know. We all have a destiny and part of mine has been to keep you safe. Safe from a world that seeks to do you harm. You are more special than you know and are destined for such great things. I'm sorry that I can't tell you yet and that I have to lie to you about who we are and where we come from.

I continued to read as Gram explained things that I now already knew. She told me that I was a werewolf and how she and my parents suspected I was the Fire Wolf. She told me what happened during the attack on Green Diamond and how we went into hiding. She told me about her background, how Cy's parents helped her, and our relation to them.

After reading the first letter, I quickly opened the second and third. They too were filled with things that I already knew. She told me about how she suppressed my wolf and the lengths she went through to make sure I was safe. It wasn't until the fourth letter that my world was rocked completely. This letter was different from the others I had read so far. It was more like a journal entry.

May 31st

Yesterday started like any other day. I had been invited to a luncheon for the Women's Club. I really didn't want to go, but Phyliss insisted that as the Secretary it would look bad if I didn't make an appearance. Of course, I couldn't tell her why I didn't want to go. It was being put on by Storme Medical, and Stefhan Storme will be there. While I have no doubt that my spell will hide who I am, it still makes me nervous to be around him. I don't like to be around wolves. It puts our cover at risk, and I can't risk anyone finding out who we are.

Mr. Storme was due to arrive in the middle of the luncheon. My plan was to get there, mingle enough to where everyone saw me, and leave before he arrived. My plan quickly was thrown out the window the second I walked in. To my horror, he was already there and standing right inside the entrance. I chanted a quick cloaking spell, not that I wasn't reeking with them already. I was nervous and doing it made me feel not as exposed. Thankfully before I made it to the door, he started walking into the dining hall. I stood outside and waited for a few minutes before entering. I wanted to make sure he wouldn't be right inside the hall.

Again, luck wasn't on my side. As I entered the dining hall, he was sitting at the check-in table with Phyliss. I thought about turning around and leaving. Before I could turn around, loudmouth Phyliss called out to me, "Betty, come meet Mr. Storme." That of course brought me right to his attention, and I had no choice but to walk to the table. At that point, it was like Selene herself was trying to make sure I crossed paths with him.

He was sitting and it gave me a clear view of his neck. I almost fainted when I saw his birthmark barely peeking out of his shirt. Of course, I knew he would have one, that wasn't what was shocking. It was the shape. A perfect crescent moon. He is Dani's mate. I managed to get through the introduction and take my seat. I find myself thankful now. The next piece of the puzzle has fallen into place. I know it's not time for Dani to meet her mate. First, she is too young still, she wouldn't be able to feel the pull and second, my dream last night confirmed it's not time. My dreams have never guided me wrong, and I have to trust in the Goddess' plan. I have to wait for the next piece of the puzzle to fall into place.

"She knew you were my mate," I whispered. I had way more questions than answers. Before Stefhan could say anything, I opened the fifth letter. It was more journal entries.

June 25th

Dani got hired at the local hospital today. She is so happy, and it fills me with just as much joy as it does dread. For years I have done everything I can to conceal who we truly are from the supernatural world. Thankfully most wolves don't care for sunny, beachy climates. My protections are going to be put to the ultimate test. The hospital Dani's going to be working at is owned by Stefhan Storme. I don't anticipate him being there often. It's not time yet.

August 31st

My assumption was incorrect. He is at the hospital more often than I thought he would be. Any doubt I had on how powerful my protection spells are have been laid to rest. Today, as I was walking through the hospital with Dani to get lunch, we ran into Carlos. I should have known that there would be at least one pack member working there. It was an oversight on my part. But thankfully he didn't recognize me. Dani invited him to eat with us, but he said he had to meet Mr. Storme. I was never more thankful that he had to decline. I would rather be around Stefhan than him. Carlos knew me when I was Ruth, and he knows my birthmark.

December 15th

I'm a nervous wreck! Dani's at a Christmas party tonight. Stefhan is going to be there. Dani's dress, while beautiful, barely covers her birthmark. My dreams are steadfast in telling me that it's not time for them to meet. I know they will eventually cross paths, I just pray to the Goddess that my protections are enough to keep her concealed from him. He is not only an Alpha, but he is also a descendant. The mate pull is the strongest emotion a wolf can feel, and I don't know if my magic is strong enough.

March 12th

Dani was promoted to head doctor today! She has worked so hard for this. She wants to get into the fellowship offered by Storme Medical. She is determined to figure out what causes the headaches. I want to tell her so bad, so she will stop pursuing it. I'm so worried that Carlos will find us out before it's time and everything will be ruined. She'll be working with Carlos more closely now. I put more protections on the house and Dani. My greatest fear is they will smell her wolf scent.

June 2nd

My dreams are still telling me that it's not time. I'm not sure how much longer I can keep this from her. It's not fair that she doesn't know who she truly is and *that her whole life has been a carefully fabricated lie. It's getting harder knowing that she's losing time with her mate. The only thing that keeps me going is knowing the importance of my role. I must trust in the Goddess.*

June 30th

My dreams told me to wait for a sign that it's time for the next step. I was told that it will come in the form I least expect.

The letters were a timeline of my life. A life I had no clue about. It was a lot to take in, but I still had one more letter that was addressed to me. As I picked it up there was a heaviness that filled me. Slowly and carefully, I opened the envelope and removed the letter inside. As I unfolded it and saw the first line, I knew this letter was going to be the most world-shattering of them all.

My Dear Sweet Dani Girl,

I'm so sorry it has to be this way. I'm so sorry that I wasn't able to tell you sooner who you are and what your destiny is. While there are many lies I have told you over the years, I wasn't lying when I told you that you are destined for great things.

I planned to sit you down, read all the letters and notes that I have, and explain everything when the time was right. Even with all my precautions and spells, we were still discovered. I was ambushed when I got home today. I was able to fight him off for a while before he captured me. I could tell that he really didn't want to do what he is here to do. I was able to get the man to start talking to me. He told me his name is Marcus White and he is under the control of the God of the Witches, Salix. He told me that his family has been bound to serve him for centuries. He told me the whole plan, and how he wanted to save you, but he didn't know how. It was then that I heard a voice tell me it was time.

Marcus truly wants to keep you from the horrible fate that his son and Salix have planned for you. I will do whatever it takes to keep you safe, including ending my life. I've come up with a plan that not only keeps you safe but also gives Marcus an alibi as to why he didn't take you. I have a syringe of wolfsbane, it's enough to kill three wolves easily. Marcus is going to inject it directly into my heart. He will then call 911, report an emergency at the house and leave.

I'm so sorry that you are going to have to see me like that. I can't risk Marcus' son coming here before Marcus can tell him that I'm dead and that they need to lay low for a while. I know that you will have Carlos prepare my body and that's when he will see my birthmark. He will instantly recognize it and call Ryland, who will in turn call Stefhan. As you already know, because you are a smart girl and have already read the other letters that I left for you, he is your mate. He will be able to help you get through the headaches of your wolf emerging and your first shift.

I know what you're thinking, and I haven't lost my mind, and you aren't in a coma dream. The reality you were raised in is just a speck of the actual truth. So much is hidden, some of these hidden things you will discover. I feel like I have failed you by keeping the truth from you for so long. Everything I ever did was with your best interest at heart. Not telling you was something I battled with for years. There were a couple of times I almost told you, but since I don't have a wolf, I had no way of proving it to you. I even thought about asking Willow and Oak to reverse the memory spell I had placed on you.

But it didn't take long for me to throw that idea out the window. You had a nightmare the same night that the thought crossed my mind. The nightmare was the only part of your memory we weren't able to erase. I knew if I had the spell reversed it wouldn't just unlock the good memories. It would also unlock the rest of the nightmare. You saw your parents die, and it traumatized you beyond belief. You didn't speak for days and then would only speak *to me for weeks after. I refused to put that back in your memories.*

I know you're scared, but you have more power inside you than you know. You just have to harness it. I am going to try and help you as much as I can. I will always be with you. Watch for signs.

I love you.

My brain couldn't process what I had just read. Marcus wasn't lying, Gram really did tell him to kill her. My eyes filled with tears as the words kept flashing in my mind. Stefhan wrapped his arms around me and pulled me into his chest. He didn't speak, just held me while I cried until I finally fell asleep.

Unforeseen Destinies

Chapter Seven

Stefhan never mentioned the letters, and neither did I. I needed time to process everything that was in them. I still hadn't even touched the other letters. Some were addressed to Willow, Oak, and Cy. I packed their letters in my suitcase, so I could disperse them when we got home.

Over the next couple of days, I took Stefhan and the kids to all my favorite places. Max was most excited about the beach. He missed the sand and the ocean and threw a massive fit when it was time to leave.

When we weren't out doing family things, I was searching through every possession Gram owned. I didn't want any more surprises. Frankly, I could go the rest of my life without another one. I searched in every cupboard and drawer; it felt strange going through her things. For days I looked, not finding anything of interest or help. We had been in Florida for almost a week. Stefhan didn't want to stay longer than two weeks. He didn't like leaving Vinnie and Cy there with him being so far away. I had already checked all the places you would think someone would hide stuff. It wasn't until I looked in the kitchen that I found something that seemed important.

I had the sudden urge to look in a small cabinet above the stove. Honestly, I didn't even know it opened. I always thought it was one of those fake decorative cupboard doors. I never saw Gram open it, but the nagging urge to try it consumed me. I grabbed a chair and dragged it over to the stove, climbed on the chair, and gave the door a gentle tug. I could tell that it was meant to open but was stuck, so I pulled a little harder and the door popped open. There was only one thing in the cupboard. A book.

The book had a layer of dust on it that I had to wipe off in order to see the cover. It was unlike any book I had ever seen. The thick black cover had carvings on the cover, but no words. Slowly, I sat down on the chair I was standing on and flipped open the cover. It didn't take long for me to realize it was a book of spells. I quickly shut it and carried it to my bedroom. There was no way in hell I was fucking with any kind of spells. I hid it at the bottom of my suitcase, covering it with clothes. Where it would stay until we got home, and I could take it to Willow and Oak.

I told Stefhan about the book as we lay in bed that night. I was hesitant to tell him about it at first. I knew once I told him what I found he would want to go back home immediately. I wasn't ready to leave, and it was for a purely selfish reason. This was the first time since we came back from California that I had Stefhan and the kids all to myself. There was no one needing Stefhan or trying to take the kids. I wanted to drag out my full two weeks, but I couldn't keep something like that from him just because I wanted him all to myself.

"We have to get home, so the Meadows can look at it," Stefhan started before I cut him off.

"I know, but can we please stay just a few more days?" I pleaded, putting my selfishness on full display. He looked at me in disbelief. I didn't give him time to say anything before I continued. "Look, I know there are a thousand reasons why we need to get back home as soon as possible. But it's been so nice with it just being us and the kids. Back home, someone always needs you for something, or someone wants the kids. I like having you all to myself, and us being our own little family unit."

As soon as the words left my mouth, regret consumed me. I sounded like a selfish brat. Again, proving that I didn't deserve him, Stefhan pulled me into his chest and kissed my head.

"We can stay a little longer," he whispered against my hair.

"We don't have to. I know we need to get back. I'm being selfish and now isn't the time for it," I told him as I kissed his chest.

He leaned back so that he could look at me.

"We. Are. Staying," he said as his eyes burned into mine.

"Why?" I whispered before I could stop myself.

"Because this is what you need. I always want you to tell me what you need from me. You and the kids are my everything, and nothing will come before you. I am your mate before I am anyone's Alpha. The problems will be there when we get back, and it's not like we're going to solve everything overnight once we get there," he replied like it was common knowledge.

Slowly Stefhan lowered us into a lying position where I quickly fell asleep, listening to his heartbeat.

I was standing back in the field. Grief coursed through me as I turned toward the bench and saw Gram. I ran full speed to her and launched myself into her arms.

"You didn't have to do that! We could have come up with another way! You should have just told me!" I sobbed as she rubbed my back.

"My sweet Dani girl, it had to be done that way. It was the only way to protect you. Let me ask you a question. Would you do anything to protect your children?"

"Of course," I answered immediately.

"So would I and I did," she told me simply before continuing. "But that's not why you're here." She was right, and I knew I didn't have much time. I couldn't waste it on things that I couldn't change.

"I went home and read the letters, and I found the book in the kitchen," I started before pausing to gauge her reaction. She just smiled at me and nodded for me to continue. "What is it?" I asked her outright. I was so over cryptic bullshit. I shouldn't have to ask the Meadows' what it is when she was right in front of me. Gram just looked at me and smiled.

"It's our family Grimoire," she said without hesitation. It was the fastest and most direct answer she had ever given me about anything supernatural. "We don't have enough

time for me to explain all its wonders to you. But the Meadows can. Take it to Willow," she continued quickly as she looked into the distance. "Remember, you can handle anything, and I love you." She placed a quick kiss on my cheek and squeezed me tight. Almost too tight.

I woke up with a feeling of dread. I went over the dream quickly in my head. I needed to fully commit it to memory before Stefhan and the kids woke up. Other than the end, there wasn't anything out of the ordinary about my visit with Gram. But I couldn't tell if I was overthinking the hug, it wasn't the first time she squeezed me a little harder than usual. I lay there going through the dream repeatedly until Phoenix started to cry. Stefhan began to stir immediately and opened his eyes.

"I'll get her. You wake up and then get Max," I whispered to him and gently placed my lips to his.

"Why are you up so early?" he whispered back.

"Later," I told him as I rolled off the bed and headed toward the door.

We had planned to go to the museum but those plans quickly changed. It was going to storm all day, and the thought of having two kids out in the storm that was coming was not my idea of a good time. So, we stayed at the house, played games, and watched TV. I couldn't get over how absolutely perfect everything at that moment was. Watching Stefhan play with

Max on the floor while Phoenix napped in my arms, I found myself thinking that this is what life would have been like if we weren't wolves.

"I thought we were past you wanting to be rid of me, child," Enya told me with a laugh after picking up on my thoughts.

"We are," I told her, returning her laugh.

Max helped me make lunch and seeing him sitting on the same counter that I did as a child made my heart ache. It brought back memories of me helping Gram cook. It always made me feel so grown up when she called me in to help. Once we ate and cleaned up, I laid Phoenix down for her nap. As I walked to the living room, I could hear Stefhan's phone ringing. Sarai had been calling every day to check on us. Well, more on the kids and to ask when we would be back. She missed them terribly. He was answering the phone right as I entered the room.

"Fern?" he said, completely surprised. I couldn't hear what she was saying, but I could feel the confusion rolling off Stefhan. "I'm fine. Why? What do you mean you've been trying to link me? You're freaking me out."

His response made me uneasy, so I walked closer to him in hopes of being able to hear what she was saying. Sensing what I was doing, Stefhan quickly stood, grabbed my hand, and pulled me into the kitchen. Once there, he put the phone on speaker.

"Dammit! I wasn't prepared for this!" Fern cried.

"What in the hell is going on?" he asked pointedly.

"Give me a fucking minute, Stefhan! I wasn't expecting to have to tell you. You should already know!" she shrieked.

"Fern, calm down and tell me what's going on. What should I already know?" He tried to keep his voice calm, but I could hear and feel his frustration.

"That our mother is dead!" she screamed.

My brain wanted to shut off. I couldn't process what I just heard. I could hear Enya's voice screaming at me.

"You cannot shut down, child! He needs you!"

I gave my head a hard shake to bring myself back into the present. She was right: Stefhan needed me, and I had to pull it together.

"What do you mean she's dead? How? It's impossible! I would've felt it the second it happened!" he roared into the phone, making the window in the kitchen shake. When his rage hit me, it took my breath away.

"I mean someone killed her! She went for her morning run and didn't come back. We found her about a mile in the forest. I have no clue how you didn't feel it, but you need to get your ass home now!"

Stefhan was already moving before she finished speaking, running toward the bedroom.

"I'll be there tonight. I'm not waiting for the plane," he growled into the phone before ending the call. His rage was growing and honestly was starting to scare me.

"Stefhan," I whispered, causing him to stop and face me.

His eyes were black voids with green swirls. Slowly I walked up to him and placed my hand on his chest. His heart was racing, he was sweating and starting to shake. I knew I had to rein him in before it got out of control, and he shifted.

"You need to calm down. This isn't the time for you to do this," I told him as I locked my eyes with his, wrapped my arms around him, and pulled him closer to me. Instinctively he dropped down to his knees, wrapped his arms around me, and buried his face in my neck. The sobs that rocked through him shattered me completely.

"Why you cry, Papa?" I heard Max's voice call from the doorway.

Stefhan took a quick breath and wiped his face before turning to Max.

"Something sad happened, and we have to go home. Don't worry, I'm okay and we'll talk about it when we get home. Right now, I need you to go back to the living room and wait for me," he explained as he hugged and kissed Max. He nodded his head and immediately went back to the living room.

"Will you please pack our bags while I get the flight arranged?" he asked me without turning.

"Of course. Anything you need," I said. I wasn't sure what to do or how to comfort him. I could feel his emotions and knew he was a complete mess. He didn't speak, he just walked out of the kitchen and headed for the living room. I sprinted to the closet and started throwing our clothes into the suitcases. Once I had us packed, I ran to the kids' room and started doing the same. I had just finished when Stefhan suddenly appeared in the doorway of the kids' room.

"We need to be at the airport in three hours. Is that enough time to make it?" he asked me, his voice a strange mix of rage and grief.

"That's plenty of time," I quickly assured him.

Truthfully it was, but even if it wasn't I would have made it. I started putting the suitcases in the living room for Stefhan to carry to the car. While he was doing that, I started breaking down the pack-n-play and gathering all of the toys. Stefhan was taking things out of my hands before I could finish packing them properly. At one point, I just stepped back and let him do it. He was like a machine, and I knew he needed to stay as busy as he could to keep his rage in check.

As he took out the last of our belongings, I started getting the kids to the car. I hadn't even closed the door behind me before Stefhan was at my side taking Phoenix from me and grabbing Max's hand. Quickly I shut and locked the door before running to the car and jumping in. I threw the car in reverse and started backing down the driveway.

The second the front tires hit the road, Stefhan grabbed his chest and roared in pain. Both kids started screaming and the windows violently shook. When his agony hit me, I almost drove into a mailbox. I slammed on the brakes just in time and threw the car in park. I immediately checked on the kids, who were okay, just scared. Thankfully the windows didn't break. I then turned my attention to Stefhan, who was still clutching his chest. Before I could speak, he turned to me.

"I'm fine. Just get us to the airport. We have to get home."

Unforeseen Destinies

Chapter Eight

CY

Dani, Stefhan, and the kids had been gone for about a week and a half. I had been spending a lot of time with Vinnie, and we were starting to get close. I still couldn't wrap my head around the fact that he was having sex with Kal. He had explained to me, after my initial shock wore off, that it was more of a convenience thing. Of course, me being a nosy bitch, I asked him how it even came to be. He told me that was a story for another day.

I was sitting on the couch, contemplating questions for the next visit. My parents were in the kitchen making lunch when the front door flew open.

"You and your parents need to pack a bag and come with me now," Jam instructed me before he was even all the way inside.

"What's going on, Jam?" I asked him without moving.

"Just do what I say, Cy, and don't ask questions. I have to get you to the packhouse. Willow, Oak! Get a bag packed, we are leaving in five minutes," he commanded as he headed toward my room.

There was something different in the way he was acting. While being different, it was familiar. It was similar to how he acted when Dani was taken. As the dots connected in my brain, I flew off the couch and ran full speed to my room. Jam was already throwing my clothes in my suitcase. He spun to face me when I entered.

"I don't have time to explain right now. I have to get you somewhere safe first. But Dani, Stefhan, and the kids are fine." His voice sounded almost frantic, but his movements were focused. "Go and make sure your parents are packing. We leave in three minutes."

I didn't question him that time, instead I did what he asked. I turned and headed to my parents' room. As I turned the corner, I could see them both packing their bags.

"I wonder what's going on?" my mom asked my dad as I ran in.

"Not a clue, but something tells me that we need to do what he says," my dad answered as he threw more clothes into a bag.

"We're leaving in three minutes," I started before Jam's voice cut me off.

"Two minutes. I'm taking Cy's stuff to the car. Meet me there."

I helped my parents grab their bags, and we ran toward the front door. Jam hadn't even bothered to close it, leaving it wide open. My parents went out ahead of me as I paused just long enough to shut and lock the door. Terror was raging through me as I ran to the car, even though I had no clue what the cause was.

Jam took the bags from my parents and literally threw them into the trunk. I threw the bags I held in the trunk too and ran to the passenger seat. My parents were in the back, looking as confused as I felt. It was times like this that I wished I was able to link Jam. I didn't like being completely in the dark. Jam was in the driver's seat and backing out of the driveway before I had my seatbelt buckled.

He raced up the forest road to the packhouse. Normally I would have told him to slow the fuck down. But the look he had on his face was one I had never seen before, and it terrified me. We sat in silence the entire ride and way faster than I thought was possible, we were pulling into the private garage of the packhouse.

"The second I put the car in park, you take your parents and go directly to Vinnie's. I'll come back later for your bags," he said sternly, causing me to jump.

Again, I did what I was told, and the moment the car stopped, I was on the move. My parents quickly got out behind me, and I guided them toward Vinnie's. I didn't look back until we were coming up to the massive door that sealed off Vinnie and Kal's rooms. My parents were right behind me, but I couldn't see Jam. I didn't have time to fully process that before I heard the door swing open.

"Hurry up and get in," Luan said as he grabbed me and pulled me inside. He shut and locked the door the second my parents cleared the frame. I took a quick glance around the room to see Vinnie, Kal, and Fern all sitting at the table. Almost as fast as Vinnie, Luan was at Fern's side. There was a protectiveness to his stance. I glanced back at my parents who still had yet to move from by the door.

"Sit down, little witch and little witches' parents. We are going to be here awhile," Vinnie said to me as he slowly stood and started walking toward me.

"What in the fuck does that mean? What's going on?" I asked him a little more harshly than intended.

"Of course, Jay wouldn't fucking tell her," Fern hissed under her breath.

"I got this, Fern," Kal quickly told her as she stood. Kal nodded her head toward her room and then at me and my parents. We followed her into her bedroom, and she promptly shut the door behind us.

"Look there isn't a delicate way to put this, so I'm just going to say it," she started as she looked at each of us one-by-one. "Sarai is dead. Someone killed her during her morning run. Dani and Stefhan are on their way back. Ryland is losing his shit and is currently in wolf form, running the forest. Fern told Jameson to go looking for him, but he refused until he made sure that you and your parents were safe. She told him to bring you all here and then to go find her dad. She wanted Luan to go too, but he refused to leave her side. We don't know what happened and Fern isn't really talking much. No one is allowed to leave the shelter until Stefhan gets here."

I didn't have time to even start wrapping my brain around what she said before both my parents gasped.

"Sarai is dead?" my mom whispered as she moved closer to me.

Kal nodded her head.

"I don't know what happened. Fern just showed up here a little bit ago and said that her mom was murdered. She said that she already called Stefhan, and they are on their way back. She said that once he gets here she will tell us what happened, she doesn't want to have to keep repeating it." Concern was written all over Kal's face. "I made some sandwiches if you're hungry. I wasn't sure if you would have already eaten before Jameson got there to get you," she quickly added. I could tell she just wanted to change the subject before I could ask any questions.

"Aren't you going to introduce me to your parents, little witch?" Vinnie nearly squealed the second we walked out of Kal's room.

It was then I realized that Vinnie wasn't the only person who hadn't met my parents. Everyone in the room had never met them. The only people who had met them were Stefhan and Jam. They had been in Crimson Diamond for months, and it completely slipped my mind that they hadn't met anyone else.

"Of course. These are my parents, Willow and Oak Meadow. Mom, Dad, this is Kal, Fern, Luan, and Vinnie," I replied, trying to keep it short.

The next few hours dragged like time had stopped. I wanted to ask Fern to link Jam, but I thought better of it. I wasn't Fern's favorite person, so it wouldn't have gone over well. I just had to wait for him to come back. Vinnie talked with my parents, asking them questions about their lineage, and Kal stayed close to Fern and Luan. Not having anyone to talk to, I leaned my head back and closed my eyes.

I was suddenly jarred awake by the loudest sound I had ever heard, followed by a lot of screaming.

"Ryland! You have to calm down!" Jam screamed.

"Dad! Please calm down!" Fern yelled

"We're going to have to restrain him if he doesn't calm down soon," Luan screamed over the other voices.

"Maybe you should have left him in the woods," Vinnie chimed in.

My eyes focused just in time to see Jam, Luan, and Fern trying to hold a feral-looking and growling Ryland still. His eyes were flashing from blue to a deep brown and his face looked stretched. He was fighting against their hold, and he was foaming at the mouth.

"We can't let him shift in here!" Fern screamed.

As the words left Fern's mouth, three things happened so fast I would have missed them if I had blinked. Ryland broke free of their hold–black fur sprouting from his skin–a breeze caressed my face, and Ryland slumped to the floor with Vinnie standing over him.

"What did you do, Vin?" Kal shrieked.

"Oh, calm down. I only knocked him out. He'll be fine. Fern just said we couldn't let him shift in here. I don't know if you were paying attention, but that was exactly what was about to happen. You should be thanking me," he snapped at her as he fixed his shirt and stepped over Ryland's unconscious body. "Someone may want to start restraining him. He probably won't be happy when he wakes up and he won't be out for long," he continued as he dramatically lowered himself into his chair.

I looked over at my parents and was shocked to see they were essentially unphased about what just occurred. They merely watched as Jam and Luan started tying up Ryland.

"Do you think rope is strong enough to hold him?" my dad asked as they started wrapping the ropes around this massive frame.

"No, but that's why we also have this," Jam answered as he held up a syringe.

I had no clue what was in it and was hoping that my dad would ask, so my curiosity would be quenched. He didn't, he just nodded in agreement.

"You're going to inject him with wolfsbane?" Kal whispered, coming to my rescue.

"We have no choice! His grief is too strong, the second he wakes up he's going to shift and go ape shit! It's either enough wolfsbane to prevent him from shifting or wrapping him in silver. Wolfsbane seemed like the more humane option. Stefhan will be here in a couple of hours. We just have to keep him under control until then," Jam explained as he prepped the syringe and injected some into Ryland's arm.

Luan and Jam moved Ryland into Kal's room and locked him in, alternating turns checking on him. Jam paced the floor and checked his phone every thirty seconds. The minutes ticked by in slow motion, and no one talked. After an hour of sitting in silence, only hearing the sounds of Jam's pacing, footsteps, and breathing, I closed my eyes and tried to go back to sleep.

"Are you sleeping?" Jam's voice whispered in my ear.

"No," I whispered back without opening my eyes.

"Can we talk? In private?" he asked.

"And where do you propose we go? We can't leave until Stefhan gets here," I told him as I opened my eyes to find his waiting.

"Vinnie said we could use his room," Jam replied with a smile. A smile that didn't quite touch his eyes.

I nodded my head in agreement and peeled myself off the couch. I followed him into Vinnie's room and closed the door behind me. Before the door was latched, Jam pulled me into his arms.

"I'm so sorry," he whispered in my ear and kissed my cheek.

"For what?" I asked him as I wrapped my arms around him.

"For how I handled this and not making sure you were okay."

"What are you talking about?" I asked him dumbfounded.

"I just barged in and told you and your parents to get packed. No explanation. You had to find out from Kal. You should have heard it from me. Never in my worst nightmares did I ever think that Sarai would not only be murdered but murdered while Stefhan is away and I'm in charge of the pack! I went into full Beta mode. I had to make sure you and your parents were safe, then I had to find Ryland and get him back here. I knew if I told you that she was dead you would ask a million questions, and it wasn't something that I was ready to face. I don't know what happened. Fern said she won't say until Stefhan gets home and as you can see; Ryland is in no state to tell us anything. I should have slowed down and told you what I knew."

I could feel his tears hitting my shirt. I squeezed my arms around him a little tighter then leaned back so that I could look at him.

"You have nothing to apologize for. You did what you thought was best at the time. I'm fine and so are my parents. If anything, they're taking all of this too well," I assured him and kissed his cheek.

"Your parents were raised in this world. They aren't as naive as you like to think they are," he replied with a strained laugh. He pulled me back into his chest and held me. I didn't move, I refused to break our embrace first. If that was what he needed, I was willing to give it to him. We stood there wrapped in each other's arms for what seemed like hours, not moving until there was a knock on the door.

"They just landed and will be here in an hour," Fern's voice called through the door.

As the minutes ticked by, the more tense the atmosphere became. Fern had started pacing; it was almost like she could sense that Stefhan was getting closer. She kept glancing at the large wall clock that hung on the east wall of the room. It was after the sixth time she looked at it that the lock on the massive door leading into the hallway opened.

"WHAT IN THE FUCK HAPPENED?" Stefhan's voice filled the room, shaking the walls.

Chapter Nine

STEFHAN

"We're the opposite of fine, boy! Fern couldn't link you; we didn't feel Sarai die! How is that fine?" Kane's pain-filled howls echoed in my head.

I didn't answer him, I couldn't. I had to concentrate all my energy on not losing my shit. I didn't want to scare Dani and the kids more than I already had. I tried to take a deep breath, but the unrelenting pain that blazed inside my chest made it impossible. I gripped the dashboard in an attempt to pull myself together. I was afraid to hold Dani's hand, feeling the rage starting to build inside me, I was afraid I would squeeze her too tight.

"She is the grounding force. You have to let her be that," Abbadon's voice lightly echoed in my head.

Timidly, I reached over, placed my hand on her thigh, and the rage began to subside. She laid her hand softly on top of mine and started to trace small circles.

"Shouldn't you have known?" Dani whispered about halfway to the airport, breaking the silence for the first time.

"Known what?" I asked.

"That your mom—"

"Yes. I should have known instantly. Just like I did with Garrett. But there was nothing, I felt perfectly fine," I quickly answered so she wouldn't finish the question. I then proceeded to tell her everything that had been running through my mind: "When Fern called, she said that she tried to link me but couldn't get through. I wasn't blocking her. Then when we pulled out of the driveway, everything hit me at once. It was like it was delayed or something. Nothing makes fucking sense. I just want to get home and find out what happened."

Dani didn't speak, just nodded in agreement, and pressed her foot harder on the gas. She drove like a skilled racecar driver, weaving in and out of traffic with what looked like minimal effort. I had the fullest faith that Jay and Luan could handle the pack, but I wasn't so sure they could handle my dad. Losing your mate was devastating, and I was sure he was losing his shit.

"Probably running in the forest," Kane said more to himself than me.

An image of Jay and Luan trying and failing to subdue him flashed in my mind. Not only was my dad a former Alpha, but he was also a descendant, so he was already stronger than both of them. Add on top of that the grief and rage he was experiencing, and they wouldn't stand a chance against him.

"I'm almost to the airport. Tell Jay to use wolfsbane, so dad can't shift," I linked Fern, hoping that whatever blocked our connection was now lifted.

"It's so good to hear you in my head again!" my sister's voice immediately answered, and a wave of relief washed over me. *"And I already did. He's in wolf form running in the forest like a wild animal. Jay refused to go look for him until he made sure Cy and her parents were safe.*

We're all at Vinnies. I've told everyone they can't leave until you get here."

"Tell me the second he's found. It's good to hear you, too."

Thanks to Dani's race car driving we arrived at the airport with plenty of time to catch the plane I chartered. I watched in awe as she navigated the massive airport with ease. We worked in perfect harmony getting the kids out and the car unloaded. It was like she could read my mind, doing the exact thing I was just about to ask her to do. We ran toward our gate and out to the plane. I watched as her face turned to shock when she realized what plane we were getting on.

"You got a private plane?" she asked me as we got settled into our seats.

"Yes. It was better and faster. Marie's going to have a stroke, but she'll get over it," I said as I put my hand on hers and squeezed.

"Why would she have a stroke?" Concern covered her face.

"When she sees how much I spent." I forced a smile.

"How much was it?" she immediately asked.

"One hundred thousand dollars. I would have spent a million and not thought twice about it," I told her honestly. I watched as her eyes went wide and bulged slightly. We never talked about money. Dani never asked, and I never brought it up. She gave her head a quick shake and squeezed my hand.

It was the longest flight of my life. Max repeatedly asked why we were going home, and I couldn't find the words to answer him. Thankfully Dani answered for me, telling him that Aunt Fern called and said that something happened, and we needed to come home.

Fern linked me a little over halfway through the fight and told me that Jay found Dad. They had him locked in Kal's room in the bunker. That made me want to get home even faster. I didn't like that they were in such close proximity to him, but I couldn't have them move. It was still daylight.

I had to keep touching Dani to keep my emotions in check. The rage simmered fiercely just under the surface, begging to be let out.

"You need to calm down. This isn't the time for you to do this." I repeated Dani's words, making them my mantra.

When the plane stopped, I flew out of my seat and started grabbing our bags. Impatiently I waited, arms full, for the attendant, whose existence I hadn't acknowledged until that very second, to open the door. Once she had the door opened and the stairs down, I was out of the plane and on my way to the car.

I sent Fern a link, letting her know that we landed and were an hour out. I raced back and forth from the plane to the car getting everything loaded. Dani got both kids in and started the ignition from the passenger side. I ran to the car and jumped in, throwing it into reverse before my door was closed. The rage became more intense the closer we got to Crimson Diamond. Placing my hand on Dani's, I repeated my mantra.

My first priority was getting my family home safely, losing my shit would come after that.

I drove over the speed limit, but not enough to make Dani say anything. Even with her race car driving, she kept it at a relatively reasonable speed. When I finally made the turn to go to Crimson Diamond, I floored it. I knew this path like the back of my hand, and it was smooth enough that it wouldn't jostle Phoenix. I only slowed down for the more serious curves–not that I needed to, but I knew it would scare Dani. I was going to scare her enough before this was done, so I was trying not to add to it.

When I could finally see the packhouse in the distance, the rage that was building inside me rose tenfold. I smashed the gas pedal to the floor and kept it there until we reached the packhouse. I slowed down to pull into the garage and looked at Dani.

"You grab Phoenix, and I'll grab Max. I'll come back later for the bags."

The moment the car was parked, Dani jumped out and opened the back door. I jumped out and grabbed Max. I grabbed Phoenix from Dani as she rounded the back of the car. I let her lead and followed close behind her. The closer we got, the faster I wanted to go. I repeated my mantra as I found myself getting irritated that Dani wasn't moving as fast as I wanted to go. When we made the last turn and I could see the door to the bunker, I moved in front of Dani and kicked the door open.

"WHAT IN THE FUCK HAPPENED?" I roared, my rage breaking the surface. Suddenly I felt Dani's hand on the small of my back.

"Not the time," she linked as she pressed her hand slightly harder against me. Sensing I was on the verge of losing it, Fern immediately launched into the story.

"She went for her morning run. Saying she was excited because she had someone to run with that morning. Before you ask, she didn't say who. Nothing was out of the ordinary until she wasn't back for lunch. Dad and I both tried to link her and nothing. Right as Lu and I were getting ready to go look for her, Dad let out the most heartbreaking howl I've ever heard. He damn near didn't make it outside before he shifted. I had no clue what was going on, that's when I first tried to get a hold of you and couldn't. Lu and I shifted and went looking for Mom. I figured if I found her, I would find Dad.

"I was right. Callie and Batté followed Mom's scent, and soon enough Dad's joined it. We followed it to the ravine. Mom's body was at the bottom, and Ajax was crouching over her. Once we were at the bottom, I shifted back and tried to convince Ajax to shift. Every time I tried to get close to Mom, he would growl and snap at me. I couldn't see if she was breathing, so Batté had to charge him. Then Batté chased him up the ravine, so I could check on Mom.

"She had no pulse, but was still warm and in a sundress I didn't recognize. There were no visible injuries or blood. She looked like she was sleeping. Batté chased Ajax far into the forest and then came back to help me. Lu shifted back and carried Mom's body to the packhouse. I linked Carlos; he met us at the back of the packhouse, so he could take Mom to examine her. He texted me a little bit ago and said that he wasn't able to find any needle marks on her body. He's still waiting for the blood work to come back.

"I linked Jay and told him what happened and that he needed to find Dad. I told him to take some wolfsbane because with how Ajax was reacting, he would probably have to force the shift. Jay said that he had to make sure Cy and her parents were safe first, and then he would go and find him. I told him to bring them here and that we would all be on lockdown until you got here. After that was when I called you. Jay found Dad and brought him back here. He's in Kal's room sleeping off the wolfsbane we had to give him."

Rage was coursing through me. I could feel Dani's hand pressing even harder into the small of my back. The only thing keeping me from tearing the entire packhouse down was her hand. I had released Max and put Phoenix's carrier down about halfway through Fern's account. My head was spinning, and I had more questions than answers.

"Get it together, boy! You have to be an Alpha now," Kane's voice growled.

I gave my head a hard shake and took a deep breath. Kane was right, I needed to be an Alpha now. For the first time, I gave the room a quick glance. Luan was standing next to Fern. Jay, Cy, and her parents were all crammed on the couch. Vinnie was in the chair, now holding Max. Their relationship didn't bother me like it once had. Vinnie really did seem to care for not only Max but Phoenix, too. Kal was sitting on the loveseat watching me, waiting for me to lose my shit.

I was having a hard time finding the words around the rage I felt. Sensing my struggle, Dani cleared her throat.

"Okay, it can take days for certain tests to be run and analyzed. It's safer for everyone to stay here until we know more about what happened and what we're dealing with. We all can't stay down here; this is Kal and Vinnie's home. Cy and her parents will stay with Jameson."

I had to stop listening. While I didn't care if Cy was on pack land, I didn't want her in the packhouse. I really didn't care if the magic she did was intentional or not. I was lost in my thoughts when suddenly my arm was shook hard. I looked down to see Dani looking at me.

"Did you hear me?" she asked as soon as my eyes met hers.

"No, I'm sorry," I confessed. This wasn't the time to get into my dislike about Cy being here.

"I asked what are we going to do about your dad. We can't leave him down here," she repeated patiently.

"I don't know yet. I need to see him first," I said after taking a minute to think.

I wrapped my hand around hers and started walking toward Kal's room. I pushed her behind me before opening the door. I didn't want to bring her in with me, but I had to. She was the only thing holding me together and keeping the rage at bay. Slowly I opened the door and stepped inside with Dani following behind me. I walked to the side of the bed where my dad lay sleeping.

"Stay back against the door," I linked Dani as I gave him a little shake. "Dad? Can you hear me?" I asked as gently as I could manage.

His eyelids twitched at the sound of my voice, but he didn't answer me. I stepped back and watched as he started to move his hand. With no other warning, not that I needed one, his eyes shot open, he shredded the ropes around him and launched himself off the bed. Directly at me. I braced for the impact right as he slammed into me. Ajax was trying desperately to take control and shift. I knew he wouldn't be able to thanks to the wolfsbane cocktail he had been given, but I still wasn't going to let him beat my ass.

I grabbed him and slammed him hard to the ground. Not giving him time to recover, I got on top of him and held him there. Dad continued to thrash and snarl at me, screaming incoherently the entire time. I could feel Dani's fear and concern mounting. I had to get this under control. There was only one way that would stop him instantly.

"DO IT, BOY!" Kane screamed at me, hearing my internal struggle. I didn't like using my Alpha voice. I hated taking someone's free will from them, but there was no other way around it.

"STOP!" I commanded him, causing the room to shake violently. Instantly he went still and submitted to me. "I'm going to let you up and we are going to talk. Do you understand me?" I commanded him again.

"Yes," he whined.

Slowly, I got up and offered him my hand. The second he was upright, Dad wrapped his arms around me and began to sob.

"Who would do something like this? She was loved by the entire pack," he cried as his heart-broken sobs filled the room.

"I don't know, Dad. But I am going to find out and they will die by my hand," I assured him before I made a plea to him, Alpha to Alpha, son to father. "I need you to keep it together until I do. You're right, the entire pack loved her, and this is going to devastate them. I'm sure that anyone who has information on who she was with will come forward. Remember, not all battles are won on the battlefield." I tightened my grip before releasing him, so I could look at his face. The pain in his eyes shattered my heart.

"I'm going to take him upstairs." Upon hearing my words, he looked around the room for the first time. When he finally saw Dani, who was pressed against the door, he sighed, and a new wave of tears rolled down his cheeks.

"I'm so sorry you had to see me like that," he sobbed as he wiped his face with the back of his hand.

"You don't need to apologize," she assured him with a warm smile. "Let's get you upstairs."

I walked him toward the door as Dani opened it. I was pleasantly surprised that Vinnie, Max, and Phoenix weren't in the living area. I glanced at Vinnie's bedroom door to see that it was securely shut. Not asking any questions, I just kept walking my dad toward the door that led out into the hallway. I was thankful that Max didn't see him like that. I still had no clue how I was going to tell Max what was going on and seeing my dad like that would just prompt all kinds of questions I wasn't ready to answer.

After taking my dad to his quarters and making sure he was okay, I headed back downstairs. Fern hadn't told anyone else that mom was dead, so I knew I would need to make the announcement soon, so we could start the preparations for the funeral. I trudged down the stairs and through the packhouse to the shelter. My head was spinning, the rage was building, and I didn't have Dani with me. It was harder to keep it at bay. I needed a release, I needed to run. Before I could stop myself, I was running full speed for the closest exit to outside and pulling off my necklace. The second I was out of the packhouse, I immediately shifted.

But not into Kane.

Running as Abaddon was strange, to say the least. Not only were we running upright, but I also had full control of our direction. I let instinct take over, and before I knew it, I was looking down into the ravine. I had no clue how to properly use this form, and I wanted to see if I could pick up any other scents that may have been left behind.

She didn't come here alone, so there had to be something. I took some deep breaths but was only able to smell the forest around me and the slight scent of my mother. As I stood there trying to find any other scents, it hit me.

"Why can't I smell Fern, Luan, or my dad's scent?" I wondered aloud.

"There are no other scents here," Abaddon answered quickly.

"That's impossible! Fern said that she followed your parents' scents to this spot. If you can still smell your mom's scent, then you should be able to smell the others," Kane countered as we all looked down into the ravine. *"Let me take over and see if I can smell anything."*

"There's no point. I'm telling you there are no other scents here," Abaddon argued.

I didn't have it in me to listen to them argue. Taking a final breath, I allowed the shift and gave Kane control. The second his paws were on the forest floor, he was on the move, looking for any other scent. He made his way down into the ravine and to the spot where my mother's body had laid. I didn't need to see it there to know this information, her scent was strongest there. Again though, there were no other scents.

I could hear Kane's internal thoughts as he tried to make sense of what was happening. I went down my own little rabbit hole, while Kane continued to sniff and theorize in vain. Scents can linger for months, depending on the conditions; outdoors they will dissipate the fastest, but we should have been able to smell them for a couple of days before there was no trace. It was like they were wiped clean.

"Get us home, Kane!" I suddenly screamed.

Sensing my urgency, Kane took off toward the packhouse. As he ran, I went over my recent revelation.

"That would take a lot of magic" was all Kane had time to say before we were on the back lawn of the packhouse.

Forcing the shift, I grabbed some sweats and ran inside, running full speed to the bunker before skidding to a stop to open the door. All eyes were on me when I entered the room, but my eyes went directly to the Meadows.

"Is it possible to erase a scent after it's been laid?" I asked a little more harshly than I should have.

"Yes, but it is very powerful magic. Not something that just any witch would be able to do. Why?" Oak asked me, concern flooding his tone.

"I went to see if I could find any scents that might indicate who my mom went running with. The only scent I was able to find was my mom's. There were no other scents. Not Fern's, Luan's, or my dad's," I started to explain before Willow cut me off.

"All magic leaves a trace. I need my book." Her words were clipped, but I could tell they weren't directed at me.

She got up and made her way to the pile of bags and suitcases sitting by the door. She rummaged through them until finding the one she was looking for. The bag was satchel style and very worn. Moving as quickly as she could, Willow went back to the couch, sat down, and started digging through the bag. She continued until she pulled out a tattered book, thumbing through the pages until finding what she needed.

"I have a spell that will tell me if someone was exposed to magic. It sounds like someone cast a selective cloaking spell, only allowing your mother's scent to remain. I can cast it, and it will tell us if Fern and Luan were exposed," Willow told me.

"You will not do any magic on my sister or Luan," I started before turning to Fern to silence the protest I knew was coming. "You can cast it on me. I was at the ravine too, so I should have been exposed." I could see the shock on both of the Meadows' faces as I spoke. They weren't expecting to cast anything on me.

"Okay. It's an easy spell," Willow quickly replied, trying to wipe the shock off her face. "I only need a couple of ingredients that you should already have in the kitchen. Is it okay if I go look?"

"Of course," Kal answered before I could.

Dani walked over to me once Willow and Kal were in the kitchen. I had noticed that Vinnie and the kids were still nowhere to be seen.

"Don't worry, I checked on them. Both kids are sleeping. Vinnie is keeping an eye on them. He knows to get me if Phoenix wakes up."

I just nodded my head and watched for Willow and Kal to re-emerge from the kitchen. When they did, I was surprised to see what Willow was carrying: water and some basic seasonings. Nothing about those items screamed magic spell to me.

"Don't let the ingredients fool you, all things hold magic when manipulated by the right person," she was explaining to Kal as they walked in, and she placed them on the table. "Please come sit," she asked me as she gestured to the table.

As I walked over and sat down, anxiety washed over me. Was I really going to let a witch cast a spell on me?

Yes, yes I was.

I could feel Kane's protest, but Abaddon was encouraging me. Willow placed the bowl of water in front of me and sprinkled in some of the seasonings.

"I have to place my hand on you," she warned before placing her hand on my head.

The words that left her mouth sounded like the most complicated foreign language I had ever heard. The words made the water swirl and change color. Without removing her hand from my head, she added the rest of the seasonings to the water. When the last one was added, the water turned black, and she gasped.

"You were definitely exposed to magic. Very, very powerful magic. Neither Oak nor I could produce magic of this caliber," she confessed as she looked at Oak with worried eyes. "I know my opinion doesn't mean much, but I would recommend staying out of the woods until we find out who's behind this. The stronger the magic, the more ancient the line. Magic this strong could only come from a direct descendant of Salix," she continued, never looking away from Oak.

Chapter Ten

JAMESON

I sat there in stunned silence as I watched her cast a spell on Stef and listened to her explanation after. Even with my shock, I kept a close eye on Fern, while Willow worked. Fern wasn't Cy's biggest fan and that crossed over to her parents. Fern blamed them for not teaching Cy how to control her magic.

"You can't fucking tell me they didn't know that it would someday bite them in the ass!" she screamed at me, while Stefhan and Dani were in Florida. In Fern's eyes, Cy wasn't part of the pack or even my mate due to us not completing the matebond. The whole thing was a sore spot for me, and I wished that people would let it go. Just because we weren't fully bonded didn't mean I loved Cy any less. I had to take whatever she wanted to give me.

"So, what do we do now? You can't tell the pack not to go into the woods without some kind of explanation," Fern told Stefhan as she stared at the onyx-black water.

"I'm pretty sure telling them that Mom was killed in the woods, and we don't know who is responsible is enough reason," Stefhan replied like she was missing the obvious.

"You can't mean that!" she shrieked.

"I mean every word. I will not lie to the pack about the fact that she was murdered. I also think that it will prompt anyone who has any information to come forward. We still don't know who she went running with. Someone could have seen something," he countered, not backing down.

"I don't think that's a good idea," she told him, also not backing down.

"Well, then it's a good thing you aren't the Alpha and I am. We will do this my way and if you don't like it, you don't have to be there," he told her simply as he glanced at his watch. "I'm going to call an emergency pack meeting and make the announcement," he continued.

"Fine. Do what you want, but if you're really going to do that, then I won't be there," she snapped at him.

"I said you didn't have to be there," he told her as his voice went an octave lower.

"Okay. That's enough," Dani quickly said as she stepped in front of Stefhan and looked at me. "Jameson, would you please take Cy and her parents upstairs and get them settled in."

I nodded my head in agreement before standing and turning to give Cy my hand.

"You better hurry, bro," Zeke's voice echoed in my head as I got ready to head down to meet Stefhan. I was meeting him by the back entrance to the main dining room at eight. I quickly glanced at my watch. It was ten till. I threw on some shoes and half ran to the living room.

"When do you think you'll be back, Jam?" Cy asked me the instant I entered the room.

"I don't know," I told her honestly. Cy and her parents weren't coming. Stefhan didn't want their presence to raise questions. "As Beta of the pack, I have to stay until Stefhan doesn't need me. Something like this has never happened before in the entire history of Crimson Diamond. Sarai was loved by everyone in the pack. This is going to devastate them. I won't let Stefhan shoulder this alone," I continued.

Dani wasn't going either; she was going to stay with Max and Phoenix. They hadn't told Max yet, so there was no way they were going to take him. I quickly kissed Cy and said goodbye to her parents before running full speed to meet Stefhan.

"You're late," Stefhan told me as I rounded the corner and skidded to a stop.

"Sorry, Stef."

"It's fine," he told me as he patted my shoulder. "Let's get this over with."

I walked behind him as he approached the door leading into the main dining room. He took a deep breath before he opened it and walked through. The dining room was filled with concerned-looking pack members, their whispers filling the massive space. I could see them craning their heads, looking for Dani. I could also see their surprise when they saw me instead of her. Stefhan walked to the microphone and took a breath.

"I know it's not often that I call a meeting like this, but something terrible has happened. My mother has been killed." The second the words left his mouth, the crowd erupted with screams.

"What do you mean killed?"

"How did this happen?"

"Where's Ryland, Fern, Luan, and the Luna?"

Stefhan gave them a few minutes to get it out of their systems before raising his hand to silence them.

"I know you all have questions. I wish I had all the answers for you, but I don't. Dani is with our children. Fern and Luan are with my dad. As you can imagine, he is in unbearable pain. His mate was forcibly taken from him. A fate none of us should have to endure. I have very minimal information on what happened to my mom. All we know is she went for a run and didn't come home. Fern and Luan went to look for her and found her dead in the forest. We do know that she planned on meeting someone for this run, but she didn't say who. Until we find the person responsible for this, I ask that no one goes into the woods. And if anyone has any information about who she was running with, I beg you to come forward."

Stefhan walked to the edge of the stage and jumped down. The moment his feet were on the floor, he was surrounded by pack members. I wasn't sure what he wanted me to do, so I jumped down and followed him as he slowly walked through the crowd. I watched as he hugged and consoled crying members of the pack. Never once shedding a tear himself, I found myself wondering how he was holding it together.

"That's because he's a true Alpha, bro," Zeke's voice echoed, answering my unspoken question.

"Thanks for staying with me," Stefhan said as we walked toward the stairs.

"Where else would I be? As your best friend and Beta, it's kinda my job," I replied and gave him a smile.

He returned my smile with a weak one of his own. The pain in his eyes was more than evident. A pain I knew all too well. When we got to my floor, he stopped and wrapped his arms around me. He didn't speak, he just hugged me for a couple of seconds before letting me go and continuing up the stairs.

It was a little after three in the morning. I figured everyone would be asleep, so I opened the door as quietly as I could. I was surprised to hear the television softly playing in the living room. I shut the door and turned to see Cy getting up from the couch.

"How did it go?"

"As well as to be expected. The pack is devastated and so is Stefhan," I replied as I wrapped my arms around her, pulling her into my chest.

"How are you doing?" she whispered as she breathed in my scent.

"I'm okay."

I took a deep breath and let her scent consume me. Smelling her arousal made me instantly hard. She pulled back so her eyes could meet mine. Before she could say anything, I smashed my lips to hers and crushed our bodies together. Without removing my lips, I scooped her up and carried her to my room.

"It's about damn time, bro," Zeke's voice softly echoed.

Ever since Cy moved in with her parents, we had very limited private time. So, any type of sexual activity was also limited. Cy also wasn't a huge fan of having sex in the forest.

"I don't like fucking in the woods, Jam! Last time a stick stabbed me in the ass," she complained the last time I tried to get her to do it.

There were no sticks to stab her now, and I knew she wanted me as much as I wanted her. I quickened my pace, almost sprinting the rest of the way. As I carried her in and shut the door, she pulled back, breaking our kiss for the first time.

"Lock the door," she moaned as she pressed her lips back to mine and wound her fingers in my hair.

I did as she asked before carrying her to my bed, laying her down gently, and running my tongue across her lips. She took a sharp breath in as they parted, allowing me to slip in my tongue, exploring every inch before moving my way to her jaw. I kissed down her neck and right before arriving where my mark would go, I stopped and sat up.

"Up and off." At my command, she sat up just far enough to pull off her shirt and lay back down. "May I?" I asked while pulling at the tiny sleep shorts she was wearing.

"Yes please," she moaned.

With one quick motion, I stripped them off, leaving her naked in the middle of the bed, taking a minute to appreciate her naked form before leaning down to continue my path, picking up just below where my mark would go and slowly kissing my way to her nipples.

I traced my tongue around an areola and grabbed her nipple bar with my teeth, giving it a not-so-gentle tug. A hiss escaped her lips, and she wrapped her hand in my hair, tugging at the roots. I sucked her nipple into my mouth and swirled my tongue around it as I massaged her other breast. Her moans got louder as I switched sides and gave her other nipple the same attention as the first. Once I was satisfied, I began kissing my way down her torso. Her body trembled as I reached just above her pussy.

"Open," I commanded as I brushed my fingertips across her legs.

She dropped her legs, and I settled in between them, snaking my arms around, locking them in place. I leaned in and grazed my lips against her inner thigh. A low hiss came from her chest and her body tensed. I waited for her to relax before flicking the tip of my tongue against her clit.

"Please," she begged as she tried to lift her hips toward me.

"Did I say you could speak?" I asked as I flicked my tongue against her clit again.

"No."

"Do you want me to punish you?" Again, I flicked my tongue against her clit.

From the long pause, I could tell she was unsure what her answer should be. As much as she loved to be punished, she was enjoying this. It had been so long since we could just enjoy each other. Instead of making her come up with an answer, I started an oral assault on her dripping wet pussy. I licked and sucked every inch and fold. There wasn't a single part of her that I didn't taste. Her pleasure-filled screams carried throughout the room; her hands clawed at every part of me she could reach. My cock was painfully hard, and I knew that Cy was getting close.

"I want you!" she screamed and started pulling from between her soaked thighs.

I let her pull me up, and the second her hands could reach, she yanked my pants down, grabbed my cock, and positioned it at her entrance. With a hard thrust, I rammed in my cock. The scream that left her mouth sent me into a near frenzy.

"Turn around," I growled at her, letting my cock slip out.

As soon as she was on all fours, I slid back inside, positioning myself and grabbing a hold of her hips. She started rocking back and forth. I squeezed her soft flesh, letting my fingers dig in deep so she knew what was coming. In response, she rocked harder. I slid my cock back to where just the tip was still inside her and waited for her to rock back toward me before ramming it inside. Only this time I didn't stop. As I rammed her over and over, her screams egging me on, I dug my fingers deeper into her skin and pulled her back against my cock as hard as I could.

Removing myself just long enough to flip her over and gathering both her hands in one of mine, I pinned them above her head. Methodically, I pushed and pulled my cock in and out of her then placed my free hand around her throat and gently squeezed, applying steady pressure as I increased my thrusts. I knew as long as she didn't use the safe word, she was okay. Her slick walls clenched around me as I rammed her with reckless abandon.

I released her hands, and she wrapped them around my neck, pulling my mouth to hers. My other hand was still around her throat. I squeezed a little harder, making her moan into my mouth.

I rammed my cock even harder inside her, causing her to explode all over me. Her juices ran down my shaft and soaked the sheets. When I was about to cum, the urge to mark her hit me like a speeding train. I forced it to the back of my mind and gave one more thrust before cumming deep inside her. Feeling completely spent, I collapsed onto the bed and wrapped my arms around her before falling asleep.

I woke up to discover I was alone. Right as I was going to call Cy's name, I heard her hushed voice coming from the bathroom.

"Of course, I want to see you."

Longing rang in her hushed words and my heart sank.

"If you're going to eavesdrop, bro, at least listen to the entire conversation," Zeke snapped, sounding rather annoyed.

"Are you sure Stefhan is okay with it?" Her words only cemented Zeke's annoyance.

"It's time, bro."

"Damn, bitch. You don't have to threaten me with bodily harm. Jam is still sleeping. Once he gets up, I'll be up."

Feeling like a total ass, I sat up and waited for her to walk out of the bathroom. Zeke was right, it was time. I still didn't want to do it. It was nothing but my own insecurities and selfishness.

"I didn't wake you up, did I?" she asked when she saw me obviously not sleeping.

"No. I just didn't want to interrupt your conversation," I started before her excitement took over and she cut me off.

"You won't believe it! Dani called me and asked me to come up to spend time with her and the kids! I'm going to get dressed and head up since you're awake." As she told me, she made her way toward her bag and started pulling out clothes.

"Can I talk to you before you go?" I asked as she pulled up her pants and adjusted her sweater.

"Sure. Is everything okay?" she asked as she came and sat next to me on the bed. I took a deep breath and just let it out.

"I know I said I was okay with it, and I was, but recently it's really been bothering me that you won't complete any kind of bond with me. Your reasons for not wanting to are completely valid, and I would never force you to or give you an ultimatum. It's hard on me not being completely mated to you. I don't feel complete. I know it's shitty timing, and I'm sorry. I'm driving Zeke nuts with my insufferable moping." I felt horrible as the words left my mouth. I should have waited. I shouldn't have dropped that on her when she was finally going to spend time with Dani.

Zeke, not missing the opportunity to call me out, *"You literally thought she was talking to another dude. It had to be done, bro."*

"Why didn't you tell me you were feeling this way?" she asked me with so much love in her eyes.

"I didn't want to put more stress on you. You're already dealing with so much."

"Enough stalling! Tell her, bro!" Zeke screamed.

"I thought you were talking to someone else," I mumbled, feeling more ashamed than I ever had.

"What? I would never, Jam!"

"I know you wouldn't. That's why Zeke has been hounding me for weeks to tell you how I was feeling. This isn't your fault. It's mine," I told her as she pulled me into her arms.

"When I get back, we'll talk and come up with something that works for both of us," she told me as she kissed my lips softly.

Unforeseen Destinies

Chapter Eleven

CY

Jam's words swirled through my head as I walked toward the living room. Brief relief washed over me when I saw my parents weren't there. I didn't have it in me to deal with the onslaught of questions they would have. We hadn't talked about what happened, but I knew it would be coming. I missed the days when they ignored me. My relief was quickly replaced by guilt. Every time I turned around, I was fucking something up and hurting the people I loved. Jam actually thought I was talking to someone else.

As I trudged my way up the stairs toward Dani's, my nerves escalated with each stair. Stefhan hadn't spoken more than maybe three words to me since Phoenix was born. Basically, acting like I didn't exist. As I turned the final corner that led to their door, I was surprised to see it cracked open.

"You don't have to keep the door open, Max. She'll be here soon."

"Mama, I wait here for Aunty Cy." Hearing Max call me Aunty Cy made me pick up my pace. I missed him wicked bad: it was harder than I would have thought to be away from him. Having kids was not something I saw for myself, but something about that boy had me wrapped. As I neared the door, I slowed down and stuck my head in; I didn't want to hit him with the door.

"AUNTY CY!" Max squealed the second he saw my head pop in. He threw the door open and wrapped his arms around my legs. Without thinking, I scooped him up and pulled him close.

"Hey, Max! You're getting so big!" I told him as I squeezed tightly.

"I'm so glad you came!" Dani called out as she walked toward us.

"I'm so glad you asked," I confessed as I set Max down and glanced around the room for Phoenix. "Where's Phoenix?"

"I just laid her down. I thought it would be good for us to talk first. Stefhan is down with Ryland," she started before Max cut her off.

"Papa say Papo sad that Sitty had to go be with Oddess Selene. Papa say we can't see Sitty anymore." Max paused, and a tear rolled down his cheek. "What if she gets lonely? What if she misses us? I sad, Mama." Dani bent down and wrapped her arms around him.

"I know you're sad little one, but Sitty is in a much better place. Don't worry, she isn't alone. She's with Selene and my Gram. She will always be able to watch over us and when it's our time to be with Selene, we will see her again. Come on, it's nap time," Dani consoled him and walked him down the hallway to the bedrooms.

Wiping the tear that escaped my eye, I sat down on the couch and waited for Dani to come back. About ten minutes later, she came back into the living room and sat on the couch with me. There was an awkwardness between us; it was the first time we had been alone together in a long time. I knew her well enough to know that there was a reason she asked me up here, and I didn't want to waste time beating around the bush. Right as I was getting ready to say something she blurted out.

"Max is having a hard time with the news. Stefhan told him right before he told the pack. Originally, he was going to wait but changed his mind after talking to Ryland." A feeble attempt to break the ice.

"I bet he is. He was close to Sarai. I'm glad he decided to tell Max," I replied. Then added on, "You said you wanted to talk. What's on your mind?" I was suddenly nervous. After what Jam dropped on me, I wasn't sure I was ready for this talk.

I could see her going through what she wanted to say and in what order she wanted to say it. Finally, she took a deep breath and shook her head. I knew that her words were going to be flying a hundred miles an hour and I would have to concentrate to catch them all.

"I hate that I don't see you every day. I hate that my kids don't see you every day. I hate that you're a shell of your former self. Seeing you like this is hard, Cy. You lost your spark. I know you feel awful about what happened. I also know that I haven't been friend of the year either. I miss you; I want us to be back the way we were, and you being the fierce bitch I know you are. And before you say anything about Stefhan, I already talked to him and told him that he can either jump on the bandwagon or stay out of the way. I refuse to lose you over something that wasn't entirely your fault. Should you have told me about your powers? Yes, but I also understand why you didn't. I told Stefhan that you and Jameson have suffered enough for this, and I won't put up with anymore."

Her words hit me with a force I wasn't expecting. For the first time in months, I felt hope. Without thinking I jumped up, grabbed Dani off the couch, and started swinging her around.

"I miss you too, bitch! I've never felt so alone. Yeah, I have Jam, kinda. But you were always my constant. Not having that has been beyond shitty," I confessed as I set her down.

"I still hate it when you do that," she told me with a smile before her face turned serious. "What do you mean you have Jameson, 'kinda'?" She grabbed my hand and pulled me back on the couch.

"Well, he dropped some heavy shit on me right as I was getting ready to come up here." I paused and took a breath. "He told me that it's really starting to bother him that I won't complete any kind of bonding with him. He woke up when I was talking to you on the phone and thought I was talking to another guy! It's giving me whiplash. Since the beginning, he's told me that he was fine with my decision and that he was happy with whatever I was willing to give. Then out of nowhere, he flips and says that he doesn't feel complete, and it's been on his mind for months. I could use some calm, just a week when something isn't happening. To just be normal." I didn't realize tears were rolling down my cheeks until Dani handed me a tissue.

"Wouldn't that be nice? I've come to the conclusion that nothing will ever be normal again. Well, at least what we would consider normal. What did you tell him?" she asked with a smile, determined to keep me from having a complete breakdown.

"That we would talk about it later. I didn't want to risk my parents being awake and asking me all kinds of questions. Their sudden interest in me and what's happening in my life is draining."

"What are you going to tell him?" she asked, ignoring my parents completely. Knowing Dani, she would tackle that later in the conversation.

"I don't know. I don't think I'm ready."

"But why? You're head over heels for Jameson," she countered.

"I am, but what if he changes his mind? We both know I'm like a LOT, and I don't want him to figure out after it's too late that he's stuck with me," I told her, repeating the words I confessed to Stefhan.

"Do you truly think that would happen?" Her voice was calm and steady.

"Don't use your doctor's voice on me," I started with a smile before going serious. "Honestly, I don't know."

"Really? Come on, Cy. Why can't you just accept the fact that he's never going to leave you, and it doesn't matter what you do? He knows you better than you know yourself. Do you think it was easy for him to tell you how he was feeling? To tell you that it's hard on him not being bound to you? He waited his whole life for you. He just needs to know that you want to be with him as much as he wants to be with you. Did you ever stop to think that you can leave him at any moment, too? He's in the same position you are. He knows that at any moment you can decide this life is too much for you and split."

I thought about it for a few seconds before responding.

"Never. Not once did that occur to me. I guess because I never thought about leaving. Well, I did think about leaving Crimson Diamond, but not without Jam. He's the whole reason I'm still here. I wanted to run back to Florida when everything first happened. He wouldn't leave and told me that if I wanted to I would have to go alone. Obviously, I stayed. But binding ourselves to each other permanently forever is a lot, and I don't know if I'm ready."

Dani nodded her head.

"That is a very valid feeling. Do me a favor though. Think about leaving Crimson Diamond without him. Think about breaking up with him."

I closed my eyes and tried to picture what she asked. A sharp pain shot through my heart, causing me to clutch my chest, my eyes shot open to see Dani staring at me.

"I think you have your answer," she told me with a smile.

"But what if what happens to you happens to me? I'm not strong enough to cope with that," I spit out before I could stop myself. Watching what she went through when Stefhan left was something I never wanted to experience. I would end my own life before I suffered like that.

"Is that what this is really about?" she asked me. Her voice was full of concern.

I just nodded my head. The cat was out of the bag, and there was no way of putting it back in.

"Cy, what happened to me and Stefhan is like a one-in-a-billion thing. He didn't leave because he wanted to. He was being manipulated. It was the only way he thought he could keep me safe. He still tries to make up for what happened, and he will never forgive himself. You can't let my experience stop you from your own happiness."

After our serious conversation, we spent the rest of the morning catching up. She told me about Florida, what she found, and gave me an envelope that had my name in Gram's handwriting. She also told me about giving Barb something to talk about for years. I told her about my friendship with Vinnie and how things were going. She told me she was glad things were going well. I didn't tell her about him fucking Kal. It wasn't gossip to spread.

We talked until the kids woke up. I played with Max and helped with Phoenix. Dani and I were cracking jokes, and everything was going great. Right around noon, the front door opened, Stefhan walked in, and my heart stopped.

"Papa!" Max yelled, jumping up from the puzzle we were working on together, and ran to Stefhan.

"How was your morning, bub?" Stefhan asked him as he swooped him up.

"So much fun! I play with Aunty Cy! She came over to play with me!" he exclaimed.

"That's great," he told Max with a smile. He then shifted his gaze to me and the smile instantly faded.

There was no doubt that I still wasn't his favorite person, and he was more than likely hoping I would be gone when he got back. To avoid any type of anything with Stefhan, I quickly got up.

"I should probably get going. I need to talk to Jam, and I haven't seen my parents yet today. I left before they woke up," I told Dani as I started walking toward her to give her a hug.

"You don't have to leave," she whispered to me. My level of uncomfortableness must have been more noticeable than I was hoping.

"I need to talk to Jam. I'll call you later," I whispered back and then turned to Max.

"Bye, Max. I'll see you later," I told him as I bent down, hugged him, and placed a kiss on his cheek. Then I kissed Phoenix's head and started for the door. Stefhan was standing by the door, but not blocking my path.

"Bye, Stefhan," I blurted out as I rushed past him.

"Wait Cy," he said as I passed. I froze. "I would like to invite your parents, Jay, and you to dinner tonight. I would like to have it here at eight. If that works for you."

I was too shocked to answer. I knew I needed to answer him, so I forced my head to nod in agreement.

"Great, I'll see you then."

Jam and my parents were sitting in the living room when I got back. I knew I had to take control of the conversation fast.

"Stefhan invited all of us to dinner tonight," I announced loudly as I shut the door before anyone could speak.

"Dinner?" my mom asked, sounding as shocked as I was.

"Yeah. He wants us there at eight," I told her with a shrug.

"How did it go with Dani? Jameson told us you went to see her," she asked nosily. So much for keeping control of the conversation.

"It went great. I got to spend time with the kids. Max is getting so big," I told her as I sat beside Jam on the couch.

"So, you and Dani got everything worked out?"

I wanted to scream. I was doing everything I could to avoid it, but she just wouldn't quit.

"Yes, Mom. We did," I told her as I closed my eyes.

"That's fantastic! Now maybe you'll get some of your power back," she exclaimed.

"What in the hell does that mean?" I asked her. I kept my eyes closed, sometimes not looking at her made it easier to digest her gibberish.

"While your powers don't come from your emotions, your emotions can affect them," she answered simply.

"I'm getting a headache. I'm going to go lay down," I told Jam as I opened my eyes and headed to the bedroom.

I could hear his footsteps behind me, but I didn't turn around. I walked into the bedroom, kicked off my shoes, and flopped face-first on the bed. I felt his weight hit the mattress beside me.

"I'm glad you made up with Dani," he whispered and started rubbing my back. "How did you manage to get us all a dinner invite?" he added when I didn't say anything.

I turned my face toward him, so he could hear me.

"No clue, but we will be there at seven-fifty. I'm not trying to give him any other reasons not to like me even more."

"He does like you, babe. He's just pissed at you. It takes him longer than most to get over something. He's just now sorta back to normal with me. Him inviting us to dinner is his way of taking the first step," he tried to reassure me.

"You weren't the one who almost killed his son," I retorted.

"In Stefhan's eyes, we are both equally responsible."

"YOU are also his brother."

"The only thing that did was spare our lives. It has no bearing on how long he's pissed for," he told me as he laid down, so we were facing each other. His eyes locked with mine, and he brushed his fingertips across my cheek. "I love having you home," he whispered.

Dani's words suddenly echoed in my head.

"You really would do anything for me, wouldn't you?" I whispered. Our faces were so close together that speaking in a normal conversational tone would have been like screaming.

"Anything and everything," he replied without hesitation.

Dani was right. I couldn't let my fears about what happened to her control my happiness. I took a deep breath and held it, once the words were out of my mouth there was no taking them back.

"I'll do it," I told him as I let out the breath I was holding.

"Do what?" he asked me, sounding totally confused.

"I guess I didn't really give any pretext, did I? I'll complete the matebond with you."

I watched as his eyes widened to the size of small saucers and his breathing got short and fast. I was starting to think he was having a panic attack until he cupped my face with his hand.

"Are you sure? I don't want you to feel like you have to because of what I said earlier. I was just in my feels, this is a huge decision and commitment. There is no going back."

Before he could start rambling, I cut him off by raising a finger to his mouth, then sat up, pulling him with me.

"Jam, I know exactly what it means. I've been letting my own insecurities and fears dictate my decision. Something Dani told me today put things into perspective. I can't and don't want to imagine life without you. I'm ready, let's do this," I told him as I turned my head and exposed my neck to him. After a few seconds of him not moving, the harsh sting of rejection started bubbling inside me. "Or not," I whispered, trying to fight back the tears that suddenly filled my eyes.

"Of course I want to! I just don't know if it's safe for me to bite you," he explained as he pulled me close to him.

"What do you mean safe?" I asked, I wasn't a fan of his wording.

"Well, I'm not sure what would happen if I bite you. If you were human, it would turn you into a werewolf, but since you're a witch, I'm not sure what would happen. There is another option though," he explained.

"Okay, so what's the other option?" I asked when it was obvious that he wasn't going to elaborate.

"We could do a binding, and when I say 'we' I mean 'you.'"

"What in the hell is that?" My confusion was on full display.

"It's something your parents told me about not long after they got to Crimson Diamond. It's the witch equivalent to the matebond. I asked them about it during the time when I wasn't allowed to mention your parents without getting hit. It's a spell that will bind our souls together forever, even in death."

"What do you mean I would have to do it?"

I wasn't worried about what the spell did, but rather why I had to be the one to perform it.

"Your parents told me that it has to be performed by one of the people who are being bound together. And you're the only witch in this relationship."

"And it won't hurt Zeke?"

"Ummm, I'm not sure. We would have to ask your parents," he admitted while the shine in his eyes diminished.

"Well, we would have to talk to them anyway. I don't know how to do the spell. Let's go," I told him as I got off the bed, pulling him with me.

"You want to do it now?"

"Yes, right now." Suddenly I was jerked to a stop, I looked back to see that Jam had stopped walking.

"Are you sure? Once it's done, it can't be undone."

I took a breath and looked into his eyes.

"I've never been more sure of anything in my entire life."

After their initial shock and making sure that Jam and I both fully understood what it meant, my parents told me what I would need to perform a binding with Jam.

"You're lucky, Cypress. I almost didn't bring it," my mom told me as she went to get our family Grimoire.

"Why would you leave it?" I asked out loud to no one in particular.

"It's not really safe to carry it around. What if someone steals what you have it kept in?" my dad answered.

"I didn't think about that," I replied honestly.

"You have so much to learn," he said with a smile.

My mom came back into the living room already flipping through the pages of a well-worn, thick, leather-bound book.

"Here!" she exclaimed as she turned the book and showed me. "You'll need to get everything on this page and follow the instructions. Then once your potion is ready, you both will drink it, and you'll recite this spell." As she explained, she pointed to each page.

"Can you help me make the potion?" I asked. This would be my first potion, and I didn't want to fuck it up and end up killing Jam.

"I can direct you while you make it, but I can't touch it. It has to be done solely by you," she told me as she marked the page, closed the book, and handed it to me. "You can do this."

Carefully, I opened the book to the marked page and read over the ingredients. They were all basic items that were easily accessible. I pulled out my phone and snapped a picture of the list. Most of what I needed was in the big kitchen downstairs.

"I guess I'm off to gather some spell shit," I announced as I stood up and gave Jam a kiss on the cheek.

After running to the kitchen and finding a large enough bowl to hold everything I needed, I glanced at my list. It was a strange assortment of items, to say the least, and they had to be gathered in a specific order. Rose petals, cinnamon, and peppercorns to name a few. It didn't sound appealing. Once I had everything I needed from the kitchen, I went back upstairs.

"You'll find the rest of what you need in my big suitcase," my mom told me when I walked back into the living room. "Don't set the bowl down," she added as I made my way to the room they were staying in.

I breathed a sigh of relief when I saw that her suitcase was already open. I wasn't sure how I was going to open it without setting down the bowl. One by one, I picked out the herbs that I needed. These had names that you would think were used in potions, like dragon's breath and powdered mushroom. Once I had everything, I made my way to Jam's kitchen. As I passed through the living room, Jam and my mom got up and followed behind me.

"Cypress?"

"What Mom?" I snapped. I was a woman on a mission.

"Are you forgetting something?"

"No, Mom. I have everything."

"Are you sure? I doubt you have the spell memorized." Her voice was soft.

"Shit! I don't have the book." Before the words were out of my mouth, I turned around, grabbed the book off the couch, and tucked it under my arm. "Got it. Let's go."

Unforeseen Destinies

Chapter Twelve

Brewing a potion turned out to be way more difficult than I thought. My first four attempts smelled like death and looked like swamp water. Frustration was starting to get the best of me as I threw my fifth attempt down the sink.

"That one didn't smell as bad. I think you're going to nail it this time, babe," Jam tried to encourage me.

"It smells like shit, Jam. Literal shit," I started before my mom cut me off.

"You're trying too hard, Cypress. Magic is about intent. You have to let your intent fill and guide you. For a binding, the intent is love. You have to let your love and devotion for Jameson consume you and push that into your potion. Rinse your bowl and try again."

I closed my eyes and took a couple of breaths. Slowly I opened them and watched the water rinse the residue of my latest failed attempt down the drain. As it went down the drain, I shifted my focus from making a potion to Jam. I dried the bowl and thought about the first time I met him. I let memories of us fill my mind as I gathered, measured, and stirred. I didn't think about what I was doing, my only thoughts were on the man I wanted to spend eternity with.

"You did it!" my mom squealed, breaking me out of my thoughts.

Before I could ask her what she was talking about, a smell filled the room. It definitely wasn't swamp water, instead, it was delicious, fresh-baked cinnamon rolls. For the first time, I truly looked at what was in the bowl. The potion was a beautiful gold. I had to fight to keep my thoughts on Jam and not break out into a victory dance. It still had to be bottled. Once the potion was brewed, it had to be used within an hour. Carefully, I poured the shimmering potion into a glass vile.

"You ready?" I asked Jam as I pushed in the cork.

"I've been ready since I first saw you," he whispered as he leaned across the counter toward me.

I grabbed the book and tucked it under my arm. I wasn't going to make that mistake again. The sudden urge to run overtook me, so I sprinted to the bedroom. I could hear Jam behind me and my mom giggling from the kitchen as I ran. I didn't stop until I was in the bedroom, Jam right behind me. I went straight to the couch and set the vile on the table. I flipped through the book to the marked page and read over the next step of the spell.

"You have to drink half first, then I drink the second half. Once I finish my half, we have to hold hands as I say this spell," I explained as I read.

Not needing any other instructions, Jam grabbed the bottle, drank his half, and handed it to me. I raised it to my lips; when the liquid touched my tongue, it was a sweet explosion. The taste was like nothing I had ever experienced, and I couldn't get enough. In just a few gulps, the contents were gone. I set the empty vile on the table and wrapped my hand around his.

"Love to love. Ash to ash. I bind myself to thee. You bind yourself to me. Forever bound, in life, in death, and beyond. Never to love another. Two souls now one. Love to love. Ash to ash."

The instant the spell left my mouth, three things happened in rapid succession: A gold cord emerged from my chest and went into Jam's, connecting us together. Then a warmth engulfed my entire body, and a bright light surrounded us. It was over in just a few seconds. When the light vanished, the cord was no longer there. It seemed anticlimactic.

"Is that it?" Jam whispered as he squeezed my hand.

Quickly I grabbed the book and flipped the page to make sure I didn't miss anything.

"I guess. There aren't any other directions," I told him and shrugged my shoulders.

"Do you feel any different, bro?" I heard someone whisper. I didn't have time to react before I heard another whisper.

"Not really."

That time I recognized the voice. It was Jam's, but his mouth didn't move. Panic quickly started rising inside me. I dropped his hand and scrambled back.

"What the fuck was that?" I shrieked as I scrambled off the couch.

"What was what? What's wrong?" he immediately asked, while he reached for my hand, his face full of worry.

"I heard someone whisper and then you answered it. BUT there is no one else here and your lips didn't move!" As I explained, it only made me panic more. "SHIT! I must have fucked the spell up and now I'm hearing things." I was getting ready to have a full-blown meltdown.

"Babe, babe, babe," he cut me off and grabbed my hand. I didn't even notice he had got up off the couch. "What did you hear?" he asked me gently.

"Why does that matter? Your. Mouth. Didn't. Move!" I snapped.

"Please tell me," he looked into my eyes and begged.

"I don't see why it matters so much, but fine. Someone whispered, 'Do you feel any different, bro.' Then your voice answered and said, 'Not really.'" As I spoke, his eyes grew in surprise.

"No way," he whispered, looking completely shocked. After a few seconds of stunned silence, he managed to spit out, "It was Zeke."

"Excuse me?" I retorted and shook my head.

"You heard my conversation with Zeke."

"I didn't need you to reword it, Jam. Do you even hear what you're saying? That's impossible! I know for sure now that I fucked something up," I started before he stopped me.

"And until a few minutes ago, I would have agreed with you. You repeated verbatim what Zeke asked me and my answer. Let's test it. Let's see if you can hear him again."

Before I could answer, I heard an irritated voice whisper.

"Not cool, bro. You're the mouth in this relationship. You can't just put me on the spot like that."

If I wouldn't have been panicking, I would have laughed.

"Of all the things you could have said. That's what you went with?" I heard Jam's voice whisper.

"You can't just throw me under the bus like that. Look at her, you're freaking her out," the other voice whispered.

I felt like I was listening in on a private conversation, but I didn't know how to turn it off.

"Can you hear us?" Jam suddenly asked out loud. I wasn't sure how to process what was happening. I was in too much shock to answer, so I just nodded my head.

"You broke her, bro."

After I recovered enough from the shock so I could think clearly, we went to talk to my parents. They assured me that I did it right and explained that each binding is different. Some couples have been able to hear each other's thoughts. According to my dad, it was said that couples who can hear each other's thoughts after binding only come from old and powerful family lines. We asked them why I could hear Zeke, but they didn't have an answer. We were the only witch-werewolf-fated mates that had completed the binding that they knew. On top of that, it wasn't something openly shared.

"It's a weakness. If your enemy knows you're bound to someone, they will go after them instead of you," my dad explained.

"Okay, so no sharing our binding status. Got it," I joked. Jam laughed. My parents didn't find it amusing.

"This is serious, Cypress. Over the next week, you may see other ways that the ritual has bound you together," my dad continued.

Not wanting to get a lecture about joking at inappropriate times, I glanced at my phone. It was almost six.

"Sorry, Dad. We're going to start getting ready for dinner. Please make sure you're ready at seven forty." I didn't give them time to answer before I got up and started walking toward the bedroom.

"We have to tell Stefhan and Dani," Jam said the second the bedroom door was closed.

"Tell them what?" I asked him, completely lost.

"That we did the binding and what it means."

I looked at him confused. Didn't he hear what my parents just said?

"Were you not listening? My parents just said not to go announcing it."

"I was listening, do you want what happened to happen again? We can't keep this from them. Our lives are forever bound; you are part of this pack now. Plus, I don't think they meant we couldn't tell family."

After much back and forth, and even pulling my parents into the conversation, my parents explained that it was dangerous for people to know. But telling your family was acceptable. So it was decided that we would tell Dani and Stefhan at dinner.

I was wicked nervous getting ready. I wasn't sure how to dress. Jam said casual was fine, but I wanted to make a good impression. This was the first time in months Stefhan went out of his way to talk to me; I wasn't going to fuck it up. I went with black leggings, a dressy deep-red sweater, and flats. But I left my hair in my usual spiky style, not wanting to come across like I was trying too hard.

I emerged from the bathroom at seven-thirty. Jam was standing behind the couch watching television. He was wearing jeans and a T-shirt. His head snapped in my direction when I opened the door.

"You look great, babe," he told me with a smile.

"Thanks. You weren't kidding when you said casual." I thought he would at least wear a button-down shirt.

"I know you're nervous, but I'm telling you, you don't need to be. Do you want to change?" he asked me gently. I glanced at my phone, it was almost seven forty.

"No. I don't want to risk being late," I answered with a nod. "Let's go make sure my parents are ready," I continued as I walked to the door.

My parents were ready and waiting for us, looking more nervous than I felt. My mom was wearing a flowing maxi dress with a flower print. My dad was wearing jeans and a button-down shirt.

"Do we look okay?" my mom asked as we walked into the living room.

"You look nice," I told her with a genuine smile.

"I'm so nervous. I wonder why Stefhan wants to have us over for dinner. We've been here for months, and this is the first time he has invited us to anything," she told me as she fussed with her hair.

"Everything will be fine, Willow," my dad assured her.

"Come on, we don't want to be late," I told everyone as I looked at my phone.

It was seven fifty on the nose when Jam knocked on the door to Dani and Stefhan's. As the door slowly opened, it was replaced by Stefhan's massive frame.

"Thank you for coming. Please come in," he welcomed us as he stepped to the side.

"Auntie Cy!" Max screamed as soon as he saw me. He was doing a puzzle on the floor with Dani, and Phoenix was in her swing. He shot up and bolted at me, knocking puzzle pieces everywhere. When he got close enough, I bent over and scooped him up.

"Max, you get back over here and clean up this mess you made," Dani scolded him as I hugged him.

I didn't want to set him down, but I did. I needed to be on my best behavior, and Dani was his mom. Looking very much like a sulking child, Max shuffled over and started picking up the puzzle pieces.

"Dinner is almost finished. We'll be eating in the dining room," Dani explained as she got up and walked toward us. "Stefhan, will you take the kids, Jameson, and the Meadow's to the dining room? Cy, do you want to help me finish up in the kitchen?" she asked as she wrapped her hand around mine and started pulling me toward the hallway, not stopping until we reached the kitchen.

"I made some of your favorites that Gram would make," she started and then listed off everything she made. Even with how much Jam and Stefhan could eat, she would have leftovers for days. She was obviously just as nervous as I was for this dinner. That's the only reason she would make as much food as she did. We talked as she finished pulling everything out and getting it plated.

"You don't have to go all out, bitch. It's just my parents," I told her as she poured soup into a fancy serving bowl.

"Fern bought all the kitchen stuff," she told me with a laugh.

I didn't need any more explanation than that. Everything Fern bought was top-of-the-line. I helped Dani carry everything to the dining room, which was thankfully close to the kitchen. I had never been in that part of the house before. The dining room wasn't small by any means, but the massive rectangular table in the center made it look small. We had to make three trips to the kitchen to grab everything. I wanted to strangle her when she turned down Stefhan and Jam's help not once but twice.

Stefhan was seated at the head of the table, Max to his right, Phoenix in a bouncy chair to his left, and Dani took the empty seat next to her. My parents were seated next to Dani. Jam and I sat next to Max.

"Dig in everyone," Dani said with a smile as she started making Max's plate.

Stefhan and Jam didn't need any other invitation and started filling their plates. I made my plate as my parents watched, not moving. I was starting to think they weren't going to eat. After a few more minutes, they finally started making a plate and eating.

"Is this your Gram's recipe?" my mom asked as she took a bite of meatloaf.

"It is. Everything is, actually." Dani replied.

"It's delicious and tastes just like hers," my dad told her with a smile.

We made small talk and were having a really good time. Stefhan wasn't acting like my best friend, but he was talking to me and being friendly. I could tell he was trying to make not only me but also my parents feel comfortable. He looked nothing like when my parents first met him. He was back to physical perfection, and I swear he was bigger than before. His size alone made him intimidating. After we finished eating, Dani and Stefhan got up to put the kids to bed. Max had already fallen asleep at the table.

"You can wait in the living room while we lay the kids down, then we can talk," Dani told me as she scooped up Phoenix and Stefhan picked up Max.

I nodded my head, and we all followed her and Stefhan to the living room. Jam had told them during dinner that we had something we wanted to tell them, but he didn't want to do it in front of Max. The thought of telling them made my stomach queasy.

My parents sat with us on the couch. Thankfully the couch was massive, so we all could fit comfortably. It took about twenty minutes for them to return. Dani barely fit on the loveseat with Stefhan, he took up that much space.

"So Jay, what do you need to tell me that you couldn't say in front of Max?" Stefhan asked once they were comfortable. I could hear the slight worry in his tone.

"I wasn't sure if this was something you would want him to know," Jam started, and the worry that was hinted at in

Stefhan's voice became evident on his face. "Cy and I did a binding." Before Jam could say anything else he was cut off.

"What is a binding?" Stefhan asked, his worry shifting to anger.

"Chill out, Stef. If you wouldn't have interrupted me, I was going to tell you what it is. It's the witch equivalent to completing the matebond. It's a ritual that binds two souls together forever, even in death. Should one of us die, the other can never be with another person. There isn't a spell that can reverse it. Cy and I are bound for eternity." As Jam spoke, I watched Stefhan's face morph from anger to shock.

Unforeseen Destinies

Chapter Thirteen

STEFHAN

After hearing Jay's news, I sat there in complete shock. While the binding did help my reason for inviting them to dinner in the first place, I now had to find a segway that didn't seem like I was only offering because of what they did.

"That's fantastic!" Dani squealed as she squeezed my leg, trying to prompt me to speak.

"Yeah, that's great," I managed to spit out.

"You don't sound very happy," Jay replied while fully taking me in.

My near rigidness didn't scream "I'm happy for you brother." Which was the reaction Jay was looking for out of me.

"I really am. It just took me by surprise, that's all. Cy has been against any kind of permanent mating ritual," I quickly told him, trying to salvage the situation.

Dani would kill me if I fucked this up. This was one of many conversations that needed to be had.

"I can't take it anymore. Will you just say what's on your mind? We all know you didn't invite us for dinner to chitchat," Cy suddenly announced, rather loudly. In fact, it was the loudest I had heard her speak in months. Not that I was around her all that much either.

"If you don't tell them, I will. It's time," Dani's voice whispered in my head.

"You're right. There is a reason I invited you tonight," I started before taking a deep breath. "I have to go back to the beginning."

For the next hour, I told them everything, not leaving any details out. I told them about the voices, what they drove me to do, and about my time trying to convince Luan to come back with me. I told them how Dani found a way to break the matebond, almost going feral in Brazil, sending Fern and Luan to find Kal, and asking them to bring Vinnie here.

Systematically I went through everything that had happened over the past three years, saving Marcus for last. Accusing the witches' God of what I was going to accuse him of was going to be the make or break. As I told them what Marcus told me, Willow and Oak both tried to interrupt me, saying there was no way. Dani quickly pulled out the letters from Gram, confirming the truth.

"But why?" Willow asked.

It was time for complete transparency with the Meadows. For the first time, I told them the full prophecy. Betrayal flashed in their eyes when they heard the part they had told Dani.

"Don't be mad at Dani, she did what she thought was right. It was the right thing to do. We have to work together if we're going to survive. This isn't just about werewolves. This involves all species and if Salix wins, we all die," I finished. Oak took a second to think about what I said before replying.

"And just how do you plan on us defeating Salix? You know you are sentencing us to death, don't you? Even combined, we aren't strong enough to kill a God."

"None of you will kill him. I will." Abbadon's demonic voice suddenly flew out of my mouth.

"What in the hell was that?" All four of them screamed in unison.

"I am Abbadon. The vessel that will kill Salix."

I let him tell his story and watched as the emotions flew across their faces. Like me, he didn't leave out any details. He told them what he told Dani when she met him. Willow and Oak wanted me to shift, so they could see this God Killer. Thankfully, Abbadon agreed with me that it wasn't the time.

"Soon, you will meet me. First, you all must get to know Stefhan's human and wolf sides. Once you are comfortable around them, then you will meet me."

"It's a lot to take in. Trust me," Dani added as a small shudder rocked her tiny frame.

"I'm confused, Stef. Why are you just telling us now?" Jay asked me, looking betrayed.

"It wasn't the right time," Abbadon answered for me.

"Okay. What do we do now?" Jay replied.

"Gram said we all have to be under the same roof," I said before Dani cut me off.

"I think it means we have to live together. Willingly. Under the same roof. It's not the same if someone doesn't want to be here; they can't be forced. Cy, Mr. and Mrs. Meadow, are you willing to permanently move into the packhouse?"

I admired her directness, but my stomach was doing flip-flops. If they said no, that was it. It would have been over before it started.

"Would we have to live with Jameson and Cy forever?" Willow asked very seriously.

"Of course not," I answered with a smile. "We can set you up in Garrett's quarters. I'll get someone to clean it, and you can move there tomorrow." The look of pure shock on Jay's face was priceless. I had closed off Rhett's quarters once his mom came and got everything she wanted. I needed to show that I was sincere in Dani and I's offer and offering them his room was just the way to do it.

"Are you sure you want me living here?" Cy asked me suddenly.

I wasn't ready to apologize to Cy, which was what Dani wanted, but I was ready to pass an olive branch.

"Yes, I want you to live here." I had to keep it simple, so I didn't fuck it up.

"Okay. I'll move in. What's the plan now?" she asked.

"To be honest, I have no clue. Everything so far has come to us in pieces. Now we have to wait for the next piece to be presented to us. What I do know is we have to be completely honest with each other. There can't be any more species secrets."

"I'm not sure how I feel about that. There's a reason we don't swap secrets like recipes," Oak said, shaking his head.

"You realize this is what Salix is counting on don't you?" Abbadon's voice suddenly erupted out of me. "Stop looking at the small picture! He knows that you all have to work together to even get to where I can kill him. He has nothing to worry about if I can't get there. Stop thinking about how to save yourself and start thinking how to save us all," he demanded.

I had to fight to keep the rage from consuming me. Dani, feeling my distress, gave my leg a squeeze and Oak cleared his throat.

"Willow and I never agreed to move in. I think it would be best if we didn't," he said. Suddenly Dani let go of my leg and stood up.

"That's fine. You don't have to stay here," she told him as she started to cross the room toward him.

"Really?" he asked, sounding a little shocked.

"Really. In fact, we can fly you back to Florida in the morning," she told him with a smile before turning back to me. "Love, will you please make sure the plane is ready to take the Meadows home?" I had no clue where she was going with this, but I could feel her anger, so I just nodded my head in agreement. "Wonderful!" she told me and then turned her attention back to the Meadows. "Please have your things ready by ten. Jameson, you and Stefhan will escort them to the airport."

"Whoa, whoa, whoa. Why are you sending us back to Florida? Salix surely knows that we know something. It would be a death sentence," Willow started before Dani raised her hand to silence her.

"According to Oak, so is you staying and helping us. We don't need you to get to the field. We need Cy, and from what I can see, she performed a very complicated ritual, so I really don't think you have to be here. If you don't want to stay in the packhouse–where we can ensure your safety–then you can go back to Florida and protect yourselves. Make your decision," Dani told Willow matter-of-factly.

Willow looked at Oak and then at Cy before looking at me. I'm not sure what she thought I was going to do. I loved it when Dani shifted into Luna mode. She was so fierce and didn't take any shit but was still compassionate and loving. After not getting a reaction out of me, Willow looked at Jay and then back at Dani.

"We'll stay."

I was mentally exhausted and just wanted the night to end. Unfortunately for me, the night was just beginning. The Meadows had excused themselves, but Dani and I insisted that Jay and Cy stay. Right at midnight, I heard the elevator door open.

"I still don't know why I had to come. I'm just the vampire in the basement," I heard Vinnie whispering to Kal.

"Because you were invited, that's why," Kal whispered harshly back.

Dani and I got up and started walking toward the hallway to greet them. Kal had been here plenty of times, but this was the first time Vinnie had ventured into the packhouse. He had only left the bunker once, to come to the hospital.

"Alpha and Luna puppies!" he exclaimed when he saw us standing at the end of the hall. I was surprised to see him dressed on the more laid-back side. He was wearing a plain black T-shirt and jeans. Usually, he was draped in sequins and feathers of some kind. When they entered the living room and Vinnie saw Cy, his eyes lit up.

"Little witch and Beta puppy, I didn't know you were going to be here!" he squealed as he took a seat in between them.

"Really, Vin," Kal groaned. Before he could reply, the front door opened.

"You could have told me it was a party, Stef," Fern complained as she and Luan walked in.

"I knew you wouldn't come if I told you everyone would be here. I don't have the time or the patience for your shit tonight, so please just come in, sit down, and listen," I snapped at her, trying to keep the rage at bay.

Fern still wasn't happy with me that I told the pack the truth, and I still didn't care. Honestly, I didn't see the point of her coming in the first place. She wasn't tied to the prophecy, Luan was. Dani told me that she needed to be here to support Luan, and it was important to her that I invite Fern. It wasn't something I was willing to fight with Dani about, so I invited her.

"No need to be so snappy," Fern mumbled under her breath as she and Luan took a seat.

"Okay, Stefhan. Are you ready to tell us what this is about?" Luan asked as he settled into his seat. Luan didn't like upsetting Fern, and being here upset Fern.

I didn't waste any time answering his question. I told them everything I told Jay, Cy, and her parents. There was only one part that we hadn't shared with the Meadows, and we did it intentionally. Dani and I agreed that only the people directly involved with the prophecy should know. We made an exception for Fern. We told them about the dreams. I even shared my dream with Lilith.

"Wait just a blood-sucking minute! You want me to believe that Lilith came to you?" Vinnie shrieked as he started to stand.

Before I knew what was happening, I was on my feet and standing directly in front of him.

"You question your Goddess, child?" Abbadon's demonic voice erupted out of me as he raised my hand and wrapped it around Vinnie's neck.

"Abaddon?" Vinnie managed to spit out as my hand began to squeeze.

"If you have to ask, you already know," Abaddon told him as he released the hold on Vinnie's neck and took a step back.

"I see you haven't got full control of him yet," Vinnie choked out as he rubbed his neck.

"Who the fuck is Abaddon?" Kal asked.

"The God Killer," he whispered. I could hear the genuine fear in his voice.

"What does that mean? And don't you fucking faint on me," she hissed at him.

If they both wouldn't have been so scared, it would have been a funny scene. Abbadon wasn't in the mood for dramatics, so he told Kal the same story he told everyone else. As he spoke, Kal started to relax, knowing that everything he was saying was the truth. Vinnie relaxed as Kal did.

"Just when I think it can't get any crazier, it does. I fucking love it," Kal said with a laugh when Abaddon was finished.

"What do we do now?" Vinnie asked me.

"I've been thinking about what Gram said and us having to live under the same roof. I think it goes deeper than just being in the packhouse together. Abaddon even said it earlier. Salix is depending on us keeping things from each other and following what we've been taught. There can't be any secrets between us if we are going to survive this. We have to become a true pack," I told them.

"Is that even possible?" Fern asked.

Honestly, I had forgotten she was there. She and Luan hadn't said a word since they sat down.

"Is what possible?" I asked her a little more harshly than was probably needed. Her habit of questioning my decisions was starting to piss me off.

"For Vinnie to join the pack? I mean, if he wants to," she said as she slightly bowed her head.

"Do you see that, boy?" Kane's voice echoed.

"Sure do," I replied.

"If he wants to, yes, it's possible. I'm the Alpha of this pack, and I decide who can join. Now I will say I don't know if we would be able to induct him the same way we would a wolf. We would have to look into that. The same thing goes for Cy," I started before Vinnie cut me off.

"How do you induct someone?"

"Well, you would pledge your loyalty to Crimson Diamond and accept me as your Alpha. I would make a cut in both of our hands with a ceremonial blade that has been used for that purpose since the start of this pack. We would then press our hands together, letting our blood mix. I would then say some Alpha-sounding shit and that's it." As I explained, I watched Vinnie's face closely. His poker face couldn't be beat.

"I won't make a decision until Kal does. We're a package deal," he told me as he looked at Kal.

"Well, shit. I guess it's time to tell my story. If I'm telling mine, you're telling yours too, Vin," Kal started before looking at the huge clock on the wall. "It's a long story and one that will prompt a lot of questions. We don't have time tonight. Come down for dinner tomorrow, and we'll tell you everything," she said as she looked at Vinnie. Their relationship was strange.

It was close to three, and I was beat. All I could think about was crawling in bed and getting a couple of hours of sleep before training. Everyone said goodnight and started to leave. I noticed Fern was standing, but not walking toward the door. Instead, she was walking toward me.

"Can I talk to you for a minute? Alone?" she asked.

"Of course," I told her as I internally groaned.

The longer she talked, the less sleep I would get, and fighting with her wasn't on the top of my favorite things to do list. She waited until everyone left, including Luan, and Dani was headed to the bedroom before speaking.

"I'm such a dick and I'm so sorry. I shouldn't have told you not to tell the pack about Mom. You don't know what it was like finding her and seeing Dad like that. I have nightmares about it. I wasn't thinking about what's best for the pack. I was only thinking about what was best for me. Just another reason you're the Alpha and I'm not."

While her apology was nice, I had no clue where it was coming from.

"You're not a dick, but I appreciate the apology. I won't lie, I'm a tad confused on where it came from. This is a complete turnaround from how you were at the start of the night," I told her honestly.

"Hearing everything that was said, this is so much bigger than any of us, and I can't let my selfishness get in the way. I promised you that I wouldn't let you down again and I meant it," she told me before a small shudder rocked through her. "That and the combination of you grabbing Vinnie by the throat and the demon voice that came out of you was enough for me."

"I wasn't that scary," I said with a laugh and a smile.

"Yes, you were. Now go to bed, you have to be up soon," she told me as she wrapped her arms around me. "Are you getting bigger?" she asked as I returned her hug.

"How did you manage to break four fingers?" Dani asked me as she rebroke each one so they would heal properly.

"Only getting a couple hours of sleep will do that to you," I told her as I kissed her forehead.

"I hate when you look like you just left Fight Club," she complained as she pushed me back so she could look at the cuts and scrapes that covered most of my body.

"I know you do, my love. I know it's not pleasant, but it's necessary–"

"I know, I know. It's better than a dead alpha," she cut in as she rolled her eyes. Dante still wasn't on her list of favorite people.

Dani and I hadn't had a chance to talk about the night before. She was already asleep when I got to the bedroom. Max and Phoenix were sleeping when I got home, so I took what could be the only opportunity we would have.

"We didn't get a chance to talk last night after everyone left," I told her as I pulled her close. I took a deep breath and let her scent consume and comfort me.

"No, we didn't, and we can't right now either. We have to finish the preparations for your mom's service. Carlos is meeting us in twenty minutes." Her voice was gentle and kind.

"How could I forget?" I groaned.

"Love, you have a lot on your plate. It's natural to forget things. When Gram died, if it wasn't for Cy, I wouldn't have gotten half of what needed done, done. Go jump in the shower, so we can meet Carlos. Cy and Jameson are going to stay with the kids. Fern and Luan are meeting us there." Her words were the life raft I needed at that moment.

I showered and threw on some sweats. Jay and Cy had just got there as I entered the living room. Dani was still telling them that the kids were sleeping.

"Bitch, I think I can figure out what to do if they wake up," Cy told her as Dani started going over where the bottles and diapers were.

"Fine, but if you need anything, just have Jameson link me."

I couldn't deny that it was nice to see them back to their regular banter. Dani needed Cy.

We walked slowly to my office to meet Carlos. Fern had taken the lead on the preparations up to that point. I wasn't sure why we even needed this meeting. When we got to my office, I was surprised to find it empty. We were almost ten minutes late, everyone should have been there. I didn't have long to ponder my confusion before Dani closed the door behind us.

"There is no meeting. We're just going to spend the day together. I have the whole day planned," she whispered as she wrapped her arms around my waist from behind.

"You're taking me on a date?"

"Yes, I am."

"I don't think that's a good idea," I started as I turned to face her. By the time I turned, she already had one hand up to stop me.

"Yes, it is. Don't fight me on this, Stefhan."

We spent the day enjoying each other's company. Kane and Enya both desperately needed to run. We shifted and they ran around the packhouse grounds. Making sure to stay away from the forest. After letting them get some energy out, we shifted back. Dani took me to our spot in the garden and we had a picnic. Even though everything else was shit, at that moment, everything was perfect. When we finished eating, we decided to take a walk. As we were rounding the corner to head to the front steps, a familiar voice called out.

"Luna Dani! Alpha Stefhan!"

"Sarah!" Dani called back to her and waved.

Sarah began to run toward us at full speed. She wrapped her arms around Dani the second she was close enough and started to cry.

"What's wrong? Why are you crying?" Dani asked her and tried to pull her back to make sure she wasn't hurt.

"My mom made me leave before I could tell you what I saw," she spit out in between her sobs.

"She made you leave where?" Dani asked her gently.

"The announcement about Luna Sarai. My mom made me leave before I could tell anyone what I saw."

"What did you see?" Dani asked her when Sarah stopped talking.

"Alpha said that he didn't know who she went running with. I was going to the packhouse for breakfast just like every day. When I saw Luna Sarai heading to the forest for her run." My heart was pounding as Sarah spoke. There was no way, no way she saw who Mom went running with. "I saw who she was with. She was with Monday."

"Are you sure it was Monday?" Dani asked her.

"I'm positive."

I didn't hear what was said after that. All my focus was concentrated on not completely losing my shit, shifting, and scaring Sarah. I closed my eyes and placed my hand on Dani's shoulder. There were so many thoughts swirling in my head that it was hard to focus. I tried to focus on Dani's scent and not the constant stream of Kane and Abbadon's thoughts. It was impossible to drown them completely out. I have no clue how long we stood there while Dani talked to Sarah. It felt like an eternity before I heard Dani calling my name.

Unforeseen Destinies

Chapter Fourteen

VINNIE

As Kal and I walked down the long hallway, a giggle escaped my lips.

"What's so funny?" she asked, lightly elbowing me in the side. "I could use a good chuckle."

"I just started thinking. If someone would have told me six months ago that I would be actually thinking about joining a werewolf pack, I would have eaten them. I must be losing my mind."

"At one point you also would have said the same about this," she told me with a giggle as she waved her hand between us. She then wrapped her arm around mine and laid her head on my arm.

"Are we going to tell them everything?" I asked her.

"We have to. I have never seen more honesty coming from someone as I did from Stefhan tonight. We have to match that honesty," she told me as she raised my hand to her mouth and pressed her lips to it.

"I need a drink."

It wasn't that I wanted to keep secrets from the puppies. Kal and I's relationship was complicated, even if you took out the sex.

"He's so fucking bossy! This better be good. I bet Stefhan didn't even tell Vinnie and Kal that we're coming early," I heard Fern's voice say as she approached the door.

"The party's starting early," I told Kal while getting up and opening it before they could knock. I assumed Luan was with Fern, but I was surprised to see Beta puppy and Cy, too. "He didn't tell us, but I'm always ready to entertain!" I told them as I dramatically swept my hand, motioning them to come in.

Knowing it wouldn't be long before there would be a knock, I stood by the door and waited, not even fully shutting it. Just a few minutes later, I heard footsteps coming down the hall. Fast. Quickly, I swung the door fully open and stepped back.

"Where's the fire, Alpha puppy? You're practically dragging the Luna puppy," I asked as he flew past me, and I shut the door.

"Lock it," a deep, almost demonic voice erupted from Stefhan's mouth.

Knowing who the voice belonged to, I did what I was told. I could feel the raw rage rushing off him in fast and furious waves. Dying at the hands of Abbadon wasn't on my list of things I wanted to experience. After locking the door, I took my usual seat. He was hanging on by a thread, and I wasn't going to be the reason it broke.

"Dani and I found out who Mom went for a run with." He paused, took a breath, and shook his head. "It was Monday."

"What? There's no way! Who told you that?" Fern shouted in disbelief.

The unique name sounded familiar, but I couldn't place it. I took a moment to scan the room. Fern, Luan, Cy, and Beta puppy all looked like they had seen a ghost.

"Someone who has no reason to lie," Alpha puppy started before being cut off by Luna puppy.

"It was Sarah. She told me that she saw Sarai walking into the forest with Monday."

Curiosity was rapidly overtaking me. While Monday rang a vague bell, I had no fucking clue who this Sarah was. I clamped my lips together in an attempt to keep myself quiet.

"After everything, Mom did for her? I don't believe it. How can we be sure it was really Monday? With all the crazy shit going on, it's not out of the question that it wasn't her!" Fern clapped back.

Suddenly the atmosphere in the room shifted, and whatever was keeping Alpha puppy's rage at bay lost control.

"YOU THINK I DON'T KNOW WHAT MOM DID FOR HER? YOU THINK I WANT TO ACCEPT THAT OF ALL PEOPLE IT WAS MONDAY WHO LURED OUR MOTHER TO HER DEATH?" The voice that left his mouth wasn't his but instead was Abbadon's.

Stefhan crossed the room in three large strides until he was face-to-face with Fern. Well, as face-to-face as they could be; he towered over her. Luna puppy ran behind him and placed her hand on the small of his back. Her small frame looked childlike against his massive one. He relaxed, but only by a fraction. She closed her eyes and pressed her hand harder against his back. Finally, he relaxed his shoulders, took a deep breath, and stepped back.

"Fern's right, we have to make sure it really was Monday," Luna puppy said barely above a whisper.

"I can't take it anymore! Who the fuck is Monday and Sarah?" The words flew out of my mouth before I could stop them. All eyes were suddenly on me. Kal chuckled quietly under her breath at my outburst. Luna puppy quickly explained who they were. But nothing in her explanation explained why Fern was so convinced that it couldn't be Monday. If I had learned anything recently, it was that anything was possible.

"Monday's history goes so much deeper with my family than her just being our flight attendant," Alpha puppy said, looking at Luna puppy. "It wasn't relevant before, but Monday's family wasn't born into our pack. Her mother showed up here pregnant and scared. She pleaded with my parents for protection. She said she was drugged and raped by some rouges, finding out shortly after that she was pregnant. She claimed her mate was abusive to her because he thought the baby wasn't his. It's VERY rare for a wolf to get pregnant by someone who isn't her mate. My dad was suspicious of her story and didn't want her to stay. Mom, on the other hand, wanted to help her. She talked Dad into letting her stay until the baby was born.

"She told him that she couldn't bear the thought of someone giving birth in the forest alone. Dad agreed but told her that as soon as the baby was born they had to go. Monday's mother died not long after giving birth. There was much back and forth between Mom and Dad on what should be done with the baby. Mom finally got him to let Monday stay. She was placed with a family in the pack, and they raised her. Mom stayed close to her, and Monday was often here spending time with her. Mom hired Monday at sixteen to be our private flight attendant."

I could then see why Fern felt so adamant that it couldn't have been Monday. She didn't want to believe that someone her mother did so much for could turn like that. I also knew how cold and cruel the world was and how easily people of any species could be swayed.

Everyone had a price.

I sat silently while everyone else talked and came up with a plan to confront Monday. Once a plan was in place, their attention turned to me and Kal.

"You should probably start, Vin. Your story is a little longer than mine," Kal told me with a smile as she walked toward the kitchen to bring out the food.

"You say it like I'm old or something," I replied as I dramatically wiped my forehead with my hand. We all made our way to the table and sat down. "Please save your questions for the end," I told them before I launched into my story.

Everyone's eyes were locked on me as I regaled them with everything I had already told Cy about my human life and how I was made. Their eyes bulged, and I could hear their sharp intakes of breath. Cy watched in amusement as they were brought up to speed. Kal casually brought the food to the table, not really listening. She already knew everything there was to know about me.

"Now that everyone is caught up on how I was made and that I killed my maker. Telling you how I killed him will also reveal a lie I told you. I lied about how I know what the sun feels like. Konstantin was stronger and smarter than me. I knew I couldn't trick him or overpower him. In my desperation, I concluded the only way would be to expose him to the sun while he slept. I snuck into his room and yanked open the curtain directly across from his bed. In doing so, I exposed my own hand to the sun. How bad and how long that shit hurt wasn't a lie."

I knew it was a lot of information and there was more coming. I needed to give them time to ask questions, so I opened the floor.

"That's so fucked up that he killed your family," Beta puppy whispered.

"You mentioned lineage and your maker having an image to uphold. What is your lineage?" Alpha puppy asked before I could respond to Beta puppy.

I immediately looked at Kal, I desperately needed her reassurance. Sharing that part of myself made me vulnerable. Very nonchalantly, she nodded her head at me and flashed a smile. I closed my eyes and took a breath.

"For the love of the fucking Goddess, Vin. Just tell them already!" Kal snapped at me after a few minutes.

"I am. Give me a minute! This isn't something I normally just go around telling people, Kal," I snapped back as I raised my hand and opened my eyes. Everyone's eyes were locked on me as they waited for me to speak. "My apologies everyone. This is something that makes me very vulnerable.

Kal is the first and only person I've told. As you all know, Crina was the first vampire created. Being the first, she was the strongest and had the closest connection to Lilith. Crina created Senta and Senta created Konstantin."

"Wait just a minute! Are you saying you're part of the first line?" Alpha puppy asked, cutting me off before I could finish.

"I'm surprised you know the term. Yes. That's exactly what I'm saying," I started before promptly being cut off again. Fern, Luan, and Alpha puppy simultaneously started shouting at me. The only person I was able to make out, mainly because it was the first and loudest voice, was Alpha puppy.

"That's impossible! The first line is dead," he shouted. After that, their voices quickly blended together.

"This is what I get for letting them ask questions," I moaned to myself before raising my hand to try and shush them.

"Will you all let Vinnie finish!" Luna Puppy shouted over them when it was clear my shushing tactic wasn't working. They immediately fell quiet. "Not all of us know what 'part of the first line' means or why it makes him vulnerable."

"Thank you," I said before giving a dramatic pause. "While I wasn't able to catch all the things being shouted at me, I'll do my best to answer them all. Now, where was I? Oh, yes!" I paused again and shifted my gaze to Luna puppy. I watched out of the corner of my eye as Kal sat down. Of all the vampire history I had told her, she found how lineage worked fascinating. "Every vampire that has, is, or will ever walk the earth is descended from one of the first five lines. And those lines are not created equal. Only the first line is considered pure."

Confusion crossed everyone's face but Kal's.

"Vampire lineage works very differently than any other species. If you recall, vampires were created as a punishment. Crina was and always will be the only pure-blood vampire. All of Crina's blood was replaced with vampire blood, not a single drop of her own blood was left behind. However, each time the Oracle repeated the process, a little more of their own blood was left behind, causing each newborn vampire to be weaker than the last. By the time the fifth was turned, they still had a quarter of their own blood mixed in with the vampire blood.

"Part of the process in turning someone into a vampire is nearly draining them of their blood and then having them feed off you. This was intentionally done by the Oracle to ensure that the blood becomes further diluted with each generation. Every new vampire is slightly weaker than the one who made it. Vampires weren't intended to recreate forever. Eventually, the vampire blood will become so diluted, so weak that the change can no longer take place."

"Wait, wait, wait. Did you just say that eventually vampires will go extinct?" Luan suddenly asked, causing my focus to shift to him. He wasn't much of a talker, so I often forgot he was even there.

"More like endangered. There will come a time when no new vampires can be created. Most vampires don't want to experience the final death. Myself included," I explained to him before looking at Alpha puppy. "The first line isn't dead, but I'm the last and I plan on keeping it that way." I watched as his confusion set in. As far as the supernatural world knew, the first line died long ago. I was genuinely curious about what he thought happened to the first line.

"What do you think happened to them?" I couldn't stop myself. I had to know how much it varied from the lie I spread all those years ago.

"Our legends don't say much, but they say that the last two were cornered and killed," he answered simply.

"That's it? Are you serious?" I shrieked, making everyone jump. "I thought at least half the story would make it. I worked really hard on it," I sulked.

"Quit stalling, Vin. Just fucking tell them. Everything," Kal told me sternly. She knew I was stalling.

"Fine," I snapped at her while throwing in an eye-roll. There were things I was hoping to not have to disclose. Alpha puppy, knowing that the first line was 'dead,' threw that out the window.

"I wasn't fully honest when I told you that Konstatin let the only other vampire he made leave," I paused and took a drink. "When he discovered our relationship, he killed her. Konstantin was a special kind of fucked up. When a vampire crossed him, made him mad, or hell even looked at him funny, he would kill them. He would lock them in a room with nothing but windows and wait for the sun to rise. I can still remember her screams.

"I'm sorry I didn't tell you the whole truth earlier, but there are some things about my life that I wanted to keep secret if I could. I'm going to tell you everything, but it can't leave this room. My lineage can make me a target, and I will kill everyone in this room before I let that happen." My voice turned raspy at the end. No one spoke, but they all nodded their heads. I took another drink to compose myself before continuing.

"Before I 'killed off' the first line, vampires from all over would show up with humans and beg for Konstantin to turn them. Every single human became a meal, and the vampire who brought them met the sun. He had no mercy and had no desire to 'muddy the line.' Unfortunately, Senta had corrupted him beyond repair before she willingly walked into the sun." I quickly held a hand to stop the onslaught of questions that I knew were coming.

"I fully plan on explaining. Crina was kind, loving, and wise. Senta was cold, conniving, and evil. She killed without thought, any human that crossed her path was destined to meet their God. Crina tried to get her to change her ways, but she refused. Crina had no choice but to cut all ties with Senta. Crina also vowed to never make another vampire. Senta, not wanting to be lonely, then turned Konstantin, teaching him to be just like her. It didn't take long for Crina to find out about Konstantin and that he was just as evil as Senta. It broke her, and that's when she decided to walk into the sun.

"When word got to Senta that Crina had willingly met the final death and why, at first, she was ecstatic. With Crina gone, she was now the purest and most powerful vampire. Together, she and Konstantin ravaged whole towns. This went on for hundreds of years. Then one day, for reasons unknown, she walked into the sun. Konstantin never offered the information, and I wasn't dumb enough to ask for it.

"When Senta died, it then made Konstantin the most pure and powerful. A title he carried with immense arrogance, and there wasn't anything anyone could do about it. Anyone that tried met the sun. One thing Senta pounded into his head was to keep the line as pure as possible. Thus ensuring that our line never dies out. After some years, he finally decided that he needed an heir. While he knew that technically he was the strongest and unbeatable, he also knew that if a group large enough banded together he wouldn't stand a chance.

"He searched for fifty years before finding me. From the moment he turned me, I knew I would never give this fate to anyone else. And when I found out he killed my family, I decided I was going to kill him. I had to bide my time and wait for the perfect moment. It was sheer coincidence that when he turned her, she would hate him just as much as I did and wanted to help me." I could tell they were curious why I wouldn't say her name, so I decided to address the elephant in the room quickly.

"It is blatantly obvious by your faces that you want to know why I won't say her name." They all nodded. "I can't. It's vampire magic, and I'm going to tell you about it later because it ties in with something else." I glanced quickly at Kal. "When he killed her, the plan was already laid out. I just had to go through with it alone. How I told you I killed him is the truth, and I did burn the shit out of my hand. Once night fell, I started massive fires all over the estate and watched it burn to the ground before fleeing. He did give me one thing to be grateful for. None of our kind that were still walking the earth knew what I looked like. He had killed all the ones that did. When we traveled, he made me wear a hood. Had me looking like *The Man in the Iron Mask.*

"I made my way to the closest town known to have vampires. All it took was telling a handful that I had heard Konstantin, and his heir were killed, and the estate was burned to the ground. Vampires are gossipy creatures, so it didn't take long for it to spread. It took even less time for some to go and look. Seeing the estate burned to nothing but a few timbers was evidence enough. His estate was as important to him as his blood status. If it was gone and he was alive, word of his wrath would have already been spreading. And that my puppies and little witch is how you kill a bloodline." I paused to give them time to process.

"WAIT A FUCKING MINUTE!" Cy suddenly screamed, making everyone but me jump. "Please correct me if I'm wrong, but are you saying that you are the most powerful vampire in the world?"

I didn't like saying it out loud, so I didn't. Opting to nod my head yes instead. I immediately shifted my focus to Alpha puppy. His face flashed so many emotions it was hard to tell what he was really feeling. It was my quote make-or-break moment.

"I understand if your offer no longer stands," I told Alpha puppy after a long time of complete silence.

"Of course, my offer still stands. My invitation didn't come with any strings. I was thinking about how it makes sense that you are a powerful vampire."

"Huh?" I was dumbfounded.

"Hear me out. The prophecy brought together the world's four most powerful wolves and one of the most powerful witches. It makes sense that you would be a powerful vampire. You being the most powerful is just icing on the cake."

"And with that, I guess it's my turn," Kal said before I could answer.

Unforeseen Destinies

Chapter Fifteen

KAL

I had to take a deep breath. Technically, what I was going to say was treason and punishable by death. There was a very high chance that none of us would survive this anyway and if there was ever a reason to die, this was it. I could feel Vin's gaze on me as I locked eyes with Stefhan.

"Have you ever heard of the Sotta la Dea?" I asked him, knowing damn well he hadn't, but I didn't have a better opener.

"No. Should I?"

"I didn't figure you would," I told him honestly. "'Sotta la Dea' translates to 'Under the Goddess.' It is a pack of werewolves that are hand-selected by the council to be the enforcers of the Goddess. The wolves selected are all very gifted, and the council has what they call Hunters who travel the world looking for gifted wolves to add to the ranks. The Hunters will watch pups from powerful families for years to see if they exhibit any special talents." As I spoke, I could see him putting the pieces together. I paused, figuring he would interrupt me.

"Is that why the council spent so much time here when Fern and I were young?" he asked.

"Yes, and you're damn lucky they didn't find out about you and Fern's gift to link no matter the distance. If they would have, you both would have been taken instantly. Chosen wolves don't get a choice." I could see the questions starting to form in Stefhan's head. "I don't know all the inner workings as I'm not part of the pack. My parents were."

"But if your parents were part of the pack, why aren't you? By law you were born into the pack," Stefhan said, cutting me off.

"I was getting to that. Just like Vin did, I'm going to tell you everything. I'm sure most of your questions will be answered." I paused just long enough for him to nod in agreement. "No one is born into Sotta la Dea. Every single wolf is selected. Selected wolves aren't allowed to take a mate, fated or chosen. It is said they exist solely to serve the Goddess. Mates and families are considered distractions. My parents were both taken at fifteen. The hunters had been watching them for years. My mother was taken because, like me, she could see lies. My father was taken because he was a descendant. He was the first male to be born in six generations and was abnormally strong. They preferred the descendants to be males. My parents discovered, when my mom turned eighteen, that they were fated mates. They didn't understand why the Goddess would make them mates knowing that they couldn't be together. But they decided that the Goddess wouldn't want them to reject each other, so they didn't. They kept their relationship a secret. They managed to complete the matebond and keep their secret for six years. When my mom got pregnant with me, they knew they couldn't hide it for long, so they came clean to the Alpha.

"They were both instantly condemned to death. The council only stepped in when it was discovered that my father was the last living descendant of our line. The council didn't want to anger Selene by killing off the line. The compromise between the Alpha and the council was that my parents would be allowed to live just long enough for me to survive on my own. It was made clear my entire childhood that they were going to be killed and I would be on my own. They were killed the day after I turned thirteen. I was told to leave and that I could only return twice a year for a week each visit. Allowing me to come back twice a year to the packland I was born on. This prevents me from becoming a rogue.

"Before you ask why they didn't keep me because of my gift, they couldn't. It would have shown mercy on my parents if they had kept me. It would have made me part of the pack. So, at thirteen, I was on my own and scared shitless. My gift saved me more than once from premature death. I had more than my fair share of run-ins with rogues. I tried to join some local packs, but they all wanted to know what happened to my pack and why I didn't smell like a rogue. I couldn't tell them the truth because it would lead to my death. When I wouldn't tell them, I was of course denied. Things got easier when I could finally shift, and Stella could protect me.

"From eighteen to twenty-one, I bounced around before finally deciding to make Corfu my home. It was there, after a night of heavy drinking, that I was attacked by rogues and Vin saved me. I'll let him go into more detail with that since it's what ties in with vampire magic. I left my family book hidden at Sotta la Dea; it was safer there than traveling around with me. Thankfully when Fern and Luan found me, it was about time for a trip back."

By the time I finished, everyone's eyes were as big as plates. I knew how unbelievable it sounded. If I didn't know it to be true, I would have thought it was made up. After a few minutes of silence, Stefhan cleared his throat.

"Just like I told Vinnie, my offer still stands. If you join Crimson Diamond, you won't ever have to go back there." Stefhan's voice was full of unshaken confidence.

"We'll see if you still feel that way when I tell you why Kal and I are a package deal," Vin whispered as we both took a long drink.

"You can do this," Vin whispered to himself before directing his attention to Stefhan.

VINNIE

"It's kind of complicated, but I'm going to do my best to explain it. I told you earlier that I can't say her name due to vampire magic. Vampire magic can only be performed by the first line," I started before Luan stopped me.

"What is a truss then?"

"If people would stop interrupting, this would be so much easier," I mumbled to myself before continuing. "Trusses are considered magic to everyone except the first line. True vampire magic has no bounds and cannot be reversed, ever, not even the death of the vampire who cast it ends the spell. Konstantin put a binding of sorts on me to where I can never communicate her name in any form." I gave them a minute to let that sink in before I laid the real bombshell.

"First, that dude was a fucker. But that doesn't explain you and Kal," Cy suddenly said.

"Yes, he was a fucker," I agreed with a laugh. "I was getting to that. I was just giving everyone a minute to process." I took a drink from my cup and then a deep breath. "You all know how I found Kal and that I nursed her back to health. What I didn't tell you is how I accomplished it. Her heart stopped once on the way to my house and then again not long after I got her there and settled. Doing CPR on a blood-covered werewolf wasn't exactly a good time. I was starting to think that it was just her time to go be with her Goddess and decided to let her go. After all, it wasn't my place to take care of dogs. But I heard a voice telling me that I had to save her. That I had to do whatever it took to save her. I didn't have time to think before her heart stopped again.

"The voice screamed at me to save her. It took me almost three minutes to get her heart beating again. The voice never stopped telling me that I couldn't let her die. I couldn't break the promise I made to myself that I would never become a maker. There was only one way other than turning her to save her, but I wouldn't do it without her permission. I was able to get her coherent enough to be able to talk to her. I told her what I was and that something was telling me to save her. She begged me not to turn her, and I told her that I had no intention of turning her. That's when I told her that I could save her and she would be bound to me, but not like a truss. She would be bound to me like a mate. Before I could fully explain the process, she agreed, saying that Stella said it was part of their journey and to trust the Goddess and for me to 'just fucking do it.'" I watched as everyone's eyes went wide. "I'd rather not go into full detail on how it was done, but the CliffsNotes version is I gave her some of my blood to help repair the damage and said a spell.

"Over the next couple of days, while she healed, I told her everything that being bound to me entailed. Most parts aren't bad. Her life isn't dependent on mine. If I die, she would be fine, and vice versa. She is free to do pretty much whatever she wants. She's not immortal and will eventually die."

"That doesn't sound bad at all," Luna puppy whispered. I knew she wasn't talking to me, but I answered her anyway.

"Oh, Luna puppy, I said most parts aren't bad. I haven't gotten to the bad part. She can no longer find her fated mate. The spell, while saving her life, made her my fated mate. She also can't have sex with anyone other than me. I, on the other hand, can have sex with whoever I want." Gasps filled the room, but no one interrupted. "I was scared shitless that when she healed enough she would turn on me. I stole her chance to find her true mate. I know what it feels like to have your life ripped away from you." I had to pause to compose myself and take a breath.

"It was then that she told me about her gift, and she could tell, thanks to our bond, that I felt horrible. We spent the next month getting to know each other. Over time, she has become my best friend, closest confidant, and lover."

"You have sex? With each other?" Fern shouted before clapping her hand over her mouth.

"Yes, we have sex. With each other," Kal answered so I didn't have to. "I was the one who brought it up. I wasn't going to go the rest of my life without it. I just lucked out that Vin is bi-sexual."

"I'd rather not talk about our sex life," I quickly added. I'm a private person and wanted to keep one thing private.

"And you shouldn't have to," Alpha puppy replied quickly, shutting down any questions. "If it was Kal's choice, then I respect it."

"Thank you," I told him before clapping my hands together and using my full speed to move beside Kal. "Let's join a pack!"

"Jay, can you go get the ceremonial blade?" Alpha puppy asked.

Beta puppy immediately stood, nodded his head, and started for the door.

"Is it safe for you to officially join the pack?" Luna puppy asked me. When I didn't immediately answer, she continued. "As a doctor, I can't help but wonder if it's safe for you to mix Stefhan's blood with yours." The genuine concern on her face made me smile.

"It takes more than a little puppy blood to hurt me," I assured her and dramatically waved my hand.

While we waited for Beta Puppy to get back, we moved to the living area to be a little more comfortable. Undead or not, my ass can only take so much time on a wooden seat with no cushion.

"Cy will also be joining the pack alongside you and Kal. She performed a binding between her and Jay," Alpha puppy started before I cut him off.

"You go, Cy! That's a hard-ass spell to do!" Her progress since I first met her was astounding, and I couldn't help myself.

"Thanks! It was wicked hard, and it took forever for me to get right. Jam's whole place smelled like swamp water for an hour."

Before I could say anything in return, Beta puppy was back and holding a box.

"That better not be a butter knife," I said to myself, causing Fern to start laughing.

"I can promise you it's not," she told me between her laughs.

"What did I miss?" Alpha puppy asked.

"Nothing. It was a joke that Vinnie pulled on us while we were in Corfu," Luan explained. Fern was still laughing hysterically.

"Let's get started then," Alpha puppy said and stood.

We lined up single file in the middle of the room. Alpha puppy opened the box and took out a beautiful blade. As he turned to face us, it was like someone flipped a switch. He started getting bigger, his aura glowing a brilliant deep red and his Alpha energy filling the room. I watched as he inducted Cy then Kal into the pack. When he took his place in front of me, I was so nervous. If my heart would have been beating, I wouldn't have been able to hear him.

"Before I can induct you Vinnie, I have to know your full name."

"Vincent Vasil Dragomir," I told him without hesitation and letting my old-world accent shine through.

"Coolest fucking name ever," Cy whispered.

"Vincent Vasil Dragomir, do you swear to protect Crimson Diamond and all that live within its borders?" he asked me as he took my hand in his.

"I do," I answered.

"Do you swear to always put the pack first?"

"I do."

"Do you swear to follow me and accept me as your alpha?"

"I do."

He released my hand and swiftly cut his palm as I raised mine to my mouth. I ran my canine across the skin, separating it like butter. As soon as I lowered my hand, he pressed his bleeding palm to mine.

"Welcome to Crimson Diamond."

"Thank you, Stefhan."

Unforeseen Destinies

Chapter Sixteen

STEFHAN

I stood there dumbfounded. This was the first time he ever called me by my name, I wasn't sure how to respond. Concern crossed his face, and I knew I needed to say something.

"You're welcome," I quickly told him.

"Are you sure?" he retorted. My tone always gave me away.

"Yes. It just threw me when you called me Stefhan. I assumed I was going to be Alpha puppy forever."

"Oh, that! You've graduated!" he exclaimed as he clapped his hands together.

"Graduated?"

"Yes, and so has Dani!" he told me excitedly. "Don't worry though, Alpha and Luna puppy will always be my nicknames for you. Only when I consider someone a true friend will I address them by their given name." He said it so matter-of-factly like it was obvious information. "May I ask a question?" he asked me very seriously. I didn't speak, instead just nodded my head. "Since I'm officially a member of your pack, do I have to stay the vampire in the basement? I haven't been outside in months, and I could really use some fresh air and exercise. Keeping this body looking this good takes work."

"Of course you can. Honestly, I think everyone could," I told him.

I for one needed some fresh air. So much information was thrown at us in the last twenty-four hours that my brain was completely mush.

"Can I meet your wolves?" Vinnie asked as we walked toward the garage.

"If you think you're ready?" Dani answered him.

"Do you underestimate me that much?" he retorted playfully.

I still had to be mindful that the pack wasn't aware of Vinnie's presence, so I guided us to mine and Dani's spot. It was big enough for all our wolves to have space to run and whatever Vinnie had planned. More importantly, it was private. I planned on introducing Vinnie once my mom's funeral was over. It was planned for the next night. The thought made my chest tight.

"Can I go full speed?" Vinnie asked me, pulling me from my thoughts.

"Yeah. This is our private area. The only room that can see it from the packhouse is our bedroom."

"Thank the Goddess!" he shouted before vanishing.

"How fast do you think he is?" Cy asked Jay.

"Faster than any of us," he answered. Hearing their back and forth made me curious if he could beat Enya in a race.

"Do you think he's faster than Enya?" Dani asked me suddenly. Like always, she knew what I was thinking.

"I was just wondering about that myself. Wanna find out?"

Dani didn't answer, instead she headed behind the statue of Selene to shift. She still wasn't comfortable being naked in front of other people. Nudity can't be avoided when you're a werewolf. At some point, you will see everyone naked. Just moments after she disappeared, Enya stepped out.

"Holy shit!" Vinnie shouted from across the field. Before I could blink, he was standing beside me and had his hand on my arm. "May I touch her?" he asked me.

"That would be up to Enya," I told him truthfully.

Enya dipped her head and walked toward us. Vinnie didn't need any more invitation than that. Slowly he walked up to her, meeting her in the middle. Enya bowed her head and lay down. Vinnie raised his hand and ran it through her fur.

"So, you're the Fire Wolf. Simply beautiful, Miss Enya, but there is no way you can beat me in a race."

Enya rolled her tongue out and huffed before standing. She motioned her head to the west and back.

"To the woods and back?" he asked her. Enya nodded her head in return.

"You're good at interpreting what she's saying," I told him as he started warming up. I think it was more for show than anything. If there was anything I had learned about Vinnie, it was that he loved putting on a show.

"Spending so much time with Stella has helped. Now if you'll excuse me, I have to go beat the fur off your wife," he said with a playful wink.

Kal made a starting line in the dirt, and I watched as they both took their places. Enya looked focused and ready to take off; Vinnie looked relaxed like he wasn't paying attention. Kal raised her hand.

"Ready, set, GO!" she called out while she sliced her hand through the air.

Enya took off at full speed, Vinnie didn't move.

"One, two, three, four, five," he counted quietly before vanishing.

Enya was on her way back, having made it to the forest edge before Vinnie even moved.

"Fastest wolf you say?" Vinnie asked me suddenly, making me jump.

Enya looked extremely confused to see Vinnie standing next to me at the finish line when she got there. She huffed and looked back at the forest.

"Let's let someone else have a try," he told her before turning to the rest of us. "Anyone care to see if they can beat me?"

One by one, we all raced Vinnie. The only one of us who even came close—and by close, I mean Vinnie didn't have time to fix his hair and clothes before he arrived—was Batté.

"Well done, Batté! That is the closest any wolf has ever come to catching me!"

Batté was almost as large as Kane, but due to Luan never taking the title of Alpha, he was slightly smaller. I honestly think if he had become Alpha, Batté would have towered over Kane. Kane disagreed with my assumption. I let Kane maintain control, and we watched as Vinnie prepared to show off. He wanted to show us what all he could do. He had us sit in a large semi-circle. I was glad that Kane was out, as I was sure my mouth would have been gaping open. His speed, agility, and ability to basically vanish was amazing to watch.

Dani was settled against Kane's massive side, holding the baby monitor that I didn't even see her grab. There were times I felt I was a failure when it came to being a parent, and this was one of them. I would have just walked out and left the kids alone.

"Don't start that shit, boy," Kane growled at me, hearing the tone of my thoughts. Before I could tell him to shut it, a soft cry came across the monitor.

"I'll get her," Dani told me quickly as she started to get up. Knowing where my head was, Kane got up to follow her.

"I got it. You don't have to come," she told us when she realized Kane was following behind her. Kane stopped so I could shift.

"Are you sure? I don't mind," I told her with a smile.

"Yeah. Just stay here and watch Vinnie show off." The smile that crossed her face didn't reach her eyes.

"Okay my love, just hurry back."

By the time the words were out of my mouth, she was already halfway back to the packhouse. I watched as she picked up her pace, ending up in an almost run by the time she made it to the door.

"Follow her," a soft female voice whispered. It was so soft I thought I had imagined it. *"Follow her, Stefhan,"* the voice whispered.

The voice was familiar, but I couldn't place it. I stood there holding my sweats and staring toward the packhouse. I was torn, part of me wanted to obey and follow Dani. The other part of me still vividly remembered what happened the last time I listened to a random voice in my head.

"Are you going to do what she told you?" Abbadon asked me.

"I'm not sure," I admitted honestly. *"Would you?"*

"I always listen to my Goddess," he answered simply. With that, I didn't need any more confirmation.

"I'm going to see if Dani needs any help," I announced to the group as I put my sweats on and jogged to the packhouse.

"She needs you. Hurry!" the voice pleaded to me as soon as I got inside. I started running at full speed, not slowing down until I reached our front door. I paused just long enough to open and close it quietly behind me. I immediately went to the hallway that led to the bedrooms. I carefully opened Phoenix's door; she was sound asleep. Next, I checked in Max's room; he was also sleeping. Finally, I went into our room. The light was on, but the room was empty, and the bathroom door was closed.

"Shut the door," the voice guided me.

This time I obeyed without question. I walked slowly toward the bathroom door. I focused on Dani, trying to get a feel of her emotions. She was blocking me.

"That's never a good sign, boy. Are you ready?" Kane asked.

Instead of answering him, I opened the door. Dani's screams and sobs instantly filled my ears the second the soundproof seal was broken. Pain and anger radiated off her in steady waves. She was sitting on her knees in the middle of the floor as if she had just collapsed there. I crossed the room, kneeled behind her, and wrapped my arms around her.

"I told you to stay outside. I didn't want you to see me like this," she scolded me as I pulled her closer.

"What's wrong?" I asked, completely ignoring her attempt at scolding me. My heart ached as her pain and anger crashed against me.

"It's not fair, Stefhan!" she yelled as she wrapped her arms around mine. The floodgates were getting ready to open. All she needed was a little prompt. She always felt so guilty for breaking down. She wanted to be strong for me.

"What's not?"

"Everything!" she cried as she turned to face me. "This prophecy is like a fucking plague! Infecting everyone it touches, going back since the dawn of fucking time! At first, I just thought it was me. I lost my parents, pack, identity, Gram, you, and my sanity there for a bit. After hearing Vinnie and Kal's stories tonight, I realized it's all of us. Vinnie's family was murdered, so he could be turned into a vampire. Kal was thrown out as a child by ADULTS who are supposed to uphold the values of Selene. The only reason she was 'saved' to begin with was so the line didn't die. Not that it mattered, the line is dead anyway. Then as if that wasn't enough, she can't even find her fated mate now!

"I don't know much about Luan's past, but I'm sure it's filled with loads of fucking trauma! Then there's you. You being the person who is supposed to kill a fucking god! And not just any god, the god of the fucking witches! Who, mind you, has already manipulated you into LEAVING me on our wedding night, so I could potentially die while giving birth to our son!" she screamed before burying her face in my chest.

I wanted to tell her that everything was going to be okay and that it would all be over soon, but I didn't. I just held her as she sobbed and waited for the screaming to start again. After a few minutes, the sobs slowed, and her breathing evened out. Without a word, I gently lifted her up and carried her out of the bathroom and into our room. She was completely asleep by the time I laid her on our bed and covered her up.

"She'll be okay, boy," Kane reassured me as I quietly walked out, closed the door, and tried to convince myself he was right.

DANI

The sunlight was blinding, but not uncomfortable. I could feel the heat on my skin, and I could hear waves crashing against the shore. I stood barefoot in the soft sand. Fear gripped me as I tried to focus my eyes.

"Please don't be afraid," a velvet voice called to me. It wasn't a voice I recognized, but it instantly calmed me. I closed my eyes and reopened them slowly to reveal a beautiful beach. There was a familiarness to it. As I looked around, I realized it was the beach that Gram

took me to. I didn't have time to think about why I was there before I saw her. Her skin was dark ebony, and her black hair flowed loose in soft curls that touched her waist. Her eyes were a bright sapphire blue. She was so beautiful, even more beautiful than Selene.

"Please don't be afraid," she repeated.

"Who are you?" I finally managed to choke out.

She smiled the most breathtaking smile and slowly walked toward me, her palms showing as a sign of peace.

"You don't know?" the beautiful stranger asked me in return. Having no clue, I just shook my head. "I knew you were powerful, but never in my existence did I think you could call me to you. Call me and not even know it," she whispered to herself. It reminded me of Vinnie. "I've been called many names over time, but I prefer Lilith."

My heart stopped and my head started spinning.

"Lilith? Goddess of the Vampires, Lilith?" I asked, feeling immediately like an idiot.

"One in the same," she answered with a smile. "Why did you call me here?"

"I didn't call you here," I said quickly.

"If you didn't call me, then how did I get here? What were you doing right before you arrived?"

My breakdown to Stefhan flooded my mind. Anger filled me and my eyes overflowed with bitter tears.

"I was telling Stefhan how this whole prophecy is like a plague and it's not fair that so many lives have been ruined because of it," I confessed as the tears rolled down my cheeks.

"Is that all?" Lilith asked me patiently.

"That's all I told Stefhan."

"What about what you didn't tell him?" That simple question transformed my anger into guilt. I didn't want to confess my true feelings out loud. They were horrible and selfish. Lilith's piercing blue eyes bore into mine with unwavering patience while I battled with my inner demons. A fresh wave of tears rolled down my cheeks as I thought about letting the ugly truth out.

"You'll feel better when you let it out," Lilith softly encouraged.

Once the words left my mouth, there would be no taking them back. I took one of Gram's deep, centering breaths.

"I don't want to do this," I whispered.

"Just let it out, Dani."

"I didn't mean I didn't want to tell you. I meant that I don't want to be the Fire Wolf. I don't want my husband to be some God Killer demon. I don't want my son to be some special wolf that can end life as we know it. I don't want to be surrounded by magic and vampires. I don't want any of it. More and more I find myself wishing that all of this really is just a coma dream. That one day I'll wake up and be in the hospital in Florida. I want to wake up and go back to my normal life. The one where I am a respected and talented doctor. The one where my best friend is a crazy bitch and gets fired for cursing out kids who pranked 911. The one where my Gram is still alive." The words felt hot and gross as they left my mouth, but they were the truth.

"You don't mean that, Dani," Lilith started before I cut her off.

"Oh, but I do! I mean every word! My life has been nothing but chaos since waking up to Stefhan at my bedside. I lost my entire world and was thrown into a new one. One I didn't ask for! Why can't it just be easy? Why can't we be normal? I wasn't made for this, I wasn't prepared for this, I'm not strong enough for this!" I confessed as the tears flowed freely.

"I can understand how you wouldn't want to tell Stefhan that," Lilith told me with a small

smile before it faded. "But that doesn't explain how you called me to you." She didn't look angry, more perplexed as she continued. "What was the last thing you were thinking before you fell asleep?" My face flushed red as the thought replayed in my mind. It wasn't red with embarrassment; it was red with anger.

"Why Stefhan? Why did you have to pick him for your demon spawn to take up residency? You could have picked anyone!" I screamed at her.

In my mind, Lilith was the entire reason my life was shit. I never thought I would ever get the chance to tell her how I felt. Abbadon made it clear that Lilith only visited Stefhan to help him make the transformation. Yet somehow, she was standing in front of me, and now that she had asked, game on.

"As Stefhan held me while I lost my shit, all I kept thinking was how this is all your fault. If you would have picked anyone else, I would have a normal werewolf relationship! Well, as normal as a werewolf relationship can be. I just want to love my super hot husband and raise my kids in a safe environment. But no! I don't get to do that because of you!" I shrieked before dropping to my knees and hanging my head

"Do you feel better?" she asked me gently. A tone I wasn't expecting.

"Not really. It doesn't change anything," I answered without raising my head. It didn't matter the size of fit I threw. Stefhan would still be the God Killer, I would still be the Fire Wolf, and Max would still be the Sapphire Wolf.

"You truly think it's my fault? That I set this course for you and your mate?" The sincere tone of her voice made me raise my head.

"Yes!"

"Oh, Dani. That couldn't be further from the truth. I didn't choose Stefhan, Selene chose you."

"But Stefhan is older than me," I spit out.

"That doesn't mean anything. Your fate was chosen long before Stefhan was born. It has always been your line that birthed the Fire Wolf. Just like Stefhan's has always birthed the Deus Interfectorem. When your parents found each other and completed the matebond, Selene deemed that their first and only child would be the Fire Wolf. At the time your parents found each other, Sarai was pregnant with the twins. There was great intrigue among the Gods and Goddesses about how powerful they would be. Some thought Selene had planned it–a claim she vehemently denied. Saying the twins' conception was purely natural. Either way, it made my job harder.

"Once it was deemed that you would be the Fire Wolf, it automatically made Stefhan your mate, thus making him the Deus Interfectorem. Normally, introducing Abbadon is easy, but this was the first time there would be two fetuses. I had to be careful that Abbadon didn't split and infect Fern. I had no clue what would happen if he did. Abbadon wasn't created to be in a woman. Very carefully, I placed Abbadon inside of Stefhan and waited for you to be born. Until you were born, Abbadon was dormant. I don't like to put wolves through living with Abbadon until the last minute." As I listened to her, Abbadon's story flashed to the front of my mind.

"But you let Abbadon kill them. He killed them all and you did nothing!" I shrieked at her.

"I can't intervene. It goes against the great design," she started before I cut her off.

"Don't give me that shit! I am so fucking sick of hearing bullshit! If you wanted to put a stop to it, you could!"

"Danielle, you don't understand. It's not that I don't want to. I can't. It's part of my punishment. My punishment for going against the Oracle. I know you were already told of my lapse in judgment and how my children are damned. My punishment was more than lore dictates. If I could take your pain and suffering away, I would. But just how I can't change what is,

neither can you. You have to become the Fire Wolf and stop letting your emotions get in the way. Salix will use it against you, and it WILL be your downfall."

Unforeseen Destinies

Chapter Seventeen

I woke up to Stefhan's arms around me and a sick feeling in my stomach. I turned my face, so I didn't wake him up, and watched him sleep as Lilith's words echoed in my head. Enya was quiet, but I knew that she knew everything. Thanks to my gift, she got an instant replay of the entire encounter the second it crossed my mind. It was times like that when I hated sharing mind space. It was hard to keep things from Enya, but it was possible. I just had to wait for her to be asleep. I reserved that time to let my selfish thoughts take over. I knew it hurt her how much I was beginning to resent this life.

Guilt consumed me as I watched Stefhan sleep. I was worried that he would sense my guilt and wake up. I needed to pull myself together, it was not the day to make things about me. Slowly, I pulled myself away from him and made my way to the bathroom.

"Stop letting your emotions get in the way. Become the Fire Wolf." The words bounced around in my head as I stepped into the shower. I had no clue how to do either of those things.

"Child, what do you mean you don't know how?" Enya asked me somewhat sternly like I was missing the obvious. Instead of answering her, I grabbed my bottle of shampoo and started working on my hair. I didn't have time to deal with any cryptic shit, and I couldn't be a mess when Stefhan got up.

"STOP IGNORING ME!" Enya roared, causing me to grab my head.

"What the fuck! Why did you do that?" I shrieked while still holding my head.

"Because you need to listen to me." Her voice was calm, but I could hear the desperation in it. She paused to see if I was going to interrupt her, and when I didn't, she continued. *"I swear, child. For a doctor, you can be really dumb. Well, not so much dumb as blind. When it comes to the people you love, you can't see the obvious. You do know how to not let your emotions get in the way. You did it every day as a doctor."* Her words made sense, but it wasn't the same.

"Stefhan isn't a random stranger that I'm treating and will never see again, Enya. You can't compare my husband and kids to strangers."

"Again, you are missing the point. I'm not trying to compare OUR family to strangers. I know every memory you have. I know exactly how you acted when Gram was brought into the ER. You may have lost it for a minute, but you pulled it together and did everything you could to save her. That is what you have to do now. You have to pull it together and fully embrace your destiny. Our destiny. Stop acting like a child who isn't getting her way."

A strange combination of Lilith's and Enya's words swirled around my head as I finished my shower and took a seat at my vanity. I knew what both of them were saying was the truth. Even if I didn't want to admit it. As I brushed my hair out, I could feel Enya's nervousness as she tried to make sense of my thoughts and where they were going. I knew I needed to embrace my destiny and, as Lilith said, fully become the Fire Wolf. The problem was that I had no clue what that meant. I couldn't see my problems being solved by just getting my head out of my ass.

"It's not, child," Enya whispered.

"Then what is it, Enya? I don't want to play the guessing game anymore. I want someone to lay out for me what I need to do."

Her silence was expected. I knew it was a fruitless request. Ever since I found out about this world, no answer was just given to me. I didn't have someone who taught me about this world. I knew that Gram couldn't tell me, but all it did was make everything more difficult. I could never say I missed my parents, it was hard to miss people you didn't remember. But at that moment, I missed them. I thought about how things would have been different if they hadn't been murdered.

For the first time ever, I let my imagination run wild with images of the life that was stolen from me. A life where I was raised in this world. A life that wasn't filled with secrets. I imagined getting to hear Enya at thirteen and making my first shift with my parents by my side, imagined Gram cooking and reading to me out of the family book. I imagined meeting Stefhan for the first time, Gram gushing about how handsome he was, and my mom helping me with wedding dress shopping.

As I thought about this life, I worked on my hair. It was finally almost as long as it was before I cut it. I was so engrossed in my fantasy and so unaware of my actual surroundings that I didn't hear the bathroom door open. Or Stefhan walking in and calling my name three times. It wasn't until he shook me gently that my fantasy shattered, and I let out a scream.

"Dani, are you okay?" Stefhan's worried voice called out to me.

"Yeah, I'm good," I answered quickly.

"Are you sure?" His eyes were full of worry as he looked into mine through the reflection in the mirror.

"I'm sure. I woke up and couldn't go back to sleep, so I decided to get up and shower. I was hoping to be done before you got up. I must have zoned out for a minute." Everything I said was technically true, so I didn't have to worry about my face betraying me.

"Okay. I'm going to jump in the shower before the kids get up. We have to meet Fern and Luan at nine," he told me as he kissed the top of my head and flashed me a smile that didn't touch his eyes.

I watched as he turned and walked toward the shower. I could feel the sting of emerging tears. Tears of guilt. This man was getting ready to send his mother's spirit to be with Selene, and instead of me comforting him, he's worrying about and comforting me while I have fantasies about a non-existent life. I waited until I heard the shower turn on to wipe the tears that were now on the verge of falling. I finished my hair and made my way to the kids' rooms.

"I love you," he called to me as I walked past the shower.

"I love you, too."

Max was already awake when I opened his door. He was sitting on the edge of his bed with his white dress pants and white button-down shirt next to him. He didn't greet me, instead he kept staring at the floor.

"Little one?" I called to him gently as I walked toward his bed. Hearing my voice, he raised his head, and his eyes met mine. I was about halfway to his bed when he finally spoke.

"I don't wanna send Sitty to be with Oddess Selene." His voice cracked as tears started rolling down his cheeks. I closed the gap between us and pulled him close.

"I know you don't. But it was Sitty's time, and you'll see her again when it's your time," I told him, trying to comfort him.

"But Sitty not old! Why it her time?" he cried into me as he wrapped his arms around me.

"Sometimes there are things that can cause people to die before they're old. Things you can't see on the outside."

"Sitty not sick, Mama! Wolves don't get sick!" he screamed.

Max never let me forget how smart he was. There were times it crossed my mind that he also had my little gift/curse. He only had to be told something once. He knew that wolves didn't typically get sick thanks to a television show where the main character died due to an illness. This prompted a twenty-minute discussion about illnesses and what caused them.

"You're right, Sitty wasn't sick like that. Sometimes there can be something wrong and it doesn't make you feel sick. You won't even know it's there until something goes wrong. Since Sitty was in the forest alone, there wasn't anyone to get her help. By the time Papo found her, it was too late. It's okay to be sad," I told him as I squeezed my arms a little tighter around him. I hated seeing him hurt like that.

He took a minute to think about my explanation before nodding his head. I was glad he accepted my answer. He had been asking a lot more questions recently, and from the tenor of them, he was catching on that something wasn't right.

"You want to help me get sissy up?" I asked him with a smile. He loved helping with Phoenix. Well, when she wasn't crying.

"Yes!"

I was just finishing up her morning routine when the best smell in the world filled my nostrils.

"Papa!" Max shouted, running to him the second he was in the doorframe. Without having to think about it, Stefhan scooped him up and swung him around.

"And how is my boy?" Stefhan asked him as he kissed his head.

"I sad, Papa. I don't wanna say bye to Sitty."

"Me too, bud. You know what might make us feel better?" Max shook his head. "Pie for breakfast," Stefhan finished with a smile.

Max looked at me for approval. Typically pie for breakfast was a no-go. I gave him a quick smile and nod of approval. Stefhan set Max on the floor but stayed bent over so he was closer to his level.

"I'm going to give your sister and mama a kiss, then we'll get some pie," he told him before walking over to me.

He kissed Phoenix on the head and me on the lips. His skin felt hotter than usual, but due to the circumstances, I didn't say anything. I watched as he turned, picked up Max, and walked out of the room.

Cy and Jameson sat with the kids, while we went to meet Fern and Luan. We walked in silence to where Sarai's body was being prepared. It was customary for the mate and children of the deceased to wrap the body in the ceremonial wrappings. I was surprised to see Ryland standing with Fern and Luan outside the door. Fern wasn't sure if he was going to be able to do it. He was completely broken.

"I refuse to let my broken heart stop me from doing my part in sending your mother to Selene," he said, his voice full of despair, before opening the door and going inside. Before I could try and follow him, Fern shut the door.

"Dad will start the wrapping by cleaning her with blessed water. Then he will wrap her with the first cloth. Once he has done that, he'll come get us," Fern explained after the door was closed.

About a half hour later the door creaked open. Stefhan grabbed my hand and without a word, he started walking inside. Sarai was laid out on a hospital stretcher. A piece of gold cloth was wrapped around her like a bikini. Stefhan squeezed my hand before letting it go for me to take my place by Luan. As their mates, we were to stand there for moral support and witness the wrapping. I watched as Fern, Ryland, and Stefhan all took turns wrapping pieces of black, red, and gold cloth around Sarai. They wrapped her entire body but left her head exposed. Stefhan had told me that they wrap the head last and either the mate wraps it, or they pick someone who meant a lot to the person. Ryland grabbed a piece of red cloth and stared at Sarai before bending down and placing his lips gently to hers.

"I'll see you when I get there," he whispered before carefully wrapping her head.

Ryland had excused himself quickly after he finished wrapping Sarai. Fern and Luan hurried after him. Slowly and silently, Stefhan and I walked hand in hand through the packhouse. It wasn't until we reached the third-floor landing that he pulled me to a stop, but didn't look at me.

"I want Marie to keep the kids during lunch and the pack gathering." His voice was just above a whisper.

"Okay."

"I'm sorry," he whispered.

"For what?" I didn't try to hide my confusion. "You have nothing to apologize for," I continued as I pulled him to face me.

His eyes were closed, and even with our massive size difference, I could see the wetness on his cheeks. He dropped to his knees and threw his arms around me.

"For not wanting them there. I'm scared that if I see Monday and you're dealing with the kids that I won't be able to stop myself." He started softly but ended with a growl.

The second Monday's name left his mouth, his grief shifted violently to anger.

"Then the kids will stay with Marie," I reassured him. "Come on, we still have to get dressed and link Marie." I kissed his head before stepping back and breaking our embrace.

I had no doubt that if left unchecked he would kill Monday without thinking twice. Monday will die by his hands, but it can't be before we get some information from her first.

"Papa, Mama! Look how handsome I am!" Max screamed with delight the second Stefhan opened the door.

I couldn't see Max at first, standing behind Stefhan's massive frame. As soon as he cleared the door, I stepped around him. Max was in a black button-down, collared shirt with black slacks. His feet were bare, and his hair was braided down his back.

"I got him ready. I figured it gave you one less thing to do. Cy is getting Phoenix ready in the bedroom now," Jameson told Stefhan with a smile.

"You should have linked me first," Stefhan replied without a smile, causing Jameson's to quickly fade.

"I'm sorry Stef. I was just trying to help."

"I know you were. However, the kids aren't going. They're going to stay with Marie," Stefhan snapped before Max cut him off.

"I don't wanna stay with Marie! I wanna go lunch!" he cried. Stefhan crossed the room and picked him up.

"I know you do, bub, but I need you to stay here," he whispered in his ear.

Before Max could argue, Stefhan set him down and started walking to the bedroom. I watched as a look of complete understanding crossed my son's face.

"Come on, little one. Let's get you changed and tell Auntie Cy that she doesn't need to get Phoenix ready," I told him as I grabbed his hand.

I didn't make it to Phoenix's room before Cy finished getting her ready. Cy took Max to get him changed, while I changed and fed Phoenix. Marie knocked on the door right as I was finishing up. I handed Phoenix off to her and ran toward my bedroom. I only had thirty minutes to get ready and for us to be downstairs.

Stefhan was sitting on the edge of our bed. His black button-down shirt was unbuttoned just enough to reveal part of his chest, and his long black hair hung loose. It was traditional to wear black to the lunch, as it represented the loss the pack had endured. The sound of me opening the door caused his head to jerk in my direction.

"Will you braid my hair?" he asked as I shut the door.

"Of course. Wait for me in the bathroom. I'll change and meet you in there," I told him with a smile and headed toward the closet.

I was stripping out of my clothes before I was even fully in the closet. By the time I made it to the floor-length black dress and matching flats, I was in my underwear. With record speed, I threw on the dress and grabbed the shoes before dashing for the bathroom. Stefhan was sitting at my vanity, watching for me in the mirror. His eyes met mine the second I stepped into the door frame. I didn't speak, I was going to let him lead.

Silently I grabbed the brush and started brushing his hair. Gently I gathered it at the nape of his neck and started to braid. As I neared the bottom, he held up a hair tie; without a word, I took it from him and secured the braid.

"Your turn," he said as he stood and turned to face me.

"Okay."

He took out my hair tie and began unbraiding my hair. He didn't move any faster when he started combing. Section by section, he separated, sprayed, and combed before carefully placing it to the side. I didn't want to rush him, but it was getting to the point where we were going to be late if we didn't leave.

"They can start without us," he said softly in response to my unspoken panic. He bent over and placed his lips on the top of my head before taking a deep breath. After a few moments, he stood up and locked his eyes with mine in the reflection of the mirror. We stayed that way for what seemed like hours before a small smile crossed his lips. He gently started separating my hair, and with slow and steady hands, he began to braid.

On the outside, Stefhan was composed and the picture-perfect Alpha. He hugged crying pack members, listened to them, and made sure they all felt heard. Sitting through lunch and the following gathering without once breaking his facade.

On the inside, he was a complete mess. His emotions had been hitting me like a battering ram for hours. At times his grief and rage were so strong that it took my breath away and nearly brought me to my knees. I cried his silent tears for him.

Chapter Eighteen

STEFHAN

I was holding on by a thread. Never in my life had I experienced the grief and rage that was coursing through me. The only thing that kept me in check was Dani's hand pressed against me. During lunch, she pressed it against my leg under the table, then in the small of my back as we greeted pack members. It was like her hand was sewn to me, I could feel the calming energy she was pouring into me. I focused on that and not the nearly overwhelming urge to burn the entire packlands to the ground to find Monday.

Fern was convinced that Monday would come to us, insisting that she would show up for the burning ceremony. Her argument being that it would cause a lot of talk within the pack if she didn't. It wasn't a secret what my mom did for Monday, and the pack would definitely notice if she wasn't there. Fern was also sure that Monday wouldn't show up to the lunch or gathering. Too social, too many opportunities for pack members to ask her questions. She was right about lunch and the gathering. Not even a glimpse of Monday.

When it was finally an acceptable time for us to leave, we made our way upstairs to get ready for the burning ceremony. As we walked, the rage slowly built.

"Soon," Abbadon whispered.

"Just a little bit longer, boy. Just stick to the plan," Kane echoed.

No one outside of Fern, Luan, Cy, Jay, Vinnie, and Kal knew what Sarah told us. I decided we weren't going to tell my dad until Monday was dead. Fern flipped shit when I told them at Vinnies'.

"What the fuck do you mean you aren't going to tell him, Stefhan? Why?" she shrieked.

"Exactly that Fern! We aren't going to tell him for a list of reasons. First, the moment we tell Dad, Ajax will take over, hunt her, and kill her. Second, we have the element of surprise. Monday has no clue that we know it was her. Third, she can't die before we find out who is behind this. We know she didn't pull this off alone. Fourth, we need a fucking plan, not a heartbroken, vengeful wolf killing the only fucking lead we fucking have!"

I went over the plan again and again in my head as we walked.

I had to stay focused. Kane and Abbadon were right, I had to stick to the plan. Dani didn't speak, instead she rubbed small circles on my hand with her thumb. I knew she had to be exhausted. My emotions had been like a rollercoaster, and I was doing a shit job of blocking them from her. When we got to the third-floor landing, she pulled me to a stop.

"If you want, I can get Max dressed. I know it's tradition for you to do it, but I also know that you may not be feeling up to it," she told me as she stared into my eyes. Those eyes, those gorgeous green eyes, full of love and understanding.

"I'll never understand what I did to deserve you. I'm so fucking thankful that Selene chose you for me." For a split second, a strange look flashed across Dani's face. But as fast as it came it was gone. "I'll get him ready. Not only would my mom haunt me for breaking tradition, but it's my duty as Alpha and his dad. If my dad can show up to wrap his mate, I can dress my son," I continued without bringing up the look. Something was telling me it wasn't the time.

"We don't need any hauntings, we have enough going on. Let's go," she said with a smile as she pulled me up the last flight of stairs.

The tears that rolled down Max's cheeks as I dressed him for the burning ceremony almost pushed me over the edge. His heartbreak not only broke my heart but also fueled my rage.

"Keep it together, boy. You have to be an Alpha first right now," Kane reminded me.

"God Killer later," Abbadon added.

They were both right of course. We were too close to the finish line for me to lose my shit. I took a deep breath and finished getting dressed.

"Why we wear white, Papa?" Max asked as I combed his hair.

"Legend says that when the first werewolf died they wore white to light his way into the afterlife," I explained as I finished combing and turned him around to face me. "Ready?"

"No," he answered with a sniffle.

"I'm not either, bub, but we have to," I told him honestly.

As a son, I wasn't ready to say my final goodbye to my mom. But as the Alpha, it was my duty to send the former Luna of this pack to be with Selene. With Kane's words, *"Alpha first,"* swirling in my head, I gently picked up Max and walked out of the room.

Dani was dressed in a floor-length, flowy dress and white flats. Her hair was in a delicate but durable braid; she looked like a goddess. Phoenix was dressed in a long-sleeved onesie and pants that had feet attached. I flashed Dani a smile as her eyes met mine.

"Ready?" I asked her.

"I'm ready if you are."

I nodded my head and set Max down so that I could take Phoenix from her. Once her hands were free, she grabbed mine and Max's hands and we headed to the event that would change my life forever.

"She's here! I told you she'd show up! She's sitting in the very last row, so you'll see her the second you fully exit the arches." Fern's voice shouted in my head right as we walked out the doors that led outside to the training grounds.

"She's here. She's in the last row," I quickly linked to Dani. I then blocked Fern as the rage started to swirl. I didn't want her commentary egging it on. Dani rubbed tiny circles on my hand with her thumb. I focused on that and the steady breathing of Phoenix, who was sound asleep in the crook of my arm.

"You can do this," Dani encouraged me as we paused at the first arch.

I took a deep breath. *"Alpha first."* Kane's words echoed in my head again as I squeezed Dani's hand, and we walked through the first arch. I kept us at a slow pace. I needed enough time to make sure I had my rage in check. As we neared the last arch, my chest tightened, but I didn't stop. I took a deep breath, pulled Phoenix a little closer to me, and gripped Dani's hand a little tighter as we walked through.

I kept my eyes fixed in front of me, fixed on the platform that held my mom's body. I didn't trust myself to look at Monday just yet. Part of me was curious if she at least bowed her head as we passed.

"She better have," Kane and Abbadon both snarled.

When we made it to the front row, Fern stood, took Phoenix from me, and guided Max to the chair next to hers. Dani and I continued to the platform and took our places. I had a speech prepared, but as we neared her body my mind went blank. The grief that shot through me almost brought me to my knees. I grabbed the platform and bowed my head. I could feel the eyes of the pack on me, waiting for their Alpha to say something. Dani squeezed my hand reassuringly. I took a deep breath; the peaceful smell of flowers and incense filled my nose. Slowly I raised my head and looked at my pack. I didn't let my eyes go farther than the middle rows.

"Tonight, we honor the life, mourn the loss, and send the spirits of Sarai and Hala to be with the Moon Goddess. My mother was an amazing Luna who treated everyone with kindness and respect. She didn't know an enemy or a stranger. She trusted fully and loved fiercely. It will take time for us as a pack to heal from this devastating loss. We still don't know what ended her life, or the person she went running with that morning, but we must take comfort in knowing that she is in the arms of Selene." Tears rolled down my cheeks as I placed my hand on my mom and leaned down.

"I love you," I whispered before standing up and pulling the lighter from my pocket. "We now send Sarai and Hala to be with the Moon Goddess. We can take comfort in knowing that we will see them again," I announced to the pack before striking the lighter and igniting the braided wick. Once it was securely lit, I placed the lighter back in my pocket, took Dani's hand, and exited the platform. We walked to our seats and sat down. Max crawled onto my lap and placed his tiny hand on my still-wet cheek.

"It okay to be sad, Papa," he told me soothingly.

I kissed his head and turned him, so he was facing the platform. I watched the fire slowly work its way toward the first satchel. The moment the flame touched it, there was a quick succession of pops and the fire blazed, engulfing my mom's body. Red and black smoke swirled, and the sweet smell of herbs and incense filled the air.

I could feel the pack's eyes on us as my family slowly stood. It was tradition for the family of the deceased to have a receiving line in front of the platform after the burning. We took our places as the first row of pack members stood. There were hundreds of pack members, and each one gave condolences. It took almost two hours to get through all the members in attendance. Dani had to take the kids in about halfway through when Phoenix decided it was time to eat and Max was getting restless. Monday was almost the last person in line. I took a breath as she walked forward.

"I'm so sorry, Fern!" she cried as she reached my sister and wrapped her arms around her.

"Thanks, Monday. I know she meant a lot to you, too," Fern cooed as she returned Monday's embrace.

Monday echoed her condolences to Luan. I didn't hear what bullshit she spewed to my dad. I didn't fully trust myself not to call her out, so I repeated my lines over and over in my head.

"I'm so sorry for your loss, Alpha," she told me as she wrapped her arms around me.

"You got this, boy," Kane encouraged as the rage simmered inside of me.

"Thank you, Monday, and I owe you an apology. I should have come to check on you," I lied, keeping my voice as calm as possible.

"Oh Alpha, you don't owe me an apology," she started before I cut her off. I couldn't listen to her bullshit and keep up the Mr. Calm and Compassionate Alpha charade.

"I appreciate you saying that, but I do. You were family to Mom, and she would be disappointed that I didn't reach out and make sure you were okay. I came across something I think Mom would have wanted you to have. Meet me in my office in an hour," I told her as I begrudgingly wrapped my arms around her, making it look like I did with all the other pack members.

"Thank you, Alpha. I'll be there," she replied as I released my arms to greet the next member in line.

"You're going to wear a hole in the carpet," Fern chided me as I paced back and forth across my office.

"I'll replace the carpet," I snapped at her. The rage was rolling off me in vicious waves–the type that drowns surfers and capsizes boats. Dani walked over to me and placed her hand on my arm, sending a blanket of calm through me.

"Trust me Stef, no one wants to beat the shit of her more than me. However, Monday will be less likely to come with us if you're all big, pissed-off Alpha," Fern retorted.

"Fern's right," Dani quickly chimed in, knowing it was going to turn into an argument. "You have to keep it together until we get to the dungeon. You've got this." Her words were followed by a knock on the door. I walked over and took a deep breath before opening it.

"Good evening, Alpha," Monday greeted me.

"Good evening, Monday. Thank you for meeting me," I greeted her in return as I opened the door wider, revealing everyone in the room. "I asked Fern, Luan, and Dani to come, too. I think it's what Mom would have wanted. Dad, unfortunately, isn't feeling up to it," I explained as I walked out into the hallway.

Fern and Dani made small talk with her as we walked. Luan and I walked in silence. When we got near the door, I heard her finally ask where we were going.

"It's a room that we keep important things in. Only Stefhan and Dani can open the door," Fern coolly lied.

I scanned my eye and let the door swing open. Fern took the lead, followed by Monday, Luan, and Dani. Once Dani was through, I shut the door and followed them down into the dungeon. Fern guided us to the same room I used for Marcus. It wasn't until she was inside that Monday finally realized where she was.

"You keep important things in the dungeon?" Her voice was cautious.

"It's where we keep traitors," I explained as I shut the door to the cell.

"Traitor?" Her voice was even more cautious, and it sent me over the edge. My vision went red, and rage burned from deep within me. I crossed the room, picked her up by her throat, and squeezed.

"Yes, traitor! I know it was you! It was you that my mom went running with. I also know you didn't do it alone." I watched as shock flashed across her bulging, terrified eyes. "There are some things I don't know and that's the ONLY reason you've lived this long," I hissed in her ear.

"Please, Alpha," she choked out barely above a whisper.

I didn't respond to her plea, opting instead to watch the color that covered her face turn from red to blue. I waited until she was on the verge of passing out before loosening my grip and dropping her on the floor. Hearing her gasp as she tried to fill her lungs with air gave me immense satisfaction.

"I didn't have a choice!" she cried as she struggled to catch her breath.

"Didn't have a choice? I don't remember commanding you, so please enlighten me."

"He'll kill me."

"You're going to die regardless. How fast and how much suffering you endure is completely up to you," I told her as I took a seat in one of the metal chairs that scattered the room.

"I swear, Alpha, I didn't have a choice. I don't want to die!" Tears streamed down her face. Black streaks of makeup stained her cheeks. Her tears and cries only pissed me off even more.

"You're going to die regardless," I reminded her.

"Can I please hit her, Stef?" Fern pleaded with me.

"Once and don't knock her out." I didn't look at my sister as I answered. Instead, keeping my eyes locked with Monday's. Conflict and fear flashed in her eyes, as she waited for me to look away. It was very disrespectful to break eye contact with your Alpha first. Fern stalked across the room. I could feel Monday's desperation as she struggled to maintain eye contact with me and not look at Fern.

"Are you really not going to look away?" Fern's voice echoed softly.

"Nope. Hit her."

As Fern inched closer, the overwhelming urge to protect herself won out. Monday turned her head just in time for Fern's punch to connect with her nose. A shrill scream filled the room.

"SILENCE!" I commanded her.

Her screams instantly turned into whimpers. I stood and moved closer to her shaking body. The fear was oozing off her; the surprisingly sweet smell filled my nose. I grabbed her shirt and lifted her off the floor, so her face was level with mine.

"Does your disrespect know any limits?" I snarled.

"I...I...I'm sorry, Alpha."

A deranged-sounding laugh left my mouth as every bone in my body ached to unleash the rage boiling within.

"Oh, you're sorry? Does being sorry change the fact that you betrayed your pack? Does being sorry bring my mom back? The person who, if you recall, saved you from being a rogue." When she didn't immediately answer me, I set her down and turned to Fern. "Make her talk."

"Please don't hit me again! It wasn't me, it was Lix!" Monday cried. She scrambled back against the wall, trying to put distance between her and Fern. Fern glanced at me as I held my hand up.

"Lix?" I snapped at Monday when she didn't continue.

"He's some kind of powerful witch. He said it was my familial debt to serve him. I told him that I had no family, and my mom was a rouge. He said that I had the White bloodline running through my veins and my father's debt had become mine."

"The White's?" I asked, somewhat shocked.

"Yes, Alpha."

"Luan, get Kal. Before this goes any further, we have to know if she's telling the truth," I called over my shoulder. I had her, Vinnie, Cy, and Jay waiting in an adjacent cell. Moments later, Luan returned with Kal.

"You're going to tell us the entire story. If you leave out anything or lie in any way, Kal will know and tell me," I explained as soon as the door was shut.

"He first came to me in a dream, right before Phoenix was born. He told me that my father was failing and that soon his mission was going to be my destiny to complete. Before I could ask any questions, I woke up. I just thought it was a strange dream. But the dreams didn't stop; about twice a week, I would dream about him. He would tell me that my father was losing his battle and soon it would be my time, and I needed to prepare. I would then wake up drenched in sweat.

"It wasn't until the fourth or fifth dream that I stayed asleep long enough to ask a question. When I asked him what I needed to prepare for, he said 'the death of your Alpha.' I told him he was mistaken. I told him that he had the wrong person because I didn't know who my father was, and my mother was a rogue when I was born. He told me he didn't have enough time to explain everything to me in a dream and asked if I could meet him deep in the woods. When I agreed to meet with him, I woke up.

"The following day, as arranged, I went deep into the forest and waited. I was about to leave when he finally appeared. That was when he told me his name was Lix and it was my destiny to help him save the world. He told me that my father was Marcus White, and he hadn't abandoned me. He said my mom ran off in the middle of the night, that my mother was a selfish wolf who ripped me away from a father who loved me. He told me that my father never stopped looking for me.

"He said he wanted to take me to my rightful pack and start my training. I told him that I already had a pack and that you are the strongest Alpha in the country. I told him that I just needed to tell you, and you would help. He said I couldn't tell you as your life was already in jeopardy. If I wanted to save you, I had to follow his instructions exactly.

"I'm not completely stupid, so I told him that without some kind of proof, I was going to go straight to you. He pulled a note from his pocket and handed it to me. He said it was from my mother to my father. I told him that since my mom was a rogue and died shortly after my birth, I had no clue what her handwriting looked like. I told him I would need more than that to betray my Alpha and my pack.

"He told me that he didn't need to provide me any more proof, and I was going to do what I was told. He told me that it was my familial obligation to serve him. He whispered something I didn't understand and suddenly I didn't have control of my body anymore. It was like when I shift, but I wasn't in wolf form. He told me to go back to my house, continue my normal routine, and wait for his next instructions.

"I couldn't tell anyone what was happening. Every time I tried, my mouth wouldn't cooperate. I even tried to tell you on the plane when you left for Florida. When I got back to Crimson Diamond, Lix was waiting for me. He lifted whatever spell he had put on me. He told me that he felt bad for how he acted and that it wasn't fair to expect me to just take this on with no support. He also said he shouldn't have forbidden me from telling you. He asked if I could bring you to the place where I had met him in the forest in one week's time. I told him that you weren't here, and I wasn't sure when you would be back.

"Lix said I could bring the Luna in your place since you were out of town, and we needed to get a plan in place for your safety. I went to the packhouse every day trying to catch Luna Sarai. It took almost the full week for me to finally get her alone. When I told her that you were in danger and what I needed her to do, she agreed. We planned to meet when she went on her morning run. I met her on the far end of the packhouse, so we wouldn't be seen going into the forest. When we got into the forest, we shifted and ran to where we were supposed to meet Lix.

"He was waiting for us when we got there. We shifted back, so I could introduce them. He said that he would take it from there and everything went black. I woke up in my bed, having no clue how I got there. I didn't have time to process what happened before you sent the mass link for the emergency pack meeting."

I looked at Kal.

"Everything she said is the truth," Kal said.

"Everyone but Dani out." The voice that left my body wasn't my own, but the blinding rage that consumed me was.

"Monday Blankenship, as Alpha of this pack, I hereby sentence you to death," I started as I felt Dani's hand press into the small of my back.

"Please, no! I didn't mean for her to get hurt!" Monday sobbed. Her tears did nothing to sway my decision.

"Even if I wanted to spare you–and I don't–our laws state that anyone having a part in a former, current, or future Luna's death, voluntary or involuntary, the punishment is death. You didn't say anything at the meeting when I asked for information. Your silence sealed your fate."

I waited for Dani to try and stop me from killing her, but she didn't. Instead, she patted my arm with her other hand and stepped back.

Unforeseen Destinies

Chapter Nineteen

DANI

I knew there was nothing I could say that would cause Stefhan to spare Monday's life. Fern explained the laws to me and how this one was absolute. If Stefhan didn't kill her, and the Counsel found out, he could be put to death. I gave his arm a gentle pat before stepping back to give him the room he needed.

"I would never hurt Sarai on purpose. I loved her! You've known me since I was born, Stefhan, you know I did. Let me fix this. I can help you find Lix," Monday pleaded as Stefhan stalked closer. I watched as his body started to shake with rage.

"You had the chance to fix this. You chose to keep the fact that you knew why she was in the forest that day to yourself."

"I was scared! I thought for sure Lix was going to come and kill me himself. I was trying to lay low; I was going to tell you once all the funeral events were over. Stefhan, after everything we've been through together, do you really think I wouldn't have told you?" she cried to him. Her last sentence confused me, but it pushed Stefhan over the edge.

"YOU WILL ADDRESS ME AS ALPHA!" he roared, causing the room to shake violently. Monday's head instantly dropped, and she revealed her neck. "Let's get some things clear. First, YES, I believe you had no intention of telling me. Second, WE haven't been through anything. I fucked you once because I was bored. Nothing more, nothing less." Her eyes went wide and shot over to me. "Don't seem so shocked. Dani knows all about my whore days. Mates have no secrets."

I didn't hear what he said next, his words had sent me into a tsunami of emotions. Yes, I knew about his whore days, but I told him I didn't want to know who all he slept with. It never crossed my mind that he would have slept with Monday. My shock quickly turned to anger as Mia's face flashed in my mind. My anger was then replaced by guilt. I was keeping secrets from him.

I was still processing my guilt when Stefhan growled, pulling me back into the present. He had closed the small gap that was between them and locked his hands around her arms. It wasn't until that moment when I realized we hadn't brought any wolfsbane with us. Slowly Stefhan's face started to morph and stretch. His nose and mouth became a snout. Claws extended from his fingers, digging into her skin. He removed one hand, placed it on her head, and pushed it so her neck was exposed.

"May Selene have mercy on your wolf's soul," Stefhan whispered before clamping his mouth on her throat and giving a hard yank. I had to stifle a gag when the sound of skin ripping and bone-crunching reached me, followed by her head hitting the ground. He dropped her body and turned to look at me. His face and hands were covered in blood. He nodded his head a single time, and I knew it was my turn. When Stefhan decided that we weren't going to tell anyone about Monday until after she was dead, it instantly meant that I would have to call her time of death. In order to stay within the law, a doctor had to be there during the execution and formally pronounce the wolf dead. I walked over to her headless body, placed my hand on her wrist, and looked at my watch.

"Dr. Danielle Storme attending. Head has been cleanly removed and there is no pulse. Time of death, 12:34 am," I recited as I dropped her hand and stepped back.

Guilt, with a twinge of jealousy, coursed through me as we lay in silence. I tried to focus on the sound of Stefhan's heart against my ear and his skin on my face.

"Please tell me what's wrong," he whispered as he wrapped his arms around me. I knew I needed to tell him, but my guilt made the words stick in my throat like they were glued. When I didn't speak, he continued. "If you're not ready, it's okay. Just promise me that you'll tell me when you are."

"Child, you need to tell him," Enya whispered, feeling my internal struggle.

"It's not that I don't want to tell you," I whispered.

"Then why can't you tell me?" he asked as I buried my face in his chest.

"It's just so selfish and horrible. Today shouldn't be about me. It should be about you,"

Gently he slid his hand under my chin and lifted my head, so his eyes could meet mine.

"You are the least selfish person I know, and every day should be about us," he whispered as he wiped the tear from my cheek. I took a deep breath, letting his scent consume me.

"But I am, Stefhan. I have the most selfish thoughts," I confessed as another tear rolled down my cheek.

"My love, we all have selfish thoughts sometimes," he told me as he shifted us into a sitting position.

"These aren't normal selfish thoughts. I'm resentful and bitter, Stefhan, and I don't want to do this anymore." I stopped to take a deep breath. I knew once I started I wouldn't be able to stop it, every selfish and horrible thought was going to spill out. I was going to tell him everything I told Lilith.

"When I was having my meltdown last night, I left some things out. I left them out because they are awful. I'm a horrible person for even thinking them."

"You're not a horrible person. I'm sure it's not that bad," he interjected and pulled me into him.

"It is that bad," I started before word vomiting every thought and feeling that had been plaguing me into his chest. "I don't want to be the Fire Wolf. I don't want you to be some God Killer demon. I don't want Max to be some special wolf that can end life as we know it. I don't want to be surrounded by magic and vampires. More and more I find myself wishing that all of this really is just a coma dream. That one day I'll wake up in the hospital in Florida. I want to wake up and go back to my normal life. The one where I'm a respected and talented doctor. Where my best friend is a crazy bitch and gets fired for cursing out kids that pranked 911. Where my Gram is still alive, and life is easy.

"My life was ripped from me, and I was handed a new one. One I didn't ask for or have a say in. Everything was chosen for me. And it's not like it's been easy. It's been nothing but chaos since I woke up to you at my bedside, and I'm tired. I live in a constant state of fear. Fear of what's going to happen next. I wasn't prepared for this! I don't even know who I am anymore. I murdered someone, Stefhan! And it doesn't matter that she deserved it. I've watched you murder two people and know of a third. I'm a doctor, I took an oath to do no harm. All I've done is harm. I'm not strong enough for this. If I could run away, I would," The hot, guilty tears rolled down my face.

"I don't want to do this either," he whispered as he adjusted me so that his face was against mine. "I know this life hasn't been easy on you. You've endured more in a few years than most do in a lifetime. I was worried that there would come a time when it would become too much. This hasn't been the life I wanted to give you. I will do anything to make you feel safe. If that means running away and going into hiding, then we will."

My head was spinning. I wasn't sure what his reaction was going to be. But that wasn't even on my long list of options. For a brief moment, I imagined us on an island somewhere. Max playing in the surf and Phoenix playing in the sand. Then Lilith's words slowly swirled in, tainting the vision. There was no running from this. The wheels were already in motion, and there were only two outcomes. Either Stefhan would kill Salix, or Salix would kill us all. It was time for me to tell Stefhan about my dream.

"We can't run. Salix will find us, too many of the pieces are in place. There's something that happened last night that I haven't told you. Lilith came to me." I knew I was all over the place, but something was telling me it needed to happen this way.

"What did she say?"

"I told her everything I just told you and blamed her for everything," I started.

"Wait, what? What do you mean you blamed her for everything?"

"I asked her why she picked you to be the God Killer. She could have picked anyone else. I told her all I wanted was to love my super-hot husband and she ruined it." Stefhan's eyes slightly darkened.

"My family has apparently always produced the Fire Wolf, and yours has always produced the God Killer. My parents finding each other and shacking up made Selene decide that I would be the Fire Wolf. By default, that made you the God Killer and my fated mate. So, Lilith implanted Abbadon in you, and I guess it was dangerous for Fern. Abbadon isn't meant to be in a lady. The fact that we weren't killed and completed the matebond kicked the fucking prophecy into full swing. No stopping the wheels from turning now!

"I'm supposed to stop letting my emotions get in the way and fully embrace being the Fire Wolf. But here's the kicker, I don't know how! If I can't figure it out, Salix will use it against us and kill us all. So many people are risking their lives for our family. I don't want to be the reason we fail." My voice sounded as defeated as I felt. Stefhan pulled me into his chest and kissed my head.

"We aren't going to fail. I refuse to think that we've made it this far just to fail at the finish line. We are figuring out the prophecy and things are falling into place. If something does go wrong, it will in no way be your fault."

"Stefhan," I said as I pulled myself back to look at him. "Look, I love that you're trying to comfort me, but Lilith's warning was real. We need to take it seriously. I need you to help me figure out how to fix it," I snapped at him.

"You're right. I'm sorry. Let's figure this out," he said with a look of determination. Then he thought for a few moments before a look of understanding flooded his face. "You weren't raised to be a Luna," he whispered more to himself than to me.

"Thanks, Captain Obvious. Tell me something I don't know," I mumbled under my breath.

"Hey! I heard that. I was still thinking it through."

"I'm glad you heard it. Do you want to share this eureka moment?"

"Yes, I do," he retorted with a smile before going serious. "If Marcus hadn't killed your parents, you would have been raised to be a Luna. The Luna of Green Diamond. It's not very often that a first-born child chooses not to take over their pack. From birth, you would have been raised to be a Luna. Your mom would have taught you all the things that a good Luna needs to possess. The most important being managing your emotions. To be a good Luna or Alpha, you have to be able to manage all feelings. You have to be able to separate yourself and do what's best for the entire pack." He paused for a second and a growl rose from his chest. "That bastard," he hissed before gently moving me from his lap and getting up.

"Who's a bastard?" I blurted out, beyond confused.

"Salix! I can't believe I didn't realize it then!" he growled as he started to pace.

"What are you talking about?" I was getting ready to ask Enya if there was a part of the conversation that I missed.

"Marcus told me that when he first met Salix, he introduced himself as Lix! Lilith said that Salix would use your emotions against you. He's the witch that was visiting Monday. It all makes sense now." I was hoping it would soon also make sense to me, but I was still lost. "He wanted Monday to bring me to him, so he could kill me. She only told him that I was out of town. That was when he said she could bring the Luna. He knew that if she said I was in danger you would go with her no questions asked." It was at that moment when the pieces that Stefhan had already put together started clicking in my brain. But I didn't interrupt him.

"Monday was just dumb enough to think he meant my mom because she already knew you, the current Luna, weren't here. Salix had no choice but to kill Mom when Monday showed up with her. She would have ruined his plan. He had to let Monday live because she was his only link to us. If he can kill either of us, that stops the prophecy dead in its tracks, and he wins."

Stefhan was right. I would have gone no questions asked, and I would have died. His arm muscles twitched and flexed as his rage started to build. My eyes were instantly drawn to the movement. I watched as it rippled to his back and across his chest.

"I'm going to kill that motherfucker!" he growled as he turned and punched the wall, causing the room to shake.

He slammed his head against the wall and let his hands swing to his sides. Droplets of blood dripped from his fingertips. I climbed off the bed and went to him. I could feel the rage pounding off him. I placed my hand against the small of his back. He let out a deep breath and his body began to relax.

"I won't let him hurt you," he promised as he turned and dropped to his knees.

"I know," I reassured him as I cupped his face with my hands and gently pressed my lips to his.

The instant our lips met, it was like an explosion went off inside me. An urgency I couldn't control. I wrapped my hands around his neck and pulled him close to me. I heard his fingers crack and pop as he wrapped his broken hand in my hair. He moaned as I grazed my tongue along the outline of his lips.

I knew there were other things I should be doing, like tending to his broken hand that was tangled in my hair. I tried to regain some composure and pull back, but Stefhan took that opportunity to kiss down my jaw. The second his teeth scraped against my mark, any composure I mustered had vanished. I dug my nails into his back as he kissed and lightly bit my mark. He wrapped his arms around me as he stood. His mouth never left my skin as he carried me to the bed. He laid me back, positioned himself on top of me, and leaned down.

"Are you sure?" he growled in my ear.

"Yes," I moaned as I pushed myself against him.

That confirmation was all he needed, he leaned back just far enough to get a good grip on the collar of my nightshirt. With one swift motion, he ripped it completely down the middle.

"So beautiful," he moaned against my neck.

I tangled my fingers in his hair as he kissed his way down, pausing briefly at my mark before continuing to my breasts. He alternated sucking, licking, and biting. While his mouth was locked on one nipple, his fingers were pinching and rubbing the other. After paying equal attention to both, he methodically kissed his way down my belly. His eyes locked with mine as he yanked my underwear off with one pull and flung them on the floor.

He adjusted himself in between my legs and locked his arms around them, holding them open. He kissed and nipped along my inner thigh. I struggled against his hold, trying to press myself against him.

"So impatient. Let's teach you some," he murmured against my skin as he inched closer to my swollen bud.

Slowly and carefully, he kissed the skin around my pussy. Every touch of his lips sent a wave of ecstasy through me. I could feel my juices running out of me and soaking the sheet. As he worked his way around, his beard grazed my clit, and I nearly came undone.

"Please," I breathed as I tried to wiggle against his firm grip. He lifted his face and stared into my eyes.

"So eager for this," he growled as he flicked his tongue across my clit. My back arched and a hiss escaped my lips. "No patience," he repeated as he slid his finger inside me. My back arched even higher, as he removed his finger and placed his hand on my stomach. "Down," he instructed me as he gently pushed me back against the bed.

When I was flat on the mattress again, he removed his hand and slid his finger back inside me. My back instantly arched and Stefhan removed his finger, once again placing a hand on my stomach and gently pushing.

"I said down." There was an authoritativeness to his voice, and it only made me want him more. I forced my back onto the mattress and locked myself into place. A small smile danced across his lips. When he slid his finger back inside me, I didn't move, only letting a moan escape.

"Good girl," he praised me as he slowly slid his finger in and out. After a few seconds, he inserted another finger. I forced my back to stay firm against the mattress. His praise stirred something deep inside me, and I wanted more.

"Ready?" he asked me suddenly.

I was so focused on keeping my back on the mattress so he wouldn't stop that I didn't notice he had not only taken his shorts off but also repositioned himself and had his cock lined up at my entrance.

"Yes," I breathed.

"Stay down," he reminded me as he placed his hand firmly on my stomach.

Excitement coursed through me. I locked my back in place and quickly nodded my head. With a single thrust, he pushed his cock deep inside. I dug my fingers into the bed as I fought against the urge to lift my back from the mattress.

"Very good," he growled, sending another wave of excitement through me. His dual-colored eyes locked with mine as he started rocking his hips back and forth. "Can you stay down if I go faster?" I eagerly nodded my head. I was willing to do anything to hear him praise me again. "Answer out loud when I ask you a question." His voice was stern, but still like velvet, and it sent a ripple of pleasure through me.

"Yes," I answered immediately.

"Yes, what?" he asked, never once breaking eye contact with me or stopping his slow and steady thrusts.

"Yes, I can stay down," I moaned in between ragged breaths.

"That's my good girl."

The words were barely out of his mouth before he rammed his cock deep inside me and proceeded to pummel my pussy. He hovered over my body, making sure his skin didn't touch mine. The words and sounds that left my mouth would have made a sailor blush, as I fought the urge to lift my back and press my skin against his. I kept one hand firmly wrapped in his hair and the other dug into his arm.

"I'm going to cum!" I screamed as he rammed his cock in and out of me. But before I could, he stopped and pulled out.

"Not yet. Not until I tell you. Do you understand?" His tone was serious, but his eyes were full of excitement and love.

"Yes. I understand," I answered. Gently he flipped me over and positioned me so that my face was on the bed, but my knees were bent, and my ass was in the air.

"Your hands stay here," he told me as he placed them above my head on the mattress. He hadn't asked me a question, so I nodded my head to show I understood. "Very good," he praised as he slid his cock back inside.

Stefhan fucked me with reckless abandon as I fought against my climax that was nearing a fever pitch. The combination of his grunts, moans, and growls, mixed with hitting my G-spot repeatedly, was making it a losing battle. All I wanted was to cum all over him. I yearned for it.

"Please let me cum!" I screamed into the mattress.

"You want to cum?" he asked me, not breaking his rhythm.

"Yes!" I cried as I rocked my hips in sync with his.

"Not yet."

He pulled his cock out of me to turn me over and pick me up. I was thankful for the reprieve, even though the curiosity of what would happen if I disobeyed him was starting to intrigue me. He guided his cock back inside as I chained my arms and legs around him. Slowly he started lifting me up and down on his cock. He kissed my neck as he increased speed. I dug my nails into his back and squeezed my legs, trying to fight off my climax.

"Cum for me," he finally called out as he slammed me up and down.

Those three words released the biggest orgasm I had ever experienced. It tore through me like an earthquake. The slick walls of my pussy locked around his cock as my body shook. Even with how great it was, I wanted more. I needed more.

"Mark me!" I screamed as I threw my head back, revealing my neck.

Stefhan sunk his teeth in, and a rush of pure ecstasy filled every cell of my body. I clung to him as he continued ramming in and out of me. I was high off the rush and craved more. When he released his bite and sealed it, I pushed his head to the side and sunk my teeth into his mark.

"Fuck!" he growled as he released his load deep inside me. I sealed my bite and kissed his neck. Gently he laid me down, got off the bed, and went into the bathroom. Moments later he reemerged with a wet washcloth and a towel. Once he had cleaned me up, he collapsed on the bed and pulled me close.

I lay there listening to the steady sound of Stefhan's breathing. Normally I would have been passed out soon after, but I couldn't stop thinking about what happened. Thanks to my limited knowledge of sex, I wasn't sure if there was a name for what that was. All I knew was I liked it. A lot. I was too wound up to sleep.

Chapter Twenty

CY

"Who is it?" Jam asked at the sound of my phone buzzing.

I didn't need to look to know who it was. It was a little before 3 AM, and only one person would text me in the middle of the night.

"Dani," I told him as I grabbed the phone off the nightstand and read the message.

Are you sleeping?

Nope. What's up? I quickly texted back. I watched the three bubbles pop up as she began to type.

"Everything okay?" Jam asked as he peered over my shoulder.

"Yeah. If something was wrong, she would call," I told him as I watched the screen.

Is Jameson sleeping? Can you come up?

No, but I'm on my way. Be there in five, I quickly typed as I got out of bed.

"Where are you going?" he asked as I pulled on my sleep pants.

"You literally were reading it as I typed it," I said with a laugh. "I'm going upstairs. Dani wants to talk. I'm sure today was rough on her," I continued as I slipped on my shoes. I leaned across the bed and placed my lips against his. "Don't wait up for me. I love you."

"I'll wait up if I want to," he retorted as he smacked my ass. "I love you, too."

I sprinted up the stairs. Dani was waiting for me at the top.

"Follow me. We're going to one of the spare rooms," she whispered as she looked behind her.

I followed her as she guided me past the kitchen and into another wing of the floor. She opened a door that lined the hallway and pulled me inside.

"What in the hell are you doing?"

"I don't want to risk anyone hearing," she told me as she pulled me toward the bed. She was almost giddy as she sat down and patted the spot across from her.

"Are you okay?" I asked as I leaned in to feel her head.

"I'm fine, Cy. I just need to talk to you about something," she started before pausing.

"Then talk, bitch," I told her after she didn't continue. I watched as she took a breath. I prepared myself for the word vomit.

"Okay. After the whole thing with Monday and we went upstairs, I told Stefhan some things that were bothering me, and it ended up in him having an epiphany within an epiphany. But that's not why you're here. It's what happened after that. He punched the wall and when I went to set his fingers... Fuck! I forgot to set his fingers. Dammit! Now I'm going to have to re-break them."

"What a second! What happened that you forgot to set his broken fingers?" The words shot out of my mouth before I could stop them.

"Well, we had a little moment, and I kissed him…"

"And?" I asked her with a smile.

"One thing led to another, and we had sex."

"I am still failing to see what the issue is. I think you need to go to bed."

"It wasn't normal sex," she said bashfully before telling me about her sexual experience with Stefhan. I couldn't stop the giggle that escaped my mouth when I realized what happened.

"Oh God. It's totally weird isn't it," she moaned at my laughter.

"It's not weird," I told her quickly.

"Then why were you laughing?" she shot back.

"I wasn't laughing because I thought it was funny. It just took me by surprise that you were soft dommed."

"Soft dommed?"

"You don't know anything about real sex. If it wasn't in a medical book, you're completely lost. You were the sub to Stefhan's Dom," I told her with a laugh.

"I don't know what that means. Just give it to me straight, Cy."

"Short version, one person, and in this case Stefhan, is the Dominator–Dom for short. The Dom takes on the role of the leader or enforcer. You're the submissive. There are a lot of types of subs, but from what you've told me, you enjoy praise. It sounds like he dabbled in punishing you, too."

"Dabbling in punishing me?" she asked, her eyes wide.

"Yeah. When you didn't listen and he stopped, he was punishing you. He probably wanted to start you off easy. Test the waters to see if it was something you'd be into. Your sex life has been extra vanilla until now. He probably didn't know how to bring it up to you without embarrassing you."

"What do you mean by 'start me off easy' and 'my sex life is vanilla'?" she asked, looking rather offended.

"Vanilla as in plain." I wanted to say boring, but I didn't want to offend her. "Everyone starts out vanilla. Typically, someone introduces you into the spicier kinds of sex. Stefhan is way more experienced than you. He didn't know how you would react to him all of the sudden taking charge and spanking you."

"Spanking?" She was practically buzzing with excitement.

"Spanking is one form of punishment."

"How do you know so much about this?" she asked me after a few minutes, looking at me with accusing eyes. I hadn't told Dani about how Jam would dominate me in the bedroom. Of course, I told her some things, but I kept out the kinker stuff. Her ears weren't ready for all that.

"Don't look at me like that! It was after I got with Jam. At first, he always let me take the lead. I dominated him like I had every other man I'd been with. Until one night he just took control and dominated me. The complete reversal turned me on in ways I can't even describe. I did have to make it clear that the only time he would dominate me was in our bedroom. I knew very little about Dom/sub dynamics at the time, so I started reading. You're going to have to talk to Stefhan."

"Talk to him and say what? 'Excuse me Stefhan, I would really like for you to start spanking me. I don't want to have vanilla sex anymore,'" she shrieked as her face went red. I couldn't believe what I was about to do.

"Calm down, bitch. You're going to hyperventilate. You do some reading, and I'll take care of the rest."

"You can't talk to Stefhan!" she howled.

"I have no intention of talking to Stefhan. I'm going to tell Jam, and he is going to tell Stefhan."

Jam was still up when I got back like I knew he would be.

"Did you have a nice talk?" he asked me as I closed our bedroom door.

"It was interesting, and I need you to do me a favor," I answered, thankful for his perfect opening.

"Anything, babe," he assured me as I climbed in bed. When I didn't take my normal spot on his chest, he sat up. "Is everything okay?" There was a flicker of worry in his voice.

"Everything's fine," I assured him. "I need you to talk to Stefhan about something."

"Of course. What do you need me to tell him?" he asked.

"I need you to tell him that he needs to Dom dick his wife down." I didn't see any point in beating around the bush and that seemed like the most direct way of saying it.

"Okay. Wait! What?" The words all came in rapid succession as he registered what I said.

"Tell Stefhan to Dom dick his wife down," I repeated. "I guess he did some really soft shit with Dani, and she loved it. She's just too embarrassed to tell him that she wants more.

She didn't even know that it was an actual thing until I told her. I gave her the basics, told her to do some reading, and I would take care of the rest."

"So…let me get this straight. You want me to tell Stefhan, my best friend, brother, and Alpha, how to fuck his wife?"

"Yeah, pretty much. I would do it, but she said I'm not allowed to tell him, so it has to be you."

"Fine, but you owe me so fucking big," he started as he laid down and pulled me on his chest. "And depending on how Stefhan reacts is how much you will be punished later," he whispered against my ear, then kissed my cheek, sending a wave of pleasure through me.

JAMESON

I didn't sleep. The mixture of my own thoughts and Zeke's commentary made it impossible. This wasn't something I could just casually bring up in conversation.

"Never again. I will never promise to talk to Stefhan without knowing what she wants me to tell him," I vowed to myself after Zeke had finally fallen asleep.

My stomach was in knots, and I was sweating. Carefully I moved Cy and slid out of bed. I made my way to the kitchen to make a sandwich. It was a little after eight when I got into the kitchen. It wasn't often that I didn't go downstairs for breakfast, but I couldn't risk running into Stefhan, knowing Cy wanted me to tell him the next time I saw him. There was no way I was going to risk seeing him, not telling him, and then having to deal with Cy. I needed to figure out what I was going to say. I grabbed what I needed to make four ham and cheese sandwiches. As I assembled them, I thought of ways to bring it up. Everything sounded awful in my head and even worse when I said it out loud.

"You up?" Stefhan's voice suddenly echoed in my head.

"Yeah. What's up?" I instantly replied while simultaneously wishing I would have ignored him. He would have just thought I was sleeping.

"Feel like working out? Dani is still sleeping, and Fern took the kids."

"Yeah. Let me eat these sandwiches and change. I'll meet you in the gym."

I only ate two of my sandwiches and put the others in the fridge for later. My stomach was doing gymnastics as I walked toward the bedroom to put on some shorts. I prayed that Cy was still sleeping, so I could buy myself some more time to figure out what in the hell I was going to say. My heart dropped when I walked into the bedroom and Cy wasn't in bed.

"Bro, you know she doesn't sleep past eight," Zeke's voice echoed in my head.

"Shut up," I snapped at him. He was getting some weird satisfaction out of my suffering.

"Going to work out?" Cy's voice hit my ears as I stepped into the closet.

"Yeah," I called out as I slipped on my shorts.

"Is Stefhan going?" she asked, her voice was closer.

"Yeah. He linked me while I was making something to eat," I answered.

"Oh good! You can talk to him about Dani since it will just be the two of you."

Even though I knew it was coming I was hoping she would just let it go for a day or two. Or forever.

I walked slowly toward the gym. I still had no clue how I was going to bring it up, let alone say the words.

"Like a Band-Aid, bro. Just rip it off."

"Right, Zeke, no problem. I bet you would be singing a different tune if you had to tell Kane how he needed to fuck Enya," I retorted, shutting Zeke up.

My heart was pounding, and my palms were sweaty. I had no clue how he was going to react. He had just lost his mother and put a pack member to death. Stefhan's temper hadn't been the best and, to be honest, Abaddon scared the shit out of me. In all fairness, anyone would be stupid not to be.

The closer I got to the gym and still didn't have a plan; it was becoming evident that I was going to have to wing it. Winging it was the last thing I wanted to do, but Cy was right. With everything that had been going on, it was rare that it was just the two of us. I paused for a moment before opening the door to the gym. Stefhan was standing in the middle, waiting for me.

"I need a favor," he called to me as I walked toward him.

"What's up?" I asked, thankful my voice came out steady.

"I need you to break my fingers and set them," he explained as he held up his hand. Three of his knuckles had clearly been broken, not set, and left to heal.

"Why didn't you have Dani set them after you broke them?" I asked as I wiped my hands on my shorts.

"We got distracted, forgot, and fell asleep. I didn't want to wake her up."

"Ready?" I asked as I grabbed his finger.

He nodded, closed his eyes, and held his breath. Quickly I snapped his finger and pushed the bones back into the proper place. Once they were in place, I moved to the second finger, following the same steps before moving on to the third.

"Thanks, Jay," he said when I was done.

"No thanks needed. You've done the same for me."

"I didn't just ask you here to fix my fingers and to work out. I wanted to talk to you," he confessed as he started to pace. I felt the sudden urge to just blurt out what Cy said, but I pushed it down and concentrated on what he was saying. "I had an epiphany last night. I'm going to call a meeting later, but I wanted to tell you first."

He explained his revelation to me as we took turns punching the heavy bag. I had to agree that it made sense. If Salix killed either him or Dani, it would be over. He then told me how Lilith came to Dani and told her that she had to get her emotions in check and fully become the Fire Wolf. On that one, I was absolutely at a loss.

"I thought she was born the Fire Wolf and that was it," I said as I held the bag while he punched.

"Apparently not and we have to figure it out," he replied.

The urge to tell him was back in full force like the Goddess herself was commanding me to tell my Alpha how his mate wants to be fucked. Fear was mixed in as I wasn't exactly sure telling him while he was already punching in my direction was a good idea.

"Tell. Him. Bro," Zeke nearly shouted at me.

"Okay. I will. Just shut up," I snapped. "Um, Stef. I need to talk to you."

"What's up?" he asked as he continued to punch.

"This is so fucking awkward and I'm sorry," I started as I took a firm grip on the bag and let the words rush out. "So…Cy talked to Dani last night and I'm using Cy's wording on this. Dani wants you to 'Dom dick it down.'" Stefhan stopped punching and stared at me.

"What?" he asked, convinced he had misunderstood me.

"Dani talked to Cy last night after whatever you two did, and Dani loved it. I guess she's too embarrassed to tell you that she wants you to take it to the next level. Cy said and I quote, 'Dani wants you to Dom dick it down.'"

Stefhan didn't speak, he just continued staring at me. It wasn't a secret that most upper-ranking male werewolves enjoy a Dom lifestyle, but it wasn't something that was openly talked about.

"'Dom dick it down,'" he repeated after a few minutes. "I can't believe you agreed to tell me," he said and flashed me a smile.

"I agreed before I fully understood the assignment," I confessed as a wave of relief washed over me.

"The things love can make you do," he mused as he started punching the heavy bag again.

"Ain't that the truth."

Stefhan fell into an easy rhythm, and for the first time, it felt like it did before the incident with Max.

Unforeseen Destinies

Chapter Twenty-One

DANI

I woke up to an empty bed, a note next to my phone, and a text from Cy.

> *My love,*
>
> *Went to work out with Jay in the Gym. Fern has the kids. Just relax until I get back.*
>
> *Stefhan*

Jam's going to talk to Stefhan, Cy's text read.

As much as I was embarrassed for Cy to tell Jameson, I was happy that I didn't have to be the one to tell Stefhan.

"He wouldn't have judged you," Enya reassured me.

"I know he wouldn't… It's just embarrassing!"

Cy was right; Stefhan was more experienced in sex— extremely. She was also right that I basically knew nothing outside the "normal shit." The few kinks I was aware of were only due to seeing bad outcomes in the emergency room. It was almost nine, and I had no clue what time Stefhan was going to be back. I needed to do some reading.

I did a quick Google search and found an article that gave me the basics. The Dom takes on the dominant role of leader, enforcer, protector, or daddy. I couldn't see myself calling Stefhan "daddy." The sub takes on the submissive roles of pleaser, tester, baby girl, and/or servant. I read that most couples keep it in the bedroom and the rules vary depending on the couple. Each couple made their own rules and typically signed contracts. I was getting ready to read an example when the door slowly swung open. I closed the browser just in time for Stefhan to see me sitting on the couch.

"I didn't expect you to be up yet," he told me with a smile as he brushed the hair out of his face, causing a memory to push to the forefront of my mind.

"Your hand! We didn't set it, and you worked out!" I exclaimed while getting up.

"It's okay," he interjected quickly. "Jay got me all fixed up."

"Good. It would've been awful trying to re-break them," I confessed. While I had re-broken many bones to set them properly, it wasn't my favorite thing to do. "Did you have a good workout?"

"Yeah, we keep it pretty light, sticking to the heavy bag. The conversation was enlightening." A sly smile crossed his lips, sending a wave of excitement through me.

"In a good way or bad way?" I asked, trying to sound nonchalant.

"A very good way." The way his eyes burned into mine set my core ablaze. I knew he could smell my arousal.

"Are you going to share?" I asked when he didn't continue.

"No," he answered with the same sly smile. "Not enough time right now. We have to get ready to meet with everyone and tell them about Salix. I'm going to jump in the shower," he continued as he walked toward the bathroom.

He left the door cracked open just enough that it didn't latch, meaning no soundproof barrier. I listened for his clothes to hit the floor and the shower to turn on. Images of Stefhan's naked body flooded my mind. My core was hot, my pussy walls clenched.

"Get your head out of the gutter, Dani," I scolded myself quietly as I forced myself up and toward the closet. I shut the door behind me, I needed to get a grip on myself. "He didn't do anything remotely sexy," I told myself as I grabbed some leggings, a shirt, and underwear. By the time I got changed and took my braid out, I was back in control. I walked out of the closet to see Stefhan standing in just a towel. The blaze in my core returned.

"Why did you shut the door?" he asked me as we passed each other.

"I just needed a minute," I told him as I quickly made my way to the bathroom.

I almost looked behind me when I heard his towel drop, but I forced my head straight. I wasn't sure how I was going to make it through the day. My sexual appetite felt as intense as when I was in heat. Only I knew it wasn't from being in heat. Stefhan had awakened something inside me, but I had to get it under control. We had too much to do for me to be acting like a horny hormonal teenager.

I sat at the vanity and started combing my hair. Concentrating on sectioning, spraying, and combing. I also sent a silent prayer to Selene that Stefhan wouldn't come in. I desperately needed time to shove my sudden need, sudden desire back into its box until I could open it at an appropriate time. Even choosing a more complicated hairstyle, so I could have more time to close the box. Once I was pretty sure my desires were securely put away, I finished up.

"I was just getting ready to come and see if you were about ready," he said, walking toward the door. "Everyone is meeting at Vinnie and Kal's. I asked Fern to drop the kids off with Marie."

"If you aren't going to let her bring them, then I need to pump before we go,"

"You didn't pump this morning when you saw Fern had them?" he asked as he stopped and turned to face me.

"I started reading something and got distracted," I admitted as I grabbed my pump and sat down.

By the time we got to Vinnie and Kal's, everyone else was already there. The moment we walked in, Cy looked pointedly at me, then at Jameson, then at Stefhan, and nodded once. I had official confirmation that Stefhan knew. I didn't have time to fully let that sink in before Stefhan took charge of the room.

"There's more to Mom's murder than we initially thought," he started before we had even sat down.

"You're telling me," Fern cut in. "I don't care what Kal says–no offense–but we know Monday was lying. There's no way she is the illegitimate daughter of Marcus White."

"The truth is subjective," Kal quickly said, interrupting Fern. "Everything Monday said she believed to be the truth. It doesn't mean that it is the actual truth. She told us everything this Lix person told her, who we don't know anything about other than they are a powerful witch."

"We may never know if she truly was related to Marcus," Stefhan called out over both of them. All heads snapped in his direction. "At this point, it honestly doesn't matter if she was. I know who Lix is. During my time with Marcus, he told me that the first time he met Salix, he introduced himself as Lix. Salix is Lix."

Stefhan then launched into his epiphany of how Salix was using Monday to lure one of us into the woods, so he could kill us. He also told them about my dream. He left out the sex but looked pointedly at me when telling certain parts.

"The Salix part makes perfect sense," Fern started after Stefhan had them all caught up. "Take out one of you and that's it. End of Prophecy," she continued. "The part about Dani... I'm at a loss. I always thought the Fire Wolf was just born that way."

"We're working on that," Stefhan responded to Fern, but he looked at me before glancing at everyone.

"Well, while you're figuring that out, I suggest we get cracking on the rest of the prophecy. We still don't have any clue what makes Vinnie be able to walk into the sun, or how Cy is supposed to open the portal," Fern stated before Stefhan cut her off.

"You're right, but we have to be careful. If Salix can get to someone as close to us as Monday was, we can't take any chances. No one is to go with any pack member alone. No matter who they are. From this moment on, the only people we can fully trust are in this room."

"That won't be hard for me seeing as I haven't met any pack members," Vinnie scoffed.

"That's going to change tonight," Stefhan countered. "I am going to officially introduce you, Kal, and Cy as part of the pack. I will also be announcing Jay and Cy's commitment to each other."

"What does one wear to this kind of announcement?" Vinnie whispered to himself.

"Whatever you want," Fern answered.

Stefhan pulled everyone's attention back to the matter at hand, and we spent the rest of the morning and part of the afternoon planning our next moves. Cy and Jameson were going to talk to her parents and see if they knew of a potion or spell that could open a portal to the field. Vinnie, Kal, Fern, and Luan were going to start on the Vinnie-walking-into-the-sun situation and if it had to be a death sentence. Stefhan was going to work with me on my emotions and becoming the Fire Wolf. The way he said it sent a shiver of pleasure down my spine.

Stefhan sent a massive link letting the pack know of the introduction ceremony that would be happening that night. The rest of the day went by in a blur, a sexually frustrating blur. Everything Stefhan did turned me on. From the way he stood, to the way he moved his hair out of his face. We were also never alone, so I couldn't act on my frustration. It was almost like he was doing it intentionally. First, it was Jameson and Cy, going over in more detail about what they needed to talk to the Meadows about. Then it was Fern, Luan, and Kal, talking about ways to figure out the Vinnie issue. Vinnie was too busy figuring out what he was going to wear.

Stefhan then made Fern and Luan walk with us to talk to Iris about food for the introduction. When I asked why he couldn't just link her, like he had every single other time, he said that with it being so last minute he wanted to tell her in person. After talking to Iris, he again insisted that Fern and Luan walk with us to the stairs. He then linked Marie on the way to have her bring the kids. Marie was waiting for us at the bottom. The kids took Fern and Luan's place as they headed to the main dining room to get started on setting up.

Max and Phoenix then demanded all of our attention, which made it easier to push the inappropriate thoughts back into their box. Stefhan insisted that I get myself and Phoenix ready first, then he would dress himself and Max. I picked a deep red, floor-length, low-cut dress with black flats. I went with a simple crimson onesie and black pants for Phoenix. When I carried Phoenix into the living room, Stefhan looked me up and down hungrily: his eyes raked over every curve.

"Come on Max," he called to where Max was playing.

"Mama, you look so pretty!" Max exclaimed when he got up and turned. "Papa don't Mama look pretty?" he asked Stefhan.

"Yes, she does, bub," he answered Max, but his eyes locked with mine. A wave of excitement ran through me, and I had to take a breath.

Without another word, Stefhan picked up Max and carried him down the hall. About twenty minutes later, they reemerged. Max was wearing a red button-down shirt with the sleeves rolled halfway up, black slacks, and black shoes. Stefhan was wearing the same, only his shirt was unbuttoned enough to see the top of his well-sculpted pec muscles. His hair was down and fell like a black waterfall. My pussy clenched and my core grew hot.

"Ready?" he asked me with the same sly smile he had that morning.

"Yes," I told him as he leaned down to take Phoenix from me.

"Later," he whispered just loud enough for me to hear.

STEFHAN

"You better tear that up tonight, boy. I didn't think wolves could get blue balls, but here I am!" Kane snapped at me when Dani emerged wearing that extremely low-cut crimson dress, revealing the swells of her breasts, driving me crazy.

Kane didn't find my antics very funny. He wanted me to take Dani the second after Jay told me what she had told Cy. I wanted to take her too, but I needed to hear it from her. Keeping this side of myself at bay had been difficult, but I knew with Dani's inexperience that I needed to take it easy.

I had been teasing her relentlessly since my conversation with Jay. I could smell her arousal, and when I got close enough, I swear I could feel the heat coming from her core. I made sure we were never alone, so neither one of us could act on the extreme sexual tension between us.

Max talked the entire way to the dining room. I was thankful for the distraction. I was walking into an Alpha first moment; my head needed to be in the game and not thinking about bending Dani over. Fern, Luan, Kal, Vinnie, Cy, and Jay waited for us by the back door to the dining room. All of them dressed in the colors of Crimson Diamond.

"When the doors open, you will all follow me, Dani, and the kids out. You'll stand behind us while I give a speech. As I call your names, you'll step forward and bow to me, then to Dani, then to the crowd. Since you aren't being inducted in front of the pack, this is the way you show allegiance to me, Dani, and the pack," I quickly explained as Fern and Luan disappeared through the door to introduce me and Dani.

We took our places on the stairs and waited for the door to open. I released Dani's hand just long enough to sweep the hair out of my face. As I locked my hand back around hers, the doors opened, and we stepped through. We took our places and Vinnie's scent started to hit the pack members closest to the stage. I watched as their noses crinkled.

"What's that smell, mommy?" I heard a child ask his mother. Before she could answer, I cleared my throat and held up a hand.

"We've been through a lot as a pack in the last year. We've had devastating losses, but we've also had some amazing additions. I've gathered you here tonight to announce that our pack has recently had more additions. I know typically they would join the pack in front of you; however, with all the recent events, I decided to bring them into the pack privately. Tonight, I introduce you to the newest pack members of Crimson Diamond: Kal Heroux, Vincent Dragomir, and Cypress Meadow." As I said each of their names, they did what I had instructed them on the stairs. The dining room erupted with cheers and clapping.

"Silence," I called out as I raised my hand. "I have some additional announcements regarding two of our newest pack members. First, Jameson and Cypress have completed the matebond. I expect you to show her the same respect you show him." The pack once again erupted in applause. I gave them a second to get it out before raising my hand again. "Second, you may have noticed a sweet smell. Vincent, who prefers to go by Vinnie, like Cypress, is not a wolf. Vinnie is a vampire." I didn't give them a chance to react before continuing. "I know you all have questions about how something like this could even happen. I can't give you all the details. All you need to know is he saved Max's life and asked me for sanctuary. Sanctuary I happily extended. I expect everyone to treat him like they would any other pack member."

"Cypress is a human. That's way different than a vampire!" one pack member shouted.

"He's not sucking my blood!" another one called out.

"Actually, Cypress isn't human. She's a witch," I confessed to them. I didn't like lying to my pack when I could avoid it.

"A vampire and a witch? Have you lost it?" someone called from the back.

"ENOUGH!" I roared, causing the room to shake. The entire pack bowed their heads to me. "If you don't trust my judgment in who joins this pack, then you don't trust me as your Alpha and you are more than welcome to leave," I told them, meaning every word.

"Can we ask him questions?" I heard Sarah's voice call up from in front of the stage.

"Well, that's up to him," I answered her before turning to look at Vinnie.

"Of course, you can, little pup." His eyes lit up as he answered and saw the line forming behind Sarah.

I could feel Dani's eyes on me as we made our rounds greeting pack members. I couldn't leave before knowing that Vinnie wasn't going to be attacked and be forced to kill half my pack. After about an hour, Phoenix was getting tired and hungry.

"I'll take the kids up and you come up when you think it's safe," Dani said as Phoenix fussed.

"Okay," I replied as I kissed hers and the kids' heads. I stared as she walked away. I knew she could feel my gaze. The sweet smell of her arousal reached my nostrils as she got to the door.

Chapter Twenty-Two

DANI

About forty-five minutes after I laid the kids down, the bedroom door slowly opened. Stefhan walked in, closing it securely behind him. We locked eyes as he sat with me on the couch. Gently he stroked his finger down my arm, causing goosebumps to cover my skin. He waited for them to disappear before placing his lips against my ear.

"I hear you like it when I call you a good girl." My core instantly blazed and my pussy clenched. "Is that true?" His voice was as soft as hummingbird wings.

"Yes," I breathed.

"As much as you deserve to be punished for telling Cy and not me about this newfound interest, we have to postpone it." A whine involuntarily left my mouth. "Oh, you're still going to be punished tonight. We just have to have a conversation first," he explained as he stood and reached for my hand. "Come with me." The sternness in his voice sent a shiver down my spine. I placed my hand in his and followed him to the living room.

"Before we do anything, I need to make sure we're on the same page," he began as we sat on the couch. I nodded my head in eager agreement. "I'm serious, my love. I don't ever want to do something that makes you uncomfortable. It's important for me to know how far you want me to take it and when it's acceptable for me to do so. It's equally as important for you to fully trust me and know that I would never do anything to hurt you," he explained as he held my hand.

He was right. In the little bit of research I was able to do, I knew this was a conversation we needed to have. I also knew I needed to be honest.

"I think I want to keep it in the bedroom, and I'm not sure how far I want you to take it. Can we just try things, and I'll tell you if it makes me uncomfortable?"

"Of course. As long as you promise you'll tell me immediately if you don't like something."

"I promise."

He leaned in, kissed my cheek, and whispered, "Are you ready?"

"Yes," I moaned against his face.

Stefhan placed his lips gently against mine before standing up. As he stood, his energy shifted.

"Stand up and follow me," he instructed as he turned toward the hallway. Excitement coursed through me as I obediently stood and followed him. He didn't look back as we walked. He stepped inside our room, stood against the door, and gestured for me to go in. I walked in, and Stefhan shut the door behind me. I was buzzing with excitement as he started unbuttoning his shirt.

"You will do what I tell you when I tell you. Do you understand?" he asked me.

"Yes," I replied as I watched him unbutton another button.

"If you don't, you will be punished. Do you understand?"

"Yes," I answered as my core blazed.

He dropped his shirt to the floor and inhaled deeply. His eyes went dark, and he strutted slowly toward me. He stood directly in front of me but made sure our skin didn't touch.

"You were a very bad girl," he told me as he took my hand, placed it on his chest, and slid it down to the top of his pants. "Do you know what happens to bad girls?" he asked me as he held my hand firmly against him. My heart was pounding so hard and fast I was sure he could hear it.

"What?" I asked him, trying to keep my voice calm.

"They get punished," he leaned down and whispered in my ear before commanding me. "Shirt and underwear off and hair down." I watched his cock twitch in his pants as I pulled off my shirt, pushed my underwear to the floor, and pulled out my braid. "Get on the bed. Face down, eyes closed, arms out, and ass up."

I went to the bed and obeyed his every command. There was complete silence for a few minutes, I was starting to think I missed a step. As I was going back over the list, I heard Stefhan's pants hit the floor. Juices ran down my leg as the bed dipped. Images of his naked body had been on repeat in my head nearly all day. I yearned to actually see him. I briefly opened my eyes to try and sneak a peek. Instead of seeing his body, I was greeted by his eyes staring into mine.

"Already not listening. Tsk. Tsk. Now I have to make it to where you have no choice," he told me as he got off the bed and walked toward the closet. Seconds later he emerged with a tie. "Sit up," he instructed me. I pushed myself off the bed and sat up. Carefully he moved my hair out of the way and started prepping the tie. "Get a good look. It's the last time you'll see it tonight."

Greedily, I looked him up and down like a piece of meat. His muscles were flexing and with each flex, his already stiff cock twitched. After a few moments, he lifted the tie, placed it over my eyes, and secured it tightly around my head. I opened my eyes to complete darkness. I felt the bed dip and him moving behind me.

"Face down, arms out, ass up," he instructed me again. His voice was firm, but still velvet.

I assumed my position and waited. And waited. And waited. I was about to speak when something smacked my ass, taking me completely by surprise. It wasn't until the second swat that I realized it was his hand. That realization made my core blaze and tighten. As the juices ran down my legs, I felt his finger slide briefly up my inner thigh, and then I heard a sucking sound.

"Does that turn you on when I spank you?" he asked me as he swatted my ass again.

"Yes," I moaned.

"I wonder what turns you on more?" he mused. "This?" he asked as he swatted my ass again. That one stung a little, but it only turned me on more. "Or this?" he asked before grazing his tongue across my clit. Instantly my hips rocked into his face. "I wonder what would happen if I did this?" he asked before burying his face in my pussy. He smacked my ass repeatedly, while he ate me like it was his last meal. When I was just about to cum, he stopped.

"Not yet," he instructed me as I felt the bed dip. Without warning, he slid his cock deep inside me. He slid his hand up my back and wound it into my hair. Gently, he pulled my head back and whispered. "You will cum when I tell you to and where I tell you to. Do you understand?"

"Yes, I understand."

"Good girl," he praised as he slowly started sliding his cock in and out of me. Every few pumps he smacked my ass, sending ripples of pleasure through me. Slowly his pumps turned into thrusts. He moved his hand from my hair and placed it under me, so it was on my stomach. I felt him repositioning his left arm before I felt him place his other arm beneath me.

"When I lift you up, wrap your legs around me. Do you understand?" he asked me as he finished getting positioned.

"Yes."

Stefhan lifted me, and I locked my legs as best as I could around him. I was still facing down, so it was difficult. He balanced me with one hand, while he quickly slid his cock back inside. He replaced his hand firmly under me and gave a test pump. Even though I knew I shouldn't move, instinct kicked in and I reached behind me to grab his arms. I felt his muscles tighten as I gripped them.

"I won't let you fall. Let go," he whispered. I clung to him for a few more seconds before taking a breath and letting go. "Good girl. Now relax your legs."

A flash of fear shot through me as I pictured myself falling face-first on the mattress. I forced myself to focus on Stefhan's arms, which felt like a sturdy table holding me up. I took a deep breath and relaxed my legs. He started sliding his cock in and out. It was so slow and rhythmic; after a few minutes, I fully relaxed against his arms. The instant he felt my body go limp, he started ramming his cock in and out like a jackhammer. Stars flashed across my eyes as pure pleasure engulfed me. I willed my body to stay relaxed, but my mouth couldn't be silenced.

"Do you like that?" he asked me in between thrusts.

"Yes!" I screamed.

The urge to scream his name was consuming me, but I couldn't call him Stefhan. I made love to Stefhan. Stefhan was gentle and soft. This was none of that. This was fucking. There was no soft and gentle. He was strong and stern.

"Do you want me to stop?" As he asked me, I knew what I was going to call him.

"No, Alpha! Don't stop!" I screamed.

"You want this cock?" he asked me as he pummeled my pussy.

"Yes!" I moaned.

"Yes what?" he growled, sending a wave of excitement through me.

"Yes, Alpha!" I screamed. My climax was begging to be released. The walls of my soaked pussy clenched around his cock as I fought to keep it back.

"Cum for me!" he roared as he pushed his cock even deeper inside. The second the words left his mouth, I released.

He never slowed his thrusts through my entire climax. After I finished, he gave one final thrust and released his load deep inside me. He took a minute to recover before he gently laid me on the bed and turned me over.

"Don't move," he whispered in my ear.

I couldn't have moved if I had wanted to, my entire body was jelly. I felt the bed dip as he got up and listened as he walked toward the bathroom. I listened to the difference his footsteps made on the carpet versus the tile. When the faucet turned off and he started walking again, I counted the number of steps it took him to get back to the bed. After he cleaned me up, he laid down and pulled me close to him.

"Aren't you forgetting something?" I asked as I pointed to my still-covered eyes.

"Nope," he told me as he pulled me closer. I could hear the sly smile in his voice. His words from earlier came rushing to the forefront.

"Get a good look. It's the last time you'll see it tonight."

When I woke up in the morning, Stefhan's arms were wrapped around me, the blindfold was gone, and I desperately needed to use the bathroom. I figured it had to be close to seven, and Stefhan would be getting up to go work out. Training wasn't set to start back up for a couple more days. It had been canceled, while Sarai's death was mourned. I waited until I couldn't hold it anymore before carefully moving his arms and ninja-rolling away from him.

When I was safely on the floor, I looked at the bed to make sure he was still sleeping. He looked more peaceful than I had ever seen him. His face was completely relaxed. The rest of his body was just as relaxed. I wanted to stand there watching him sleep forever, but my bladder had a very different idea of what I should be doing.

Once I took care of my bladder, I decided to jump in the shower. I was covered in dried sweat and sex and my hair looked like a haystack. I didn't need Max asking any questions about my appearance, and he would have. I was combing my hair when Stefhan walked in. He was glowing.

"Good morning," he greeted me as he got in the shower.

"This may be a dumb question, but why are you taking a shower before you work out?"

"I'm covered in dried sweat and sex. It would be a little rude to ask Jay to spot me," he replied with a wink that sent a shiver up my spine before stepping into the shower.

I finished my hair and then threw on a flowy top, leggings, and flats. I heard the shower shut off as I opened the bedroom door. Phoenix was getting ready to fuss when I opened her door.

"Mama's here, bug," I gently called as I walked to her crib.

I deftly got her changed and started to feed her. Stefhan came in right as we got settled and gave us each a kiss before leaving to work out.

Once we were alone, I couldn't help but think about how different my experience being a mother had been with Max and Phoenix. I tried not to think about those dark days, but I couldn't always keep them at bay. Stefhan wasn't the only one of us that harbored guilt. Before I could get too carried away, I heard Max's voice in the hall.

"Mama must be in Pheenick room. I scare her."

Trying to scare people was his newest thing. It only took Stefhan doing it once to Fern and it became Max's obsession. I could hear his little feet thumping against the carpet. As he got closer, I prepared myself to be "scared." I leaned my head down, looked at Phoenix, and waited.

"Roar!" he screamed as he jumped into the room seconds later.

"Oh my!" I called out and placed my free hand on my heart. "You scared me," I told him as I took exaggerated breaths.

"I scare you so bad, Mama!" he exclaimed with a look of triumph across his face.

"Yes, you did. But do you remember what we talked about?" I asked him gently. His nose crinkled as he thought about it.

"Don't scare people in Pheenick room, or when they are holding her," he told me after a few minutes.

That rule had to be established after he ran up behind me and pushed me, while I was changing her, causing me to almost fall on top of her.

"I sorry, Mama."

"It's okay, little one. Once I finish feeding your sister, I'll make breakfast. Do you want to wait in here or in your room while I finish up?"

"I wait here," he answered as he sat on the floor next to us.

I decided to make pancakes, eggs, sausage, bacon, mixed berries, and toast. As much as I loved Iris's cooking, I wanted to cook for my family. I didn't have a lot of normal in my life, and cooking for my family felt normal. Max loved helping me cook. I let him do all the pouring like Gram had with me. He mixed the berries as I washed them and put them in a bowl. Everything took twice as long, but I loved these moments with him.

"Where are you?" Stefhan's voice softly popped into my head.

"In the kitchen making breakfast."

"Is it done, or do I have time to shower first?" he instantly asked.

"You have time to shower."

Even if it was done, I would have told him that he had time. I didn't want to smell his workout funk while we ate. I had just pulled the eggs off the stove when Stefhan came into the kitchen.

"Papa!" Max squealed before running to him.

"Hey, bub. Did you help Mama make breakfast?"

"Yes, Papa. I mix the berries and all the pouring," he told Stefhan with a smile. They kept talking while I got everything put on platters and onto the table.

"How was your workout?" I asked him as we started eating.

"It was good," he answered as he shoved a piece of sausage in his mouth. "We went a little more intense since training is starting back up soon. Jay said he and Cy are going to talk to her parents today."

"We can talk about that later," I told him as I glanced pointedly at Max.

"Right."

Stefhan still had to tell Ryland about Monday. He was adamant that he was going to do it alone. He had no clue what Ryland's reaction would be, and he didn't want anyone to get hurt.

"I need to be there too, Stef! I get you're the Alpha, but they are my parents, too. And I can take care of myself," Fern argued as a single tear rolled down her cheek.

"You're right. You can come," Stefhan started before Luan cut him off.

"If Fern goes, I go." There was no tone of negotiation in his voice. There was no way he was going to let Fern be in any kind of danger.

"Let me guess. Now you want to go, too?" Stefhan turned and asked me.

"I would like to be there to support you, but I don't want to give you anything else to worry about. If you want me to stay home, I will," I told him honestly.

Stefhan worried about my safety more than anyone else's. Not just because I was his mate, but because I had zero self-defense training, human or otherwise. My size also didn't help. I was the smallest adult pack member.

"I do want you to stay home, but you are also the Luna of this pack. If Fern and Luan are coming, then it's only right for you to come. If you want to."

While I did want to support Stefhan, the kids had spent more time with other people than us since we got back from Florida. I also wasn't totally sure I wanted to see Ryland's reaction. I ultimately decided to stay home, a decision that was solidified when Stefhan returned. He was covered in cuts, deep gashes, and blood.

"I'm so glad you stayed here. He went completely nuts and shifted in the living room. You can thank Ajax for my current state. He wasn't responding to my Alpha commands. I really thought I was going to have to shift. He attacked me and Luan; I got the worst of it. Thankfully Fern stayed out of the way. I ended up having to inject him with wolfsbane and calling in Carlos to give him something to knock him out," he explained as I cleaned the deeper gashes.

"I wish you would let me stitch some of these. They are really deep." I was trying not to imagine him being attacked by a giant black wolf.

"Would it make you feel better if I did?" he asked me gently.

"Yes," I confessed as I continued cleaning.

"Okay. Go ahead."

I was so shocked that I nearly dropped my sterile water. After I recovered, I grabbed my suture kit and got to work. Even though it had been years since I had to suture someone, it was like riding a bike. There were five places that were too deep for my liking. I fell back into an easy rhythm as I closed them.

"All done," I said with a smile.

Chapter Twenty-Three

We were waiting for any kind of update when Stefhan got a link from Jameson, saying we needed to come down to the Meadow's. I hadn't seen them since giving them the ultimatum. I felt slightly nervous as we walked down the stairs to the third floor. Jameson already had the door open and was standing in the hallway waiting for us.

"I think we might have the next part!" he exclaimed as he guided us in and shut the door. Before we could ask what he meant, Oak cleared his throat and stood up from his seat.

"Stefhan, I owe you and Dani an apology. I let my own fear of Salix get in the way. We are willing to do anything we can to help. There's a spell that can open a portal to the field. It's one of the most complicated spells that I've ever seen. There are multiple elements you have to do in order to achieve what Cy and Jameson told us. Our grimoire doesn't have all the elements. It only has the spell for opening the portal. Not the one for allowing you or Vinnie to walk through it," he said as he grabbed an old-looking book and started thumbing through it. I could feel Stefhan's frustration building.

"But we know where the other elements are," Willow quickly chimed in and looked at me. "They're in yours."

Until that moment, I had forgotten about the dusty spell-filled book I found in Florida. With everything that had gone on, it completely slipped my mind. I quickly ran upstairs to retrieve it. While I was in the closet grabbing the book, I also grabbed the letters that Gram had addressed to the Meadow's. Once I had everything, I raced back downstairs.

We moved to the dining room table, so we could look at both books simultaneously. I was hesitant to open the worn cover. Stefhan gave my leg a reassuring squeeze as I slowly opened it. Carefully, I flipped through page after page, looking for the spell. After about five minutes of looking, I finally found it.

"To walk with death," I whispered as every head looked in my direction. There was a small paragraph above a list of ingredients. "I don't know what half of these things are," I sighed as I read the very complicated-looking spell.

"We do," Willow said softly as she started to read over my shoulder. "This is the most complicated spell and potion that I've ever seen. It's going to take a month to brew the potion alone. That's if you can even get all the ingredients."

"What do you mean by 'if' we can get them?" Stefhan asked her.

"Well, this flower," she started as she pointed to an ingredient, "is only found in one place in the world."

"My plane can get us to wherever we need to be," Stefhan interrupted her.

"Getting to where you can find one is the easy part. Finding one is another story," she told him as she ran a nervous hand through her hair. "Rafflesia arnoldii, the stinking corpse lily or corpse flower. It's native to southeast Asian rainforests and is practically impossible to grow anywhere else. They are the largest individual flower blooms in the world. They can get as big as three feet, have blood-red dotted petals, and emit the smell of rotting flesh. This says you have to pick it when it is in bloom. They take years to bloom for the first time. Then once they do, they only bloom once a year and the bloom only lasts for five to seven days. No one really even knows when they bloom. Theories say everything from after a heavy rain to sometime in July. And if finding one wasn't going to be hard enough, this says it has to be picked on the fourth day of the bloom."

The more Willow spoke, the more defeated I felt. It was a near-impossible task. I had to stop listening.

"Don't think that way," Enya's voice echoed softly. I was trying to, but the cards were definitely stacked against us. Oak, Jameson, and Stefhan talked strategies of how to track down the flower. The more they talked, the more the defeated feeling inside me grew. I was beyond relieved when Phoenix's feeding schedule caught up to me and we had to leave.

"What's wrong?" Stefhan asked me the instant we were in the hall and the door was securely shut.

"Can we talk about it later?" I asked in return. I didn't have it in me to tell him what was on my mind and then go straight to the kids.

"Of course," he answered as he leaned down and kissed my head.

We went through our normal evening routine. Max insisted on spaghetti, garlic bread, and salad for dinner. I went through the motions like I was on autopilot. More than once, I had to ask Max to repeat his question because I wasn't listening the first time he asked. When it came time for bed, we did our usual divide and conquer.

I knew the second I walked into the living room that Stefhan was going to ask me if it was later. I prolonged laying Phoenix down for as long as I could after she fell asleep. I hated admitting my insecure feelings to him. I walked slowly to the living room. Stefhan was waiting for me on the couch.

"Is it later?" he asked softly as he patted the space next to him on the couch.

"I guess it is technically later."

"Okay, and?" he asked when I didn't continue. I took a deep breath and let his scent fill my nose.

"It's just every part of this is more impossible than the last," I confessed as I breathed out.

"And we've figured out every other 'impossible' part," he reminded me.

"This is impossible in a different kind of way. And if we're being honest, the other parts kinda fell in our laps. We aren't going to just happen across a corpse lily flower on the fourth day of bloom in Oregon. What are we going to do, Stefhan? Send someone to just hang out in a southeast Asian rainforest for months and hope they come across one?"

I could hear the bubbling panic in my own voice.

"Come with me," was his only reply as he stood and offered me his hand.

Stefhan silently led me to the bedroom and then guided me to the bed. He had me sit in the middle and then disappeared into the closet. When he reemerged seconds later, he was holding a tie. Before I could tell him that it wasn't an appropriate time for sex games, he sat in front of me and whispered.

"Just trust me." Gently he tied it around my eyes, taking my sight. "Now take a few deep breaths," he instructed me. I took a few deep breaths and felt better. I just couldn't figure out why I needed to be blindfolded. "Imagine yourself in your happy place. Let yourself get fully immersed," he instructed once my breathing and heart rate were normal.

I pictured a beach with the waves crashing against the shore. I tried to imagine the sun on my skin and the sand between my toes. I found myself wanting to lay down. Before I could say anything, Stefhan slowly pushed me back, placing my head on my pillow. I imagined laying in the sand, the water lapping around me, and a beautiful blue sky above. Slowly my body fully relaxed; as I felt myself falling asleep, I couldn't help but think of Gram and how I could use one of her hugs.

I was standing in the field. A brilliant sun was shining on my skin and the smell of the wildflowers filled my nose. I wasted no time before looking toward the bench. The moment I saw her white hair, my feet took off full speed toward her. I launched myself into her arms, wrapped mine around her, and started crying.

"My sweet Dani girl why are you so upset?" she asked me as she hugged me tight.

"It's impossible Gram!" I sobbed.

"What is?" she asked gently.

"Finding the corpse lily for the potion."

"Well, that is a bit of a challenge," she mused as she rubbed my back.

"A bit?" I asked as I pulled back so that I could look at her. "Gram, this is beyond a bit of a challenge. Not only do we have to find a rare flower that only exists in one place and blooms once a year, for only five to seven days, but we also have to pick it on day four of the bloom. Oh, and did I mention that no one knows when it blooms?"

Gram looked at me with nothing but patience and love, while I got it all out of my system. When she was sure I was done, she wrapped her hands around my arms. "I know it seems impossible, but you're on the right track. You have to use all the magic available to you."

I looked at her like she was speaking a different language. I couldn't believe what I was hearing. Anger bubbled in me as I continued to stare at Gram.

"What do you mean 'use all the magic available to us? What do you think we're doing with the Meadow's and Cy living in the packhouse? A decision Stefhan wasn't thrilled about either," I shrieked at her.

"My sweet girl," she started before looking at me with more love than I thought was possible. "That only sounds like one kind of magic to me. You have to look all around you."

"I really wish–just once!–you would come out and just say what I'm supposed to do," I *confessed as a hot, frustrated tear rolled down my cheek.*

I watched as Gram thought about my words. I knew she wasn't going to give me any real answers, but I felt better just getting it out. She was silent for a long time before she took one of her deep, centering breaths.

"I kept too much from you for too long. The only regret I have is not telling you the moment I knew Stefhan was your mate. I will tell you what I do know. You have the five of seven and you have to tap into your collective magic. I know it's hard, but you have to embrace not only your own magic but also the magic that flows through each one of your friends. You have to stop thinking that things aren't possible. Nothing is impossible when you have as much magic at your disposal as you do. You have to fully embrace who you truly are."

"I don't know who that is!" I cried.

"You listen to me," Gram started as she gently grabbed my face in her hands and her tone went regal. "You are Dr. Danielle Emerald Storme. Daughter of Liam and Citrine McKenna. Granddaughter of Jennings and Ruth Solace. Wife of Stefhan Storme. Mother to Max and Phoenix. Luna to one of the most powerful packs in the world. You are the Fire Wolf and half of the mezze anime. You have double alpha blood

and witch magic running through your veins. You're kind, compassionate, resourceful, tough when it's needed, and loyal." She leaned in and kissed my forehead. "You, my sweet Dani girl, are amazing."

"I don't feel very amazing," I whispered.

"You have to stop feeling sorry for yourself and focusing on what you don't have. Let go of the past. You are surrounded by people that would do anything for you and your family. Do you remember what you used to tell me when you were a child?"

"That I didn't like brussels sprouts?" I answered her sarcastically.

"No," she said with a laugh. "You would tell me that when you grew up you wanted a career, a family, to be neighbors with Cy, and to be someone important. Look around you, you have all of those things and more. Are you really going to let someone take that from you?"

I woke up to Stefhan's arms around me and Gram's words echoing in my head. Silently and carefully, I unwrapped myself from his grip and made my way to the bathroom. I sat at my vanity and looked around. The memory of my first time ever being in this space flooded my mind. That memory triggered another and another. My entire life since coming to Crimson

Diamond played back like a movie in my head. I was so engrossed and focused that I didn't hear the door open.

"Are you okay?" Stefhan's voice suddenly called out, bringing me back to the present.

"Yeah," I replied automatically before turning to look at him. When my eyes locked with his, everything clicked. "I'm just really dumb for being a doctor," I finished as Gram's words truly sank in.

"What?" he asked me, totally confused.

"I'm having an epiphany. Gram came to me and said that I need to focus on what I have and not what I don't," I started as I stood up so I could pace. As I spoke, I felt a shift deep within me. "I've been focused on what I've lost, Gram, my career, my old life. So focused that I didn't appreciate everything I've gained." I stopped pacing and looked at Stefhan, who was wearing just a pair of basketball shorts, looking hotter than anyone had a right to. He was also staring at me with slight concern.

"My love," he started before I cut him off. I was finally moving past my trauma.

"I mean look how hot you are!" I exclaimed as I waved my hand in his direction. "Never in my life did I think I could get someone like you. You are one of *People Magazine*'s most beautiful people. I'm married to one of the top ten hottest men on the planet and we have not one but two beautiful children. Family and friends that would do anything for me. My best friend lives one floor below me and I live in a fucking castle! Take that, Courtney!" I clapped my hands together at the end like I had just made some major point. Stefhan's look of concern had yet to leave his face. If anything, he looked more concerned and confused.

"I'm not sure what's happening, or what I'm supposed to say. So, I'm going to say, 'Thank you' and then ask a question. Thank you, and who is Courtney?" His voice was soft and gentle. I could tell he thought I was having a mental break.

"What's happening is that I'm realizing what I have and that overall, I'm pretty damn lucky. To answer your question, Courtney Beach, she was my bully in school. She's actually the reason Cy and I became friends. She lifted my dress up on my first day of school, and Cy punched her in the nose. She made my life miserable until graduation," I told him as I shrugged my shoulders.

"What do you mean by miserable?" he asked cautiously as he slowly started walking toward me.

I didn't talk much about my childhood trauma, and when I did, it was kept pretty vague. I glanced at the window, the sun was beginning to peak in. It probably wasn't the best time, but it was the right time. I needed to let go of the past.

"You know that I didn't have the best experience in school. If it wasn't for Cy, I know it would have been worse than it was. Courtney was the ringmaster of my torture. She knew better than to lay a hand on me, so she stuck to verbal insults and assisted me in being accident-prone. She would tell me how I was going to end up being a cat lady, how no one would want to be with me because I'm a freak. She even tripped me at graduation as I walked up the steps to the stage." I watched as Stefhan's face morphed from pain to anger. "You want to hear something I've never told anyone?" I asked him suddenly.

"Yes, I do, but let's go sit down," he answered as he took my hand in his. He guided me to the couch in the bedroom. "Okay, I'm ready," he told me as we got settled.

"I didn't even tell Gram this," I started as I took a breath. "The reason I came back to Florida for my residency and to work is because I wanted to show Courtney that I made something of myself." The words flew out as I released my breath. It felt amazing to be letting it out, so I continued. "I saw her once at the hospital, it was during my residency. Her dad had been brought in with a possible heart attack. I was standing in an empty trauma bay covered in throw-up when she walked by. She made a comment about how she wasn't surprised that I was covered in puke to her mom."

"And then you went in and saved her dad's life," he said, trying to hide the pain in his voice. Even if he could have hidden it, his eyes would have given him away.

"Hell no. I was covered in throw-up, I was in no condition to be seeing patients. I needed to shower. Plus, I was mortified, that wasn't how I pictured seeing her for the first time since becoming a doctor. I didn't have a chance to rectify it either. The possible heart attack turned out to be gas, so her dad was discharged just a few hours after he arrived, and I haven't seen her since. I know one thing though. She would fucking die if she knew that you are my husband, and I would pay money to see that," I told him with a laugh.

"You said Gram came to you. What else did she say?" he asked suddenly, totally changing the subject.

I told him everything Gram said. Stefhan didn't seem shocked that she said we needed to use our collective magic. He said that we needed to talk with everyone as soon as possible. We didn't have time to talk about much else before the kids woke up and he had to go to training. He came home just long enough for me to set his broken fingers and shower before going to his office. He had pack and Storme Medical work that needed to be done.

Chapter Twenty-Four

STEFHAN

Were there a million other things I should be doing? Yes. Was I doing any of them? No. Instead of calling an emergency meeting and telling everyone about Dani's dream, I was setting up my mate's revenge.

"Are you really going to do this?" Kane asked me as I made my way to my office.

"Yes, I am, and honestly I'm surprised you aren't more on board with it," I answered.

"I'm not on board because this is the last thing you should be focused on. Plus, you don't even know if it's the same person! But if it is the same person, I will support you," he retorted.

I didn't answer him, instead I picked up the pace. When I arrived at my office, I went straight to my computer and signed into the Storme Medical employee database. After a quick search and a few clicks, there she was Courtney Beach. After a few more clicks, I confirmed that she graduated the same year and from the same high school as Dani.

"Is this enough for you?" I asked him as I stared at her employee profile.

"Fine, but you know you can't pull this off alone," Kane snapped.

As much as I wanted to do this without help, I couldn't. I had no choice but to bring in reinforcements. I linked Jay and asked him to bring Cy and meet me in my office.

"Everything okay, Stef?" Jay asked me the second the door closed behind them. It was out of character for me to request to see Cy.

"Yeah. I need your help," I said looking at Cy.

"From me?" she asked as she looked behind her like someone else was going to suddenly materialize in the room.

"Yes, from you. But you can't tell Dani." I watched as she thought about my words.

"It depends on what it is. If you're having an affair, then I'm going to tell her." I couldn't stop the laugh that escaped my mouth.

"I'm not having an affair. Dani told me about someone who made her life miserable growing up. When she told me her name–" I started before Cy whispered.

"Fucking Courtney."

"Yes, Courtney Beach. I was shocked that it was a name I knew. There is a Director of Human Resources within Storme Medical with the same name," I told her as I turned my laptop to show her the photo listed in Courtney's employee file.

"Courtney Fucking Beach. I see she finally got her nose fixed. I don't mean to be rude, Stefhan, but I don't think showing Dani that is a good idea," Cy whispered as she looked at the photo.

"So, this is her?" I asked Cy. I needed to be one hundred percent sure.

"Yes, that's her. That is the dumb bitch that tormented Dani for years. Why?"

"Dani is going to get her revenge. That's why," I told her with a smile.

"Um, Stef. How exactly do you plan on doing that? From her file, she works in Georgia. Dani won't go to Georgia, not with everything that's going on," Jay said as he read her file.

"I don't need to take Dani to Georgia. Courtney will come to Oregon," I started as I turned the laptop and made a few clicks before turning it back around. "This," I told him as I pointed to the screen.

"The Storme Medical charity ball?" Cy asked.

"Yes. Every year Storme Medical throws a huge charity ball in Portland. Every Director in the company is invited. No one ever turns down the trip. It is fully paid for by Storme Medical." I turned the screen back and made a few more clicks. "She's already RSVP'd for the event."

"But that doesn't explain how you are going to get Dani to go to Portland," Jay countered.

"I'm going to tell her the truth. That I've been slacking on my Storme Medical responsibilities, and this is an important event that we need to attend."

"Okay, so what do you need my help with?" Cy asked after hearing my simple yet direct explanation.

"I need you to convince her to go."

"What?" she asked automatically. I knew my response was going to throw her off, but I was prepared.

"I already know that she's going to come up with a million reasons why we or she shouldn't go. Shit, there's a million reasons I can come up with why we shouldn't. But, when Dani told me the things that Courtney did to her and how she made her feel, it made me want to do something. She told me that Courtney would die if she knew that I was her husband, and she would pay money to see that. So, I'm going to make it happen for her. For free," I confessed to Cy.

"Shit, I would pay money to see that. She will be there, even if I have to drag her to Portland myself."

I didn't have much time to get Dani on board with going: I had less than a week. I knew I couldn't waste any time in bringing it up. Once Jay and Cy left, I started on the actual work that I needed to do. I wasn't lying when I said I had been slacking. It was already dark, and the kids were in bed by the time I got upstairs. I had tried to prepare myself for any questions or concerns she would bring up.

"Can I talk to you?" I asked her as soon as I stepped into the bedroom and shut the door.

"Of course," she answered as she patted the spot next to her on the couch and turned off the cooking show she was watching. "Is everything okay?" she asked me as I sat next to her.

"Yeah. I just need to talk to you about Storme Medical," I told her as I took her hand in mine.

"What about it?"

"With everything that has been going on the past couple of years, I haven't exactly been CEO of the year. I've kept everything running, but I haven't been going to events that I would normally attend. I'm getting pressure from the board to attend the annual charity ball in Portland," I explained.

"Okay. I don't see what the problem is. I know that technically you shouldn't leave, but Storme Medical is what pays the bills. We don't need rumors starting in the human world that you vanished, and paparazzi showing up at the gates." Her response wasn't what I expected, but it actually helped me.

"You aren't worried that Salix will try something?" I asked her, trying my best to keep my voice in the proper tone.

"I honestly don't think he would try anything. He isn't the type to attack directly. Plus, I don't think he would want to get the attention of the human world." I took a breath and looked into her eyes.

"I want you to come with me."

"Why?" she asked, looking completely surprised.

"Because you're my wife."

"You can't just show up with me and be all 'this is my wife'!" she shrieked at me.

"Why can't I?" I asked her, totally confused.

"For multiple reasons. First, you are a notorious bachelor. Second, no one even knew you had a girlfriend. Third, no one knows you got married. Fourth, you can't just show up with a wife out of nowhere!" I could hear the panic bubbling in her voice.

"Do you really think that I didn't tell anyone I got married?" I asked her as a pain shot through my heart. She didn't answer, only nodded her head. "I have to admit my feelings are a little hurt," I confessed as I grabbed my phone did a quick Google search on myself, and handed it to her. "Read this." I watched as she clicked on article after article, the *People Magazine* story that announced our engagement and then wedding. She held onto my phone as she looked at me.

"How?" she whispered.

"I told the board about us the day after you agreed to be my wife. The publicist for Storme Medical called *People*, *TMZ*, and a couple of other magazines. I have never been one to give interviews, have always maintained a low profile, and kept my private life private. It wasn't shocking that I would get engaged before anyone knew I even had a girlfriend," I told her as she clicked on my Wikipedia page.

"'Stefhan Storme, thirty-five; wife, Danielle Storme; two children; net worth, seventy-seven billion. Stefhan is a very private man who fiercely protects his wife and children's identities,'" she read aloud before stopping to look at me. "You're worth seventy-seven billion dollars?" she shrieked, shoving the phone toward me.

"Give or take. And technically, WE are worth that," I told her as I lifted my left hand, showing her my wedding band. "But that's not what we're talking about," I continued before she could totally lose it. "Will you please go with me?" I asked as I looked deep into her eyes.

"I'll go. When is it?" she whispered.

"Saturday."

"Saturday? Which Saturday?" she asked as the color drained out of her face.

"This Saturday," I replied as I gently squeezed her hand.

"Nope. Not going." She was already standing before the words finished leaving her mouth.

"Why? It's not like we haven't been in public together before."

"This is different," she replied as she paced.

"How is this different?"

"No one knew who you were!" she retorted, never breaking her stride.

"Are you ashamed to be in public with me where people do know who I am?" I asked her as I stood up.

"No one in their right mind would be ashamed to be in public with you, period," she snapped.

"Then why won't you go?" I asked, letting some sadness seep into my words. I wasn't below begging at this point. I had to get her to Portland.

"You could let me try, boy. My puppy eyes are hard to ignore," Kane whispered.

"This is really important to you, isn't it?" she asked me gently, as she stopped pacing.

"Yes, it is," I replied with nothing but honesty in my voice.

"Okay, I'll go," she finally agreed. If she hadn't agreed, I was honestly considering letting Kane try his puppy eyes. I walked over to her, dropped to my knees, and wrapped my arms around her. "I do have some questions," she continued as she embraced me.

"You ask, and I'll answer," I whispered as I let her scent fill my nose.

"Who is going to keep the kids?"

"Fern and Luan or Cy and Jay."

"How far is Portland from here?"

"About two hours."

"How long would we be gone?"

"Three days. We will go to Portland Friday afternoon and come back on Sunday."

"Where would we be staying?"

"Wherever you want."

"What all does this event entail? I don't want to be surprised with anything."

"The charity benefit starts Saturday at four-thirty and usually ends around eleven. There will be dinner and dancing, followed by an auction."

"That's it?"

"Yep."

"Then why are we going on Friday? We could leave Saturday morning."

"Well, we could, but I don't want to." I was hoping she would leave it be.

"Why not?"

"You can never just be surprised. I want to take you on a proper date. Our entire relationship I have never just been able to take you out somewhere. Like a normal couple," I confessed. She pulled back so that she could see my face. She looked like she had just won the lottery.

I only had three days to get everything set up for our trip to Portland. The next morning, I made some phone calls. The board was ecstatic that not only was I coming, but that I also was bringing Dani. I made the hotel reservations, called some fancy restaurant in town, and reserved a table for Friday night. I got Fern and Luan to keep the kids Friday night and Jay and Cy on Saturday. I also called Coral, a call I wasn't expecting to make. When Dani found out the ball was black tie, she said she wanted to wear the red dress she wore for her Luna Ceremony. I was surprised that she wanted to wear it, but I didn't question it. She needed it taken in since she wasn't pregnant.

I called a meeting with everyone, so Dani could tell them what Gram said about using our collective magic. Vinnie wanted to do some research; he said he remembered reading something a long time ago that referenced combining magic. Since the pack finally knew about Vinnie, he was free to move about the packhouse, like any pack member, so I gave him access to the restricted section of the library. Typically, I wouldn't give anyone outside of my family access, but there was nothing typical about our situation. Coral arrived on Thursday to work her magic, and within a couple of hours, Dani's dress fit her perfectly.

Dani wouldn't let me see what she packed for our date. She said she wanted it to be a surprise. Fern also insisted on giving me pointers.

"I already know that I need to open her car door for her," I snapped at Fern, after an hour of her telling me what I needed to do and not do.

"How many women have you taken on a date before?" she snapped back.

"None, but that's beside the point. I'm not taking some stranger out. I'm taking out my mate. I know how to be a gentleman, Fern," I told her, trying to sound a little calmer. I knew she was just trying to be helpful.

"Why can't she be helpful somewhere else?" Kane mumbled grumpily.

"I guess that's true. I'll let you finish getting packed," she said before coming up close, grabbing me by my shirt, and yanking my face closer to hers. "You better not have fucked any of the women who are going to be at this event. If Dani comes home and says she had anything other than a stellar time, I will beat the shit out of you," she whispered before giving me a kiss on my cheek and turning to leave. Dani walked into the closet right as Fern was walking out.

"How are you still not done packing?" Dani asked me when she saw my suitcase still sitting open on the island. "You've been in here for an hour."

"That's my fault. I was talking to him," Fern answered on my behalf.

"Oh, okay," she replied to Fern before turning to me. "I'm going to pump one more time before we leave."

"Sounds good. I'm almost done," I told her as I continued packing my bag. I needed them both to leave before I could pack the last item.

On top of Max not being happy that we were leaving the packhouse and not taking him with us, Dani insisted on showing Fern, Luan, Cy, and Jay where everything was. Literally everything. We didn't get to the garage for almost another hour.

"This isn't the first time we've been in your house, bitch. Stop stalling and go enjoy the weekend. The kids will be fine," Cy had finally told her when she had started to take them into the kitchen.

"And you wanted me to wait in the car," I told her with a laugh as I helped her into the car and shut the door.

"I just wanted to make sure they knew where everything was," she replied when I got in. I could feel the nervousness pouring off her.

"I know you're nervous about leaving the kids. I promise they will be fine," I said, trying to reassure her.

"That's not why I'm nervous," she confessed as I pulled out of the garage.

"Then why are you?" I asked her gently.

"It's nothing, really. It's silly," she answered.

"There is nothing silly about your feelings."

"It's just that this will be the first time that we're together in a professional setting. Everyone is going to know who you are. Everyone is going to know that I'm there with you," she started before taking a breath. I knew she was going to continue speaking, so I waited patiently for her to be ready to say what was bothering her. "I'm not going to be what they expect," she whispered.

"What do you mean not what they expect?" I asked as I intertwined my fingers with hers.

"Come on Stefhan, don't be stupid. Everyone expects your wife to be some tall, tan, supermodel. I'm not any of those things," she confessed before adding, "And I heard Fern."

My heart sank. I immediately pulled the car over to the side of the road. I put it in park, got out, walked to her side, opened the door, and placed my hands on her face.

"First, they shouldn't have any expectations. The only woman who I've ever taken to an event is Fern. Second, I don't want a tall, tan, supermodel. I want you. And to what Fern said, I haven't had sex with anyone that works at Storme Medical. I kept my whoring strictly to the pack and close neighboring ones." By the time I was finished, my face was so close to hers that I could feel her breath on my skin.

"That's not true," she whispered.

"What's not true?" I asked, a little offended. I had been nothing but honest.

"That you haven't had sex with anyone that works for Storme Medical. Last time I checked, I'm still a current employee," she said with a giggle.

"You wait until later," I told her with a growl as I smashed my lips against hers.

Chapter Twenty-Five

DANI

To say I was nervous would be an understatement. I was sure
Stefhan could hear my heart pounding as we pulled into a
swanky hotel. Before the car was even in park, the valet was
standing at the driver's side door. Stefhan put the car in park,
popped the truck, opened his door, and got out.

"Mr. Storme, it's been a long time! It's so nice to see
you, welcome back," the valet greeted him with a smile. He
was an older man, probably about fifty, with salt and pepper
hair.

"It has been a while. It's nice to see you too, Arthur,"
Stefhan greeted the man as he made his way to my side of the
car. Arthur in close pursuit. Stefhan opened my door. "I'd like
to introduce you to my wife," he told Arthur as he helped me
out of the car. "This is my wife, Dr. Danielle Storme." Stefhan
had such a look of love and pride on his face as he spoke.
"Love, this is Arthur. He's been the valet here for years," he
continued

"It's very nice to meet you, Arthur," I said as I extended
my hand out to him.

"It is a pleasure to meet you, Dr. Storme," Arthur told
me as he gripped my hand and gave it a firm shake.

By this time, a bellboy was coming out to help us with our bags. Stefhan handed Arthur a one-hundred-dollar bill and walked to the back of the car to meet the bellboy.

"Welcome, Mr. Storme. My name is William. I'll be getting your bags," he greeted Stefhan as he started loading our bags onto a cart.

"Thank you, William. This is my wife, Dr. Danielle Storme," Stefhan told him as he moved so that William could see me. He immediately turned to greet me.

"I am so sorry, Dr. Storme. I didn't see you. Welcome!" he told me with a very apologetic smile. Stefhan handed William a one-hundred-dollar bill before guiding me inside.

As we walked to the front desk to check in, Stefhan matched his stride to mine. It seemed like he was purposefully making sure that he didn't block me from view. He squeezed my hand slightly as we approached the desk. There was a very pretty, petite woman working; her deep auburn hair was just below her shoulders.

"Checking in?" she asked as she looked up from her computer. I could hear the gulp as she took in Stefhan. As her eyes raked over him, she took a deep breath and swept her hair back. I could tell that she was completely taken off guard. I really hoped that wasn't what I looked like the first time I laid eyes on him.

"Yes. The reservation is under the last name, Storme," he told her as he gripped my hand a little tighter.

"Mr. Storme!" someone suddenly yelled. I turned to see a middle-aged bald man approaching us. "Amy, please get the keys to the Presidential suite. Mr. Storme is one of our most prestigious guests. Congratulations on your marriage. I read the article," the man continued as he got closer.

"Hello, Joe. I'd like for you to meet my wife," Stefhan greeted him and stepped aside, so I was in full view.

"Oh, Mrs. Storme!" Joe started before Stefhan stopped him.

"It's Dr. Storme."

"My apologies, Dr. Storme. It is such a pleasure to meet you!" Joe told me as he shook my hand.

"Here is your key, Mr. Storme," Amy's voice suddenly called out. "If there is anything you need, please don't hesitate to ask." Stefhan grabbed the key and thanked her, making sure not to make eye contact.

Our room was larger than some houses I had been in. It was a one-bedroom with a living room, kitchen, and huge bathroom. The shower was big enough that Stefhan and I could both fit inside comfortably. The whole place screamed money and luxury. I was in complete awe and slowly walked through the space. By the time I made it to the bedroom, Stefhan was already unpacking his bag.

"Is everything okay?" he asked me as I stood there looking around.

"Yeah. I've just never been in a hotel room like this before. It's super fancy," I confessed as I pulled out the garment bags that held my dresses. As we unpacked and I continued to look around, my curiosity started to get to me.

"It's rude to ask him how much this cost," I scolded myself.

"Why is it rude?" Enya asked.

"Because it's not my business how much of HIS money he spends," I told her.

"Are you sure everything is okay? You haven't moved in like five minutes." I could hear the concern in his voice.

"I'm okay. I was just arguing with Enya," I told him.

"Can I ask what about?"

"We were arguing about if something was rude or not," I replied, hoping but knowing he wouldn't leave it at that.

"If you want, I can be the tiebreaker," he told me as he locked his eyes with mine and smiled the smile that made my world stop.

"Is it rude to ask someone how much they paid for something?" I blurted out before realizing what I was doing.

"That depends on who and what it is. If it's your husband and you want to know how much they paid for a fancy hotel room, that is perfectly acceptable," he said with a shrug.

"How much was it?" I asked.

"A little under four thousand," he answered.

"Total?" I choked out.

"No, per night. Total was about eight thousand dollars," he told me. Outside of purchasing my cars, I had never spent that kind of money on one thing. I could feel the color draining from my face; I took a couple of deep breaths. "Dani?" his voice called to me as I closed my eyes.

"Give me just a second. I'm trying to wrap my head around the fact that you spent eight thousand dollars on a hotel room for two nights. But when you have seventy-seven billion dollars, I guess it really isn't that much. Seventy-seven billion…" I rambled.

The second the words were out of my mouth, Stefhan's arms were around me.

"Did you truly not know how much money I have?" he asked me gently.

"I knew you were rich, but I had no clue you are a multi-billionaire," I confessed, feeling suddenly really stupid.

"You never Googled me?" I could tell he was shocked that I genuinely had no clue. It was public information after all.

"No. I never thought about it honestly. But in my defense, I did think that I was in a coma dream."

"I'm sorry I never told you. I shouldn't have just assumed you knew. Seeing how you've reacted to the amount I spent on the room, I need to warn you," he started, and I took a deep breath. "I'm going to be spending a lot of money this weekend," he continued.

"How much is a lot?" I asked him, not being sure I wanted to know the answer.

"During the last auction, I spent over a million dollars." I choked on the air I was breathing. He let me go, dropped to his knees, and cupped my face with his hands. "Breath," he whispered as I desperately tried to stop the panic attack that was fighting its way to the surface. I took a deep breath and let his scent fill my nose. I concentrated on that and the sparks that danced across my face where his skin touched mine.

"That is so much money, Stefhan. There are people without houses and food." Images of the needy families I had helped in the past flashed through my head.

"I know it's a lot of money, and it goes to a good cause. Each year a different charity is chosen to receive the money raised," he told me.

"I'm sorry, I'm making a bigger deal out of this than there needs to be," I quickly apologized. "If I would have done what any normal person would have done and googled you, I would have known this years ago. It just never mattered to me. I was more focused on maintaining a coherent conversation with you and not drooling," I continued more for myself than him.

"Let's just enjoy the weekend and when we get home, I will go over everything with you. It's just as much yours as it is mine."

"Okay," I agreed.

I made Stefhan get dressed in the bedroom, while I got ready in the bathroom. I didn't want to admit how excited I was to go on a real date with him. I loved our picnics in the garden, but this was going to be my first true date. I braided my hair in an elegant French braid, pulling out pieces to frame my face. I kept my dress a surprise: I brought the powder blue dress I had worn to Le Palais Rouge. Not only was it one of the fancier outfits I owned, but it reminded me of Stefhan. Even though I hadn't seen him there, knowing he was there in my mind connected the dress to him. I put on some light makeup, slipped on my shoes, and gave myself a quick once-over before walking out the door to meet Stefhan.

He was waiting for me in the living room and wearing a teal long-sleeve, button-down shirt, with black dress pants and shoes, and his hair was loose. His eyes went dark with lust as he looked me up and down.

"You tempt me like this when we have places to be," he growled softly, making my core tighten. He glanced at his watch and gave his head a hard shake. "Come on, love. The car will be waiting for us," he said as he took my hand in his and started walking toward the elevator.

"Car? What car?" I asked as we walked.

"I hired a driver for the weekend," he answered simply.

"Why?"

"You'll see."

We walked in silence to the front entrance. When we got outside, there was a large, black SUV waiting for us.

"Mr. and Mrs. Storme?" an older gentleman asked.

"Yes. I am Mr. Storme, and this is my wife, Dr. Storme," Stefhan corrected him.

"My apologies, Dr. Storme. My name is Jorge, and I will be your driver for the weekend."

"It's okay, and it's very nice to meet you," I told him as I extended my hand.

Stefhan helped me into the car and once he was inside, he pulled me close to him. He lifted my dress just enough to lightly trace patterns on my thigh with the hand that wasn't tangled around me. Every so often he slid his finger under the fabric. I had to use all my focus to remember that we weren't alone.

Stefhan's fingers never actually touched anything other than my leg, but he came dangerously close. Close enough that my core was on fire and my pussy was throbbing. Relief washed over me when Jorge announced we were at the restaurant. I needed a distraction, and dinner was a good one. Stefhan helped me out of the car and wrapped his hand around mine as we walked into the very fancy restaurant.

The woman at the hostess stand basically had the same reaction to Stefhan that Amy at the hotel had. Her eyes went wide as she raked them over his body before landing on his face. She had yet to even glance in my direction. She swallowed hard and gave her head a shake before speaking.

"Good evening and welcome. Do you have a reservation?" she asked him, still not acknowledging I was even there.

"Yes, I have a reservation for me and my wife. Last name is Storme," he told her politely. It was the voice he used when he talked to pack members. I had to stifle a giggle.

"Yes, Mr. Storme, here it is. Right this way," she replied as she gave me a quick glance. She guided us through the beautiful space to a very private table. It was a booth tucked into a corner of the dining room. "Your server will be with you shortly," she told Stefhan as she set down our menus.

"Thank you," he told her, using the same tone he had earlier. This time I couldn't stop the giggle from escaping my lips. I sat down and scooted to the middle of the semicircle seat, so I was facing the dining room. He sat down and scooted right next to me. "Do you want to share what was so funny?" he asked as soon as the hostess was out of earshot.

"I just never realized that you have a doctor's voice," I told him with a laugh.

"What?"

"Cy always tells me that I have a specific voice I use on my patients. She calls it my doctor's voice and she hates when I use it on her. You have a tone that you use when you're talking with people at home. It's calm and polite, and you totally just used it on the hostess."

"I'm glad it sounded that way. I wanted to smack the taste out of her mouth," he told me as a wave of anger rolled off him.

"Why?" I asked him, totally confused. I hadn't felt any anger coming from him at all until that moment.

"I'm used to the staring and the comments that women make toward me. You would be disgusted by the things people will say when they think you can't hear them. I've gotten to where I can ignore it and keep a professional front. But it is rude as fuck for them to just ignore you. Both the check-in girl at the hotel and the hostess never acknowledged you until I said something," he explained as he pulled me closer to him. I could feel his anger radiating.

"In all fairness, love, you take people off guard. Not only are you enormous, but you are also twelve out of ten hot. I was actually hoping that I didn't look like the girl at the hotel the first time I saw you," I confessed and placed my hand on his leg.

"You looked nothing like that. You were adorable," he told me as he started to calm down. Before I could reply, a man with short, dark hair approached our table.

"Hello, Mr. Storme. My name is Bernard; I'm the manager. I wanted to personally greet you and speak with you about your special request."

"It's nice to meet you, Bernard. What about my request would you like to talk about?" Stefhan asked him.

"I was just curious as to why you requested a male server?" Bernard asked quietly. Hearing his question, I was curious too. It seemed like a strange request to make.

"I requested a male server so what happened with the hostess doesn't happen the entire time we are here," he told him bluntly.

"What happened with the hostess?"

"Well, she stared at me like I was a piece of meat and didn't even acknowledge my wife's presence until I said something. And then only glancing in her direction, not speaking directly to her once. I don't appreciate my wife being treated like that. Now, are you able to honor my request from when I made this reservation, or do I need to take my business elsewhere?"

"Of course we can, Mr. Storme. I am so sorry for your experience with the hostess, Mrs. Storme," Bernard started before Stefhan corrected him.

"It's Dr. Storme."

"I apologize, Dr. Storme. I will personally make sure that the hostess is spoken to about what happened. Your server will be with you shortly," he quickly told me and Stefhan before walking away.

"Really, Stefhan? A male server?" I turned to ask him.

"Yes, really. I told you, this is a common occurrence for me. It was something I was hoping to limit your exposure to. It doesn't feel very good to see your mate being hit on," he whispered.

The memory of when he showed up at the hospital in California, right after I had been asked out, played in my mind. I gently squeezed his leg and moved closer to him. In response, he lifted my dress, just like he had in the car, and lightly traced designs on my skin. The sparks danced and my core tightened.

"Good evening. My name is Vani, and I'll be taking care of you this evening," a voice called out, making me jump. "Can I start you out with something to drink?" I looked up to see a man in his early forties standing at our table. He was about six-foot and bald.

"I'll have the most expensive bourbon you have and water please," Stefhan told him without looking at the menu. Quickly, I scanned the wine list.

"I'll have the apple wine and a water please," I answered, trying to maintain my focus. Stefhan's hand never stopped moving, and his fingers were dangerously close to grazing something other than my leg.

"I'll give you a few minutes to look over the menu while I get your drinks," Vani told us with a smile before turning and walking away.

"Dr. Storme, you smell amazing." Stefhan leaned in and whispered in my ear. Before I could gather my thoughts to respond, Vani was back with our drinks.

"Bourbon, apple wine, and two waters. Are you ready to order?" he asked us with a smile plastered on his face.

"We're going to need a few more minutes," Stefhan told him politely as I grabbed and opened the menu that was still sitting in the same place the hostess had set it. When the server came back a few minutes later, I was ready. Stefhan ordered the surf and turf with about eight sides. I ordered the steak with mashed potatoes and green beans.

I'm not sure how he pulled it off, but Stefhan managed to keep one hand on my leg for almost the entire meal, only removing it once to cut his entire steak. I had to force myself to focus on eating. My stomach muscles were tight, and my core felt like a fucking volcanic eruption was about to take place. Stefhan kept trying to make small talk, I answered tersely. I was afraid if my mouth was open too long that I would moan.

Stefhan finished eating about ten minutes before I did. He used that time to continue tracing lightly on my leg. He already had his card out and four one-hundred-dollar bills in his hand when the server came with the check. He tucked them in the check presenter without looking at the bill and handed it immediately back to the server. I could hear the soft growls emanating from Stefhan's chest as my arousal hit a fever pitch. The sexy underwear I had on were soaked, and I was praying that I didn't have a wet spot on my dress.

I didn't have to see the server to know when he was on his way to our table. Stefhan was watching across the restaurant in the direction Vani had walked to pay the bill. About five minutes after he walked away, Stefhan adjusted his erection and started to scoot out of the booth. Like a choreographed dance, Vani made it to the table right as Stefhan was out of the booth. Without taking the bill presenter from

Vani, he pulled his card out of the top, stuffed it in his pocket, and held out his hand to guide me out of the booth. I could tell he was working really hard to not drag me through the restaurant as we walked. As we neared the hostess stand, I heard someone calling out "Mr. Storme." Stefhan didn't stop walking, he just glanced behind us.

"How can I help you, Bernard? We're in a hurry," Stefhan called out as we kept walking.

"I just wanted to make sure that everything was up to yours and Dr. Storme's standards," Bernard called out. Stefhan stopped, let go of my hand, and turned around.

"The service Vani provided was excellent, so excellent in fact, I gave him a four-hundred-dollar tip. The food was good, not the best I've ever had, but good overall. I just really hope that you talked to the hostess about her behavior. If she would have treated my wife like she was in the same room, I would have given her a four-hundred-dollar tip as well. Have a nice evening," Stefhan replied casually. We were close enough to the hostess stand that she overheard him. The look on her face was priceless when she learned how much of a tip she would have gotten–if she *only* would have spoken to me.

Stefhan didn't wait for Bernard to respond; instead, he turned, grabbed my hand, and started marching for the door. Less than fifteen seconds after we got outside, Jorge pulled up in front of us. Stefhan opened my door and helped me inside before practically running to his side and jumping in. He leaned forward and whispered to Jorge.

"If you can get us back safely to the hotel within ten minutes and without scaring my wife, I'll tip you five hundred dollars."

"Are you serious, Mr. Storme?"

"Very," Stefhan replied as he pulled out his wallet and removed five crisp one-hundred-dollar bills.

"You got it. Please buckle up," Jorge replied after looking at the banknotes.

He drove like Ricky Bobby as he raced to the hotel. If it weren't for Stefhan picking up right where he left off at the restaurant, tracing lightly on my leg, I would have been terrified. When the hotel appeared in the distance, Stefhan's fingertip grazed against my swollen and throbbing clit. I had to clamp my mouth shut to keep myself from screaming. After almost two hours of his foreplay game, all I wanted and could think about was him deep inside me. I slid my hand up his pants and across his cock, a quiet hiss escaped his mouth. Jorge pulled into the hotel, and before the car was even fully stopped, Stefhan was already on the move. He handed him the money, took off his seatbelt, and opened the door the instant we stopped moving.

Within seconds, he was at my door. He was so fast that I didn't have time to take off my seatbelt. When he opened the door and saw this, he quickly reached across me and hit the release. He lifted me out of the car and gently placed me on my feet.

"Thank you, Jorge. Please be here tomorrow at four to pick us up," Stefhan said to the driver as set me down.

"My pleasure. I will see you then, Dr. and Mr. Storme." The words were barely out of his mouth before Stefhan was shutting the door.

"Come on, Dr. Storme. We're late for a meeting," Stefhan told me as he took my hand and marched us into the hotel.

"What meeting?" I asked him as he guided me through the lobby and to the elevator. He didn't answer me as he pushed the call button. "What meeting, Stefhan?" I asked him again. I told him I didn't want any surprises.

When the elevator doors opened, Stefhan pulled me inside, hit the button for our floor, and the button to close the doors. As soon as they were closed, he lifted me up and started kissing my neck. Electricity flowed through me like a lightning bolt each time his lips caressed my skin.

"This meeting," he breathed against my neck as he pressed his rock-hard cock against me. My core blazed anew and my pussy clenched. He kept kissing my neck as he started to lift up my dress.

"What if someone sees us?" I moaned into his hair. Not really caring enough to try and stop him.

"This is a private elevator. It only goes to the Presidential Suite. I could take you right now and no one would know," he growled as he lightly bit my mark.
That little bite sent a wave of sparks through me like I had never experienced. In response, I grabbed Stefhan's face, lifted it to mine, and crushed my lips against his. I ran my tongue across his bottom lip, instantly he parted them. I took advantage and slid my tongue in his mouth, then pressed

myself as close as I could to him and wound my hand in his hair. I was only vaguely aware when the elevator doors opened. Stefhan carried me off the elevator and straight to the bedroom where he set me gently on the bed and took off my shoes.

"Stand up, I don't want to ruin your dress," he told me as he started taking off his shoes. I stood up, reached behind my back, and pulled on the zipper; it didn't move. I pulled a little harder, still nothing. By this time, Stefhan had his shoes off and looked at me just in time to see my third attempt. "What's wrong?"

"My zipper is stuck," I told him as I turned around.

"I'll get it," he said and gave it a tug. Nothing. He adjusted his grip on the tiny tab and tugged again. "It's not moving," he explained as he gave it another forceful tug.

"Rip it off me," I told him as the fire in my core blazed once more.

"Are you sure?" he asked me as he tried the zipper again.

"Rip. It. Off. Me. Stefhan," I commanded him as I turned around to face him. All I wanted was him inside me, and this dress was in the way.

"If you say so," he said before turning me back around and grabbing the fabric next to the zipper.

With one swift motion, he ripped the fabric to just above my ass and let it fall to the floor. He turned me around, lifted me up, carried me to the bed, and laid me down. Then he quickly unbuttoned his shirt and took off his pants. While he was working on that, I unsnapped my bra, slid off my underwear, and threw them on the floor.

"So beautiful," he whispered as he positioned himself on top of me and pressed his lips to mine. Slowly and methodically, he kissed his way down my body. As he kissed, his hands explored, there wasn't a spot left untouched. As his skin caressed mine, my core felt once again like a volcano that was ready to blow. Ripples of pleasure flowed through me like hot lava as he traveled.

I wrapped one hand in his hair and clutched his arm with the other as he inched his way past my breasts and down my stomach. I could feel the juices flowing out of me. I let out a little whine when he stopped so he could reposition himself in between my legs.

"So impatient. For this?" he hummed as he flicked the tip of his tongue across my clit. The lava ebbed and flowed as he repeated the motion. His hands locked around my legs, holding them open as he started his oral assault. Heat waves of pleasure scorched every inch of my skin Even where his wasn't touching mine.

Tangling one hand in his hair and grabbing his shoulder with the other, he continued to eat my pussy like the last supper as I screamed and dug my nails into his flesh. Right as I was getting ready to cum, he stopped and got on his knees. He positioned his cock at my entrance, pushed just the tip in, and pulled it out. Before I could protest, he slid it back in, but just a little bit further, then pulled it back out. He repeated this pattern over and over. Each time only going a little bit deeper inside me. Each time he would pull out and re-enter me, the heat intensified.

When he was finally all the way inside me, he only increased his speed slightly. I clawed at his back as the heat consumed me, my entire body buzzing. Slowly he increased his speed as I wrapped my legs around him. He gently gripped my hips and lifted my bottom half slightly.

"Are you ready?" he asked as his eyes locked with mine.

"Yes," I moaned and pushed myself against him.

He adjusted his grip and did a test pump, making a few more adjustments to his hand placement and how he had me positioned. Each change got a test pump. When he was finally satisfied, he started to ram me full force. Each powerful thrust hit my g-spot. Between that and the pleasure current that consumed me, within seconds I was ready to cum.

"I'm going to cum!" I screamed as I clawed at any part of him that my fingers touched.

"Come for me," he commanded as he continued to punish my pussy in the best possible way.

Two thrusts later my pussy clamped around his cock and my body started to twitch. My orgasm was an eruption in every aspect, I shook uncontrollably, I saw stars, and my skin blazed. I pulled him against me as my juices ran down his shaft and rode the high. A few thrusts later Stefhan growled and released his load deep inside me. He collapsed beside me and laid his head on my chest.

"Let's get cleaned up," I said after a few minutes.

"We will when we're done," he told me without moving.

"When are we going to be done?"

"That was only round one. I'm just catching my breath," he answered as he sucked my nipple into his mouth, setting my core instantly ablaze.

We never made it to the shower. I fell asleep on his chest as we were catching our breath after the sixth round.

Stefhan ordered room service for breakfast that was actually closer to lunch. We didn't wake up until almost eleven. We watched TV while we ate, then we showered. My hair was a snarled mess and took me way longer than usual to tame it. It was three forty-five when I carefully unzipped the garment bag that protected my dress. Even though he didn't ask, I knew he was curious why I chose that dress. I'm glad he didn't–it wasn't a question I had the answer to. I knew I shouldn't want to wear it, but I felt the most beautiful I had ever felt in that dress. When I was standing in our closet trying to decide what to bring, something told me to wear it.

I didn't want people to think I was trying too hard. My makeup was simple and light. Stefhan braided my hair in a Stefhan original. I was speechless when he finally told me that most of the styles he did on my hair were his own creations. I stepped into the crimson, floor-length dress and zipped it up. I couldn't believe that Coral was able to alter it in time. I asked Stefhan if he was sure she wasn't part witch. He said she wasn't, but I'm not convinced.

I slid on my matching flats and walked to the living room to meet Stefhan. He was looking out the window with his back toward me. As he turned, it was like time slowed down. He was wearing a black tux with a shirt and cufflinks that matched my dress and his hair was down.

"Goddess, you are so beautiful," he whispered as he took me in. "I have something for you," he continued as he reached inside his jacket pocket and pulled out a jewelry presentation box.

We walked toward each other and met in the middle of the room. Without another word, he handed me the box. I waited a moment to see if he was going to say anything, but when he didn't, I opened it carefully. Inside was the most stunning necklace I had ever seen. A giant red stone was nestled in an outline of small black stones.

"It's gorgeous. I love it," I finally managed to spit out, knowing that my words didn't do it justice.

"I'm so glad you like it. It was my mom's, and before you say anything, Fern wanted you to have it too," he said softly as he took the necklace from me and placed it on my neck. "It's a cushion cut ruby surrounded by black diamonds." He glanced at his watch and then back to me. "It's time to go. Are you ready Dr. Storme?"

"No, but let's go."

Chapter Twenty-Six

"There may be some photographers taking pictures as we get out of the car and walk into the event," Stefhan told me as we made our way through Portland.

"What?" I asked him. While I had never been invited to the event before, I had read articles about it. There were never any pictures.

"This is the first time I'll be at an event with you. Everyone is curious to know who Stefhan Storme married. Plus, I think the board is trying to get an updated picture of me for my employee bio," he answered as he pulled me closer to him. My anxiety was nearly out of control. "Breath," he whispered to me. "I will get out first, you will slide to my side, and I'll help you out. Just keep a smile plastered on your face and your hand in mine. We're almost there," he continued as Jorge pulled onto SW Morrison.

It didn't take a genius to figure out where the event was being held. There were at least thirty photographers standing outside The Nines and a line of cars ahead of us. I watched as they snapped pictures of everyone getting out of their cars. It made me feel a little better that we weren't going to be singled out. When we got to the front of the building, Stefhan turned to me.

"Are you ready?" he asked with a smile.

"Nope, but let's do it," I replied and forced a smile.

"That looks painful. Don't use that one for the pictures," he whispered in my ear and kissed my mark, sending a shiver up my spine.

He took a breath and opened the door. The sound of camera shutters filled the air. The second he was visible, the yelling started.

"Stefhan! Can you look over here?" one photographer yelled.

"Is it true you brought your wife?" another shouted as Stefhan turned to help me out of the car. Stefhan gently helped me from the car and securely grabbed my hand.

"We are going to walk as fast as you can," Stefhan linked me as I put what I hoped was a natural smile on my face. I squeezed his hand in response.

"Mrs. Storme! Look this way!" someone yelled as we quickly walked.

"It's Dr," Stefhan corrected them without turning his head.

Before anyone could yell anything else, we made it inside. We followed the signs to a beautiful ballroom that looked like it could hold hundreds of people. There were about two hundred people already there, and every single one turned to look at us as we walked in.

"Stefhan!" a short woman with brown shoulder-length hair called out as she practically ran toward us.

"Baylor," he greeted the woman before turning to me. "Dani, this is Baylor, she's the head of the board." He then turned back to the woman. "Baylor, this is my wife, Dani."

"It is so nice to finally meet you! You look stunning!" she told me as she held out her hand.

"Thank you. It's nice to meet you too," I told her as I let go of Stefhan's hand to offer her mine.

"Follow me, the rest of the board is waiting," she told us as she turned and glided through the crowd.

A stream of names were thrown at me as I was rapidly introduced to all twelve members of the board. I was trying to make sure I caught every name, so I could play them back later. They all complimented me and called me every version of pretty I could think of. I thanked them, knowing the only reason they were saying it was because of Stefhan. I had been the keynote speaker at events and not gotten as many compliments on my looks as I did with the board.

"I'm sure we'll be seeing you all later. There are some people I would like to introduce Dani to," Stefhan told them after a few minutes of small talk. We walked around the room and Stefhan introduced me to a dozen more people. He was saying the names so fast that I couldn't catch them all. I said a prayer that I wouldn't need to remember them later.

"Please be ready to take your seats in fifteen minutes. Dinner will be served shortly," a female voice announced. I glanced to the stage to see Baylor standing with a microphone.

Stefhan guided me through the space and occasionally introduced me to someone. I met people from every part of Storme Medical, and each one kissed mine and Stefhan's asses. It got annoying real quick.

"Is this how it always is?" I had never been more thankful for the ability to link than I was at that moment.

"Unfortunately, but it's part of being the top wolf," Stefhan's voice said inside my head.

"The saying is top dog," I corrected him without thinking.

"I prefer not to talk about myself that way. It's not exactly an endearing term to wolves."

Stefhan kept looking at his watch, like he was waiting for something. He had looked at it four times since Baylor's announcement. After checking it for the seventh time, he started guiding me to the one part of the room we hadn't been to yet. He led me to a group of about forty people and to a middle-aged man with short blond hair.

"Mr. Storme!" The man exclaimed as we got closer. "I didn't know you were coming. I can't believe I didn't see you."

"It was a last-minute decision. With two little ones at home, it's harder to get away," Stefhan told the man as we closed the remaining space between us. "Bob, I'd like for you to meet my wife, Dr. Danielle Storme. Dani, this is Bob, the VP of our Human Resources Department."

"It's so nice to meet you, Bob," I said as I extended my hand.

"The pleasure is all mine, Dr. Storme."

"It looks like you have the majority of your team here," Stefhan said as he looked at the group.

"Yes, all fifteen of my directors are here," Bob said proudly.

"That's fantastic! I don't think I've met some of them before," Stefhan replied.

"Let me introduce you!" he told us before turning. "Team! If you could all gather round. Dr. and Mr. Storme are here to say hello," he called out to get their attention. I couldn't see anyone who was on the other side of Stefhan.

"Hi, Mr. Storme," I heard a voice I could never forget saying to Stefhan. "My name is Courtney Beach, Director at the Georgia office. It's so nice to meet you."

"It's nice to meet you. This is my wife, Dr. Storme," Stefhan responded as he stepped back to reveal me. She made a strange choking sound as she shook her head.

"It's nice to meet you, Dr. Storme," she finally spit out after giving her head a violent second shake. Before I could respond, Baylor announced it was time to eat and for us to all take our seats.

"It was a pleasure meeting all of you. I hope you all enjoy the rest of the evening," Stefhan said as soon as the announcement was over.

"Yes, it was so nice to meet you all," I called out as Stefhan guided me away from the group. I could feel Courtney's eyes burning into my back.

I didn't have time to wrap my head around what was happening before discovering that our table was directly next to Courtney's. I thanked the Goddess when we were seated with our backs to her. While it stopped me from having to look at her, it didn't stop me from being able to hear her hushed conversation.

"You do not know her," the woman sitting next to her whispered.

"Yes, I do, since kindergarten," Courtney told her.

"Well, she certainly didn't act like she knew you," the woman retorted, and I had to stifle a laugh. I forced myself to stop listening and focus on my own table. We were seated with members of the board, so it would have been rude to not be present.

"Stefhan, are you going to bring Dani on?" I heard Baylor ask when I checked back into the conversation.

"Well, that would be up to her. We have a lot going on at home with the kids. Our youngest isn't even six months old yet," Stefhan answered politely.

Stefhan talked with the board members as we ate. They were talking about Storme Medical things, and I had no clue what any of it meant. I mainly listened, only chiming in enough that I stayed involved. After we were done eating, Stefhan stood up.

"Will you dance with me?" he asked as he looked lovingly into my eyes and held out his hand. I took his hand and stood.

As he led me to the dance floor I whispered, "How is this going to work?" Anytime I had danced with him previously, it was impromptu, and he either picked me up or got on his knees. Neither option seemed appropriate in this situation. He didn't answer, he just kept walking and that made me nervous. When we got to the dance floor, he got on his knees and placed his hands around my waist. I could feel every eye in the room on us.

"Everyone is looking at us. Please get up," I begged as embarrassment flooded my cheeks.

"Just focus on me," he whispered against my cheek as he pulled me close to him. I shut my eyes, trying to block out the feel of hundreds of pairs of eyes, and let his scent consume me.

As we swayed back and forth, the eyes I could feel on us lessened. I could hear people joining us on the dance floor and starting to dance. I kept my eyes firmly shut as the song finished. Stefhan gently placed his lips on mine as the last note played and then slowly stood. When I opened my eyes, I wasn't surprised to see Courtney watching us, she was standing by the bar. Her eyes stayed locked as we strolled around the room.

"Do you want to get a drink before the auction starts?" Stefhan asked me.

"Sure. I'm going to the bathroom. I'll meet you at the bar," I told him as I looked to see Courtney still in the same spot.

"I'll save you a seat," he replied as he leaned down and kissed my cheek.

As I followed the signs indicating where the bathrooms were, I heard footsteps behind me. I didn't look behind me to see who they belonged to. I had to go around a corner and down a corridor. I was just about to open the door to the bathroom when I heard more footsteps, and they were coming fast. I turned my head to see Courtney barreling toward me.

"Are you really going to act like you don't know me?" she snapped. I didn't answer, opting to open the bathroom door instead. "Since when do *you* get to ignore *me*?"

"Why is it so important to you that I acknowledge you?" I asked her.

"It's not important to me. It's just rude," she retorted.

"It wasn't my intent to be rude," I told her politely. I knew she was trying to goad me. To get me to say something stupid that she could use against me later.

"Do you think you're better than me now?"

"I don't think I'm better than anyone," I told her calmly.

"Good, because you're not," she sneered at me.

"What do you want from me, Courtney?" I asked her as I pinched the bridge of my nose, trying to keep myself from screaming at her.

"I want to know how you did it," she snapped.

"Did what?" I asked, completely confused.

"Don't play fucking stupid. Stefhan Storme," she practically shouted.

"What about Stefhan?"

"Geeze! You used to be a lot smarter. You at least knew how to answer a simple question. But since I apparently have to spell it out for you. How did you convince Stefhan Storme to marry you? Hell, how did you even meet him? I'm pretty sure he's not into women that are covered in puke."

"Are you being serious? We're adults now. Can we act like it?" I knew the instant those words left my mouth it was going to set her off.

"Yes, I'm being serious! Us being adults doesn't change the fact that there is no way in hell that you could score a guy like Stefhan Storme without having some kind of dirt on him. There is no way he would choose to have sex with you," she hissed at me through her teeth. I took a deep breath before responding.

"While it's none of your business how I met Stefhan, I will tell you it had nothing to do with blackmail."

"Oh, come on! You may be able to fool all those people that don't know you," she told me as she pointed in the direction of the ballroom. "You may be Dr. Storme now, but I know who you really are."

"And who would that be?" I asked her as I felt rage building inside me. Rage that didn't belong to me.

"Damn Smell, the freakshow."

"What did you just call my wife?" Stefhan's voice suddenly asked, filling the small corridor. I watched as the color drained from Courtney's face.

"It's not what you think, Mr. Storme!" she cried as she turned around to see Stefhan standing at the end of the corridor.

"It's not is it?" he asked her as he walked and stood a few feet away from her. His massive frame took up so much room that there was no way for her to go around him.

"We, we were just talking," she stammered before looking at me, "Right, Dani?"

"Is that true, my love?" he asked me out loud before linking, *"I heard everything."*

"If you call asking me how we met and what blackmail I had on you to convince you to marry me? Then yeah, we were talking."

"That's not exactly how it went," Courtney quickly said. I watched as a small smile crossed Stefhan's lips.

"You say it went differently. Okay, let's hear it then."

"I was just playing. We know each other, I didn't realize she didn't know I was joking," she explained with the same plastered smile on her face that she had when we were kids. The one she used to get herself out of trouble.

"Was that before or after you called her stupid? Or was it when you said I would never choose to have sex with her?" he asked her as her eyes went wide. "You see, my wife may not want to tell you how she met me, but I will. I met her while she was head doctor at a Storme Medical Hospital in Florida. I was there on business and was going to see the dean. I ran into her in a hallway and thought she was the *most beautiful* woman I had ever seen. We didn't even get each other's names before parting ways. I thought I'd never see her again. She was then selected to be in the Fellowship. When she arrived, she met and became close with my sister, which in turn made her cross paths with me. *I* pursued *her* relentlessly, and after months she finally gave me a chance." Stefhan then leaned down and put his face close to hers. If it wasn't for the pure rage radiating off him, it would have seemed romantic.

"Let me fill you in on a little secret. I have sex with her every chance I get, six times last night as a matter of fact," he whispered in her ear before straightening back up. "Follow me, Miss Beach."

A look of pure shock rocked Courtney's features as she processed what he said. I was glad she wasn't able to see my face, I was sure it looked just as shocked as hers. Stefhan didn't wait for her to respond, he just turned around and started stalking back toward the main hallway.

"Where are we going?" she asked as she followed in his wake.

"To find Bob. I need to inform him about your immediate demotion," he told her as he turned to face her. "My love are you coming?" he asked me when he realized I hadn't moved.

"I still need to use the bathroom," I told him as I pulled on the door.

"We'll wait for you," he told me with a smile.

I quickly made my way into the bathroom. Thanks to Courtney's ambush, my bladder was ready to explode. I struggled for five minutes to get my dress up so I could even sit on the toilet. I almost linked Stefhan to ask for help but thought against it. Ten minutes after I went in, I finally made it out of the bathroom. Courtney looked a strange mix of scared, embarrassed, and shocked. Stefhan was standing with his arms crossed and a brilliant smile on his face.

"Ready?" he asked me as I walked to the main hallway where he was waiting for me with Courtney.

"Ye–" I started before he leaned down and pressed his lips against mine.

I was keeping a mental list of questions to ask Stefhan once we were alone. I added the kiss to my list. He slowly straightened up and wrapped his hand around mine. He didn't even glance at Courtney as we walked back to the ballroom. The second we walked in, over two dozen people turned to look at us. Thanks to the look on Courtney's face, they stayed glued on us. Stefhan looked around the room and quickly found Bob. I could hear people whispering as we walked by. They were all wondering what was going on.

"Bob, I need to talk to you," Stefhan told him as we approached. It was beyond evident in the tone of his voice that he wasn't happy.

"Of course," Bob hastily answered. "Is everything okay?" he asked as he saw Courtney.

"No, Bob, it's not," Stefhan answered.

"What's going on?" Bob asked as he continued to stare at Courtney.

"Effective immediately, Miss Beach is demoted to file clerk," Stefhan told him sternly.

"What? She's one of my best employees. Why?" Bob asked, completely shocked.

"I think that is a conversation best had later," Stefhan told him. I could feel the pure rage pouring off him.

"No disrespect Mr. Storme, but if you are going to demote my best director in the region to a file clerk at a charity event, I think I have a right to know why." Slowly, Stefhan let go of my hand and took a step closer to Bob.

"If you insist," he told Bob before yelling, "BAYLOR! BRING ME A MICROPHONE." He then turned back to Bob. "We'll make this a teaching moment for everyone." The color drained from Bob's face, moments later Baylor appeared with a microphone.

"Are you sure you want to do this, Stefhan?" Baylor asked as she handed him the microphone.

He didn't respond, just took it and raised it to his mouth.

"Attention ladies and gentlemen. May I have your attention please?" He waited for the room to quiet down. "I want to inform you all of an incident that happened tonight involving my wife and an employee. This employee thought it was okay to ask my wife personal questions about our relationship and call her very inappropriate names. A severe line was crossed and there will be consequences. I want you all to know that I will NOT tolerate this type of behavior. Not only against my wife but also anyone that works within Storme Medical. I do not tolerate bullying, and if anyone in this room or within the company feels the need to be one, they don't have a place here." He handed the microphone back to Baylor and looked at Bob. "I could fire her for what she said. Things I heard with my own ears. I don't want someone like that working in a leadership role, especially in Human Resources. I am beyond fair, Bob, you know that. The only reason I'm not firing her is because I believe that everyone deserves a second chance."

"I understand, Mr. Storme," Bob told him before turning to Courtney. "I want you in my office at 9 AM Monday."

We didn't stay for the auction. Stefhan wrote a check for two million dollars and gave it to Baylor. Steady waves of rage were pouring off his body, and I wasn't the only person who was feeling it. It was like a forcefield around him, the crowd gave us a wide berth as he led me out of the ballroom. We walked in silence to the lobby and outside to wait for Jorge.

Stefhan pulled out his phone, sent a text, and two minutes later Jorge was pulling up.

"Same deal as last night," he told Jorge after we were in.

"You got it," Jorge said with a smile as he shifted the car into gear and hit the gas.

This car ride was the polar opposite of the night before. Stefhan's rage was hitting me like a prized boxer. I held his hand and rubbed tiny circles with my thumb, trying to calm him. He was taking deep breaths, but the rage didn't relent. Jorge got us to the hotel in record time. Stefhan handed him the money and quickly got me out of the car. The silence continued as we walked through the lobby and to the elevator. On the outside looking in, it probably looked like we were having a fight. The look on Amy's face as we walked past the front desk confirmed my thoughts.

"Do you know how hard it was to not lose it on Courtney?" he asked me when the elevator doors closed.

"I'm pretty sure anyone within a thirty-foot radius could tell," I told him as I squeezed his hand.

"Hearing her talk to you like that and what she called you," he whispered as a tear rolled down his cheek and his rage flared. When the elevator doors opened and we made it inside, I decided to start asking the list of questions I had been compiling. I chose the one that aligned with what he had just said and not the one I was most interested in.

"What's the real reason you didn't fire her?" I asked him as we walked toward the bedroom.

"There were two reasons: First, what Bob said is true. She is one of the best HR directors in the southern region. That leads me to the second reason, I didn't want her coming after me for wrongful termination. Demoting her took that off the table. I personally have only fired one person. It was about five years ago, and it was my secretary. She was stealing money from me. Not Storme Medical, me directly. She was stealing my personal checks and filling them out to cash. Then using the stamp of my signature to endorse them, she would get them cashed. Marie brought it to my attention after she noticed three checks for fifty thousand dollars each were cashed over the course of two months.

"I called the bank and had them pull the video. I saw her on video cashing them, so I fired her and pressed charges. She came after me for wrongful termination, saying I gave her the checks to cash. It went through the courts for months. With everything going on, I didn't want to risk it."

"Okay. What did you say to her while I was in the bathroom?" I asked him.

"She asked me what I see in you. She really is stupid. I told her that you are perfect to me, and I am damn lucky that you tolerate me. I also told her that I eat your pussy like a buffet and fuck you until you scream my name very regularly."

"You did not!" I hissed at him.

"I did. I also told her that if she told anyone they would never believe her," he said with a sly smile.

I was suddenly exhausted and didn't have the mental capacity to deal with everything that had gone on. Stefhan helped me out of my dress, and I laid down. Once he was out of his tux, he laid next to me and pulled me close. I laid my head on his chest and breathed in this scent as I drifted to sleep.

Unforeseen Destinies

Chapter Twenty-Seven

I woke up to an empty bed and the smell of sausage in the air. I got up and threw on some leggings and a shirt before making my way toward the delicious smell. Stefhan was sitting at the beautifully set table, wearing only basketball shorts.

"I want to take you somewhere before we go home," he told me as I sat down at the table. His eyes were dancing with excitement.

"Am I allowed to ask where?"

"Nope, and all I'm going to tell you is that you can wear what you have on and there won't be anyone else there." I could feel his excitement and it was making me excited. We quickly ate and got packed to check out.

I almost had a stroke when the woman at the counter told Stefhan the total. He didn't bat an eye, just handed her his card and gave my hand a gentle squeeze. By the time we got outside, our car was waiting, and the bellboy was putting our bags in the trunk.

"I hope you enjoyed your stay," Arthur said as Stefhan helped me into the car.

"We did, Arthur. Thank you," he told him as he handed him and the bellboy each one hundred dollars.

"Are you ready?" he asked me excitedly once he was in the car.

"Let's do this," I answered with a smile.

Stefhan drove for over an hour. We headed in the direction of Crimson Diamond, but then he went west. Almost an hour and a half after we left the hotel, he pulled up to a tiny house on a beautiful lake. It reminded me of my house in Carmel. He pulled into a makeshift driveway, put the car in park, and shut off the engine. He got out, came to my side of the car, and opened my door.

"Come on," he said with a grin as he helped me out of the car.

"Whose house is this?" I asked him as he guided me to the front door.

"Yours," he answered as he reached into his pocket, pulled out a key, and put it in my hand.

"What? Mine? Stefhan, no," I rambled as I wrapped my hand around the key.

"Yes, yours. Look inside before you say no." His voice enveloped me, warming me from the inside out.

Slowly I put the key in the lock and opened the door. I walked in, looked around, and was shocked to see my furniture from Carmel. I walked slowly through the space. The living room was decently sized, and the dining room had a patio off it that overlooked the lake. The kitchen was on the smaller side, but I could reach all the cabinets. It had three bedrooms. The primary bedroom had its own bathroom and a patio that also overlooked the lake. The lake had a beach that wrapped halfway around, and lush forest surrounded the other half.

"Do you like it?" he asked me as we made our way back into the living room.

"I love it. I'm just really confused," I told him honestly.

"I bought it for you."

"Why?" I asked him, still confused. Stefhan walked over to me and dropped to his knees, so he was face-to-face with me.

"A few reasons. First, I know you miss the beach. Second, when we were in Florida, you said you liked it there because you had us all to yourself. You said we were our own little family unit," he explained as his dual-colored eyes burned into mine.

"That still doesn't explain why you bought me a house," I said as I tried to wrap my head around it.

"Now we have somewhere we can go with the kids where it's just us. We can be our own family unit. I know it's not the real beach, but I thought it was a nice compromise." I could feel the anxiety building inside him.

"You bought me a lake house, so we have somewhere that I can have you and the kids all to myself?" I asked him as my brain fully comprehended what was going on.

"Yes," he whispered. Tears filled my eyes and quickly spilled down my cheeks.

"I love you," I cried as I threw my arms around him and yanked him close to me.

"I love you, too. More than anything."

After I stopped crying, he walked me outside, so I could see the lake. As we walked, questions started popping into my head.

"How far are we from home?" I asked him as we stood on the beach.

"About forty-five minutes. I wanted somewhere that was close in case there was an emergency, but far enough away that we could actually get away."

"Who else knows about this?" I asked as I stared out at the water.

"I had to tell Marie that I was buying some property since she makes sure all the bills are paid and would have seen the check go through. I didn't tell her where it was. Outside of her, no one," he answered.

"How much property did you buy?"

"About one hundred acres. The back of it butts up against Crimson Diamond. If we went to the far southeast corner of the property, we would run into the security wall," he explained as he pointed to where I assumed was southeast.

I didn't ask him how much it cost. I didn't want to know.

We arrived home right before dinner. Cy was getting ready to feed Phoenix, and Jameson was playing with Max, who promptly stopped playing the second we walked into the room.

"Papa! Mama! You back!" he screamed as he ran to Stefhan.

I was thankful that Cy hadn't already heated up a bottle. I didn't want to mess with pumping. I took Phoenix and went to her room to feed her. Once we were settled, there was a knock on the door. A few seconds later, the door opened, and Cy walked in.

"How was the charity ball?" she asked me as she sat on the floor.

"You won't fucking believe what happened!" I told her before launching into the story.

"He demoted her to file clerk? I would have paid damn good money to see that," she said with a laugh when I finished.

"Speaking of money! Did you know Stefhan is worth seventy-seven billion dollars?" I shrieked at her.

"Yeah, anyone with Google does," she replied as she took in my face. "Don't tell me you never looked," she continued as she realized that this was new information to me.

"I never thought about it. I was more concerned with maintaining a coherent conversation with him."

"You also thought you were in a coma dream or had a tumor," she mused, making me laugh.

We kept talking while I fed Phoenix and changed her for bed. Cy gave me a recap of the entire weekend. I wasn't ready to lay Phoenix down yet, so I carried her to the living room where Stefhan promptly took her from me.

Cy and Jameson left after dinner. By the time they left, it was Max's bedtime. Stefhan took Max, while I took Phoenix. She had fallen asleep in her swing, so I just had to lay her down. Afterward, I went to the bedroom to change and wait for Stefhan. I threw on one of his tee shirts, plopped on the couch, and turned on the Discovery Channel. About twenty minutes later, he finally walked in and sat next to me on the couch. He pulled me close and took a deep breath. My core instantly ignited.

"Are you fucking kidding me," he suddenly whined as he pulled back. "Fern thinks they may have figured out how to find the corpse lily. She wants to come up with Luan, Vinnie, and Kal. This will have to wait," he continued as he pressed his rock-hard cock against me. I reluctantly got up and headed to the closet. "Don't change." His words sent a wave of excitement through me.

It took almost ten minutes for them to get here. Stefhan kept making comments under his breath about how if they didn't hurry up, he wouldn't be responsible for what they walked into. He had already pulled me onto his lap and started lightly biting at my mark when the living room door opened.

"We can come back later," Fern started as soon as she walked in and saw Stefhan's face buried in my neck.

"You're here now, and we'll be busy later," he told her as he repositioned me on his lap, but not moving me.

"Why are we still standing in the hallway?" Vinnie's voice called out from somewhere behind Fern.

"Because my brother needed to cover his erection."

"That was a little more than I needed to know," Vinnie told her as they filed in.

"Let's just get on with it. You said you think you figured out how to find the corpse lily," Stefhan told them, redirecting the conversation.

"Well not me, Lu," Fern told him as she looked at Luan.

"Before I begin, I need to tell you some of my history," Luan started, looking only at me. "You're the only person I haven't shared this with yet," he continued before taking a deep breath. "Years ago, my pack was attacked by a group of vampires. My little sister was killed in the attack. I vowed revenge. That is why I didn't become Alpha; I was hunting vampires." Images of Vinnie turning to smoke and appearing on Stefhan's back flashed in my mind. "Hunting vampires isn't easy, as I'm sure you can imagine. I was constantly looking for something to help me find them." He paused before looking at Stefhan. "I heard a story about a very remote pack of wolves in Borneo that vampires refuse to go anywhere near. It is said to be surrounded by the final death," he started before Stefhan stopped him.

"So, it's surrounded by the sun?"

"May I?" Vinnie cut in before Luan could answer.

"Of course. You're the one who confirmed it wasn't merely a story," Luan told him.

"I don't have personal experience, so it could still be just a story. But it is one that is known to vampires, and we don't go there," Vinnie corrected Luan before turning his attention to Stefhan. "About two thousand years ago, stories started floating around about vampires going missing after traveling to what is now Borneo. The few that made it back said the air smelled like death and their powers were affected. They said they weren't able to move as fast, but it wasn't just their speed. It was every advantage that a vampire has.

"About a thousand years ago, I met someone who claimed they had gone there with their partner. She told me that when they first arrived everything was fine. She said as they traveled into the rainforest the smell of rotting flesh began

353

to fill the air. They ignored it, thinking it was just some animal that met its end. Circle of life and all that. She said as they walked deeper into the rainforest, the worse the smell got.

"They decided to turn around when the smell still wasn't getting any better and they started to feel disoriented. Right as they turned to run back the way they came; a wolf attacked her partner. It is impossible for anything to sneak up on a vampire. She said neither one of them heard it. When she ran, her speed was no more than a human's. If there had been another wolf there, she wouldn't have gotten away. Moral of the story: Vampires that want to live don't go to Borneo."

"Okay, so we know that vampires don't go there, but that doesn't have anything to do with the flower," Stefhan said after Vinnie was done. I could feel his irritation.

"During my travels, I ran into a friend from an ally pack," Luan explained. "I was talking to him about it. He's the one who told me that the entire pack lands are lined with enormous red flowers that smell like death. He said there is something about the flowers that is a natural repellent to vampires. I know it's not a total confirmation, but it's better than nothing."

"So, what's the plan then?" Stefhan asked him.

"Fern and I will go to Borneo, find the pack, and see if it's the right flower. If it's not, we will at least be in the right place to find it."

I watched as Stefhan thought about Luan's plan.

"While I'd rather know for sure it is before you go running off, we don't have much of a choice. You're right, it's all we've got, and it has to be looked into. I don't want you to take the plane all the way to Borneo in case someone is watching you. Find somewhere close that you can fly into and then fly to Borneo from there."

I tried my best to stay in the conversation, but Stefhan's fully erect cock pressing against my pussy made it difficult. Every so often he would shift slightly, causing it to rub against me. My panties were soaked, and I knew the shirt I wore had a wet spot. Stefhan was completely composed, seemingly oblivious to the situation in his lap.

For the next twenty minutes, they talked about when they should leave and where they would land first. They debated the pros and cons of flying commercially the entire way. But they decided that Fern and Luan were going to fly into Indonesia on Stefhan's jet and then to Borneo commercially.

"You'll leave in a week. This will give us enough time to secure your flight and for you to put together a plan for when you get there. You don't need to be trekking aimlessly through the rainforest," Stefhan told them as they made their way to the door.

"Sounds good, see you tomorrow. Have a good night," Fern replied as she wiggled her eyebrows. That little motion made me think of something I hadn't thought of before and pure embarrassment flooded me.

"What's wrong?" Stefhan asked me as soon as the door was shut.

"Can all male wolves smell when I'm horny?" I asked him as I felt my cheeks turning red.

"No, only I can smell how turned on you are for this," he whispered into my neck as he pressed his cock against me. A soft moan escaped my lips.

Without a word he stood up, picking me up with him, and started walking toward the bedroom. On his way, he paused at each of the kids' rooms, opening the door to make sure they were sleeping. The second he stepped across the threshold of our room, there was an instant shift in his energy and my core blazed. He set me down in front of the bed and stood in front of me, his massive frame towering.

"You will do what I say when I say it. Do you understand?" he asked me, a sexy authoritativeness saturating his tone.

"Yes," I immediately answered, excitement coursing through me.

"What happens if you don't?" he asked as he pulled off his shirt.

"I get punished."

"Good girl," he praised me. "Shirt off," he continued. I was slightly confused that he wanted me to keep my underwear on, but I did what I was told. He took half a step back, looked at me, and tilted his head to the side. "Take your hair down." He watched, keeping his head tilted as I took out my braid and shook out my hair. I could tell he was debating on what he wanted to do next. I just stood there waiting for his next command. After what seemed like an eternity, he straightened his head and locked his eyes with mine. "Undress me. Slowly."

A wave of excitement coursed through me as I took a step forward and placed my hands on him. As I slid my fingers down his perfectly sculpted chest, a soft growl escaped his lips. I traced along his V-line before slipping my fingers in between the waistband of his shorts and skin. My fingertip grazed the tip of his cock as I positioned my hands. I hooked my fingers around the fabric of his shorts and started to pull them down. I had to slide one hand over to make sure the elastic band cleared his cock. When I had them low enough, I let them fall to the floor. I could see the precum on his tip, and the urge to lick it bubbled inside me. I fought the urge and waited, my eyes never leaving his glistening cock.

"Do you want to lick it?"

"Yes," I immediately answered. He took a step forward, so the tip barely grazed my lips. I didn't move.

"Yes, what?"

"Yes, Alpha." As I answered, my lips grazed his tip. I could feel his precum on my lips.

"Go ahead." The second the words were out of his mouth, I licked my lips and flicked my tongue across the tip. Excitement coursed through me as a hiss escaped his mouth and he placed his hands on my shoulders. I wrapped a hand around his shaft and sucked his head into my mouth. "Fuck," he hissed as I slowly slid down his shaft. I took as much as I could comfortably before pulling my head back. I closed my eyes and swirled my tongue around the head.

Slowly I slid my mouth up and down his cock a couple more times before increasing my speed. He tightened his grip on my shoulders and growled. I took as much of him as I could, using my hand to stroke what I couldn't.

"Don't stop," he commanded. My eyes were watering, and I could feel the spit running down my chin. I felt his cock twitch in my mouth as his hot cum shot down my throat. I kept sucking until I was sure I got every drop before releasing him. He bent over, grabbed his shirt, and wiped my face.

"Get on the bed." I instantly complied and sat in the middle. Stefhan didn't follow me, instead, he went to the closet. A few moments later, he emerged with a tie in one hand and the other behind his back. He climbed on the bed and sat behind me, making sure I never saw his other hand. "Close your eyes," he whispered in my ear, sending goosebumps across my skin.

He positioned the tie over my eyes and laid me back. Something soft touched my face, causing me to jump. "Relax," he whispered as the same soft thing traveled down my neck and grazed against my mark. The sensation caused chills to cover my body. The softness slowly traveled down my arms and across my breasts. As it made its way to my stomach, I realized it was a feather. When the feather reached my underwear, it was replaced with Stefhan's hands. Deftly he slid them off and the feather continued its journey.

Lightly it traveled down and up my right leg before moving to my left. I could feel my juices soaking into the sheet under me as he ran the feather along the inside of my thigh. Suddenly his beard grazed against my breast before I felt his lips on my mark. It was exhilarating not knowing where he would touch me next. My pussy throbbed as the feather went across the skin directly above my clit, then I felt his beard graze against my thigh; my body tensed, and my hand started to raise.

"So impatient. Relax," he breathed against the skin on my inner thigh. I took a couple of deep breaths, letting his scent fill my nostrils. I lowered my hand and focused on relaxing. When I was fully relaxed, I felt his lips brush against the tender skin of my inner thigh. I willed myself to stay relaxed as he kissed his way closer to my aching bud. Suddenly his tongue flitted across my clit, a moan escaped my mouth, and sparks shot through my body. I continued to focus on relaxing as he languidly licked my clit and increased his speed. When he slid a finger inside me, I nearly came undone. My pussy walls clenched around his finger and my body tensed.

"Not yet. Relax," he commanded me between licks. I took a deep breath and focused, once again, on relaxing. When I relaxed, he removed his finger and moved away from me. Before I could fully register the change, his finger was replaced with his cock. I moaned as he filled me completely. Slowly he pushed and pulled his cock in and out.

He grabbed my hand and wrapped my arm around his neck. He increased his speed and hungrily kissed my neck. Each thrust and kiss sent explosions through my body. My walls clenched around him as he rammed me with reckless abandon. My orgasm was building, and I wasn't sure how long I could keep it back.

"Do you want to cum?" he asked me right as I was losing the battle.

"Yes!"

"Yes, what?" he roared as he continued to slam his cock in and out of me.

"Yes, Alpha!" I screamed

"Cum for me!" he commanded. My orgasm exploded with the force of an atom bomb. My body shook and I saw stars. Stefhan kept his vigorous speed, while I rode out my orgasm. As I was coming down, he gave one more hard thrust and came deep inside me.

Chapter Twenty-Eight

STEFHAN

The next week was full of heavy prepping and light planning. Once Fern and Luan's flight from Indonesia to Borneo was booked, there wasn't much else that could be planned. I wasn't comfortable with them just trekking through the rainforest, trying to find some mystery pack that we had no confirmation even existed. The night before they were leaving, I was a bundle of nerves.

"You're going to wear a hole in the carpet," Dani called to me from the bedroom doorway.

"I got a few more miles before there's any real damage," I told her with a forced smile. She shut the door behind her and walked to where I was pacing.

"They'll be okay," she assured me as she wrapped her arms around me. I dropped to my knees, wrapped my arms around her, and buried my face in her neck.

"We have no plan other than how they are getting there. I don't like the idea of them walking aimlessly through the rainforest," I confessed into her hair.

"I'm sure Luan knows how to survive in the rainforest."

"But Fern doesn't!" The words popped out of my mouth before I could stop them. Dani leaned back, so she could look at me. I had been keeping my fears to myself. I didn't want to risk speaking them into existence.

"Is this what all the worrying is really about?" she asked softly.

"Yes, and before you say it, I know she's an excellent fighter and can take care of herself."

"Then why are you worried?" she asked when I didn't continue. I took a deep breath, letting her scent fill and calm me.

"Fern has very minimal real-world experience. She's only left Oregon to go on family vacations and only left the US when they went to find Kal. If she gets separated from Luan...."

Images of the horrible things that could happen to her flashed in my head. I shuddered at the thought of what all could go wrong.

"That's a valid reason to be worried."

"It should be me going with Luan," I whispered. It went against the Alpha in me to sit on the sidelines, but I understood why I couldn't.

"I know it's hard, and it's okay to be worried," she comforted me. "Let's lay down."

Slowly I stood and followed her to the bed. She pulled me close to her, and I took a deep breath, trying to calm my nerves.

"I swear to the Goddess, Stefhan!" Fern shouted at me after I asked her for the fifth time if she had everything.

"I just want to make sure," I told her as Luan put their backpacks in the car.

"She can only take about eight things. She didn't forget anything," Kane grumbled at me.

"Link me the second you land in Indonesia and when you get to Borneo. I expect daily updates." I could feel Dani's eyes on me as I told Fern my expectations.

"I'm going to be fine, Stef," Fern answered and pulled me in for a hug.

"Daily. Updates. Fern," I repeated.

"I'll link you so much you'll tell me to shut up," she laughed before linking, *"I know you're worried about me going and you think it should be you. You know why it has to be this way. Lu won't let anything happen to me. I'll check in every day."*

"I know, but it doesn't make it easier," I replied as I pulled back and opened her car door. She turned and hugged Dani before getting in.

"We'll be back before you even have time to miss us. Love you!" Fern called out the window as they left.

"Now what?" Dani asked as we watched their taillights disappear out of the garage.

"We make sure Cy can do her part when they get back."

I didn't like that so much was depending on Cy. Dani had more faith in her than I did. She was getting better at harnessing her magic, but she wasn't near where she needed to be. If she couldn't brew the potion and open the portal, we were fucked. She was training six days a week and the Meadows' were having her make all kinds of potions and practice different types of spells. One of these potion-spell combos turned Dani's hair brown for two days.

Fern actually sent me daily updates. After arriving in Borneo, they tracked down a local pack and found out that the mystery pack did exist. Their pack lands were a four-day walk into the rainforest.

FERN

I discovered very quickly that I didn't like extreme hiking. The humidity was intense, and the air was thick. We walked in human form during the day and shifted to eat and sleep. Callie and Batté were much better equipped for those tasks in the rainforest. I asked Lu why we couldn't let Callie and Batté handle the trekking, too. He said being in wolf form could come across as a threat.

I sent Stefhan his daily updates. They were boring until we were two and a half days into the rainforest. The smell of rotting flesh began to float in with the breeze. I never thought I would be happy to smell rotting flesh, but it meant we were going in the right direction. There were times I was worried that we were walking in circles.

As we walked, the smell got stronger. After another full day of walking, the smell was overpowering. The rainforest became eerily quiet as we walked.

"We're not alone," Lu's voice suddenly echoed in my head. *"Keep walking and act natural."*

"Who are you and what are you doing here?" a voice called out.

"My name is Luan, and this is my mate, Fern. We are looking for a special flower," Lu answered the voice.

"What is your pack and who is your Alpha?" the voice asked. It was impossible to tell where it came from.

"Crimson Diamond and Stefhan Storme," Lu answered as his eyes searched the thick trees and brush.

"You don't sound like you are from an American pack," the voice countered.

"I am originally from Lago de Ametista. I joined Crimson Diamond when I met my mate," he explained.

"That's not common," the voice mused. "Why would you leave your pack?"

"I don't see how that is relevant."

"It's not. I was just curious," the voice responded. "You said you were looking for a flower. What flower are you looking for?"

"We are looking for the stinking corpse lily."

"Why are you looking for that flower?" the voice asked him.

"If you want to know, you'll have to come out of your hiding place." A man stepped out from behind a tree about twenty yards away and strolled toward us.

"Why are you looking for the stinking corpse lily?" the man asked again.

"It's a rather long story," Lu started before the man cut him off.

"Short version."

"Short version. My mate's nephew is the Sapphire Wolf, and we need it to help fulfill the prophecy," Lu told him bluntly and I nearly choked.

"Is this true?" the man asked, looking at me.

"Yes," I answered.

"Wait here," he commanded us suddenly before disappearing into the thick trees and vines.

"We are not alone," Lu linked me as he sat down against a tree. I followed his lead and sat across from him. We sat there for over an hour waiting before the man returned.

"My Alpha wishes to speak to you. Follow me," he told us before turning back the way he came.

We followed the man deeper into the rainforest. We walked for almost twenty minutes when I saw the first signs of civilization. The path was well-worn, and the thick trees and brush started thinning. As the man guided us through the village, it reminded me of Lago de Ametista. He took us to a large hut and knocked on the door before opening it.

"Welcome to Bulan Hitam. I am Alpha Cempaka." The most beautiful woman I had seen welcomed us as we walked in.

"It's a pleasure. I am Luan and this is my mate, Fern," Lu greeted her as we both bowed in respect.

"Bissam tells me that you are related to the Sapphire Wolf. Is this true?" she asked as her dark brown eyes locked with mine.

"Yes, it is. My brother and his mate are the parents of the Sapphire Wolf," I answered.

"Your brother's mate is the Fire Wolf?" she asked.

"Yes."

"And you are both descendants of the first four?" Cempaka asked as she looked back and forth between us.

"Yes," Lu answered.

"Lopes or Heroux?" she asked him.

"Lopes and Red Storm," he answered as he pointed from himself to me.

"Do you have the fourth and the walking dead?" Cempaka asked him as her eyes filled with shock.

"I'm not sure what you mean?" Lu asked in return. I could tell he wasn't comfortable with the line of questions anymore.

"Have you found the fourth descendant and the vampire?" she asked us bluntly.

"Yes," he answered her before linking me. *"Something is telling me to be honest."* No sooner did he finish before Cempaka gasped.

"This is it," she whispered to herself before turning her attention back to us. "I apologize for the strange questions, but I had to make sure it was really you. I've been anticipating your arrival," she told us as she dug through a drawer in her desk.

"Anticipating our arrival?" Lu asked her, completely puzzled.

"Oh, yes. You see, a few years ago the Moon Goddess came to me in a dream. She told me that two strangers would come and need a stinking corpse lily. She told me that I needed to help these strangers, but I had to make sure they were the right people. She told me that you would be descendants, and you would be related to the Sapphire Wolf. She said that when you arrived here, you would already have all four descendants and a vampire. I thought it was just a dream. Imagine my surprise when Bissam told me that you were here," she explained as excitement danced in her eyes.

"So, you will help us get the stinking corpse lily?" I asked her.

"Of course. It is Selene's will. I assume there is more to this than just guiding you to them."

"We need to pick it on the fourth day of bloom," I told her, excitement stirring inside me. This was turning out to be easier than we thought.

"Then I hope you have some time to spare," she told us as she walked to the window.

"How much time are we talking?" Lu asked her.

"Anywhere from three to six weeks. You are more than welcome to stay here in my guest hut until the bloom."

STEFHAN

"I got good news, and I got bad news," Fern's voice echoed in my head. *"Which do you want first?"*

"The good news," I replied as I gently shifted Dani off my chest, so I could go into the bathroom.

"We found the Bulan Hitam pack, and Alpha Cempaka is going to help us. She said Selene came to her in a dream a few years ago and told her that me and Lu would be coming and she needed to help," Fern explained.

"What's the bad news?" I immediately asked.

"The stinking corpse lily isn't due to bloom for another three to six weeks." A wave of relief washed through me as Fern delivered the bad news.

"That's honestly better than what I was imagining," I confessed as I walked back to bed and laid down, pulling Dani close to me.

"Do I still need to check in every day?" Fern asked as I got settled.

"It would make me feel better if you did," I told her honestly. I knew that Luan would keep her safe, but for our entire lives it was my job to look after her, and I wasn't going to stop.

"Okay, Stef. I'll let you get to bed," she started before I cut her off.

"What does Bulan Hitam mean?" I asked her. I knew that would be the first thing Dani would ask me, so I wanted to make sure I knew the answer.

"Black Moon. Tell Dani and the kids I love them. Night Stef, love you."

"I will. Love you, too."

Dani couldn't get over the fact that Black Moon had a female Alpha. "How does that happen?" she asked me as we talked after Fern's week three, day two update of still no blooms. Fern had taken to delivering them like diary entries.

"The same way a male becomes Alpha, by birth or force," I told her as I pulled her close.

"Why does Fern send you updates at almost midnight?"

"To irritate me," I said with a laugh.

"I need to talk to you," Dani said seriously, changing the entire tone of the conversation. I knew something had been bothering her, but when I asked, she said she wasn't ready to talk about it. Which meant she thought it was going to hurt my feelings.

"Okay," I told her as I pulled her a little closer.

"With Phoenix getting her scent"–she had gotten her scent the week before– "it got me thinking about my heat. How often do they come?"

"Are you feeling okay?"

"I feel fine. I just don't like not knowing my own body and how it works."

I didn't have a scientific explanation like I knew she wanted. I took a deep breath.

"It's different for every couple, and there isn't an explanation," I told her, knowing she wouldn't be satisfied.

"What does that mean?" she asked as she adjusted herself to look at me.

"Every wolf is different. My mom only had one heat, and you've had two. I think this may be a better conversation for you to have with Carlos. Heat one-oh-one wasn't in my Alpha training," I confessed before adding, "Do you want to have another baby?" I watched her face as she thought about it.

"I don't know," she finally answered after a few minutes. "I'm not totally against the idea. I just don't think it would be a good one until we complete the prophecy." Excitement coursed through me as she spoke. "Do you want to?" she asked me suddenly.

"I want to have as many as you do," I told her.

"I'm being serious, Stefhan."

"So am I. I would have a litter of pups with you if that's what you wanted."

Aside from the kids, I spent the next three weeks alone, waiting for Fern's updates. Dani took my comment about talking to Carlos seriously. Once I got home from training, she would start studying werewolf medicine. She spent basically every waking moment reading and taking detailed notes. It made it easy to picture what she had been like in medical school.

Jay was helping Cy with her magic. While I was in a better place with Cy, I still limited my contact. And Cy was spending a lot of time with Vinnie. Along with her parents, he was helping her with her magic, thinking he would be able to give her pointers since he also had to learn how to harness his magic later in life. Kal was wherever Vinnie was. My dad didn't want company.

Chapter Twenty-Nine

JAMESON

Bleach had nothing on the smell that had taken up residence in my quarters. It was like nothing I had ever experienced. The near-nauseating mix of failed and successful potions clung to every surface, there was no escape. There was also no way to get rid of it. It had to dissipate on its own, and that wasn't going to happen anytime soon. Cy was making at least ten potions a day. She would make the same one over and over until she got it right. When they were right, the smell was amazing, but until then it was the opposite of amazing.

"Can you please ask her to take a break, bro?" Zeke pleaded with me.

"There are multiple reasons I can't do that, and you know them all," I reminded him. Not only would it get me hit, but Stefhan made it clear that she needed to be ready when Fern and Luan got back with the stinking corpse lily. And she had nowhere else to practice. Vinnie wouldn't let her brew potions at his place after it took two days for the smell to be completely gone.

"I know, but it smells so bad," Zeke whined.

"You think I don't know that? Try smelling it firsthand! Just focus on the good-smelling ones," I snapped at him right

as another failed attempt made its way to the living room, causing the room to spin.

"SHIT! That was worse than the last one! How is that even possible?" I heard Cy shriek from the kitchen.

I faked a link from Stefhan, so I could get some fresh air. I was pretty sure Cy knew I was lying, but she didn't call me out. At first, I had no destination in mind, but eventually, I decided to go to the gym. I stopped in the big kitchen and grabbed a couple of waters and a muffin. I ate the muffin as I walked. I was feeling back to normal by the time I got to the gym. I threw the door open and was surprised to see it wasn't empty.

"Beta puppy!" Vinnie called to me as he clapped his hands.

"Hey, Vinnie!" I called back as I walked toward him.

"How is Cy doing with potion making?" he asked me as he lightly punched the heavy bag.

"She's improving," I told him as I moved into position and held it for him.

"Improving?" he asked as he raised his eyebrows. "Beta puppy, you smell like a swamp and smelly gym socks. That mixed with your natural wet dog scent is making for an interesting combo," he continued as he wrinkled his nose.

"I said improving, not perfect," I laughed.

"You know your house is going to smell forever." Vinnie started hitting the bag a little harder.

"I didn't know vampires worked out," I said, trying to change the subject.

"Most don't, we don't technically need to." He hit the bag with a little more force.

"Then why are you working out?" I asked him completely dumbfounded.

"It's a good stress reliever. Whichever human said that was right," he answered me and then mused to himself. We took turns for the next twenty minutes holding and hitting the heavy bag in silence. "Do you think she'll be ready?" he asked me suddenly as we switched places.

"What?" I asked, trying to figure out if I missed something.

"Cy. Do you think she'll be ready by the time Fern and Luan get back?" he clarified.

"I think she will be," I answered way too fast.

"How many first-time successful potion and spell combos has she achieved?" his eyes held a small glimmer of hope.

"None," I said honestly and watched the glimmer vanish.

"I don't want to die."

"You're not going to d–"

"You don't know that Jameson!" Vinnie shrieked at me. I was so shocked that he called me by my name that I couldn't respond. "Kal tells me to think of the victories and not the struggles, but it's not that easy. So, what if she can harness and focus her physical magic? It means nothing if she can't brew the potion correctly. She won't have unlimited practice runs!" He was nearly shouting at me by the time he finished.

I didn't know what to say, he was right. Vinnie was able to help her harness her physical magic in a little over a week. She could now manifest and choose the intensity at will. But in the grand scheme of things, it meant nothing, and he had every right to be worried. Cy would have one shot at brewing the potion correctly. And we wouldn't know if it was right until Vinnie drank it and she cast the spell.

"I would be scared shitless if I was him, bro," Zeke softly whispered.

"Luck has been on our side for this long," I tried calming him.

"Oh, cut the shit! We can't depend on luck! Luck runs out. Do you call what happened to Stefhan's mom or the former Gamma puppy lucky? I can't depend on luck, I have to depend on Cy and her getting it right," he said before taking a breath. "I'm sorry, I shouldn't have freaked out on you. It's just a lot."

"It's okay. I did interrupt your workout. I kinda asked for it," I said with a laugh. While Vinnie was always dramatic, it was hard to see him like that.

"No, there is no excuse. I knew what I was signing up for when I lost my mind and joined this werewolf pack. I've known for more years than I care to remember that this could be my end." There was a resolve in his eyes that told me he was preparing for the worst.

"Can I ask you a question?" I asked him quickly.

"Of course you can. It doesn't mean I'll answer it," he replied as he grabbed the heavy bag for me to start hitting it.

"Who's the coolest person from history that you've met?"

"Well, that certainly didn't go where I thought it was going. Let me think," he said as I started punching the bag. "If I had to pick one, I would have to say Vlad Tepes," he answered after a few seconds as he looked at me expectantly. "You have no clue who that is, do you?" he asked me after a few more seconds of me not responding. "I swear you all need to read more. I can't even joke with you," he continued.

"Joke?"

"Yes, joke. Vlad Tepes was better known as Vlad the Impaler or Dracula," he explained with a sigh.

"I read and I know who that is. I just didn't know his real name," I told him defensively.

"Okay, okay, no need to get all huffy," he told me with a laugh. "Truthfully though, I don't have one. I didn't go around crashing parties in ancient Egypt or anything. I kept to myself. Survival was my number one priority," he continued with a shrug.

"What happens if you don't eat for longer than four days?" I knew I shouldn't ask him, but I was curious. He never said what would happen, just that we wouldn't like it.

"I'm surprised it took someone this long to ask me," he mused to himself. "I will start to go into blood lust. I'm just going to assume you don't know what it means and break it down for you. As you know, vampires must consume blood. What you don't know is why. It's not for nutritional value, it keeps us from going into blood lust. It's a preservation tool to make sure we can't starve ourselves to death. Once a vampire is in full-blown blood lust, there is no reasoning with them. They will feed on anything with blood. I would kill Kal without thinking twice."

"How long does it take to go into full-blown blood lust?" I was completely intrigued, and it was smart to know these things.

"It depends on the vampire. It affects everyone differently. I have never gone completely off the deep end. I've only gone without eating for longer than four days once, and it wasn't long after that I killed my maker. I wanted to see if he was lying to me about what would happen. It started out not that bad. I was just cranky, but who isn't cranky when they're hungry. As the hours slowly passed, all I could think about was eating. I went for a walk and quickly had to turn around. I could hear the blood flowing through the veins of the people I passed on the street. I found myself thinking about how fast I could drain someone. Even when I didn't have a donor, I never killed my meals after I killed my maker. I made it six and half days before I killed a sheep to come to my senses long enough to make it my donor."

"A sheep?"

"Yes, a sheep. I said anything with blood, the source doesn't matter. Out of everything I said, that's what you get hung up on," he said as he rolled his eyes.

"Can I ask you something else?" I knew I should probably shut up, but I had so many questions.

"Go for it," Vinnie laughed as we switched places, and he started hitting the bag.

"How strong are you?"

"I'm not sure," he answered between hits.

"How can you not know how strong you are?" my mouth asked before my brain could stop it.

"Honestly, I haven't had to use it. With the other gifts I possess, I don't need to overpower someone." As he answered, a thought crossed my mind.

"Don't be stupid, bro," Zeke's voice echoed in my head as he saw where my thoughts were going.

"Wanna find out?" I asked him, ignoring Zeke completely.

"And just how do you propose I do that? I don't think Cy or Stefhan would approve of me breaking you," Vinnie replied with a smile.

"Not hit me, the heavy bag," I told him and Zeke. I wasn't so dumb that I would let him hit me. I watched as Vinnie thought about it for a couple of minutes. His poker face was like nothing I had ever seen before. Utterly blank.

"Let's do it. Do you want to hold the bag, or do you want me to just hit it?"

"I'll hold it," I replied as I adjusted my stance.

"Okay. Do you have a good grip on it?" I gave him a firm head nod and tightened my grip. He took a step back, and a deep breath, before drawing his arm back.

The next thing I knew, I was being lightly smacked in the face and Vinnie was calling my name.

"What happened?" I asked as I realized I was laying on the ground.

"Well…when I hit the bag, you flew back about twenty feet and hit your head. Are you okay?"

"Yeah, I'm good," I told him as I sat up and looked around. I was halfway across the gym from the heavy bag.

"Come on Beta puppy, let's get you up," he said as he offered me his hand. The hairs on my neck instantly stood on end when my skin touched his. I ignored it and tightened my grip as he pulled me up with ease. "I'm going to head home, one concussion is my limit," he continued when I was on my feet.

"I should probably get home, too," I told him as I gave my head a shake to clear it.

The smell had not improved when I got back to my quarters. Vinnie's comparison of swamp water and smelly gym socks was pretty spot on. Cy was cursing in the kitchen; I shut the door loud enough that she would hear it. I headed to the kitchen to check on her progress or lack thereof.

"Did you take care of what Stefhan needed you to?" she asked me as I walked in.

"Yeah. How's it coming along?" I replied quickly to take the attention off of me. I hadn't come up with a reason why Stefhan needed me.

"I finally got the last one right after eight tries. This is attempt three on this one," she answered as she dumped something into the pot she was stirring. I watched quietly as she added more ingredients and continuously stirred. "The last ingredient, if I did it right, will smell like candy and turn green," she whispered as she dropped in what looked like coarse salt. The second it hit the potion, it turned a bright red and the smell of rotten eggs filled the air. "Son of a bitch!" she yelled as she grabbed the pot to dump it. "I don't fucking get it, Jam! I did everything exactly how it says," she told me as she pointed at the book she had propped up.

"You'll get it, babe," I said as I wrapped my arms around her waist.

"It shouldn't be this hard to make a potion that will make sweet things sour." She sounded so defeated.

"Your parents said potions work is hard. You'll get it," I encouraged her.

"What if I don't?" she whispered as she hung her head.

"You will." I turned her around and lifted her face, so I could look into her eyes.

"You don't know that. I've been nothing but a fuck up my entire life. I wasn't lying about that."

"Don't say that" I started before she covered my mouth with her hand.

"I have literally one fucking shot to get this right, and the only way we will know is to sacrifice Vinnie. I have exactly zero first-time solo successes in magic. I don't want to kill my friend," she said as the tears rolled down her cheeks.

"I don't think you will. I may not have magic, but I've seen how far you've come. You got this, just remember what your mom told you," I reassured her from behind her hand.

"What do you mean you don't have magic? You literally turn into a wolf," she told me as Zeke whispered, *"She's got you there, bro."* I ignored him and focused on what Cy was saying. "I do remember what she said. I have let my intent fill me. All I do is focus on how I don't want to kill Vinnie, and you've seen how that's panned out."

"That's it! That's what you're doing wrong," I nearly yelled as it hit me.

"Care to share?" she snapped at me when I didn't immediately continue.

"You said you are focusing on not wanting to kill Vinnie. You should be focusing on wanting to learn magic. Once you learn, you won't have to worry about killing him," I explained, and her face started to soften. "What's it going to hurt to just try it?" I continued.

"I'm willing to try anything. Let's do it," she said as she turned around and grabbed her pot. She took deep breaths as she rinsed the last remnants of the bright red potion down the sink, then carefully dried and set the pot down. I watched as she added and stirred the ingredients. She hesitated slightly as she grabbed the coarse salt and added it to the pot. The room was instantly filled with the smell of sour candy and the potion turned a brilliant shade of green. Without breaking her concentration, she carefully bottled the potion and handed it to me. "I did it!" she squealed as soon as she withdrew her hand.

"I knew you could," I told her with a smile. We were taking turns trying the potions, and it was mine. I lifted the bottle to my lips, opened my mouth, and dumped in the contents. The sudden taste of sour coated my tongue before instantly disappearing. Cy handed me a spoon with a little bit of sugar on it. I touched it with the tip of my tongue–I learned after the first potion I tried that less is more. It was like I had licked straight malic acid; my face puckered and my eyes watered.

"Are you going to tell Stefhan, bro?" Zeke asked me softly, making sure he blocked Cy from hearing. It was strange having to block our thoughts from her now.

"I'm going to wait. She's only done it once. I don't want to jump the gun," I told him. While Cy still wasn't one of Stefhan's favorite people, he was talking to her. I wasn't going to fuck that up by telling him she was ready before knowing for certain.

"Why don't we clean up and watch a movie?" I asked her once I could talk again.

"I really should keep practicing, Jam."

"You can practice tomorrow. You don't want to overdo it." I wanted to end the night on a high note, and my stomach was slightly upset from all the potions I had consumed throughout the day.

"You're right. Let's do it," she said with a smile.

Chapter Thirty

DANI

We were approaching the week four mark and still no bloom. I knew as much as it frustrated Stefhan that there wasn't, it was also a relief. The longer it took to bloom, the longer Cy had to practice. He didn't like that everything was so reliant on her. He also wasn't thrilled that she only had one chance to make it. He hated that Vinnie was essentially a guinea pig. It went against the Alpha in him, he was supposed to protect his pack, not let them potentially walk to their deaths.

I couldn't watch Stefhan wear a hole in the carpet as he waited for updates. I chose to use my time a little more productively. I read. I alternated between books I got from Carlos and Gram's grimoire. In all honesty, I should have been focusing on the grimoire, but I was over not knowing how my body worked.

I learned that essentially werewolf genetics are extremely similar to humans. Which I kinda assumed based on the fact that I thought I was a human for thirty years. Female wolves have monthly periods but don't ovulate. Once they complete the matebond, fated or chosen, it triggers ovulation. Ovulation is what causes the heat. There was also no way to tell how many times a she wolf would ovulate.

"Mama, Papa needs you," Max's voice called to me suddenly. My head automatically snapped to the direction of the sound. His speech had improved tremendously during the time Fern had been gone. I dragged myself away from my pile of books and made my way to the living room. I walked in to see a familiar sight, Stefhan pacing.

"Is everything okay?" I asked him as I walked toward him.

"What if they can't get back in time with the flower?" he asked me as I got closer.

"What are you talking about?" I asked, completely confused. He was talking like we were in the middle of a conversation.

"I've been thinking about Cy and her brewing the potion," he started. I was well aware of his concerns. But before I could say anything, he continued. "I've been so focused on if she could even do it that I didn't think about how long we had to make it." I could see the worry in his eyes as they locked with mine.

"As long as we want," I whispered as the recipe in the grimoire flashed in my mind. Stefhan looked at me confused. "The grimoire says the flower has to be picked on the fourth day of bloom. It never says that the flower has to be used in a certain amount of time," I quickly explained.

"Are you sure?" he asked me as hope flickered in his eyes.

"I'll double-check," I told him then ran back to the kitchen. While I knew with absolute certainty that it didn't say it in the recipe, I needed to make sure it didn't say it anywhere else. I grabbed the grimoire and flipped to the page with the spell to open the portal. I looked at the pages before it and after to make sure there wasn't some obscure hidden line. I linked him once I was sure that it didn't specify when the flower had to be used. *"There's nothing that says we have to use the flower in a certain amount of time."*

"Come on bub, it's time for bed." I heard Stefhan telling Max as I walked back into the living room. Max ran to me and flung his arms around my legs.

"Night, Mama. I love you," he told me as he squeezed.

"Night, my little one. I love you too."

Stefhan took Max to his room as I grabbed Phoenix and inhaled her sweet honeycomb and cinnamon scent. I carried her to her room, changed her, and settled us into the rocking chair. As I fed her, I ran my fingers through her red curls. Closing my eyes, I started softly humming and let my mind wander. A thought that crossed my mind more than once pushed to the forefront.

"I think it's time to tell him, child," Enya whispered softly.

"I know," I told her as the thought bounced around my head like a ping-pong ball. Once Phoenix was asleep, I laid her in her crib and trudged to my bedroom.

"What's wrong?" Stefhan immediately asked when I walked in.

"Well," I started before taking a deep breath. "I can't get over this almost nagging feeling that we're missing something."

"Then let's go over what we have and go from there," he told me as he wrapped his hand around mine and guided me to the couch. I sat down and started running through everything we knew. Stefhan sat in silence, listening to me talk it out with myself. It was one of the few times I was thankful for my gift. I replayed every part of the prophecy and everyone's collective contributions.

"Why do we all need to be in the field?" The question flew out of my mouth the second it popped in there.

"What do you mean?" Stefhan asked me. I had finally paused long enough for him to actually speak.

"We already know that you are going to be the one who kills Salix. But what we don't know is why we all need to be there," I explained. When he still looked confused, I continued. "Me and Cy brew the potion and say the spell to open the portal. Vinnie escorts you in and you kill Salix. So why do we all need to be in the field? It seems extremely risky and dumb to have people there that don't need to be. But everything says we all have to be there, clear down to Vinnie's dream. We have to know what part everyone plays, and we have to figure it out before we open the portal," I told him with a confidence I couldn't explain. I watched as he thought about what I said before taking a deep breath.

"You're right. We have no clue why Luan and Kal even need to be there. It would be stupid to needlessly potentially sacrifice even more people." I could feel the worry pouring off him.

"That settles it then. Tomorrow we start working on finding out," I said as I placed my hand on his and gave it a squeeze. "Let's go to bed."

I was standing in the field and looked at the bench. Seeing it empty, I made my way over and sat down. After a few minutes, I started to get nervous, it had never taken this long for someone to show up. The feeling I was being watched suddenly overtook me. I felt exposed. I quickly stood up and looked around. I didn't see anyone at first, but then a slender man with light brown hair stepped out from behind a tree about fifty yards away. I couldn't make out his features due to the distance.

"I never thought I'd get you here," he called to me. His voice was soft and friendly, but it caused the hairs on my neck to stand up.

"I'm sorry, I don't mean to be rude, but who are you?" I called back, using my doctor's voice. I wasn't going to offer up anything until I knew who I was dealing with.

"I'm surprised you don't know. You are plotting to kill me after all," he said as he took a large step toward me.

"Salix," I whispered as the realization hit me. Slowly, he sauntered closer, a furtive smirk on his face.

Everything was telling me to run, but I was frozen in place.

"Kylan was right, you are smart. But not smart enough to kill me. I brought you here to offer you a deal." He was close enough that I

could finally see his features, and he was nothing like I had pictured. I pictured an old man with leathery skin. He looked about twenty-five and was the most beautiful man I had ever seen. Even more beautiful than Stefhan. "Do you want to hear it?" he asked me when I didn't respond. I was too busy staring at his face.

"Yes," I immediately answered as his hazel eyes locked with mine.

"You give me the Sapphire Wolf and I'll let you, your family, and your friends live," he offered as his eyes burned into mine.

My first instinct was to say yes.

"Don't do it," Gram's voice suddenly whispered in my mind. I closed my eyes and shook my head. The second I broke eye contact with him, I realized what I was about to agree to.

"You want me to give you my son?" I asked him with my eyes still closed. I realized I shouldn't make eye contact with him again. I had to make sure I didn't do anything stupid before I could wake up.

"He is the Sapphire Wolf, and I need him to fulfill the prophecy and set true balance to the world," he explained gently.

"He may be the Sapphire Wolf, but he is still my son," I told him, keeping my eyes firmly closed.

"He is destined for things that you can't help him with. But I can." His voice was like velvet, it called to me like a siren, begging me to open my eyes.

"You don't know that. You aren't my god," I snapped, pushing the very believable thought that I should trust him out of my head.

"Oh, but I do and I partially am. You forget so easily that you are part witch," he told me as I felt his finger graze the back of my hand.

"Don't touch me." I yanked my hand away, still keeping my eyes firmly shut.

"Would you talk to Selene like that?" he asked me, still keeping his gentle tone, but I could tell he was using great effort to keep it that way.

"Yes, and I have."

"I see why Selene chose you. I can feel your Alpha energy, shame you can't control it. I wonder…" he mused. I fought the urge to open my eyes. "I can help you harness the true power inside you. Would you be willing to accept my offer if I allow you to come, too?" His words wrapped around me like a cocoon. Everything in me was screaming to say yes, but right as I was about to accept, Gram's voice shouted in my head.

"Don't trust him!"

I gave my head a shake to clear it. "No, thank you." I forced the words out through gritted teeth.

"Are you sure?" he asked me as the overwhelming urge to agree hit me again.

I knew I couldn't trust my mouth, so I just nodded my head. I knew I needed to wake up. The longer I stayed here, the greater the risk I would do something stupid. I focused on wanting to wake up and internally screamed for Stefhan. I'm sure I looked crazy just standing there, eyes closed and completely silent. I could hear Salix trying to talk to me, but I ignored him and kept screaming for Stefhan.

"DANI!" I heard Stefhan scream, ripping me from the dream. My eyes shot open to see him hovering over me with his hands around my shoulders. "Are you okay?" he asked me as I sat up.

"I saw him. I saw Salix," I spit out trying to catch my breath. Once I was composed enough, I told Stefhan what happened.

"That bastard thought you would just give Max to him?" he asked when I was done.

"That's the scariest part, I was going to. I wanted to do what he asked. If I hadn't heard Gram telling me not to trust him, I would have," I confessed as shame washed over me.

"That's why we need Kal!" he suddenly shouted, causing me to jump. "I'm sorry, my love," he quickly apologized before continuing. "We need her, so she can tell us when he's lying. He must have been using magic to try and get you to agree. You said Gram told you he lies. What can Kal see?"

"Truths and lies."

His revelation clicked in my head.

"Exactly! She'll be able to make sure we don't fall for his tricks." While it made me feel a little better that my dream was able to help us, it still terrified me.

"How did you know to wake me up?" I asked him as he pulled me close.

"It was the strangest thing. I was sleeping and all the sudden I heard you scream my name. When I woke up, you were sleeping, but you were tossing and turning. Suddenly I heard you call my name again, and that's when I started trying to wake you up," he explained as he ran his fingertips up and down my arm.

Stefhan didn't like that Salix was able to call me to him. He decided that we would sleep in shifts. This way if either one of us was in distress the other could wake them up immediately. He insisted that I sleep first, and he kept tracing designs on my arm until I fell into a dreamless sleep.

I was surprised to wake up to the sun coming in the window. Stefhan's arms tightened around me as I rolled to face him.

"That wasn't exactly taking turns," I said as I looked at the clock on his table. "And you have to be at training in less than an hour!" I scolded him.

"It was only two hours, and I'll be fine. I can nap when I get back. I'll sleep on the couch while the kids play," he said as he kissed my forehead.

"Fine. Go get ready, the last thing you need is to be late. If you hurry, I can braid your hair," I told him as I kissed his cheek. Once Stefhan was gone and I had both kids up, fed, and settled, I texted Cy.

"What a fucker," she whispered to me as she made a disgusted face. "What do we do now?" she continued as she glanced over at Max.

"We'll need to sleep in shifts."

"What do you mean in shifts?"

"If you wouldn't have interrupted me, I was getting to that," I said as I rolled my eyes. "You and Jameson will take turns sleeping. This way if you start showing signs of distress he can wake you up and vice versa. Stefhan is even having Fern and Luan do it." I spoke in a whisper, so Max couldn't hear me.

"I wonder if he could even do that," Cy mused to herself more than to me, but it made me curious.

"Do what?" I asked her as I watched her think.

"Pull a non-witch into a dream," she began before I cut her off.

"We know that it is possible because Lilith has appeared to both me and Stefhan."

"I was getting to that part before you cut me off," she retorted and mimicked the eye roll I gave her earlier. "Anyways. You have both seen Selene and Lilith. I think they were able to come to you both because you are connected to them both. Selene is the goddess of all wolves, and Lilith is death. You are both wolves and eventually, Lilith will guide you to the afterlife. Salix came to you, but not Stefhan," she explained and looked at me to see if I was catching on.

"You could have something there. It makes sense that only a god you are connected to can appear to you," I said as I thought about it.

"That's what I'm saying," she confirmed as she looked pointedly at Max, who was staring at us.

Cy stayed until Stefhan got back. His injuries told me exactly how tired he was at training. He had four broken fingers, and while he denied it, I knew he had a cracked rib. I set his fingers and forced him to let me wrap his ribs at least while he took a nap. By the time he was settled on the couch and sleeping, it was time for the kids to take their naps. Once both kids were sleeping, I went back to the living room and sat in the chair nearest to Stefhan. Then I turned on the Discovery Channel and leaned my head back.

I was standing in the field, and I froze. "You had one fucking job, Dani!" I scolded myself as I took a breath.

"Danielle Emerald, you better watch your mouth," Gram's voice called to me. I instantly looked at the bench to see Gram.

"Oh, Gram!" I nearly yelled as I ran to the bench and threw my arms around her.

"What is going on, my lovely?" she asked me as concern saturated her features. I quickly explained to Gram my encounter with Salix, Cy's theory, and the whole sleeping in shifts. She looked at me as she thought. After what seemed like a lifetime, she grabbed my hand. "If he has presented himself to you once, it won't be long before he does again. Cy is right, he can't appear to anyone who isn't part witch. Having everyone sleep in shifts is a really smart idea. Even just one percent of witch blood is enough for the connection to be made.

He is acting desperate, trying to get you to surrender Max to him shows that he is grasping at straws. He knows you're getting close to opening the portal. You all must be on high alert and make sure you are always aware of your surroundings. You won't have much time to put everything into action. You must complete the process and fully become the Fire Wolf," Gram told me as she kept scanning the tree line.

"I still have no clue what that means," I confessed as I hung my head.

"You must embrace what you would have been if your parents hadn't died and your pack wiped out," she instructed me as she suddenly looked over her shoulder like someone called her name. "You'll figure it out, my lovely. Just keep

*on the path," she whispered as she leaned in and
kissed my cheek.*

I immediately looked at the couch, Stefhan was sound asleep. I
glanced at the clock and realized I had only slept maybe twenty
minutes. I thought about what Gram said as I stared at the TV.
I wasn't sure what she meant by who I would have been. I
began replaying everything I knew about my parents and Green
Diamond. Suddenly something Stefhan said burst to the front
of my mind.

"We're Alphas," I told Enya as the thought swirled in
my head.

"Yes, we are, child," she replied simply.

*"Is that what Gram was talking about and if she was,
how are we supposed to embrace it? A pack can't have two
Alphas,"* I mused as I tried to figure out what Gram meant.

*"What if it's more about a state of mind and not the
title,"* Enya's voice echoed in my head after a few minutes.

*"That makes sense, but how would I get into an Alpha
state of mind?"* I asked her after thinking about it.

"I'm not sure, but I know we will figure it out."

I sat there thinking about how to get into an Alpha state
of mind until Phoenix's soft cries grabbed my attention.

The rest of the day was pretty uneventful. Stefhan had
gone to Vinnie and Kal's on his way to training and told them
about the dream and sleeping in shifts. I was on the fence about
when to tell him about my dream with Gram. I didn't want to
confess that I had fallen asleep, seeing as it was my only job.

Enya wanted me to tell him right away, but I wanted to wait until it was my turn to sleep. I won.

I was nervous as we made our way to bed. I hadn't thought about what would happen if Salix visited me again. I ignored Enya's comments about how she told me to tell him earlier. I was trying my best to keep my nerves at bay, so Stefhan wouldn't feel them, but I knew I wasn't doing a very good job.

"What's wrong?" he asked as he closed the bedroom door behind us. Those two words opened the floodgate. I told him about how I fell asleep, what Gram said, and what Enya and I had come up with so far. "I'm not sure either," he told me after he thought about it for a minute. "But I know we will figure it out. You get some sleep." He guided me to the bed and lay beside me. I let his scent fill me as I drifted to sleep.

Chapter Thirty-One

It had been almost five weeks since Fern and Luan had been on bloom watch and a week since sleeping-in shifts started. I was still no closer to figuring out how to get into an Alpha state of mind. I wanted to ask Carlos, but I couldn't risk it because he was not part of the prophecy. I opted instead to get every book related to Alphas and Alpha training. I spent days reading and trying to make some kind of connection. But the more I read, the further away the answer seemed to be.

"Are you going to come to bed?" I heard Stefhan's voice call to me from the hallway.

"I might as well," I answered in frustration as I shoved away from the kitchen table. For the first time I glanced in his direction; that glance turned into a stare. He was only wearing basketball shorts, and those shorts were hanging dangerously low on his hips.

"I'm sorry you haven't found what you're looking for," he said as I shuffled toward him. I refused to let him help me because something was telling me I needed to figure this out on my own.

We walked in silence to the bedroom. It wasn't until I was inside that I finally looked at a clock; it was just past midnight. Guilt washed over me. Stefhan always gave me the first shift. He also made sure I got at least four hours of actual sleep before waking me up, even though I told him not to. I wanted us to get equal sleep, but he wasn't having it. I knew if he wouldn't trade me shifts, he wouldn't sleep at all until after training.

"I'm not sleepy yet, why don't you take the first shift," I told him, hoping he would go along.

"I'm not either. Sounds like we're in quite the conundrum," he said with a sly smile.

"It makes no sense for us to both be up doing nothing. I know you have to be sleepy," I replied, trying to convince him.

"What should we do then?" he asked me, ignoring the second part of my statement. My core blazed as his eyes locked with mine, and I forgot what I was going to say. "I think I have an idea," he continued when I didn't answer. Slowly he guided me to the bed and motioned for me to lie down as he went to the closet. I lay on the bed and waited. "Clothes off," he commanded me from the closet. I quickly did what I was told and laid back down. Excitement was coursing through me by the time Stefhan exited the closet. He held his hands behind his back. "Do you trust me?" he asked as he stood at the edge of the bed.

"Yes." I knew that no matter what he had planned I would be fine.

"Sit up and face away from me," he instructed as he flashed me a smile. I did what I was told and waited. When the fabric of the tie entered my line of vision, I closed my eyes. Stefhan secured it around my head and laid me back.

I waited for the feather, but nothing came. I lay there completely naked and blindfolded for what seemed like hours before something finally grazed my skin. I knew instantly it wasn't the feather. I tried to figure out what the object was as he gently ran it up and down my body. When I thought I finally had an idea of what it was, it felt completely different. Sometimes it felt like a spatula, and other times it felt like a bunch of strings. I concentrated on the smells since touch wasn't giving me any clues.

I had to smell around Stefhan's scent. Once I was able to do that, I could smell leather, wood, and plastic. It seemed like an odd combination, and I couldn't think of anything that would have those smells and feel the way it did on my skin.

"Turn over and get on all fours," he commanded as I kept trying to figure out what the object was. I did as I was told, and as soon as I was in position, something swatted my ass. It stung slightly, but it turned me on. I waited for the next swat; I wanted to make sure I was focused. After a few seconds, I heard a soft whistle and a smack. Immediately after the smack, I felt a sting on my other ass cheek. As he alternated sides, I noticed the sound was slightly different depending on what cheek he was swatting.

I finally figured out that he was smacking me with both ends of whatever he was holding. Suddenly the smacking stopped, and his hands gripped my hips firmly. Feeling the tip of his cock brushing against me, I remained still and waited. Gently he placed his lips on my neck as he rammed his cock deep inside. The stark contrast between the kiss and him penetrating me sent an electric shock through me and a moan escaped my lips.

"Do you want me?" he asked against the skin on my back.

"Yes," I moaned.

"Yes what?" he growled softly

"Yes, Alpha," I answered as I pressed myself against him.

Once the words left my mouth, Stefhan rammed his cock in and out of me like a jackhammer. Each pump sent electricity shooting through me. When I tried to move myself against him, he tightened his grip on my hips.

"Still," he commanded as he never broke his stride. Slowly he slid his left hand up my back and tangled it in my hair, pulling my head back gently, so my throat was exposed. He then slid his right hand up my back and around to the front of my neck. Excitement coursed through me as I understood what he was about to do. I locked my arms and legs in place, so he wouldn't need to worry about me falling.

He squeezed my throat gently as he kept ramming me with his cock. I could still breathe, but the sensation it created made my head spin. My pussy clenched around him and without my permission, my juices exploded all over. Before I was done, he pulled his cock out and flipped me over. I hadn't fully registered what happened when he slid back inside me and wrapped a hand around my throat again. I was amazed how he could squeeze my throat so gently but fuck me with the speed and intensity that he used. I could feel another orgasm building.

"Cum for me," he commanded as it reached a fever pitch. My pussy clenched around his cock as I released my juices all over him for the second time. Right as I was coming down, he growled and gave a final pump, cumming deep inside me.

I felt him drop next to me and heard his labored breathing. Once it returned to normal, I felt him roll off the bed. I counted the steps as he made his way to the bathroom and back. He quickly cleaned me up and pulled me into his chest.

"Aren't you forgetting something?" I asked him as I pointed to my still blindfolded eyes.

"Nope. Goodnight."

I woke up to the sound of Stefhan's alarm going off. My face instantly flushed, and I was beyond relieved to see I was alone. Stefhan came running from the bathroom and turned off the alarm.

"I'm sorry, my love. I thought I turned it off before I went in to shower," he started before fully taking me in. "Are you okay?" he asked, noticing my bright red cheeks.

"Yeah, I just need a shower," I told him as I got out of bed and headed to the bathroom. "I'll braid your hair when I'm done," I continued before I shut the door.

"You should tell him," Enya encouraged me as I replayed the dream in my head.

"Hell no! Plus, I don't think he seems like the type," I replied as I let the water run down me, and the image of me spanking Stefhan played again in my head. I gave my head a violent shake and grabbed my shampoo. By the time I showered, I had the dream tucked safely away. I braided Stefhan's hair and shoved him out the door. I was thankful he

didn't ask any more questions. I wasn't ready to tell anyone about the dreams that I had been having recently.

Once I had the kids up and settled for the morning, I went back to studying. I brought some of the books into the living room to read and was in the middle of a book called *Traits of an Alpha* when a passage jumped out at me: "Being dominant creatures by nature, most Alphas and high-ranking male wolves indulge in a more dominant style of sex. Being able to completely dominate their mates helps them achieve and maintain balance."

The words played in my head on repeat until Stefhan got home. For the first time ever, I was glad he needed medical attention. It took my mind off the thoughts that wouldn't stop swirling. After rebreaking and setting three fingers and his shoulder, he took the kids outside, so Max could get some energy out while I kept reading.

"I really think you should just talk to him, child. He's an alpha, too. He will understand your needs," Enya told me as I tried to block her out.

"And just how do you propose I bring it up? Casually tell him I want to tie him up and spank him?" I snapped her

"That would work," she answered calmly. I didn't respond, just kept reading.

The book didn't talk about female alphas, only males. I had no way of knowing if all the things in it were even relevant for me.

I insisted Stefhan slept in the bedroom since he got no sleep before training. When it was time for the kids to take their nap, I laid them down, went into the bedroom, and turned on Food Network. But I wasn't watching what was on. I was thinking about my dream and if I was just being stubborn by not telling Stefhan.

STEFHAN

I knew there was something Dani was keeping from me. I was also sure I knew what it was. Thanks to her talking in her sleep and Kane's comments, it wasn't hard to put two and two together. Unfortunately, just because I knew didn't mean I could say anything. It was something she had to decide on her own. I couldn't lie that the thought of her taking control and commanding me made me have to adjust myself.

My anxiety had been on high alert since Salix came to Dani. I wanted to get the whole thing over with, but everything so far had been hurry up and wait.

"Things happen when they are supposed to, boy," Kane said for the thousandth time as I paced the living room waiting for Fern's update. Abbadon agreed with Kane. He let me know more than once that we weren't ready to face Salix. *"Just because you can get there doesn't mean you can catch him,"* his voice would echo in my mind.

Dani had read every book we had on Alphas, werewolves, and magic, but was no closer to figuring out why Luan needed to be in the field. She finally let me start helping when we were pushing the six-week mark from when Fern told me three to six weeks. Dani moved her base of operations to the restricted section of the library, so we could look at more ancient texts and scrolls. I was reading an ancient scroll when something jumped out at me.

"'Just because one can open the portal to reveal a god doesn't mean they can catch a god. In order to kill, you must capture first. Undead-like speed, knower of lies, double alpha, demon of death, and witch's true,'" I read out loud before looking at Dani. "What in the hell does that mean?" I watched as she thought about it before taking the scroll from me and rereading it.

"I think this partially explains why we all have to be in the field," she whispered as she looked up from the scroll. "Kal is the 'knower of lies,' I am the 'double alpha,' you are the 'demon of death,' and Cy is the 'witch's true.' So, by order of elimination, Luan is 'undead-like speed,'" she continued as she pointed to each item on the scroll.

"Okay, but it doesn't tell us what we are supposed to do," I said as I sighed in frustration. Before Dani could respond, Fern's voice filled my head.

"Day I don't fucking know, nor does it matter. The flower started to bloom. It's officially day one."

Rhiannon Hailey

www.ingramcontent.com/pod-product-compliance
Lightning Source LLC
Chambersburg PA
CBHW021847010726
47493CB00005B/1597